EVERY LONGING HEART

EVERY LONGING HEART

A Christmas Gothic Vampire Romance

BONDS OF BLOOD
BOOK II

CLAIRE TRELLA HILL

This book is a work of fiction. Names, characters, places, and incidents are the product of the author's imagination or are used fictitiously and are not to be construed as real. Any resemblance to actual events, locales, or persons, living or dead, is coincidental.

EVERY LONGING HEART

"In the bleak mid-winter
    Frosty wind made moan,
Earth stood hard as iron,
    Water like a stone;
Snow had fallen, snow on snow,
    Snow on snow,
In the bleak mid-winter
    Long ago."

CHRISTINA ROSSETTI, "A CHRISTMAS CAROL"

Prologue

NOVEMBER 1880, LONDON

When the blood bond severed, she felt it. Pain washed over her, but she bore it, bracing herself against the sensation of the cut as one did for the pain of amputation in order to separate a diseased limb that would kill if left on.

Then the pain lifted. Genevieve gasped, her first free breath in twenty years.

"Genevieve? What is it?" Elspeth asked from the other side of their small, dark bolt hole. Her quick needle hovered over the frayed hem of Genevieve's cloak.

"It's—gone," Genevieve stammered. "Gone—" Her hand scrabbled convulsively at her chest, as if to hunt for the end of the broken, intangible tether.

Elspeth's face blanked—and then set. "Then you must go. Go now," she urged. She tied off the last stitch and snipped the thread, thrusting the cloak towards Genevieve.

"I—but what about you?"

"Genevieve," Elspeth said, her colorless eyes flashing red in the dark, "*Go.*"

Genevieve Dryden wrapped herself in the voluminous cloak and fled the dark depths of London.

She recalled little of her flight, stowing away in baggage cars, sleeping when she had to, clutching her hood tight about her, ignoring the cold winds that blew.

Need drove her on. Need—and desperation.

Her journey ended on a bleak street in Oxford as she stared up at the lit windows of a small house. But as she gazed through the cloudy glass, she did not recognize the man who pored over a book in the study. Small footfalls and children's laughter rang out from the upper floor.

Her heart, which she had thought long dead, seized in her chest.

The neighbors in the surrounding houses were all different. And she could not call on any other familiar acquaintances. Not after twenty years.

She searched the college as a last resort, but no familiar figure lay asleep in the library over a translation or sat beneath the trees to watch the constellations.

Genevieve finally drifted through the streets to the church-yard. And in the moonlight, as snow began to softly fall, she fell to her knees in front of the tall hewn stone and sobbed bitterly, her threadbare gloves clawing at the words inscribed there under an open book:

> In Memory of Ezra Dryden, who died Nov. 23rd,
> 1879, Aged 78 Years. Beloved Husband to
> Constance. Faithful Father to Genevieve.
>
> *"Naked came I out of my mother's womb, and naked shall
> I return thither: the Lord gave, and the Lord hath
> taken away; blessed be the name of the Lord."* Job 1:21

She was too late.

Chapter One

After dark had fallen—early, for wintertime, and doubly so for all the coal smoke and smog that filled the air—a woman swathed in black disembarked from Paddington Station and merged with the foot traffic on the streets of London. Ignoring the cries of shopkeepers and flower sellers, she moved slowly through the thick, choking fog, heading east towards the poorer districts, the narrow thoroughfares where no one looked up, the alleys devoid of light.

Genevieve walked past crowded omnibuses and cabstands, staring sightlessly ahead. It was cold, but she couldn't feel it. A part of her not numbed by grief rebelled against the path her feet trod—but where else could she go? What was left for her now?

At her elbow, someone tugged. Her hand clamped atop the grimy paw before she thought.

"Cor blimey, miss, you moved fast," the urchin said. Two green eyes stared up at her from under a ragged cap. "And you don't half smell. What *is* that?"

"It's the dye," Genevieve rasped. She had paid a woman in Oxford half of what was in her purse to do the dyeing of her dress. It felt senselessly wasteful now—but at the time, it had seemed like the most important thing in the world.

"Where you been, Miss Dryden? The tykes been missing you."

"I've been away, Fletcher," she whispered. "A—death in the family." Her voice caught. Genevieve hurried on, even as the boy called after her.

In a lonely, putrid street with houses leaning crookedly against each other, she held her breath and willed her body to still. *See me not*, she thought.

Then she passed between two large men who stood at either side of a house's open basement entrance. Neither one registered her presence. Inside the basement, she walked to the back and pushed aside a grate that a woman of her slight build should not have been able to lift. She descended into the bowels of London.

Genevieve trod along a narrow walkway without light. She followed the path until it met with one of London's underground rivers that had become a sewer and then took that track until she reached a hidden door in the brick. Pushing it aside, another feat she should not have been able to accomplish, she passed through.

Several minutes later, she stepped into an underground cavern teeming with people. She moved past the cavern's inhabitants and staggered down a familiar narrow passageway, fumbling as her vision blurred.

"Genevieve?"

She stopped and braced herself against the stone transom, like it would hold her up.

Elspeth stepped out of a crack in the passage that led to their bolt hole. She reached up a hand and self-consciously patted her blonde hair, making sure she had pinned it to cover the sides of her head. "What are you doing back here? I thought—has *he* called you back?" Her voice trembled.

Genevieve shook her head and pulled off her old-fashioned bonnet, hands shaking, revealing her short dark hair that just brushed her chin. "It was no use. I was too late." Her voice broke.

Genevieve covered her face with her gloved hands. *A whole year too late.*

"Oh, no." Elspeth's arms came around her. "Oh, my dear, I'm so sorry."

The tears that Genevieve had valiantly tried to hold back escaped. Blood trickled down her cheeks as sorrow crashed over her in waves. All her hopes to which she had clung for so long—dashed. Shattered around her like miniscule slivers of glass, never to be put back together. Determined to slice her to ribbons if she moved. *Oh, Papa.*

"Why did you come back, Genevieve?" Elspeth murmured. "I had hoped you would seize your freedom."

"All I wanted was to find my father. Without him, where could I go? This place... It's the only home I have left."

"What an awful thought," Elspeth said on a broken laugh.

"And I thought you would need me," Genevieve admitted.

Elspeth pulled back and looked her in the eye. "Dear, we've leaned on you most shamefully for support, and when you were no better off than the rest of us. You deserve your time to grieve. Let us be strong for *you* for once." She handed Genevieve a fresh handkerchief. "Here, or you will stain your gloves."

That produced a fresh wash of tears. Genevieve mopped her eyes and stained the cloth red. "But what about you, Elspeth?"

Elspeth shook her head. "I am still bound, but others felt their bonds part as well," she whispered. "No one really knows what happened. But there's some disturbance tonight. Sparrow went to see what was happening—here she comes." They both looked up.

A patter of rapid footfalls announced Sparrow's arrival. "Elspeth! Elspeth—oh! Genevieve," Sparrow fluttered. She had taken the name because of her diminutive height and her high voice. "You've come back! I didn't realize."

The noise from down the passageway grew louder.

"What is it?" Elspeth asked.

"You must come—both of you! They're saying that the Draugodrottin is dead!" Sparrow exclaimed.

Genevieve exchanged a shocked look with Elspeth. The master of all the vampires in London and much of England, *dead?*

Rupert, the Draugodrottin, had taken control of the vampires of England for twenty years, coming to power just before Genevieve and Elspeth had been turned. She had heard that Rupert had taken the chance to kill the prior master, Theron, after part of the prior master's power base had been slain by another. Styling himself with the mythic title "Draugodrottin" instead of the traditional "Master," Rupert had removed strictures on turning new vampires to increase his power base but had exerted ironclad control over everyone else.

Sparrow twisted her hands together. "Everyone is converging in the main hall!"

The old role of marshaler and mother hen felt familiar, even as black despair tried to pull her under. "Well, we must go and see, I suppose," Genevieve whispered.

She balled up the bloody handkerchief and put her bonnet back on before she and Elspeth ventured out into the hubbub of the main hall.

Sparrow nodded to the group approaching the cavern's makeshift dais, one that the Draugodrottin always used to sit upon in a great chair he had styled as a throne to look upon his thanes and thralls. "They arrived not long ago, gathering all the loners and far-flung ones. They're about to make an announcement." Sparrow pressed a hand to her throat.

Elspeth seized Genevieve's hand, holding it tightly.

A tall man with long hair unbound around his shoulders and a blond beard stepped onto the dais. His face was set and resolute. Though he could not be older than middle thirties physically, something about his eyes looked ancient. In his hand, he held a naked sword, its long blade gleaming in the scant light.

Genevieve had never seen him before.

Most vampires had a distinctly feline look to them, thin and whip-like. If they were cats, this man was a lion. He was broad-shouldered and well-muscled. A warrior in a frock coat.

Strange. Most strong emotions in vampire eyes showed as red. His eyes glowed yellow.

His voice rang out, silencing the whispers in the cavern.

"The man you called 'Draugodrottin' is ash now. I killed him. He forfeited his position long ago. The missing ones among you he sold to humans in exchange for gold. He violated any trust you had in him."

If Genevieve's heart had been able to beat, it would have pounded.

"Is *that* what happened to Otto?" Elspeth whispered. "Here one day and gone the next?"

Whispers circulated. Out of the crowd, a thin, wavering voice asked, "Who are you?"

"Some know me as Kendrick. I have watched the decline of leaders over the centuries, and I say to you no more. I lay claim to the throne of the Ossuary. Are there any here who would challenge me?"

Genevieve and Elspeth looked to Sparrow in confusion. In a whisper, Sparrow explained, "In order to become the next Master, he must defeat any challengers in single combat, or the title will not be truly his."

That made sense. From what Genevieve had seen, vampire politics were brutal and bloody. But *centuries* of leaders? "Could he really be as old as all that?" Genevieve murmured.

"None of *us* have ever seen him before," Sparrow said. All across the chamber, murmurs spread.

Kendrick gestured to himself. "Are there none among you who will challenge me?" He scanned the assembled vampires, then turned around to stare at the crude runes behind the dais that the Draugodrottin had set in stone to pontificate about his power and might in poor Anglo-Saxon grammar. Kendrick made a face.

He can read it, Genevieve realized with a start.

Out of the crowd, a figure flew forward, a knife outstretched.

Kendrick pivoted faster than the eye could follow. In one smooth motion, his sword thrust pierced the heart of the vampire who had tried to stab him in the back. The knife clattered to the floor.

The room fell silent.

Kendrick frowned. "In the back? Is this the sort of honor that the vampires of London possess?" He pulled the sword free. The body fell to the floor. He brought his sword down once more to part the head from the shoulders, and the body slowly crumbled to dust and bone.

"Who else covets the throne for their own or thinks me unfit to rule? Who will challenge me, face-to-face?" Kendrick demanded.

There was no answer.

"Do you then acknowledge me as ruler of the Ossuary?"

All around the chamber, vampires knelt in obeisance. Genevieve and her fellows did the same. "Master," the London vampires whispered. "Master of the Ossuary."

A grimace flashed across his face, there and gone so fast, Genevieve thought she might have imagined it.

"For too long," he said, "the Ossuary has been ruled with fear, intimidation, and dishonor. I will make you a vow to be different. Keep your faith with me, and I will keep faith with you."

Genevieve swayed under the nearly physical impact of his voice. It rolled over the crowd like a wave, and she could see the effect on the faces around her. His words flowed like hot butter, rich and thick, assuring them of his good intentions, swaying them into acceptance.

The people around her stared in awe, murmuring in amazement and disbelief.

Genevieve's eyes narrowed. He sounded like a vampire accustomed to getting his own way. As if true transformation of a broken and corrupt system could be accomplished simply on his say-so. What did he know about what London's vampire Ossuary needed? Who *was* he?

"Now what?" she whispered to Sparrow.

"Now he's the Master," her friend said.

"That's it?"

Sparrow stared at her, her brow furrowing. "What else is there?"

"An indication of *how* his rule will be different?" Genevieve suggested.

Sparrow just blinked at her.

Kendrick turned. He dug his fingers into the stone behind the dais and with one large hand, he wiped out the crude runes. With his finger, Kendrick dug into the rock and began to write.

Genevieve's lips parted in shock. He was writing new words into the stone. Ones that made her throat tighten with emotion.

> Sceal þeodna gehwylc þeawum lifgan,
> eorl æfter oþrum eðle rædan,
> se þe his þeodenstol geþeon wile.

How did he know that phrase? And did he mean to live up to it?

"Genevieve," Elspeth whispered, "you're crushing my fingers. What does it say?"

Genevieve swallowed, belatedly releasing Elspeth's hand. "It's from an Old English poem. It says, 'Let every leader live aright, earl after earl in honor rule, who thinks to thrive and his throne maintain.'" Her shattered hopes sliced like a knife.

"We shall know a man by his fruit," Genevieve murmured as Kendrick finished the phrase.

Chapter Two

DECEMBER, THREE WEEKS LATER

"Master. You're needed."

Kendrick looked up from his copy of *Wolfhead Tree* by E.D. Saxon, which he was reading by the light of the glowing lamp. He had taken a break from poring over the poorly kept and piecemeal law codes he'd found in the Ossuary to reread a favorite tome.

"What is it?" he asked the vampire at his door, masking his distaste for the appellation of "Master."

"Markham has the madness. He's killed two humans by the East End exit—nearly in the main thoroughfare. We have restrained him and brought him down for your judgment." Joseph stared at him with no expression on his scarred face.

Joseph had been one of the vampires to apprehend Kendrick and his friends in Yorkshire when Rupert, the previous master of the London vampire Ossuary, had attempted to crush the knowledge that he had sold his own vampires to human scientists and graverobbers in return for gold. Kendrick did not believe Joseph had had strong loyalties to the previous master—but that didn't mean he had any loyalty to Kendrick, either.

"Will you come?" Joseph asked, his mouth firming in a line.

Kendrick set aside the book and stood to his full height, which was well above average for a man of his time. He picked up the longsword gifted to him during that Yorkshire misadventure and slung it over his shoulder. "Lead the way."

Joseph led him from the chamber down the rough corridor of stone and brick. It smelled of earth and damp and rock, plus the tang of blood and death. These were the passageways of the dead, a honeycomb of tunnels carved out below London, at first merely a handy connection between fine Mayfair houses but expanded throughout the city as the rivers were paved over and enclosed underground. If he listened hard, he could hear the susurrus of the water—and likely, sewage—as it flowed to the Thames and out, ever onward, towards the whale road, the swan's riding place, where his people had sailed...had it been his people?

Kendrick probed the thought like a bad tooth. Memories faded and crumbled with age like old parchment, and he had been a part of the world lit by heaven's candle for a comparatively small portion of time, more than a thousand years ago. Something like a thousand. He knew the tongues of the Saxons, the Celts, the Normans, the Danes, but which he had learned at a mother's knee? All that had passed away, but stories... Ah, the stories told around hearth fire, the tales of men and monsters—those, he remembered.

It was a monster he encountered in the main chamber of the Ossuary, the gathering place where a ruler more pompous than himself would call his people to him at his every whim to make demands and pronouncements. Five vampires held a frothing fellow down by arms and legs and barely kept him still. The vampire's eyes glowed red, and his clothes were drenched in blood. Other vampires in the room stared furtively at the spectacle in front of them, hanging back, creating an uneven circle around the tableau.

"Speak," Kendrick said. "Where are the witnesses?"

"I, sir." A vampire with a cleft chin stepped forward. His Adam's apple bobbed as he swallowed. "I guard the easternmost door."

"What is your name?"

"Orson, sir."

"Say on, Orson."

"Markham went out at dusk, sir," he said. "He had…a strange countenance. I did not like it. Not long after, a cry went up. I left my counterpart, Anne Wright"—he gestured to the woman beside him—"and went to see. He had killed a beggarwoman, and a man had come upon them and cried out. By the time I had reached him, he had torn the human's throat out with his teeth. I detained him long enough for Miss Wright to call for reinforcements. With their help, we were able to wrestle him back belowground."

Kendrick paced around the monster named Markham. The vampire growled, his eyes completely red.

"Come in from the cold dark," Kendrick said, "or be lost to it evermore."

Markham made no response. The vampire threw himself against his fetters, growling wordlessly.

He was well and truly lost, then.

"Markham has broken the law. He has killed not one, but two humans. He has endangered the secrecy of his brothers and sisters. His life is forfeit."

At Kendrick's nod, the vampires wrestling their mad brethren let go and jumped free with inhuman speed. Markham hissed and whirled on the only vampire within reach—Kendrick. He readied himself and sprang—

Only to find the end of Kendrick's blade.

The body fell one way, the head another. That was the surest way to end a vampire. Part them from their head.

Kendrick flicked the dark blood from the blade. "What was done with the bodies aboveground?"

"We removed them to a different neighborhood, Master."

"Good. Their people, if they have any, should have the chance to claim them." Kendrick wiped the dark blood from the sword as the body before him slowly crumbled to dust. "How old was he?"

"Sixty, Master."

"*Sixty?*" Kendrick repeated, eyebrows flying up. He should not have lost himself to the madness. Vampires burdened by the weight of centuries in the dark were the ones who lost some necessary part of themselves and succumbed to the bloodlust. It should not have occurred in one so young.

I am failing at this, Kendrick couldn't help but think. From the reports he had read, incidents of madness had spiked in recent years, vampires younger and younger succumbing. Perhaps they could have done something to hold Markham back from the madness and the dark. But if there was something, he didn't know it.

When he turned on his heel and left the spectacle in the chamber, Kendrick thought the bloodshed for the night was over. But that was not to be.

A knife came at him from the dark.

Not again.

Back in his rooms, Kendrick eyed the dark blood on the blade of his sword and glowered.

Etienne handed him a cloth. He had arrived at Kendrick's door with Addie, his fiancée, after news of the night's events reached them. "That was closer than I would like, *mon ami*."

With quick, efficient movements, Kendrick cleaned the blade. The action was as deeply ingrained in him as blinking. Then he pulled the scrap of paper from his pocket, read it again, and crumpled it in his hand. "And yet someone knows before word reaches our ears," he murmured.

Beware Safina and Titus. They are conspiring to kill you, the note read.

Just like the previous two notes.

And the conspirators had indeed attacked him in a dark corner of London's vampire Ossuary, but they had forgotten, like the other schemers, that he carried the sword with him everywhere he went. Vampires were strong and powerful but grew set in their thinking. Adaptation was not one of their strong suits. He'd probably be putting down plots years from now, dealing with holdouts from the old regime who had been too cowardly to challenge his right to rule from the start.

"At least you are doing something to combat the overpopulation problem," Etienne said with rueful dark humor. He pulled pince-nez glasses he did not need from his nose and polished them with a silk handkerchief.

"What I want to know is how the informant is getting this information."

The quarters were the finest in the catacombs, from what he had seen. They had belonged to Rupert, and Kendrick had only moved in after a thorough cleaning. He had a fine four-poster bed with rich coverlets and treasures scattered about the room. If he so desired, he could have fine clothes and any woman he wanted and all the blood he could drink. A king's privilege.

He felt lonelier here than he had in all his years wandering.

"Do you mean to look a gift horse in the mouth, as the English say?" Etienne asked. "I should think you would welcome someone watching your back among these saboteurs."

"Well, I have you, don't I?"

"I am not enough, and you know it, *cher ami*," Etienne said, turning serious.

Too right, but Kendrick did not like to dwell on it. It hurt to think of old friends long gone. "Who else is there who knows me, besides you and Salem? It feels like the whole Ossuary is full of spotty youths under a hundred."

"What about Dominic?"

"Dominic? He's in London?"

"You *have* been gone a long time. Rupert liked to keep the older vampires close and under his thumb. Dominic and many others were forced to relocate years ago. I'll find his direction for you."

"Thank you." He and Dominic went back a long way; it would be good to see him again. Kendrick tapped the note. "Back to the matter at hand—beyond their knowledge, I can't fathom how no one saw them come and go."

"Worrying, if this mysterious note-leaver can breach your chamber. Can others?" Etienne mused.

"Well, it isn't like I lock the door," Kendrick muttered. "Even so, the notes could have been slipped under the door. But I can't even catch a scent from the scrap of paper. Nothing to identify the sender."

"You ought to thank her," Addie said from her chair at the end of the table. "She's saved your life." She set her head in her hands.

"Yes, but how is she learning of these plots?" Etienne asked.

Kendrick said, "*She?*"

"The handwriting," Addie said, rubbing her eyes with her fist.

Etienne moved to her side. "Do you have the headache, *mon chaton?*" He ran a hand over the crown of her head, stroking her hair.

"I don't like it down here. Everything echoes off the stone and it's all close." She shivered.

"Then we shall go. Kendrick, can you manage to stay alive another night?" Etienne asked. "I will take Addie home."

"Home to Brompton?" Addie lifted her head hopefully.

"For now, *mon ange*, but I have secured us apartments on a basement level of a house. Only a little more time until the work is finished, and then we can take up residence."

"In time for Christmas?" Addie sat up straighter, her eyes sparkling.

Etienne kissed her hands. "Perhaps. I had meant to surprise you but then thought better of it. I will take you to see it, and then you shall beggar me furnishing it to your taste."

"A real home of my own," Addie said wonderingly. "With you all to myself."

"To be sure, *ma chère*."

Kendrick noted with some amusement that Etienne's eyes were suspiciously moist behind his pince-nez. He ribbed Etienne cheerfully in French, and advised, "Take a cab. It will be light soon." He waved them both off.

With his sword set close at hand, Kendrick reached for the note again and spread it flat on the table, staring at the script once more.

Fashionable handwriting style and script changed from century to century, but it *could* have been a woman's. It was a quickly scrawled cursive hand—an attempt to disguise a known script, or dashed off in a hurry?

He brought it to his nose and breathed in again.

No scent.

Who could have left it?

He had not had much to do with the vampire women in the underground Ossuary besides Addie, and Gisela, who had been Rupert's woman. He suspected she would not spit on him if he were on fire, though she uttered all the right blandishments when he came upon her in passing. He could not bring to mind any other woman's face with clarity, though there were many down here—more than the men. And several had given him looks he could not misinterpret.

Kendrick leaned back, fingering the scrap of paper. He had not had a woman in several decades, and it would be a good long while before he had another, he suspected. If he was *de facto* lord of the London Ossuary and its surrounding demesnes and stayed as such for an extended period, those he took to his bed would seek to gain what status and gifts they could from him, so he would have to be choosy and politically minded about it. Not go through the Ossuary like a randy lord bedding his house servants.

Not that he was randy. Nothing had sparked his blood for years, though in long ages past, he had had animal spirits in abundance. All things passed away, it seemed.

Was the note-leaver an innocent bystander or somehow tangled in a web of conspiracy? Did he need to worry over her safety? *Why wouldn't she just speak to me, instead of leaving cryptic notes?* he wondered. *I'm not going to eat her.*

Well, she wouldn't know that, would she?

Not many vampires knew him at all anymore.

Kendrick pondered the note again. It was not a neat piece of stationery. It looked more like a corner of dirty newsprint ripped free. He squinted at the ragged edges and brought the paper to his nose again.

There was no *vampire* scent to the note—but there was the faint scent of stone, damp, horses, and the live scent of whoever had sold the paper. If he could track the human, that might provide a clue.

That was what he would do. Just as soon as dusk fell again, he'd take to the streets and see what scents he could follow. After all, it had been some years since he had prowled this city. It was time to make himself known to London again.

Chapter Three

It's a mean little pub, Kendrick reflected. Small and cramped and smelling of all the things that were a part of human life. But the ale was appreciated by all those who put their pennies on the bar and got a mug in return. Much of the crowd consisted of unfortunates who probably had no place to lay their heads but scrounged enough coin from begging or day work or other means to satisfy their need for drink. The other patrons were the residents of this neighborhood teetering on the edge of desperation.

He normally would not appear in such a place—he preferred a larger locale for more anonymity. But the storyteller by the fire was a good one.

Kendrick had made a survey of all the newspaper stands and news sellers from Mayfair to the East End, it felt like. He had searched every night this week for the scent, sometimes with Etienne in tow. He had seen the fine folk pile into their carriages for their parties and soirees and had seen them return in the wee hours of the morn. He had even gone to Fleet Street, clogged with printers and the smell of ink and glue and pulp filling the nose.

Vampires had habits, patterns. They found themselves on a worn path trod again and again. In an ever-changing world, they liked the routine, the familiar. Even in a city as teeming with life as London and choked with coal dust and sewage and dirt and odor, he should have sensed *something*.

Kendrick could question the Ossuary sentries. No one entered or exited the Ossuary without permission from the door wardens, to keep unsuspecting humans from wandering where they shouldn't and finding the hidden entrances to the catacombs. But Kendrick felt a strange reluctance to relinquish the paper slips to the scrutiny of someone he did not trust. Besides the need to keep the warnings a secret, to prevent any impression of weakness, and to keep the note-keeper safe, since the members of the conspiracies were unknown, there was no guarantee a door warden would even be able to detect the scent. Etienne had been hard-pressed to detect anything at all on the notes, much less pursue it.

But the true reason was Kendrick wanted to keep it to himself. It was faint, barely detectable. But it compelled him. Vampires liked perfumes—rich florals, heady bergamots, or patchoulis—the women in particular. But the note leaver wore no fragrance. The faint scent he could detect smelled like water over stone, overlayed with the human aroma of life—smoke from cooking fires and body odor and boiled cabbage. It bothered him. It intrigued him. What other vampire smelled like *life*?

Yet he couldn't find her.

It was like he sought a ghost.

This was not unlikely in a city as old as Londinium. He was not quite old enough to remember the red crests' dominion over the island, but he recalled the ruinous former towns and tumbledown buildings, collapsed stone covered over with brush and earth, relics and remnants from Rome's collapse that littered the landscape of Britain. He recalled the change in the rivers, the shift to the skyline, the razed portions of the city after fire and flood had done their work. Ghosts, should they exist, gave the city of London its soul, imprinted into the stone and mortar. The world was full of unexplainable things, and he was one of them.

Wasn't there a book about ghosts at Christmas? Salem, with his hoard of tomes, probably knew it.

Kendrick lifted the tankard to his lips and pretended to drink. Etienne had offered him Salem's direction the previous night when they had searched Covent Garden.

"Salem doesn't read letters from the Ossuary," Kendrick had said, as music had spilled out into the street from one of the song and supper rooms.

Etienne had shrugged. "Faelad and Ophelia do. They have settled in Ireland, near where Faelad's people originated. I thought you might like it."

"Even if I write, he won't write back."

Unbothered, Etienne had handed him the slip of paper. "In case. Or if you desire to write Faelad."

Kendrick had the paper in his pocket now—Kilkenny, Ireland. But there was no point in writing. Salem wanted no reminders of London; he had been very clear on that.

By the fire, a fiddler with middling skill and a better voice gulped from a tankard, taking a break after leading the pub in a rousing chorus of "Good King Wenceslas," new words to an old tune Kendrick recognized. A man with a gray head not too far into his cups was telling the tale of Kate Crackernuts. His voice still carried the unique accent of an Orkney man, and the story the details from that region, but the teller put his own flairs and embellishments into his words, giving the story its own life. Kendrick let the words wash over him, feeling the emotions, the echoes of the past melding with the present.

When the story concluded and the fiddler took up his bow again, Kendrick left his untouched mug and slipped out the door.

Stepping onto the street, he could see no moon or stars above for all the fog in the air tonight. He slung the wrapped sword over his shoulder and freed the hilt, should he need it, and continued down the dark street. A stray cur on the street cut a wide berth around him, growling low in its throat. Kendrick ignored it.

London was situated in a basin, a bowl for all the unhealthful odors and low-lying smog, collecting the dregs of the whole of society, with no way to scramble out for so many of the millions of people in London. He had never seen Englishmen so damn small and sickly as he had in these last few years. You could practically taste the coal dust in their blood. They died sooner, their bodies full of drink, their lungs full of smoke. His sojourn to Yorkshire brought the distinction into sharp relief between the hale countrymen and the wasting city dwellers.

And if the city is so unhealthful for the living, what is it doing to the dead? No wonder in such bleak and dreary environs, vampires like Markham went mad.

Kendrick passed one of his kind on the street—like recognized like. The black man, who looked little older than a youth, though that was no indicator of his real age, dipped his head and didn't meet Kendrick's eyes until Kendrick motioned him over.

"Yes, Master?" the vampire asked.

Kendrick felt once again the distaste for the appellation, but asked, "Where would a woman feed?"

"Sir?" the vampire blinked at him.

"A female vampire, who isn't afforded the ability to go everywhere men can. Where does someone like her find her meals? I thought near the theaters, but women don't wait there anymore."

"A woman without a family? L-Likely, she finds dossers or those who look for women alone after dark," the vampire stammered.

"What does family have to do with it?"

"A woman with a house and vampire family has servants, tradesmen who come to the house, callers..."

"No. This woman buys newssheets from the hawkers," Kendrick said with some certainty.

"Then she likely takes her meals where she can get them," he murmured.

"What is your name?"

The man looked up in surprise. "Marshall Cutter, sir."

"Thank you, Mr. Cutter. A good evening to you."

"A-And you, sir." The young man dipped his head and ventured, "And good hunting."

Kendrick flashed him a smile and turned up the collar on his coat so he would not appear different from others hunched against the wind's sharp knife of cold. Perhaps not every vampire in London wanted to stick a knife in him. First his mysterious note woman, and now Mr. Cutter.

He just had to find her.

Chapter Four

Genevieve knew she was dreaming because sunlight trickled through the curtains of her childhood home. She sat on a comfortable sofa beside her father and listened as he read, blinking at the patterns of light on the rug. The warm rasp of his voice soothed her, even if she couldn't understand the words. Lips as soft as a cloud brushed against her cheek as slim, feminine hands curled around Genevieve and her father from behind.

"She's falling asleep, Ezra; it's time for her nap," Genevieve's mother murmured.

"She wants to hear the end of the poem," her father objected.

Her mother replied with fond amusement, "Dear, you're reading in Old English; she doesn't understand. She just likes the sound of your voice."

Genevieve came awake slowly, the flicker of a candle stub replacing the memory of the sunlight's brightness. Her throat ached with the pressure of unshed tears.

It was a happy dream. A happy memory, she insisted, rubbing eyes that felt filled with sand. *Don't ruin it. Hold on to it.*

She sat up in her corner of their earth-and-stone bolt hole and drew back her cloak. The sun must have gone down below the horizon. She could feel her body waking up.

Their bolt hole was a pocket in the rock and clay of the catacombs, barely big enough for the three of them together. As vampires, they no longer had to eat or relieve themselves or suffer many of the human indignities that cropped up when one lived on top of another, but they still had to sleep when the sun rose, and they all barely had a place to lay their heads. But it was like that everywhere in the catacombs.

Elspeth was already awake—she had been the one to light the candle. She faced away from Genevieve as she pinned her blonde hair, the texture of fairy floss, carefully over her ears. Then she settled her bonnet on her head. Genevieve had bought her the blue bonnet with the first coins she had earned.

"Good evening," Elspeth whispered, mindful of Sparrow still curled up at the back of their bolt hole. "Sleep well?"

Genevieve nodded. "You?"

"I stayed up too late finishing the lace, but I did rest well afterward." Elspeth pulled out the finished lace and displayed it for Genevieve. "Isn't it lovely?"

"Gorgeous." She marveled over the tiny, intricate stitches that would make anyone other than Elspeth go blind.

"You could pull it through a ring," Elspeth said proudly.

Genevieve hugged her. "I can get you more thread today."

"Here." Elspeth bundled up the lace. "Take this with you."

"To sell? But you should—"

"Silly; I'm not going to wear it down here, am I? And coin will help us more."

"I don't have to sell it today," Genevieve protested. "You ought to have time to be proud of your accomplishments." When Elspeth frowned, she added, "Bacchus is gone, you know."

"And glad I am of it. But Laurent isn't." Elspeth turned away, her face shadowed.

Genevieve bit her lip.

She could recall with perfect clarity walking home that last day in Oxford, just a week before Christmas. It had been raining, and darkness had come early. She'd wanted to get home. Her head had felt curiously light, and she'd kept reaching up to feel the hair that had brushed against the nape of her neck. Still unused to what she'd done for Hetty, her friend in need, only a few days earlier, she hadn't noticed the two young men emerge from an alley until they'd laughed.

She had thought them university students who had had too much to drink. She could even remember what they had said as they had loomed closer. "The doxy's cut her hair. Nothing left to sell, mm? Come along with us, girl. We'll pay for your time."

She should've run. Should've done anything else other than drawn herself up and given them a tongue-lashing worthy of a governess, haranguing them for their drunkenness and impaired discernment.

They hadn't appreciated the scolding.

She remembered that all too well. It was everything after she couldn't recall.

There had been pain, she knew that. Blood. Fear. Darkness in the place she was held—and Elspeth. Elspeth had always been the constant, her hand to cling to in the dark. And then after, when the fools had drunk too deep from their veins and wounded too badly to heal, and hadn't wanted to lose their playthings, Elspeth had still been there when clarity had returned after death.

Now Bacchus, Genevieve's maker, was dead. He had been the one far more likely to hunt them down in the Ossuary and cause mischief. And he had been far more gleeful in ordering Elspeth about. He had no blood tie to her to force Elspeth's compliance, but each had commanded those of their bloodline to obey the other crony, and they gained far more enjoyment from that than puppeteering their own progeny. Only in the last few years had Bacchus grown bored with them and turned his attention elsewhere, allowing Genevieve to start using her talents to earn coin for them.

But Laurent, Elspeth's maker, remained—somewhere. Lurking. An unseen threat. With Genevieve's bond broken, she also was no longer beholden to the command to obey Laurent. But Elspeth's fetters remained.

"All right," Genevieve conceded, taking Elspeth's hand in her gloved one. "I'll sell it and bring you back more thread. How much? And is there anything you'd like? They're your earnings, you know."

"Bought with *your* earnings."

"There is no ledger between you and me," Genevieve insisted. "You *know* that."

Elspeth squeezed her hand. "I do."

Sparrow rolled onto her back and stretched, propping her legs up on the wall. Her skirts rode up and revealed her patched and threadbare stockings. Genevieve made a mental note. *Stockings for Sparrow.*

Her brown hair loose around her head, Sparrow yawned, her small fangs glinting in the candle's light. "I dreamed about roasted chestnuts. I saw a hawker selling some when I fed last evening, and then I dreamed the exact taste. Roasted chestnuts always make me think of Christmas."

"It was a good Christmas when we had a roasted goose," Elspeth said. Genevieve nodded her assent in silence.

In years past, Elspeth had tried to conjure a little Christmas for their bolt hole, a way to keep spirits up and mark the passing of the year, even if it was simply recollections of happier times. But Genevieve had little heart for the season—and none at all this year. *Truly a bleak midwinter*, she thought, remembering the scrap of poem she had read from a book propped open in a bookseller's window the year before. Would she ever find hope for Christmas again?

Wooden heels on stone announced their visitor. "You'll never guess," Winnie announced, rounding the corner without preamble.

"All right." Elspeth folded her hands in her lap.

"Well?" Winnie demanded, hands on her hips.

"You just said we'd never guess," Sparrow pointed out in her chirping voice.

"Someone tried to kill the new master again last eve. And what does he do about it? Nothing!" Winnie threw out a frustrated hand that nearly clipped Elspeth on the head. "Honestly. I think the conspirators might have the right of it. He's of no use at all."

"I wouldn't say that very loud if I were you," Genevieve said, with a warning look at her. "All the assassins who have come for him have been summarily dispatched."

Winnie sniffed. "How is he any better than what we had? I don't want to live in this hovel forever," she grumbled. "If the bully boys at the Mayfair entrances would let me use them, then I could lure a few wealthy men into a dark alley and come out with pounds in my pockets for new dresses. This is last year's fashion!" She stared in disgust at the dress she wore.

Genevieve glanced down at her badly dyed dress that had been made to accommodate a crinoline and didn't say anything.

"You ought to do the same," Winnie said pointedly to Sparrow. "You could use your talent to make any man in the street empty his pockets to you." Sparrow had begun to develop a basic persuasive talent. So far, she had only managed to coax the guards into looking the other way when she returned later than she ought.

"That would be *stealing*." Sparrow's mouth twisted and a hand snuck towards the pocket where she kept her small, brass crucifix. Even small sins smote her desperately because she could no longer go to confession. Genevieve had once gently suggested that drinking blood was not all that different than the Eucharist, and the look of horror Sparrow had given her had closed her mouth.

"You don't *understand*. You're *Protestant*," Sparrow had insisted, tears in her voice. Genevieve had conceded that she didn't and had apologized, turning to keeping Sparrow's mind occupied and not turning inward to brood. She modified her mental note to *Stockings and something else? For Sparrow.*

"Your soul is to perdition, anyway." Winnie sniffed.

"*Winnifred*," Genevieve said warningly as Elspeth patted Sparrow's shoulder.

"What? Why not? The gent is planning to pay for what he thinks he's taking you down an alley for, anyway. Why not dip your hands in his pockets while you take a drink from him? But if that's too extreme, maybe you should charge for that childminding, Genevieve."

"I do." Genevieve set her bonnet on her head and tied the frayed ribbon under her chin.

"Pennies," Winnie said scornfully.

"Charging more would take food from the babies' mouths, when their mothers can barely afford what they pay me now." Genevieve got to her feet. "Speaking of, they will be expecting me."

"You think you're special because you can get out without a problem." Winnie's face soured.

"No. I think that if this is my talent, that I have the responsibility to use it for others."

"Responsibility." She snorted. "The way you talk, I would've thought your father had been a vicar and not some fusty old professor!"

Genevieve's lips twisted in a snarl. "*Don't* talk about my father."

The women all froze.

"You keep his name out of your mouth. Do you hear me?"

Winnie quailed under the force of Genevieve's red-eyed glare.

"Winnie, cut line," Elspeth said briskly, wrapping her lace in a cloth and handing it over. "You've already said that you have no interest in sharing our space or pooling resources. Therefore, you have no say on how we earn money or what we do with it."

Winnie sniffed and flounced out of their crowded bolt hole, which eased the space considerably.

Genevieve's shoulders relaxed, her sudden fury draining away, leaving her empty.

"Why does she act like that?" Elspeth asked lightly, snipping a thread with her teeth. "Does it make her happier to spread her vitriol to others?"

Genevieve said, "We all wear thin down here in the dark. Does anyone need anything?"

Both Sparrow and Elspeth shook their heads.

"Don't forget to go and feed by the north gate," she reminded them. "I heard that Rafe will be on duty tonight. He won't give you any trouble."

Sparrow stared at her hands, but Elspeth nodded. "We'll go." She would make sure Sparrow got sustenance.

Genevieve checked her bonnet ribbons again and took up the bundle. "I'll be back before daylight."

⁂

Genevieve slipped the coin from the sale of Elspeth's lace into the inner pocket of her skirt as the shop's door jingled shut behind her. She stood on the stoop and marveled at the spark of joy that flared within her. *Stockings and thread*, she reminded herself, setting off down the street. *Before the shops close.*

She bought a pair of sturdy but soft stockings for Sparrow and two more spools of thread for Elspeth at the milliners. The shop windows had begun to decorate for Christmas, though December had just begun. In a few weeks, carolers would crowd the streets, and they would all hope for snow to cover the dirty thoroughfares.

At a nearby bookseller's, she paused to stare at the stacks in the window. They did not have her favorite, but *The Wife of Weland* was in stock, next to a stack of copies of the popular Dickens novel. Part of her imagined walking into the shop and laying down the price of the volume, to be able to say she owned it. To hug it to her chest as something rather than nothing.

Foolish. They needed the coin for far more important things. But if there was one tome she'd do so for, it would be *Wynnflaed's Knight*. And she knew it practically by heart.

"Oh! *A Christmas Carol*! Louis, that is my very favorite book! Do say you will purchase a copy," a woman passerby said, tugging on the arm of her escort. They entered the shop, the bell jingling. A more appropriate purchase for the season, to be sure.

Genevieve chuckled suddenly. "'Genevieve Dryden was dead, to begin with.'"

Her smile faded as the scent of humanity suddenly swelled, her senses heightened. The hungry urge made its presence known, raking at her insides, wanting to be unleashed.

She turned away from the shop window and headed east.

What would you think of me, Father? Genevieve wondered as a carter followed her down an alley, away from the street's light. The carter walked a little too close to her, but she had implied that she would give him a favor in return for shifting a fictitious trunk.

"It's just there." Genevieve pointed.

The carter, a man with a square face and a square body under his warm layers, frowned and moved past her. "Where?"

Genevieve didn't bother to answer. She seized him from behind and bit his neck, hand over his mouth to stop any cry. The man tried to fight her at first, but his strength was no match for hers. Then the bite's effect took over and he slumped against the wall.

She drank her fill; he would not miss it. And the horse that pulled his cart would appreciate a lighter hand at the reins and whip.

She let him slide to the ground, groaning, and set his cap over his eyes. He wouldn't remember this. Wiping her mouth, she walked to the end of the alley, emerging onto the street. Genevieve adjusted her bonnet, waiting for a horse-drawn omnibus to go by.

A boy appeared at her elbow. "Miss Dryden!"

"Fletcher!" Had she managed to wipe all the blood away? Had he seen her? "What are you doing here?"

"Walkin' you to your job," he said, squinting up at her.

"How thoughtful," she said. There was a smear of blood on her glove. She balled that hand into a fist. "How are you this evening?"

"Bloomin' marvelous, mum," he said. A bold claim for a street urchin, but he was Cockney.

"Have you eaten?"

It was a fair question. Fletcher was, as far as she could ascertain, an orphan of perhaps ten who did a variety of things to feed himself—street sweeping, begging, pickpocketing. Possibly even housebreaking. She did not ask. She did not know if he was under control of a gang and thus had access to shelter or if he slept rough. But he had attached himself to her a year or so ago, and she saw him most nights.

"Ain't takin' your money, mum," he said firmly.

She had been too blunt. For a street orphan, Fletcher had a lot of pride and was extremely canny. Inspiration struck. "I only ask because I thought I would stop for a twist of roasted chestnuts, and I know you know the best vendors. In return, you could have a few, as a finder's fee." *Thank you, Sparrow.*

His suspicious eyes peered at her from under a thatch of hair of an undetermined color and a grimy cap that had once been a sort of brown. "Long Tom's got the ones with the most flavor," he allowed grudgingly.

"Wonderful, but I'm not familiar with Long Tom," Genevieve said briskly. "Which is why I need your assistance. Is he on the way to Sally's?"

Fletcher nodded. "This way."

"Lead on, then, good sir."

What would you think of me, Father? Genevieve followed the boy through the throng of people still out in the early winter dark. She would give Fletcher a portion of the roasted chestnuts, but not so much he would think she was being overly charitable, and the rest to the children at Sally's—a small Christmas gift.

She lifted her face to the black sky above, most stars obscured from the smog and smoke. How could it be a Christmas without the hope to which she had clung for so long? How could it be Christmas when nothing was changing in the Ossuary?

As much as she hated to admit it, Winnie was correct—their new master hadn't changed anything yet. And what good was a new ruler without change?

Chapter Five

Kendrick stared up at the innocuous house. It looked the same as every other house on the street—except for the black fabric wrapped around the door knocker. He checked the direction Etienne had scrawled on a card with the name on the house. Fernside. He slipped the card in his pocket and ascended the steps.

The knocker thudded against the door, muffled by the fabric. Kendrick waited.

An aged human butler carefully opened the door.

"I'm here to see Mr. Dominic Penrose," Kendrick said.

"The family is not receiving visitors, sir," the butler said in an apologetic whisper.

Kendrick caught his eye and smiled. "Tell him it is Kendrick."

The butler blinked and opened the door. "Will you wait in the blue salon, sir?"

Kendrick glanced around the home as the butler ensconced him in the salon before disappearing. It was just as innocuous as the outside, except that all the mirrored surfaces were covered, and all the drapes tightly closed.

Except for the butler's footsteps, the house was silent. Not even the ticking of a clock disturbed the air. They had probably been stopped as part of this era's mourning practices. But Kendrick could smell the house's inhabitants. Several humans lived here. Even one who was nursing.

The door swung open. "Kendrick. I had heard you had returned."

Dominic Penrose looked just as Kendrick had last seen him twenty-five years ago, and as he had known him for the last four hundred years, though he wore his brown hair shorter in recent times. Kendrick hoped he liked the change because, frozen in time as vampires were, it would not grow back. Ironically, he looked younger this century with no beard to hide the cleft in his chin and the line of his jaw. Dominic always had a serious, unsmiling mouth, as befit a man who had lived and died during the Wars of the Roses, but now his colorless eyes regarded Kendrick with sorrow—nearly despair.

"I had not heard you were in London, old friend, or I would have called sooner. I thought you were still in Cornwall." Kendrick crossed to Dominic and clasped his arm. Dominic returned the gesture, but he moved like a sleepwalker, one beat behind.

"Yes. Rupert...liked having us all under his thumb." Dominic gestured half-heartedly around him. "As you see." He stared into the distance, unseeing.

"Dominic. What's happened?"

"You didn't know?" Dominic wandered to the unlit fireplace and ran his fingers over the mantle, staring at the dust that came away on them. "Cornelius had joined Rupert's cadre. He was there, in Yorkshire. He is no more."

Kendrick stilled. "I did not see him there. I am sorry to hear it, Dominic."

"He was taken in by Rupert's crowd. He...chafed against our

rules. But he was our blood. Little fool," Dominic whispered. "Godfrey is...taking it hard."

"And you?"

Dominic made a little gesture as if to say once more, *"As you see."*

Vampires had family units, after a fashion. Bonds connected vampires who made others of their kind. Makers had a responsibility to train and look after those they turned, and Dominic was a man who felt responsibility keenly. He had been made by Godfrey, and so he looked after his sire. He had made Cornelius a bit more than a hundred years ago and had cared for him as a son.

"In all honesty, it is a relief, you being here." A ghost of a smile flickered over Dominic's face. "I thought you had stayed away because..."

Because I had ended him. "No, old friend. I would have searched you out and brought you the news in person had that been the case."

Dominic nodded mechanically. "Rupert managed to corrupt so much in just a blink of time. I thought it was simply a phase. Children grow out of phases. But his grip was strong, and his tongue was sly, the power he offered a...tempting lure."

"Will you tell me some of what Rupert did in the last twenty years, Dominic? I hadn't even known you resided here now."

Dominic's lip curled, showing a hint of fang. "The worst vices and excesses with the most ridiculous pageantry. Rupert always liked to claim more years than he had. He tied us all to him with a blood oath and then used it to wield his will indiscriminately. Bullying and manipulation were the bywords of the court he gathered around himself, and he traded power and support for a blind eye to their behavior. No check on turning so he could strengthen his power base, and all the young, impetuous ones left to run wild with no guidance. I am afraid they are all ruined."

"And the victims?"

Dominic blinked at him. "Victims?"

"The ones turned and abandoned."

"Penned up in the Ossuary. I have not ventured to the catacombs except when Rupert demanded an assembly, but I believe it is bad." Dominic shook his head, as if to clear some of the cobwebs from his mind. "Is this what growing old is like, Kendrick? This...desperate unhappiness?"

"No," he said gently. "That is grief. And if *you* are old, what am I? No, you have a while to go before age catches up with you, Dominic, and a good thing, too. There are precious few to help me besides Etienne. Fending off the constant attacks is a bit tiresome."

Dominic's colorless eyes slowly focused on him. "Attacks?"

"Yes, four in the last few weeks. Come, walk with me and I'll tell you about it. Or—let us go find a fencing academy. I'll even concede to using the toothpicks you like so much."

Dominic's eyes widened a fraction. He licked his lips. "Fencing? Where?"

Kendrick hid a smile of satisfaction. Dominic had been in Spain for the rise of the rapier and loved the weapon irrationally. "If memory serves, there was some place down the street from Gentleman Jackson's—Bradon's or Bradley's or some such. It may still be there."

"Why?"

"Because you need to get out of this house a while, and soon someone who actually knows what end of a sword to hold will try to kill me. I'd rather practice with someone who isn't actively trying to end me. Unless you've got a secret grudge."

That seemed to wake him up a bit. "No grudge, Kendrick. You're one of the few honest men I know."

"What a compliment." Kendrick laughed. "Get your coat."

Brendan's Fencing Academy did still exist, though it was much smaller and shabbier than Kendrick remembered. It seemed to be the trend for everything in London, along with a thick layer of coal dust. However, this slide into genteel poverty ensured that the proprietor was more than happy to take Kendrick's money to open back up for the evening for two nameless gentlemen, no questions asked, and not intrude on the practice session. A small dose of Kendrick's persuasion helped reinforce the coin.

Kendrick doffed his hat and coat. "Foils or rapiers?"

Dominic shot him a narrow look. "What need have we for foils?" He chose a rapier, feeling the edge. "Not as sharp as I'd like, but it will do." With a sword in his hand, Dominic recovered a bit more of his vampiric liquid grace, shedding the stilted movements Kendrick had worried over at their reunion.

Kendrick picked up one of the light rapiers to test its balance. "You'll go easy on me, won't you?"

A slow smile crossed Dominic's face. "Where's the fun in that?"

Kendrick grinned. "*En garde.*"

Kendrick let Dominic make the first thrust and parried with the slim rapier. They had to temper their strengths to not snap the blades—another reason why he preferred a stronger, wider blade—but that was part of the challenge and skill. Kendrick disengaged and made a feint at Dominic before a thrust of his own. Then the blades flashed silver, advancing and retreating faster than a human could follow.

Dominic grinned as Kendrick was forced to parry his attacks. "You say some have tried to kill you? I assume they haven't come at you with a rapier, or they would've done some damage."

"Funny," Kendrick said, advancing with a thrust that Dominic jumped backwards to avoid.

"There are dueling rules, you know," his friend complained.

"My attackers don't follow dueling rules. They come at me with a knife in the dark, children trying to use the element of surprise. It's very tiresome. But I expected that." Kendrick defended against Dominic's riposte. "I didn't expect them to run mad."

"Madness?"

Kendrick explained about the regressions, getting a hit in on Dominic's shoulder. "What's strange is that none of them are older than a hundred. We never saw ones that young losing their minds."

Dominic acknowledged the hit. "*Touché*. In recent years, I have heard of a higher rate of recidivism with regards to human attacks, as well as an uptick in madness."

"Do you know why?"

"No. No one does. That's why Rupert ordered all the exits from the underground guarded a few years ago."

"Did that help?"

"No."

"So he penned up everyone who had no home."

"Yes. He thought every vampire should be under a master's thumb, with his thumb being the largest. Those of us with the money or position to establish our own households had a measure of independence, but Rupert wished to keep an eye on what he termed 'rabble.'"

I'll need to do something about that, Kendrick thought, retreating against Dominic's lunge.

"Even at the very start, he insisted all vampires who had sworn a blood oath to him make their homes in London," Dominic said. "And then after he lifted all restrictions on turning, those newly-turned ones were disenfranchised and dependent."

"Who supported Rupert?"

"Those who never wanted to leash their base urges."

"No one did anything about it?"

"We don't deal well with change; you know that. We assumed it would sort itself out. Then Rupert or his cronies dusted those older than him who might've stood against the injustices. He made commands via the blood oath so we could not oppose him. And everything seemed so…futile." Dominic's gaze turned inward.

Kendrick's blade sliced through Dominic's sleeve. "Another hit. Stay with me, old friend, or I might skewer you."

Dominic's eyes narrowed. "The day you manage to skewer me with my favorite weapon, consign me to the grave."

Kendrick's teeth flashed in a grin.

❧

"You've pinked me." Kendrick watched the skin over his collarbone close.

"You let me through your guard," Dominic said.

"I was getting tired of not breaking this." He set the sword back on the rack. His heart did not beat, but his lungs did heave to go along with the exercise. Vampires did not need to breathe, but human bodies continued to work as they were designed to, even without need. He took a breath and controlled what in a human would have been signs of exertion.

Dominic stared at the sword in his hand, and some of the sorrow settled back on him again. "What was the point of coming here?"

Kendrick picked up his coat. "Seducing you into coming with me so that maybe some night, you'll be willing to use something more substantial than that pig sticker." *And so maybe I will not lose you to the dark as I am losing other vampires.*

Dominic raised an eyebrow. "You mean stand there while you try to hack me in two with a broadsword or stab me with a spear? No, thank you."

Kendrick tilted his head. "There's a thought. Do you think any smith in this cesspit of a city could make a decent spear?"

"Save me from your barbaric instincts."

"Maybe next time, I'll convince Etienne to show up."

"Maybe pigs will fly," Dominic drawled.

Kendrick laughed and clapped his hat on his head. "Really, old friend—I need allies. Your help would be invaluable. Right now, the only ones I can count on are Etienne and Addie—as well as a mysterious correspondent."

Dominic raised an eyebrow in inquiry. Kendrick explained about his note-leaver.

"A woman, you say?"

"Addie believes so. I have searched for her for a few days now, but no progress yet."

"You have a secret admirer. How quaint." Dominic half-smiled. "Well, there hasn't been a London Master of Vampires whom I've respected in centuries. I suppose I shouldn't squander you."

Kendrick led the way to the exit. "I appreciate that. Now, I'd better get back to the Ossuary before any more would-be assassins miss me."

Dominic stopped in the doorway. "You're staying in the Ossuary?"

Kendrick turned to look back at him. "Where else would I stay?"

"Rupert had a house. He inherited it from the previous master."

"See, this is why I need you. A house—where?"

"Mayfair. There's a tunnel that leads from the Ossuary to the house."

"Convenient."

"Something else, Kendrick," Dominic said. "Do you remember before you left for the Continent, you stored some belongings with me?"

"Yes, but I assumed they'd be in Cornwall."

"No. We brought everything with us because..." He sighed. "Because it didn't seem likely we'd be allowed back anytime soon. Your trunks are in the attic. You're welcome to get them whenever you like." He slanted a look at Kendrick. "Now that you have a house to put them in."

Kendrick clapped him on the shoulder. "Incentive to search out the mysterious dwelling. Thank you, old friend."

A mysterious dwelling. A mysterious note leaver. Mysterious assassination plots. To think I believed ruling the Ossuary would be simple.

Chapter Six

"Now, Peter, tell me what letter this is," Genevieve instructed, wiping baby Mary's mouth and hands free of gruel.

Peter, a dark-haired boy of seven, squinted dubiously at the slate she had propped up on the table. "G," he finally decided.

"Good. Tell me some words that start with 'g.'"

Peter sighed deeply.

"Ennui is unseemly in one so young," Genevieve said. The baby attempted to grasp the slate and chew on it. "Oh, Mary, that is not for chewing, dear."

"Teeth coming in," Hannah said, worldly wise at five in the way of babies.

"Prodigiously so," Genevieve allowed, handing the baby a handkerchief soaked in cool water to gnaw.

Justin, just two, banged the wooden spool that Genevieve had found for him on the floor.

"Perhaps Hannah could tell us a word that starts with 'g,'" she prompted. "I am sure she could tell us what sound it makes."

"Guh," Hannah obediently intoned. "Does goose start with 'g,' Miss Dryden?"

"It does. Very good, Hannah."

The little girl beamed, showing the large gap between her two front teeth.

"Gun," Peter said, clearly unwilling to be shown up by a younger pupil, and a girl at that. "Gout. Gusto."

"Well done, Peter," Genevieve said. "Only think, in some languages, they use a completely different alphabet to write with."

Peter pursed his lips and sighed. He had no patience for other alphabets when the modern English one was giving him fits.

The children she looked after from dusk until the early hours varied from day to day, but usually, Peter and Hannah were her regulars. Some nights their mother, Sally Blevins, went around to the pub. Other nights, she went elsewhere. There had been a Mr. Blevins at some point, but he had "piked off"—Sally's words—and she had not found herself another suitable man with whom to split household costs and live in semi-respectable commonality, as many did in the East End. She took what work she could get, whether day work or charring to put food on the table and to pay the rent on the one-room lodging the family occupied, but often what brought her coin was done between dark and early morning.

Other children of women in similar straits to Sally's were often dropped off for Genevieve to mind for a time in the evenings. They were glad for a safe place for the children, as well as what spontaneous schooling Genevieve could offer, since for many, even the national schools cost too much for their purse strings to stretch. Genevieve only charged a penny or two per child, mindful of those who needed food and shelter and clothing and money to supply it all.

She had started the child-minding as a way to gain some measure of independence—both physical and financial. Bacchus had liked to have her ask him for every little thing, even for his leave to go out and feed. When her talent had developed and she and Elspeth had begun to trust that their makers would not appear at odd hours or demand her appearance through the bond,

Genevieve had begun sneaking out of the Ossuary. It had taken a little time to build trust with those like Sally, and then she had earned enough coin for basic things like new gloves and bonnets —their original ones had been falling apart.

Now she earned enough to buy the needlework supplies Elspeth wanted and was able to sell her work to the shops. She had gotten a tidy profit from the lace, and now a new skein of thread and a good amount of coin waited in her pocket. The seamstress shop had also said they would have piecework ready for her to pick up tomorrow and complete—something for Sparrow's hands to keep busy with.

Maybe one day, they could afford lodgings outside the Ossuary. Her bond to Bacchus had been broken by his death, but Elspeth was still fettered, and Laurent had set down that she might not leave the Ossuary without his permission. And of course he had not shown his face since the coup, for he had been one of the main toadies of the Draugodrottin.

And it would be just like Laurent to spitefully deny Elspeth's request in any case, Genevieve knew. He would do it just to cause them pain. Because he liked that.

So, she waited and minded the children and tried not to hope too much. Because where had hoping gotten her?

They reviewed two more letters—the dreaded 'h,' which many of the children in this corner of London could not hear, and 'i'— before baby Mary began to fuss and Genevieve had to call a pause to lay her down on a pallet. And then of course Justin began to rub his eyes.

"Who would like a song?" Genevieve asked, patting Justin's back.

"Oh, please Miss Dryden, a Christmas song," Hannah pleaded. "Isn't Christmas coming soon?"

"It will be here in a few short weeks." *And what kind of Christmas will you have, Hannah?* Genevieve wondered, thinking of convivial years long past with gifts exchanged and family all around. Her ruined hopes cut like a knife. *There is no "peace on earth, good will to men" for either of us.*

But the child deserved to hope, even if there would be no presents or Christmas treats. Everyone deserved hope. Genevieve swallowed back the pain and sang through the first two verses of "While Shepherds Watched their Flocks" as Mary's and Justin's eyes drooped.

"Why don't the two of you get to bed?" she whispered to Hannah and Peter. "Your mother will be home before long."

"What about a story?" Peter mumbled.

Genevieve swept his hair back from his forehead. "Yes, I can tell a story. I shall tell you one of my very favorite stories. It's about a brave girl named Wynnflaed."

The words flowed from memory out of the past and into the tiny room that smelled of that night's supper and one of baby Mary's napkins, but judging by the looks on the children's faces, they were smelling the scent of heather and rain as Wynnflaed pulled from the swift-flowing river near her dun a wounded stranger clad in warrior raiment, which would change her destiny forever.

By the time Sally had returned with Ruth, Justin's mother, and Colleen, Mary's mother, all children but Peter were sound asleep. The boy would nod off for a time, but every half hour would rouse to wakefulness, as if he could not rest easy until his mother was home.

"Lord bless you, Miss Dryden," Sally said in a loud whisper after the two other women had taken their children and left Genevieve with their pennies. "I've told the girl on the second floor that you'll watch the little ones—her husband died two months back, and they've been barely scraping by. She needs to get herself another man, but the grief is powerful. But she has a boy and a baby girl, so perhaps she'll bring them by some night. A good mother, she is. Not like that Myra Stubbins." Sally shook her head. "Poor woman, she's got the trouble with drink."

"Yes, I know all about that," Genevieve murmured.

"If she don't watch it, she'll be on the streets or maybe the workhouse, and then how will she get them back?" Sally clicked her tongue. "You know, if you were willing to watch the little ones during the day, Miss Dryden, I know other women what could use you."

"I'd like to, Sally, but I have other obligations during the day," she murmured. "But if your friend brings her children by tomorrow night, I'd be happy to have them." Genevieve tied the threadbare ribbons of her bonnet below her chin. "You take care, Sally."

"Bless you, Miss Dryden," Sally said.

Outside the tenement building that hovered at the edge of neighborhoods in truly desperate poverty, Genevieve walked past night soil men and their carts as well as a few weaving figures coming back from the pubs. She ignored them. She had already fed tonight; it was her practice upon leaving the Ossuary to feed immediately. She had never been tempted when caring for any of the children, but she thought it best not to leave anything to chance. Harm to a child at anyone's hand was not to be borne. Especially not her own.

"Miss!"

She stopped as the figure of Fletcher appeared from the corner by a much-frequented doss house.

"Early tonight," Fletcher said as a greeting.

"Sally came home early," she said. "If you ever desire to learn a few letters, Fletcher, you are always welcome."

"Naw," he said in tones of deep scorn.

"You ought to be asleep," Genevieve chided.

"I got to see you home, don't I? That's what you said a toff does."

"That's very kind of you." Genevieve smiled faintly. She had never realized the boy had latched so strongly on to what she had said as a passing comment months ago. "Have you got a place to stay tonight?"

"I got lots of places to go," Fletcher said, glaring. "Why don't you buy some dress that don't stink to high heaven?"

Ah, the bluntness of children. "You know very well that the dye smell has faded," Genevieve said, smiling in spite of herself. "Besides, mourning requires one to wear black."

"Buy a new black one, then. Who died?"

"My father," Genevieve whispered. "I suppose I'm an orphan too, now."

"Where'd you say you was from?"

"Oxford."

Fletcher thought about this. "Cor blimey," he muttered. "I ain't never been farther than Tyburn."

"Go to bed, Fletcher," Genevieve said as the gas streetlights grew more plentiful. "I will make my way from here."

The boy was stubborn and followed her for two more blocks, but Genevieve ducked around a corner ahead of him and held her breath, stilling everything about her. He darted past and looked around in confusion, his eyes skating over her without seeing. It was unfair to trick the boy so, but he would follow her directly to the door of the Ossuary if he could. He was that persistent.

On silent feet, Genevieve kept walking towards her destination. *Be safe, Fletcher.*

❦

There were many entrances to the Ossuary all around London, though some were harder to get to and a few areas had been rerouted due to the construction of the London Underground. But they were all secret, and under a rotating cycle of guards.

Genevieve's lip curled. That hadn't changed much since the Drau—since *Rupert*'s reign. So much for the change that they had hoped for.

Sparrow had told her once that centuries ago, no vampire had truly lived in the tunnels—they had just been handy byways between houses, and the vampire residents had kept to their cellars and storerooms in the homes where their people had resided. Some smaller vampires with less prestigious families and resources would take a house together, and those with no monies had frequented the graveyards. But the Great Fire had occurred, and it had become prudent to have a safe refuge to which to retreat. And later the population had soared, and graverobbing had become more common, and then Rupert had come to power and set the restrictions upon the doors. No one could leave without their maker's by-your-leave. It was a leash yanked whenever their creations fell out of line.

If told to stay, they had to stay. And there were guards at the entranceway to make certain of it. Safety, security, secrecy were the bywords.

More like strangulation, Genevieve thought.

Wrapping her talent around her like a cloak, she stepped silently up to the vampires on guard at the entrance closest to St. Paul's. The door was not propped open, so she would have to wait. She stood for a good, long time, but she was used to that. Finally, the doors that barred the way to a long, rickety basement stair opened and someone exited. Moving rapidly, she slipped through the doors just as they swung shut.

She relaxed. They had not seen her.

But then, no one ever did when she used her talent. "Passing unseen," Elspeth called it.

Genevieve passed through into the Ossuary's tunnels and followed the snaking paths until she reached a crevice with a convenient stone for sitting and settled in. Vampires had very good hearing, and from this position, she could hear the comings and goings of those who went in and out of the Ossuary. She called it her "listening post" and she had several places in the Ossuary she would sit and listen to those around her without being seen. Sometimes she did rounds through the Ossuary, making sure that no one was causing trouble or bothering those who could not speak against them.

She watched the Ossuary dwellers come and go, creeping up to the doors and humbly requesting to go and feed or complaining to the guards that the policies were unfair. She also saw those who were able to come and go without any questions—the aristocrats of vampire society, those who did not live in the Ossuary but came to view their creations and walk among the rabble.

Many nights, it was a fruitless endeavor, sitting alone in the dark. But some nights, she got lucky. Like tonight. Under the far-off, rattling roar of the Underground that had become a regular occurrence, she heard someone snap, "—Suppose we'll just have to try again with a quicker dagger this time!"

The corners of Genevieve's mouth turned down in grim unsurprise.

"It isn't wise," a woman replied. She sounded as if she were trying hard to hold on to her temper.

Genevieve's eyes widened. She knew that voice—everyone did. For all Genevieve's time as a vampire, that voice had been synonymous with the Draugodrottin's. Gisela, the prior master's woman.

"You'll just let him sit on Rupert's throne—"

"*Let*, after three attempts, the last only a week ago? We need a new approach."

Footfalls came closer, and Genevieve stood and pressed hard against the side of the passage. *See me not. See me not.*

The woman passed close enough for her to feel the whisper of her gown, and the man carried a cane that he tapped nervously against the pavement. She did not recognize the man. After they passed, she turned and followed.

The man insisted, "If we could get a large enough group together, rather than just one or two at a time—"

"And what if he takes us all out in one fell swoop? What then, Horace?" Gisela asked in a flat voice as the train noises died away.

There was no answer. After dying once, vampires became very cowardly about the process.

Horace. Genevieve didn't know that name. it was possible it wasn't the name the man was currently using. Her old master had commanded her to address him as "Bacchus," but his name had originally been Cuthbert.

Gisela continued. "He is gathering people to him. Etienne Flambeau, Dominic Penrose, Joseph—"

"Joseph? That traitor—"

"He was always too soft. But Kendrick's support is growing."

"So we must strike now, before he grows stronger—"

Gisela snapped, "We're *not* discussing this here. Come." She turned down the path that would lead out of the Ossuary.

Genevieve stayed still and silent until she could no longer hear them.

Kendrick had shown no inclination to take on any of the problems that beset the Ossuary—a bitter pill to swallow—but neither had he exerted his will in any onerous way over its inhabitants. And if he passed out of existence, one of *them* would take his place.

A phrase written on a wall in a language that no one else could read was too weak to hang her hopes on. It had simply been a quote from the poem "Widsith," after all, something to counter Rupert's rough declaration of power.

But how had he known it? Was he a scholar, or was he really as old as the Exeter Book that contained the only version of the poem? And oh, if it had been a portent, a true promise...

"'Þæt wæs god cyning,'" she murmured to herself. *That was a good king.*

Genevieve patted her pockets. She had just enough of a newspaper left to leave one more note.

Chapter Seven

Kendrick pulled the ribbon from his hair as he stalked down the Ossuary's corridor, spearing his fingers through the thick strands in frustration.

After fencing with Dominic, he had spent several more hours scouring likely doss houses by the Ossuary entrances and any other likely places for female vampires to find opportune meals, but he hadn't picked up any scent from the notes he had received. Frustrating in the extreme. He had forgotten how London teemed with humans, over three million of them, and adding more all the time from workers pouring in from the country, immigrants from overseas, and the high fecundity of all people everywhere.

He *had* managed to learn the extent of his domain well during these nightly rambles, he admitted to himself, loosening the cloth around his neck. Some small benefit.

He mentally reviewed the notes he had received once more:

There is a plot against your life. Be wary of Winslow.

Take care—Derwin and Mars mean you harm.

Beware Safina and Titus. They are conspiring to kill you.

All three found in his room, on his desk.

He didn't lock the door except when he was in it—there was nothing he was concerned about losing. Etienne had suggested posting a guard to the door, but that would cause more problems than it solved. It would send the impression that he needed help protecting himself and embolden the attempts against him.

Plus, Etienne was right, damn it. If someone had to watch his back, it had to be someone he could trust—and that list was very short. Etienne and Addie had their own home. Getting Dominic to relocate would be a feat—and then that would leave Godfrey alone. Not wise in a vampire that old. Too many friends had encountered the wrong end of Rupert's temper in recent years, and even more had met the sun in the last century.

Kendrick sighed, feeling the weight of years upon him as he approached his rooms. No one told you how hard it was enduring long past all sense or reason. So few things could hold your interest.

But the note-leaver held his attention.

If he could not sniff her out on the streets of London, he could lay a trap, lie in wait for her to come around. She obviously came during the night while he was out and left no sign. He could—

The nearly silent click of boots on stone reached his ears.

Kendrick stilled. The noise came from the hallway of furnished rooms. The hallway where only he resided.

He reached for the sword at his shoulder and advanced in silence.

As he rounded the corner, he heard—and *saw*—the door to his room click shut.

In an instant, he ran forward to jerk open the door of his room, naked sword in hand.

It was empty—but a new slip of paper waited on his desk.

He snatched it up and ran to the hallway, searching up and down the passage.

No one was there.

Kendrick stilled himself and *listened*.

That was close. Too close.

Once around the corner and away from the light that spilled out of the master's room, Genevieve leaned against the wall and let out a slow breath. Her bones had felt like water as Kendrick had run forward like a marauder and thrown the door open, passing within a foot of her. She hadn't even dared blink as she had inched away from his frightening visage, complete with sword in hand.

She hated coming to this section of the Ossuary because it was a lie. The corridors and passages here looked far more like a real dwelling. Rooms had doors, and the walls were planed smooth. Sconces hung from the walls, and the lights and lamps were lit and replenished. The higher-up vampires used these rooms if dawn rose too soon for them to return to homes not connected to the Ossuary.

As far as she knew, Kendrick had used it exclusively since his takeover. No one else had wanted to get near him, and the other high-up vampires were keeping their distance until they discovered which way the wind blew.

Genevieve passed a hand over her face. Using her talent usually felt as easy as drawing a curtain over herself. Now she felt too shaky to even reach for the invisible drapery.

Too close, she told herself, setting off back into the darkness. She had become too comfortable, too confident in her invisibility.

No other vampire had ever been able to sense her when she was near or following them through the Ossuary. He must have senses keener than a bat. Next time, she would not risk passing him a note. Next time, he would have to take his chances with no warning and—

A strong hand clamped around her arm and swung her around, pushing her back against the wall.

"You have some explaining to do, miss," Kendrick growled, his gold eyes shining in the dark. "Who are you, and why have you been leaving me these notes?"

Chapter Eight

If Genevieve's heart could still beat, it would have been seizing in her chest. Her lungs gasped as she wrenched unsuccessfully at the grip of his hands.

He felt like stone—immovable. The old panic rose in her throat.

He was frowning, saying something, but she could not hear him over the roaring in her ears. Her lungs kept doing the completely unnecessary heaving. She was dead; it didn't help anything. They were not susceptible to reason, it seemed.

You're dead; nothing can hurt you, Winnie sometimes said, but Genevieve knew that was a lie.

Kendrick's free hand came around her waist, and he lifted her, whisking her back to his room. He shut the door and set her down. Genevieve fumbled instinctively for the doorknob and yanked on it, but the weight of one large hand held it shut. Kendrick didn't touch her again. He was still talking.

Her ears stopped roaring.

"Easy, love," he was saying. "I mean you no harm."

Genevieve clenched her hands together, feeling the small hole in her left glove rub against her finger. *I need to mend that*, she thought, swallowing. She'd do it tonight. Envisioning the neat, tiny stitches she'd use calmed the tremors in her body, and her lungs came back under her control. No help for feeling like a shivering, panicky fool in front of this man, though. As terror left, embarrassment and anger with herself flooded in. She hadn't had a bad turn like that in years.

"There," he said, in a voice like smoke. "Better?"

She pursed her lips and lifted her chin. She would not fall to pieces in front of a stranger. Or not any further. She threw her shoulders back and turned to face him.

From far away, the man had seemed larger than life. This close, he took her breath away—even after the panic had subsided. His mane of hair filled her vision. She had never seen a man with such long hair before. Broad shoulders strained the seams of his shirt—of a rougher quality than she'd expect for the master of the Ossuary, who could afford the finest London's tailors could supply. But his coat was working man's tweed, a support against the elements, and his waistcoat corduroy. He wore no cravat or collar—only a cloth wound around his neck—again, a working man's attire. His bright-gold eyes fixed on her with interest and a too-canny insight. What did he see in her?

He gripped the sword still. A man out of time, as all vampires were. A warrior, a fighter.

He looked as though he might have stepped directly from the pages of *Wynnflaed's Knight* or *Finwold Law*, tales of heroism in early Britain, before the Norman conquest, when the Saxons and Vikings had invaded and come to make the land their own, mingling with the British tribes and carving kingdoms from the heather and bracken.

He had lifted her with one hand. The rational part of her knew that was vampiric strength. Another part thought he probably could have done it when he had been human, too.

A smile curled over his mouth. "I have been combing the news sellers and the printers for my mysterious note-leaver, and here she comes to see me, instead."

Her eyes widened.

The smile broadened, his teeth flashing white in his closely trimmed beard. "Your eyes are very expressive. Did you know that, Miss...?"

"Dryden." She forced the word through her throat.

"Pleased to make your acquaintance, Miss Dryden. Will you tell me his name?"

Her brows drew together. "Who?"

"The man who put that look on your face."

Her suspicion deepened. "Why?"

"So I can kill him."

ॐ

The woman was tall enough to nearly look him in the eye, her head covered by a badly dyed black bonnet. Her worn gown, also dyed black, looked nearly two decades old. The woman's colorless eyes were blown wide with panic, and her face was bloodless, even for a vampire.

Kendrick kept his expression deliberately calm and warm, even though a knot of anger burned in his gut and grew stronger by the second.

Someone had frightened her very badly in the past. Hurt her, almost certainly. The knowledge lit a fuse in him. What it led to, he had no idea.

Her lips pinched, her eyes narrowing with disapproval. "Is that your only approach to problems?" she shot back. "Killing them?"

Her tart response increased his fascination. He lifted a sardonic brow. "Because swinging a sword is the only thing I know how to do? I confess that it was my main function for many a year. I am very good at it." He looked down at the weapon in his hand and set it on the desk, the naked blade gleaming in the lamplight. "But I am a man of many talents."

She lifted her pointed chin at him in challenge. "I am sorry to inform you that he is already dead. In fact, it's likely you dispatched him a month ago." Her gaze sharpened as if to ask, *Now what?*

Good. A dark surge of satisfaction flared in him—shocking and surprising. "Ah, efficiency—another of my talents."

She snorted.

His eyebrows shot up. "You disagree, madam?"

She stilled, a mouse in front of a lion.

He didn't like it. The flash of spirit she had displayed had intrigued him, and her height put him in mind of a shieldmaiden. So who had made this woman feel so small?

"I assure you, Miss Dryden, you have nothing to fear from me. I only decapitate vampires *after* they've tried to kill me."

Her lips pursed. "Or those whose names I give you."

He acknowledged this with a tilt of his head. "I feel sure you will bear the weight of this responsibility with good sense, Miss— what is your Christian name?"

"It isn't appropriate to address me by my Christian name."

He grinned. "Ah. Propriety, Miss Dryden? At this late date? Tell me, do you always sneak into men's bedrooms to deliver clandestine notes?"

She drew herself up very straight. "Only when someone is trying to kill them. Do you always grab women and sling them around?"

"Only when they ask nicely."

Her eyes sparked ruby for less than a second—but he saw it.

There you are, sweetheart.

"All right, Miss Dryden. Suppose you explain why you were leaving me notes about murder plots? I would love to know how you came by your information."

"Should I not have bothered?" Genevieve snapped, confused and furious with herself. She should have turned around and walked away. Let him fend for himself for once. Instead, he had caught her—he must have had ears like a bat!—and she had reacted like a frightened animal. All because he had touched her arm.

"It does raise the question of how you've managed to intercept the plans of—three? four?—separate conspirators."

"I am not involved, if that is what you mean," she forced through numb lips.

"Don't look like that, Miss Dryden," he said, unrolling her last note. "I have told you; you are quite safe. Tell me, how do you hear these whispers? 'Horace and Gisela plan new attack. Watch yourself.' Thank you. I suspected Gisela was not as pleased with me as she pretended. But who is Horace?"

"I don't know."

"You don't know?" His eyes narrowed. "Then how did you hear this name? For that matter, how did you come by this information at all?"

"I overheard them speaking in the dark and heard her call him by name."

He pondered this. "Why should I trust you, Miss Dryden?"

"Besides the fact that I have not been wrong yet?" She lifted her chin. "I have a talent for not being noticed. People are more loquacious when they believe they plot in secret."

He raised an eyebrow. "That would be why I saw no one in the passage when I opened the door?"

Genevieve pursed her lips.

"It's a useful talent to have," Kendrick acknowledged. "And impressive. I didn't sense anything until your foot scraped on the stone around the corner. I've never encountered anything quite like true invisibility. All right. We've covered how. Now let's address why."

Genevieve frowned. "What?"

"Leaving the notes. Why bother warning me?"

"Because you obviously need help!" she snapped.

He raised an eyebrow. "Do I now?"

"Yes! If I happen to overhear such plots muttered, how many are voiced that I do *not* hear? Have you considered they're trying to kill you because you aren't *doing* anything?"

"No."

"*No?*" Her mouth dropped open in outrage. Why was he smiling?

"Firstly, because I *have* been 'doing things.' Second, vampires don't like change, and *I* am the change that they don't like. So ergo, they are trying to dispatch me before I do any more... things."

She scoffed. "That won't turn back time!"

Kendrick said dryly, "They don't seem to have realized that yet. However, I am interested by your assertion."

She paused. "Why is that?" she asked slowly.

"It may not be what the rest of the Ossuary believes, but I think it is what *you* believe. What is it that I am not doing, Miss Dryden?"

Her pent-up irritation with his tenure so far as ruler warred with her survival instincts, ones who screamed standing up to male vampires and telling them they were wrong only invited pain and suffering.

Irritation won.

"It's your laws," she finally forced through her teeth.

Amusement glinted in his eyes. "My laws?"

"Yes."

"What about them?"

"You haven't made any."

His head jerked back.

Genevieve forged ahead before he could resume his arrogant, vaguely amused air. "You have ousted the previous master, true, and you keep order, but so do occupying armies. You have made us no oaths. We have nothing to depend on."

He tilted his head to the side. "What oaths would you like, Miss Dryden?"

"At the very *least*? An assurance of peace, prohibiting all ranks of men from wrongful deeds, and justice and mercy in all judgments. And that is the bare minimum." Genevieve clenched her firsts. "Binding yourself to keep your own laws would not go amiss, either. Kings should not be exempt from justice."

He asked gently, "Do you think me unwilling to make such oaths?"

She threw out a hand. "I don't know! None of us know! You are a stranger to us. And we have gotten *less* than nothing for all the years that I have been a vampire! I have *not* known peace, and wrongful deeds still persist, and *where* is the justice and mercy? Where is it?"

"Miss Dryden—"

"What is the *point* of you?" she demanded. "If all you plan to do is enforce the status quo that we have had for years and which has helped no one and hurt many, go ahead and fall on your sword, let those assassins overtake you. See if I care."

She choked to a halt. At some point in her tirade, she had reached out and seized him by the open collar of his shirt, the better to rage at him. Her hand was fisted in the material, and she stood close enough that she could feel the heat of him through his clothes.

Vampires were not supposed to be warm.

What had she done? She had behaved as if she were still Genevieve Dryden, confirmed bluestocking and daughter of Ezra Dryden, tutor, writer, and expert in ancient languages for Oxford students, able to speak her mind to any man who condescended to her.

"I—I'm sorry," she forced out. She unclenched her hand from around the fine linen and stared at the crisp, curling hair that showed through the partially undone plackets, the skin that somehow still carried the memory of the sun, even centuries later.

She had never touched a man like that. Not since—well, she had never touched a man like that.

Kendrick intercepted her hand and held it loosely in his own. She stared at her glove—dingy, and with that hole coming through —held in his broad, capable hand, hair curling where his cuffs were turned back. "You don't have to retreat from me, Miss Dryden. I was telling the truth when I said I only smite people who try to kill me first."

Genevieve swallowed under the weight of very male interest. She could recognize looks of desire, but usually, they carried an element of superiority. As if bestowing their interest on her was a favor.

This man stared at her like he beheld a queen and a conundrum all at once. It made her knees shake.

"My experience has been that vampires do not like women who talk back."

His face darkened. "I would never hurt a woman."

"You killed Safina."

"As I said, she tried to kill me first. And I let her slice me before I ended her. I think that was more than fair." His free hand came up to run his thumb over her cheekbone, a feather-light caress that abraded her nerves. His voice turned smoky and persuasive. "You don't need to fear me, Miss Dryden. Won't you tell me your given name?"

"Saying that in a honey voice doesn't automatically make me trust you," she said tightly. "May I go now, please?"

Chapter Nine

Genevieve stumbled back to her bolt hole, a hand pressed to her face. Vampires did not blush—so why did it feel like her face was aflame? Chagrin and bafflement warred within her.

Vampire men did not like mouthy women who did not know their place. They especially did not like sharp-tongued spinsters who grabbed them by the shirt placket and harangued them! All her experience thus far in the Ossuary bore this out. There was a hierarchy to be obeyed. Old vampires were at the top of the social ladder, then those men of noble birth, followed by women of noble birth. Then everyone else trickled down in order of time in the dark and the rest of England's class structure. As men of noble birth and status before their deaths, Bacchus and Laurent most of all had been opposed to anything that smacked of opposition. Genevieve clenched her gloved fists.

Yet Kendrick, their new master, had watched her with an interest she could not begin to fathom. And he hadn't lashed out when she had taken him to task. He had...asked her opinion? Held her hand gently? And he had escorted her out of his room when she had asked to go. He hadn't demanded her given name, only asked. He hadn't punished her for impertinence.

And he had bowed over her hand before bidding her a good night.

Genevieve pressed her hand to her chest. Ducking her head to clear the low overhang of her shared bolt hole, she said, "Elspeth, you will call me every kind of fool—"

She broke off at the sight of Robbie MacPherson sitting beside Elspeth, the two of them hastily leaning away from each other. "Oh. Forgive me, Mr. MacPherson."

Robbie MacPherson was a flame-haired Scotsman who had died at Culloden and had come south to London after the Highland clearances had shattered many of the communities he had depended on to stay hidden. He had been kind to Genevieve and Elspeth when they had first been turned, offering what knowledge and assistance he could without their makers' knowledge. He was one of the few men in the Ossuary whom Genevieve would term a friend. Elspeth might have called him something else.

"I beg your pardon, Miss Dryden—my visit has gone on for too long," Robbie said, reaching for his crutch to lever himself up to his one leg. He had lost the other below the knee. While vampirism would repair injuries sustained after death, it could not regrow limbs or mend wounds sustained before they were turned.

"No, no, please. Don't mind me." Genevieve collapsed across from them in an ungraceful puddle of skirts as her knees gave out. "I've just been a pea goose of the highest order, that's all."

"Pea goose? You?" Elspeth asked, taking Robbie's crutch and leaning it back against the wall. "Do tell, Genevieve."

Robbie cleared his throat, tugging at his collar. His red hair gave the impression of a blush, even if his skin stayed pale and gray. "I can—"

Genevieve squeezed her eyes shut. "I just gave the new master a tongue lashing. Nothing to worry about."

And I ogled *him!* He appeared again in her mind's eye, the glow of his regard, his hair loose about his shoulders, burnished in the light of the candle flame, his corded neck visible through his opened shirt. The feel of his thumb on her cheekbone. She blinked rapidly to dispel the vision.

Elspeth gaped. "*You*? Scolded him? How did you even *encounter* him?"

Genevieve took a deep breath and explained about the overheard plots and the notes, and how she had been caught. Robbie knew of her talent and could be trusted. Loyalty was one of his best qualities—next to his silent constancy towards Elspeth.

She gulped and finished with, "And I was so—unsettled, and irritated with him, I told him what I thought of his management so far. So, you see. Pea goose."

"Gracious," Elspeth murmured.

Robbie leaned forward. "Kendrick's a good man. His ego won't be pricked by a lass's honesty, Miss Dryden."

Elspeth turned to him, alight with interest. "You *know* him?"

"Know *of* him, aye. He's old—older than anyone else I can think of. Knows his Erse," he added with a grin. "Been here and there, goes as he will. Never been involved with politicking before that I remember. He's old friends with Etienne Flambeau and Salem."

Etienne and Salem were the other two vampires who had contributed to Rupert's death and downfall, Genevieve had heard. Etienne, she knew of—a blond Frenchman, always very correct—but he didn't come to the Ossuary often. Salem, she had never seen. He was a bit of a legend among the underground. He had toppled the power behind the previous master, Theron, which had allowed Rupert to swoop in and usurp Theron. Which she was sure had always stuck in Rupert's craw.

"He is older than Godfrey de Bayeux?" Elspeth asked. "Or Bohémond, who died during that impenetrable fog several years ago when he fell into the Thames just before daybreak?"

Godfrey de Bayeux was reputed to be a former Norman lord, and Bohémond—

"Not *the* Bohémond de Terente, surely?" Genevieve put in. "The *crusader?*"

Elspeth frowned. "I don't know. He was quite old, but—might it have been someone using the name?" Vampires freely changed their names as the fancy took them.

Genevieve pressed a hand to her forehead and giggled, the emotions of the night suddenly overwhelming her. "Was he extraordinarily tall, slender of waist and flanks, with broad shoulders and chest, but perfectly proportioned, conformed to the ideal of Polykleitos, and the skin of his body very pale? Did he breathe freely through nostrils that were broad, worthy of his chest?"

Robbie said, "Every vampire is very pale."

Elspeth tilted her head to the side, her brows furrowing. "I never saw him. Did you?"

"No. Anna Komnene describes him in her *Alexiad*, and—never mind," Genevieve muttered. "*If* that's who he was—you think Kendrick is older still?"

Robbie nodded. "He might be as old as the land's henges or the White Horse."

Elspeth murmured, "Surely not."

"I'm not sure," Genevieve whispered, thinking of his visage in the candlelight, the way he held his sword like a warrior of old. "I'm really not."

"What are you going to do now?" Elspeth asked.

"*Do?*" Genevieve repeated, wrapping her arms around her knees. "Why must I *do* anything?"

"Well, he knows who you are now," Elspeth said practically. "Will you speak to him again? Or will you just continue to slip clandestine notes into his bedroom?"

Genevieve made a face at her. "I regret telling you that. Why would I speak to him again?"

"To tell him what needs to be done with the Ossuary."

Genevieve shook her head, her shoulders slumping. "You know as well as I do, Elspeth, that any suggestions from the Ossuary rabble on the proper governance of London's vampires would be shot down immediately."

"Yes, we know that," Elspeth said cryptically, "but does he?"

"She did what?" Etienne laughed. "*Incroyable*! Called you onto the carpet like a governess dressing down a pupil. And resisted the famed Kendrick persuasion into the bargain."

Kendrick frowned at him. "You don't have to look so delighted about this."

After Miss Dryden had left his rooms—she had clearly not wanted him following her, and he suspected she had used her talent once she'd been beyond his sight—he had decided to find Etienne instead of pacing the length of his room until dawn. Etienne had sent him the direction of the terrace house down a small, quiet lane that he had purchased. It was home to several families, Etienne had said, but the basement apartment would be for him and Addie. It was a good place for a vampire, small windows up high that could be easily curtained, and quiet. The basement was fairly empty at the moment, only a few chairs and a table in the main room that had belonged to a former occupant, but Etienne had told him Addie was choosing furnishings.

Some indefinable quality allowed women to transform a place from a building with a bed in it into a home. The addition of curtains and embroidered cushions on chairs and patterned rugs on the floor, some men would say. But it wasn't just an accumulation of things. It was a kind of...softness. A shelter from the cold.

Now Etienne chuckled as he cleaned the lenses of his spectacles and replaced them on his nose. "You cannot deny that your mystery woman had a point."

"Stop that; you don't even need those things," Kendrick said in deep disgust. "And *what* point?"

"You've had discussions with Dominic and with Addie and me about what to do about the state of London's vampires, but the general populace doesn't know that. All they have seen is one dramatic speech where you wiped Rupert's crude 'might makes right' motto from the wall of the Ossuary, and then they heard of you offing assassins." He shrugged.

Kendrick glowered. "I thought I had time to contemplate ruling. It's been nine hundred years since I had anything to do with vampire politics. And now this...this *woman* insists I upend the whole Ossuary right now."

"We are very much prone to inertia," Etienne acknowledged. "But all the more reason to listen to this—what is her name?"

"Miss Dryden." Devil take it, what was her Christian name? He had never gotten it out of her.

In the span of only a few minutes, Miss Dryden had gone from wooden to deeply terrified to impassioned, and Kendrick would be lying if he said it didn't fascinate him. But after seizing him by the collar, as if he were a small boy caught filching an apple, she had retreated within herself, her eyes fixed on her toes.

Because of some man who was dead now. Etienne would say it was primitive of him to feel viciously satisfied about that. So be it. His very bones were primitive, and surviving this long had earned him the right to own it.

Black didn't suit her. She should have been in lovely raiment— a dark blue or ruby would suit her coloring, not freshly dyed crow-black, with threadbare cuffs and fraying bonnet ribbons and a hole in her glove. Her silhouette was out of date. All the women in the fashion plates and on the street wore artificial rumps and tails now, but her skirts were still cut in the old style to accommodate round layers of crinoline and hoops. Was the new color to cover the stains and signs of wear on an old gown? Or was it for mourning?

For whom does she mourn? Kendrick wondered, his hand clenching around his sword hilt.

"So, what was her suggestion?" Etienne asked, buffing a brass finger plate that, based on the entwined roses, led to a bedroom.

"She said…" Kendrick paused in sudden realization. "What she said sounded like the coronation oath of Edgar."

"*Qui diantre est Edgar?*"

Kendrick shot him a wry look. "A Saxon king. You wouldn't know him. It was before your people's time."

Etienne scoffed. "You think my people came from Normandy? *Mais quel Ostrogoth.*"

"Now who's wrong?" Kendrick gestured crudely and Etienne laughed. "It's odd, though," Kendrick added. "It sounded too similar for coincidence."

"A student of history, is she?"

"Perhaps."

Where did she bide? What justice had been denied her?

She was a puzzle he wanted to solve.

If she were his woman, he'd buy her new gloves.

Etienne lifted his coat and brushed it before sliding his arms through the sleeves. "So her suggestion, based on a coronation oath. What was it?"

"Peace, forbidding wrongdoing, and just and merciful judgments." Kendrick mulled this over.

Etienne gave a Gallic shrug. "It does not seem an unreasonable request, *cher ami.*"

"I *intend* to deal fairly with all concerned." He frowned.

"As far as I know, no vampire has developed mind-reading as a talent," Etienne said dryly. "Therefore, how would they know that?"

"It's very irritating when you're right," Kendrick said, narrowing his eyes. "And she is right as well. My intentions are not laws." He fell into a brown study, musing over the problem.

Etienne broke the silence. "Where does your mysterious Miss Dryden live?"

"Given that she is able to slink around and overhear plots and slip me notes, I would assume somewhere in the Ossuary."

"Ah. Then it probably does feel urgent to her."

"What about that makes it urgent?"

"No one likes living in the Ossuary." Etienne held up a hand. "Before you ask me more questions to which I do not have the answers, why not come and have a bite with me? Tomorrow night, find your lady and ask her about the problems that plague her and what she believes could be done about them. Ladies have a managing instinct that should not be discounted."

"Fine," Kendrick said, picking up his sword and swinging the baldric over his shoulder. Maybe slaking his thirst would take his mind off the woman.

❧

Slaking his thirst did *not* take his mind off the woman.

"You are still stewing, *mon ami*," Etienne said, eyeing him warily.

Kendrick realized he was stalking down the dark street like a marauder and both humans and horses were giving him a wide berth.

"If you continue like this, I shall have to use my talent to keep the humans away," Etienne said, likely only half-joking.

Kendrick halted at a street corner. He ran his tongue over his teeth, tasting the blood of the young dandy who had had one drink too many. After helping himself to the falling-down-drunk dandy's blood, Kendrick had poured the man into a cab. He probably would have had his purse and anything else in his pockets stolen in a twinkling otherwise. Closing his eyes, Kendrick inhaled the sharp wind flavored with smog and the smell of sewage and horse droppings and cookfires into his lungs. The strong and clashing scents cleared his mind and helped him focus.

Talents developed at need. Etienne had come into his talent early for a vampire. His ability obscured him and threw up "keep away!" warnings of danger, making humans and to a lesser degree, vampires, avoid his immediate area. A way to hide since Etienne had been turned during the bloodshed of the French Revolution.

Miss Dryden had a talent for true invisibility.

What had caused her to need to hide? And if a man who had hurt her was dead, why was she hiding still?

Etienne asked, "So. What are you going to do about your little harridan?"

"She isn't little," Kendrick said absently, eyes still closed. "She's as tall as me."

"What are you going to do about your giantess?" the French vampire asked without missing a beat.

"Find out her name."

"And then?"

"Begin swearing oaths, I suppose."

"I can guarantee you will never be bored, my friend."

Kendrick turned his head. "With what?"

"Setting the Ossuary to rights," Etienne said with studied innocence. "What else?"

He would never be bored watching Miss Dryden's face. He wanted to watch the emotions play over her features. He wanted to know what she looked like when she smiled.

"Ask your mystery woman her thoughts about that." Etienne grinned. "If she wants to help, Kendrick, let her. You could use more allies. I can verify her latest note, track down this Horace person. Just think about it," he coaxed.

Kendrick had a feeling he would be doing little else.

Chapter Ten

"I want your opinion on this house I have inherited," Kendrick told Dominic the next night. He had arrived on his friend's doorstep a half hour after dusk. "I could find the tunnel entrance, but I'd like to see it from the street as well."

"I know where it is," Dominic said. "But we'll need keys to avoid looking like housebreakers to humans."

"Who would have the keys, if all Rupert's cronies are dead or fled?"

"Not all," Dominic said, giving him an odd look. "There is Joseph."

"I wouldn't describe him as a crony," Kendrick said, thinking of the silent man who had alerted him to the onset of madness in a vampire.

"Perhaps not," Dominic murmured.

"Where would we find him?"

The dingy chop house teemed with clerks and laborers eating bread and meat after a long day. Men sat elbow to elbow at long tables, putting away food as efficiently as possible. Kendrick spotted Joseph towards the back, staring into the middle distance with a tankard in front of him.

Kendrick weaved through the crowd and stopped in front of the table. "What are you doing here, Joseph?" Kendrick asked conversationally, doffing his baldric and swinging a leg over the bench to sit.

The human masticating his bread beside Joseph stared at the sword Kendrick rested on the table. He lifted his head and opened his mouth.

Kendrick caught his eye and shook his head.

The man blinked and looked down, sliding farther away. Dominic silently sat in the open space.

Joseph blinked, focusing on Kendrick. "I'm listening," he murmured at a pitch only the vampires would be able to hear in the cacophony. "The petty squabbles, the earnest conversations, the bad jokes... They make me remember being alive."

"Good," Kendrick said. "Those who forget go mad. Have you heard of any more madness incidents?"

"No, thankfully," Joseph said. "These last few years, there have been far more than usual."

Kendrick leaned forward, resting his forearms on the table. "Do you know who would have the keys to Rupert's house?"

Joseph shot him a long look. Finally, he said, "I have them, Master."

The word churned in Kendrick's gut. "Not 'Master.' I don't choose that title."

"What, then, if not Draugodrottin?" Joseph asked quietly.

Rupert's title, though stupid, had been designed to instill a mythos of fear. Master, though—that was a brutal, bully's title. A master implied that those under him were slaves, Kendrick realized, disquieted. *That* was why the word stuck so in his craw.

"I don't know, but not 'Master,'" Kendrick said firmly.

One long blink from the scarred man. Then, "Yes, my liege."

Kendrick nodded, his shoulders easing.

"We'd like to look at the house," Dominic said, picking up the thread of conversation.

Joseph put his palms flat on the table. "I can take you there now."

Kendrick picked up his sword and stood. "Let us go."

Joseph led them to a grand, terraced townhouse in Mayfair, just off Berkley Square. It had a fine façade and impressive stonework, and the nameplate by the door read, "Carmine House." It loomed over the houses on either side like a shadowy vulture. No lights lit the windows. Joseph placed a great iron key in Kendrick's hand.

Ascending the steps, Kendrick turned the bolt. The door opened with a low groan of protest from the hinges, as if unused to anyone passing this way.

Past the threshold, Kendrick stepped into silence. Not the sorrowful, neat silence of Dominic's Fernside, or the cozy quiet of Etienne's new abode—but a held breath. Like a silent sob.

Here and there, conspicuous furnishings were missing, Kendrick noted as he walked through the hallways. The silver was gone from the butler's pantry—if they had ever had any to begin with—and any small ornaments or porcelain knickknacks that had been in the house had disappeared. Pictures were missing from the walls. As if any residents or servants had scarpered with whatever they had been able to set their hands on.

It was in the upper floors, the non-public rooms, where Kendrick smelled the fear and the blood. And it was in the attics that he found the stained straw pallets, and the shackles. Some iron. Some silver.

Someone had broken them open and let the prisoners loose. *Good*, Kendrick thought, his clenched fingers twisting the metal shackles into something unrecognizable. He should have come here sooner. He should have sought out the cancer of Rupert's reign sooner. He took hold of the silver chain and squeezed. His flesh sizzled against the metal.

A floorboard behind him creaked. "My liege," Joseph said in a carefully neutral voice.

"Did you unlock these chains, Joseph?" Kendrick asked. His skin slowly turned red and blistered from the silver.

"Those that still remained when we returned from the north, yes."

"*Good.*" Kendrick threw down the mangled chains and straightened. "Why were they imprisoned?"

"Punishment for various infractions, my liege. Or in the case of the humans, as food. Or entertainment." Joseph's voice was very dry.

"And no one did anything?"

"He was the Draugadrottin. We were all bound to him."

That was obfuscation. "What function did you serve in his court?"

"Broadly, I was his majordomo. It allowed me to..." He faltered. "I did what I could. For them." He glanced towards the chains.

"And for us, too, if I am not mistaken."

Joseph shot him a look.

Kendrick raised an eyebrow. He had not forgotten that Joseph had spoken up for Ophelia when they had all been captured by Rupert's woman, Gisela.

"It wasn't enough," Joseph burst out. "It was *never* enough."

"We have the chance now to do more. The both of us," Kendrick rumbled. "Will you help me?"

Joseph stood there a long moment in the dark before he bowed his head. "Yes, my liege."

"It occurs to me," Kendrick said, "that I am not truly your liege lord. Not yet."

Miss Dryden's words about oaths and laws came back to him. The Ossuary had functioned on a bloody principle of strength for centuries. But maybe he could forge a different way. Not based on vampire traditions, but human ones. A master could do whatever he liked to those under him because he wielded absolute power over their lives. A liege lord or king, however, owed his subjects security and justice. "I shall have to do something about that." He offered Joseph his hand, and after a second of hesitation, Joseph clasped it.

They descended the stairs to find Dominic. On the second floor, Kendrick heard a far-off chorus of voices lift in song. He went to the window, and when he found the curtains were nailed down, he yanked, ripping them back. Through the dingy glass, he could see a church steeple a few blocks away. He lifted the stiff latch and pushed the window open.

> *"God rest you merry, gentlemen*
> *Let nothing you dismay*
> *For Jesus Christ, our Saviour*
> *Was born upon this day,*
> *To save us all from Satan's power*
> *When we were gone astray..."*

"Caroler practice," Joseph said. "At St. Alban's."

"That's right," Kendrick said. "It's December, isn't it?" He let the curtain fall back as Dominic paced up the hallway towards them.

"It's a good thing you have the keys because the door down into the Ossuary tunnels is locked. But the back half of the house and the basements are disgusting," Dominic said without preamble. "Absolutely abhorrent. Was Rupert continually feeding off his household staff? And there are...bodies. Old ones."

"Why does that not surprise me?" Kendrick muttered. "The attics are similarly foul."

Anger animated Dominic, his eyes flashing red. "Did he have *no* care for his household?"

"They were human," Joseph said, which seemed to be the only answer.

"Human or not, you don't do this kind of thing to your own people. By God, you don't do it to anyone. We have *laws* about killing humans!"

Joseph passed a hand over his face. "Laws do not apply to you if you are the one making them."

"You're right," Kendrick said. "Laws should apply to everyone, or they are not truly fair or just. I have taken over as ruler of the Ossuary, but—as someone recently pointed out—I have not made it clear how my rule will be different. I want to make oaths to the populace and receive their oaths, to bind us together." He flexed his hands, feeling vigor flow through him, as if he were waking up after a long time asleep. "I also want to find all the laws set in place for the vampires of London and discover out just what I am expecting the populace to obey so I can make changes if needed. I'd like your help, the both of you. I have found several of the law books in the Ossuary, but they are old and incomplete. I don't know if there are any in this house. And if it's as disgusting as you say—"

"You'll need to scour the whole building," Dominic said darkly. "I'd suggest fire, but flame is not kind to London or vampires."

"And for such a large building, we'd need a lot of help. Let me think on it," Kendrick said. "But if the both of you are willing, we can comb through the law codes and find which are still in effect, and what—if anything—Rupert was using to govern."

"Yes," Joseph said immediately.

"It will be a large undertaking." Dominic rubbed his chin in thought.

"I am confident," Kendrick said, "that you are up to the challenge."

They left the house the way they came, and Kendrick re-locked the door.

"I will not ask you to name names of the survivors who left

this place," he told Joseph. "And I would not ask them to return. But for the humans—they will keep silent?"

"The few still alive?" Joseph nodded. "They were controlled by fear, the threat of death to any they cared about. They will do their best to disappear. I did not know, at the time, what number of Rupert's circle were still extant, and I told them so. Besides," he said heavily as the wind picked up, "who would believe them?"

Kendrick bade them a good night and walked east, past the fashionable streets and carriages coming and going, through the throngs of people still out in the late evening.

Even though he walked through their spaces and moved through their crowds, he was still at a remove from humanity. As if they were all inside a warm and cheerful pub with a crackling fire and good company, and he watched them from outside the window, the sound tricking to his ears with a muffled quality as rain chilled him to the bone.

What a painful thought.

After a millennium, was he still lonely?

He didn't even remember his own humanity.

But he saw it, every day, through the window.

The trouble was, some vampires simply stopped looking and went on their own way, into the dark. And because of it, a necessary part of them died.

Kendrick kept walking, unbothered as the wind picked up and cut through his layers of clothing like a knife. He had never been able to resist the lure of a good fire and a story told around it.

Chapter Eleven

Genevieve took special care leaving the Ossuary, though she remained as unseen as ever. Kendrick had given her a scare. She dropped off Sparrow's piece work with the shopkeepers and received the meager wage in return. After, even shrouded in her talent, she walked carefully up to a man sleeping rough in an alley. He never realized she was there, even when she sank her teeth into his wrist, above the line of grime around his cuffs. She only took a little blood from him because he tasted strongly of drink, and it was just early evening.

At Sally's, there was no Justin or Mary to watch, but Peter and Hannah squabbled all night. A very fractious and contentious assemblage. Genevieve forwent most of the alphabet lessons and instead asked what sort of story they would like to hear.

"Exciting, with battles. And not a girly story, neither," Peter said in a sullen voice.

"Not a girly story." Genevieve sighed. He had not been as enthralled with Wynnflaed as she and Hannah, then. "Hmm. Shall I tell you of a monster called Grendel, who haunted a lord's hall in years long past, and the hero who did battle with him?"

"Yes."

Genevieve raised an eyebrow.

Peter ducked his head. "Yes, please, mum."

"All right. Now, Grendel…" The words transformed the small room into a lord's hall that smelled of peat smoke and ale, of a night full of monsters, but among the hall's inhabitants: heroes.

Partway into describing the battle against Grendel, an insistent knock sounded on the door.

Peter and Hannah stilled.

Unforeseen knocks were never good. Genevieve stood, smoothing her skirts. "I'll see who it is," she said, gliding to the door on silent feet. The back of her neck tingled, and she flexed her hand. She could deal with any human threat. When her hand rested on the knob, the scents on the other side of the door registered. Blood. Blood and—

She drew back the bolt. "Fletcher? What's happened?"

The urchin swiped his hand under his running nose and gestured to the small boy beside him and the hiccupping baby he carried. "The baby's bashed her head in, miss."

Genevieve crouched to look at the baby, who was bleeding from a cut on her head. "Oh, poor darling," she murmured. The baby twisted away from her to hide against her brother's neck. They must have been siblings; they had the same green eyes and towheaded hair. "What's your name?" she asked the boy. He could not have been older than seven.

He shot her a look and swallowed.

"He's the tyke what lives up the second floor," Fletcher said. "Augie and June."

"August," the boy whispered.

Genevieve's gaze widened. "I think Sally—Mrs. Blevins— spoke to your mother about me. My name is Miss Dryden. I look after Peter and Hannah at night. Would you like to come in, August? I can help you bandage up June's head. She's not too heavy for you?"

"See, I told you she was a good 'un. Go on," Fletcher said, backing away from the door.

Genevieve straightened. "Fletcher, won't you come in?"

"Naw," he said, swiping his sleeve over his nose again and sniffing.

"Just to warm yourself by the fire? You can wait and escort me home," Genevieve coaxed.

"Got something to do, miss. I'll be back." He disappeared down the stairs.

Genevieve sighed, her shoulders slumping. "That boy." She motioned August inside. "Would you like to give June to me? Let's see what we can do about her head. You banged it hard, didn't you, dear?" she murmured, taking the girl's weight and settling her on her hip. She was big enough to crawl but perhaps not walking yet.

June howled at the transfer to a stranger, twisting towards her brother.

"Shh. It's all right. Look, August is right here." Genevieve patted her small back, checking her over quickly. She was small but clean, in a neat flannel gown, and the blood had slowed to a trickle, though the drying blood was all over her head and she'd certainly come out in florid bruise colors soon. The children's names were decidedly not Cockney. Hadn't Sally said something about their mother coming down in the world? How far she must have fallen for her family to land in the East End. "Hannah, there's a bit of supper left. Bring me that bowl and let's see if June is interested in a bite to eat."

The girl did as she'd asked. Peter looked on silently, arms crossed.

"Thank you, dear. August, do you know Peter and Hannah?" she asked over June's howls. "I think Hannah is your age. We've gone over our letters tonight—all the way to 'p,' and I had begun a story. See if June—yes, there you go." August had carefully scooped up a bit of food from the spoon and poked it into June's crying mouth. The wailing stopped as she chewed.

Genevieve smiled and reached for the clean cloth beside the washbasin. She wrung it out and carefully cleaned the cut before wiping away the blood. "It must've been frightening to see your sister get hurt. But see, it's only a little cut. Head wounds tend to bleed prodigiously because there is a lot of blood in the scalp."

"Pro... Prodid..." August repeated in a whispered.

"Prodigious—'huge,' 'colossal,' 'immense.' 'Quite a lot,'" Genevieve defined. "There. Peter, do you know where your mother would keep bandages?"

Peter shook his head.

"Well, no matter." Genevieve dug a handkerchief from her pocket and folded it into a bandage before tying it around June's head. "There. Better, dear?"

June just opened her mouth for another spoonful.

"August, would you like to hear the rest of this story?"

He cast a glance at the door.

"I don't know when your mother plans to return, but I will listen for her," Genevieve promised. "I don't want her to worry. Why don't you finish up that pot?" She shifted June to rest against her shoulder and patted her. "Peter, where was I in the story?"

"They was fighting with the beast," he said immediately.

"Ah, yes. So, Grendel, a great monster who had long harrowed the Hall of Heorot, was sought by Beowulf, a great hero of the Geats. Beowulf did battle with Grendel..."

When Beowulf had vanquished both Grendel and Grendel's mother and gained great renown and Hannah and June had fallen asleep, Genevieve heard footfalls on the stair. But it was Sally who bustled into the small room. "Brr, wind's picking up," she said, unwinding her shawls. She held her hands out to the fire. "Were you good for Miss Dryden, my duck?" she asked Peter, who was yawning.

"Yes, Mama."

She pressed a kiss to his head and straightened to goggle at June and August. "Well, bless her! She finally brought the tykes around?"

"No, August brought his sister over. She had a bit of an accident, but all is well now." She decided not to mention Fletcher.

Sally clucked over the both of them. "They can stay here until their mum gets home. I'll watch them. You'd best be going before this wind turns to a storm, Miss Dryden."

Genevieve was impervious to wind and storms, but Sally didn't know that, and it was kind of her to think of it. She transferred the sleepy weight of June to Sally and settled her cloak around her shoulders. "August, tell your mother that I said you are both welcome anytime," Genevieve told the boy, patting him on the shoulder. He was too young to take care of a baby on his own, but needs must. "I am very glad I could help. Don't be afraid to knock on Sally's door if you need it."

"Thank you, Miss Dryden," he said shyly.

"You're very welcome, dear." She re-tied her bonnet ribbons. "Take care, Sally."

When she stepped out onto the street, Genevieve looked both ways for a small waif with a mulish expression on his face, but Fletcher did not appear. Sometimes he didn't, but she felt foolishly disappointed. Perhaps whatever he had had to do had taken longer than he'd expected. She hoped wherever he was, he was safe and warm on this cold night. A deceptive chill hung in the air that boded either rain or snow if temperatures dropped low enough.

A strong gust of wind buffeted her, and one of her frayed ribbons snapped. Her unsecured bonnet flew off her head.

Genevieve lunged after it, but the wind carried it past her reach.

Then a hand snatched it out of the air.

"*Beowulf*, Miss Dryden?"

Kendrick stepped from the dark shadow of the house, looking

for all the world like a human laborer walking home from the pub —if a laborer walked with a sword slung over his shoulder, that was. "I believe you've lost this."

Genevieve swept her short hair out of her face, gaping at him.

His boot heels clicked against the cobblestones as he approached, and she knew it was only because he allowed it. This man could be silent as the grave when he wanted. Genevieve pressed her lips together. *Pun intended.*

Large hands gently brushed back the hair the wind had disarranged and settled the bonnet on her head. She clapped a hand on it to keep it in place.

Kendrick tilted his head to the side, staring down at her. "Conversations do require a second participant, in my experience, Miss Dryden."

❦

Miss Dryden's hair was short, dark, and soft, ending just an inch or two below her chin. Had she been ill before she'd died? Why had her hair been cropped? Short hair had not been the thing for women since the beginning of the century. Come to think of it, was that why she wore the outmoded bonnet all the time? Kendrick noted the way she clapped it to her head. The worn ribbon trailed down her shoulder.

Miss Dryden licked her lips. "What would you like me to say, sir?"

"Kendrick," he corrected her, and added, on a whim, "Or, if you like, Cyneric. That's what they called me when this land was young." He wanted to hear her say his name.

"What are you doing here?" she asked warily. "How did you find me?"

"I have your scent now. It makes you much easier to track than residue from a note." At her look of wide-eyed alarm, he said, "I do not think many others could find you thus, and I mean you no harm, Miss Dryden. I wanted to see you again. To let you know my plans and see if they meet your approval."

"*Plans?*" she said sharply.

"It occurred to me tonight that you were correct. I have not made any oaths and have not received any, so I cannot expect loyalty or obedience. So far as I know, the Ossuary has never given or received oaths...but that doesn't mean we can't start now. I want to give the vampire population a thorough understanding of the laws I expect them to obey, and what they can expect from me as their lord. You are owed both security and justice, and I will provide both."

"A very elementary step," she said, though she seemed somewhat mollified by his words.

"Everything must begin with a single step. But tell me what you believe the next few to be and I will give them every consideration." He offered his arm.

After a brief hesitation, she took it. Her hand was small on his arm. That damn glove still sported a hole, and he caught a brief flash of skin. Ladies' hands were soft, were they not? That was the purpose of a glove?

"Something must be done about the Ossuary," Miss Dryden said. "It is an extremely unhealthy dynamic. People live on top of each other and in the most primitive conditions. Vampires don't need human facilities or cookfires, but everyone should have a place to lay their head. Tempers flare and quarrels crop up nearly every night, sometimes leaving those involved bloody or dead. Vampires who make trouble of any kind are either leashed into compliance by their makers or summarily dispatched. It's crushing and dark, and you never feel so far from humanity as when you must crouch in a hole like a rat." She paused apprehensively, glancing at him from the corner of her colorless eyes. "Why are you looking at me like that?"

"I like the sound of your voice. It's lovely. Keep going," he assured her. "I'm listening."

She eyed him warily but continued, warming to her theme. "Vampires are trapped in the Ossuary because they have no money, no resources, no friends or family with whom they could lodge outside it. If they could go out at night, they could earn or beg or steal money to improve their lot, find a place to live outside the underground, but they cannot get out either because of the guards on the door or their makers' decrees on them that they must always return to the Ossuary. So they are trapped below, utterly cut off from the flow of human life, and they have nothing to do, no industry, and with nothing because they have no money."

"Much like the lilies of the field, they neither toil nor spin," Kendrick murmured.

Miss Dryden turned an acerbic glance on him. "This is not the moment for levity."

Kendrick hid a smile. "You are right, Miss Dryden; I apologize. Carry on. What did Rupert do to combat these problems?"

"Anyone who had a natural aptitude for pain or bullying, he recruited for a door guard or one of his lackeys. Anyone who made too much of a fuss was turned over to their maker for punishment. It didn't *fix* anything."

"What would you do?" he pressed. "Have you given the matter some thought?"

She sniffed and continued. "I would say the vampires with power never saw a problem with our lack of resources and industry because they were nearly always upper class and never had a trade or profession to begin with. They never felt the pinch of funds because they always had money in the bank, and whoever changed them wanted the wealth and power they afforded. They were never cut off from that indolent lifestyle, and so now we have a problem. The British upper class only functions because they receive rents and profits from their farms, and they live off this income."

"Less so now than in days gone by," Kendrick added.

She raised an eyebrow. "Well, you would know."

He laughed. "Is that a dig at my age, or my beginnings, Miss Dryden? I was no manor lord, you know. I remember that much. I was far closer to the toiling serf. I was able to swing a sword better than the next boy, and I was big. But I take your point. Vampires have no tenants or fields."

"And I do *not* suggest such a thing to enrich the higher class of vampires," she said firmly, "but to break the cycle of poverty. It is the same for humans. To get off the street, a body needs money, but to get money, one must work, and to get good work, one must have a strong body or the right clothes, and stay fed, and how can you save for lodgings without safety, without support? If we could give the Ossuary vampires either a way to earn money or a way to break their blood bonds, we could vastly improve the quality of life among the vampires of London."

"So you want to find something to give the people purpose?"

"We all need something to live for," she said quietly.

"An odd choice of words."

She lifted her head to meet his eyes. "Is it?"

He acknowledged this with a dip of his head. "These are very weighty, well-thought-out arguments," Kendrick said. "I thank you for your perspective, Miss Dryden; it has been extremely enlightening. Tell me, what do you do with the rest of your nights? After you mind human children and teach them letters and tell them stories." He watched her face, what little he could see of it under the bonnet's brim.

She licked her lips. "I go home. I deliver new piecework and sewing supplies to the ladies with whom I lodge. Then I check on people. Listen for trouble."

"What does that entail?"

"Less now than it did," she allowed reluctantly. "You have winnowed down some of the troublesome personalities. But I like to make sure..." She trailed off, biting her lip.

He gave her a long look. "Are there many vampires who make life difficult for others with regularity?"

"Unfortunately, yes."

"And Rupert never did anything about it."

"No. He favored a top-down approach to ruling and so didn't care what a maker did to those of their blood. Besides, most vampires of status try to pretend we don't exist." Her lips pursed.

"They abused those of their own making?" Kendrick asked. The burn started in his chest again. "I can see by your face that they did." And it was entirely possible that Miss Dryden had been on the receiving end of such hurt. He came to a decision. "May I accompany you on your rounds, Miss Dryden? I would like to get to know the portion of my population some would prefer I pretend not exist."

Chapter Twelve

Am I really doing this? Genevieve kept asking herself the question as she and Kendrick approached the Ossuary entrance and the guards at the door.

One of the guards reflexively held up a hand before he realized who was with her. "S-Sir," he said.

"What is your name?" Kendrick asked.

"A-Athos, sir."

"Ah, a Dumas aficionado. Well met, Athos." Kendrick smiled affably, but his keen gaze warned onlookers to be wary. The broad shoulders and sword hilt didn't hurt, either.

"Thank you, sir." The guard's gaze flickered from Kendrick to Genevieve and back again. "Ah..."

"Yes?" Kendrick said. His smile grew sharper.

"Begging your pardon, sir, th-the woman did not exit by this door."

"Lady." Kendrick's growl sent a shiver down Genevieve's spine. "The *lady* did not exit by this door. But now she is returning through this door. With me. Is there a problem?" His voice made it clear that if there were, he would not be keen on the result.

Cowed under the weight of personality, the guard bowed and

stepped out of the way. His counterpart did the same, staring silently.

"That was an example of guards exercising control, I suppose?" Kendrick asked once they had passed down into the tunnels below.

"We are not supposed to exit and enter by different doors. The guards keep track to monitor that all who have left return. Those with repeat infractions are reported to their makers and eventually to the Master. You now, I suppose."

"And what happens then?"

"Punishment."

Kendrick's face hardened, but he did not press for clarification. "You did not come via this door?"

"I did. They just didn't see me leave." Genevieve met his eyes steadily.

"You are a woman of many hidden depths, Miss Dryden." A reluctant smile spread over his face.

"A veritable catacomb's worth," she said in a dry voice.

His laugh boomed out, rich and deep, echoing through the tunnels. It sent shivers of heat down her spine.

"It's just down here," she said quickly, not wanting to dwell on the sensations that his laugh conjured within her. "Let me—" She let go of his arm and hurried forward along the narrow passage. "Elspeth! Are you there?"

"Is that you, Genevieve? You're back early—"

"We have a visitor," Genevieve said hurriedly, poking her head into the bolt hole. "Is everyone decent?"

"Yes, of course," Elspeth said, frowning.

Sparrow looked up from her mending. "Who?"

Elspeth looked beyond Genevieve and her eyes widened.

"Your Christian name is Genevieve?" Kendrick rumbled.

Genevieve turned sharply.

"'Woman of the tribe,' or 'woman of the family.' It suits you." He looked beyond her and bowed. "Pleased I am to meet your acquaintance, ladies. Please, do not stand on ceremony," he said, as the women started to scramble to their feet. It would have been a difficult feat in the small space. "In truth, I am a man of humble origins." He went to one knee and took Elspeth's hand in his, bowing over it. "I am Kendrick."

"This is Miss Elspeth Gibbins," Genevieve said, taking the reins of the introductions, "and this is Miss Sparrow." Sparrow had eschewed her former name.

"Miss Gibbins, Miss Sparrow." He tipped his hat to Sparrow, declining to encroach farther into the small, cramped hole.

Genevieve flushed with embarrassment for how he must have seen it—a small cave in the stone and dirt, barely small enough for three people to fit, and not tall enough for her to stand up straight in. The remains of candlewax dripped down the walls, and one lone flame flickered to light the space. No belongings or furnishings. They slept wrapped in their cloaks during the daylight hours and owned little more than what they could keep in their pockets. Elspeth and Sparrow shared a small basket of sewing supplies that they guarded carefully, and that was all there was to the space.

"How do you do, sir?" Elspeth said carefully. Sparrow stared at him, wide-eyed and silent.

"Better than I have in many nights. Miss Dryden has kindly allowed me to accompany her on her rounds this eve."

His voice had a honeyed quality to it. Genevieve had noticed it before, the first night they had spoken. With only a few sentences, he was quietly coaxing words out of Sparrow and politely inquiring how they found life in the Ossuary, how long they had lived under vampire rule—a kinder way of asking when they'd died, perhaps?—and what they were desirous of to see changed.

Sparrow mentioned the door guards. Elspeth said nothing, but Genevieve put in, "Oversight into the use of blood bonds."

Kendrick shot her a keen glance but did not comment when

Elspeth ducked her head. "I won't take up any more of your evening," he said, rising to his feet. "I appreciate you speaking to me. It was a pleasure to meet you both."

They both assured him, slightly starry-eyed, that the pleasure was theirs.

Once Genevieve had turned the bend of the hallway, she stopped and said, "What on earth did you do to them?"

"Do?" Kendrick seemed genuinely puzzled.

"That—*voice* of yours. Is that your talent? Did you manipulate them?" she demanded.

Realization dawned on his face, and his expression grew grave. "I assure you, Miss Dryden, I did not. But persuasion is where my talents lie, and after so many centuries, a good deal of it is instinctive and bleeds out into much of what I say and do."

Centuries, Genevieve thought. *Gracious.* "So you didn't—"

"I did not compel your friends to speak. They simply became...more at ease with me. Because I meant what I said." He met her eyes seriously. "This, I swear to you."

She lifted her chin a fraction in the air. "And you're not using your talent to persuade me now?"

The corner of his mouth ticked up. "If I were, you would know it. Indeed, you *did* know it, the first night we were introduced. And you pushed back against it. The fact is, anyone can push back on my persuasion unless I bring the full force of my will against them. And I rarely do unless the need is great. You can trust me, Genevieve," he said quietly.

"I have not given you leave to use my Christian name," she said, striding off again.

"Ah, but it is beautiful and rolls off the tongue. Genevieve, Genevieve, Genevieve."

"*Miss Dryden*," she corrected him, steeling herself against the way her name dripped from his tongue. Like a caress.

He laughed. "All right, Miss Dryden. Carry on."

She stopped in at many of the other domiciles she regularly

checked on, introducing to Kendrick apprehensive huddles of women who relaxed into wide-eyed wonder at his solicitous inquiries and clumps of glowering, suspicious men whose faces cracked into grins when he shook their hands and made jokes. He was correct; it was less a direct use of power and more an aura of personality that infected people. Any other night, those men might have come to blows over something inconsequential as their tempers wore thin, or the women shut down before a male authority. But not now. Because it was sincere.

Could this be real? Do we finally have a ruler who cares? Genevieve thought.

Around a bend, she came upon Robbie, probably making his way towards their bolt hole to spend a little time with Elspeth. "Are you acquainted with Mr. MacPherson, Kendrick? Sometimes I think he knows everyone in the underground."

"I have not had the pleasure." Kendrick held out his hand, and Robbie switched his crutch to the other arm to shake it. "Mac-Pherson. Any relation to Cluny?"

Robbie nodded, squeezing his grip in the way men did. "He was my clan leader, and Culloden where I fell."

"A bloody business," Kendrick said. "Bloodier when soldiers are promised invincibility and a way to turn a battle's tide and receive only dust in return." His face was grim.

"Aye," Robbie growled. "And then to lie in the dark of Cluny's Cage for nigh eight year, good for naught else than guarding, with only one leg. T'was after he decamped for France that I came south."

"I am surprised we have not crossed paths before, but much of that century, I was in Wales," Kendrick said. "It is good to meet you, Mr. MacPherson."

"It's Robbie I am, sir."

"Robbie."

Genevieve supposed Robbie would have said more, but along came Winnie down the passage, and he excused himself in favor of visiting Elspeth. Robbie and Winnie were not friends, and as much as Robbie could not find it in himself to be rude to a woman, he avoided her as much as possible. According to Elspeth, Winnie had once said something deeply cutting within his hearing about being half a man.

And her so newly made, and turning so hard and uncaring already, Genevieve thought, watching Winnie advance coquettishly upon them. Sometimes she wondered whether a side effect of vampirism caused such cruelty. Other times, she believed it had far more to do with inner character.

At least Kendrick has his wits about him, she thought as she performed the introductions with a neutral expression. The man was discerning and canny, and he tempered whatever magnetism spilled out of him from a warm exuberance into a pleasant politeness as he bowed correctly but did not take Winnie's hand. "How do you do, Miss Cunningham?" Kendrick said.

It was like the man stuffed all the force of his personality under his hat.

Winnie, for her part, gushed.

Was she trying to throw herself at him or communicate her sophistication? Genevieve wondered. Perhaps Winnie was not quite sure herself, as she several times glanced at Kendrick's yeoman garb doubtfully. For all her social-climbing ambitions, Winnie did not have much in the way of practice.

Kendrick did not allow his thoughts on this clumsy attempt at machination to show, but Genevieve thought he might be amused. *Sort of like a kitten batting at an old tom's tail.* She bit the inside of her cheek.

Mid-sentence, Winnie stuttered to a stop, her hand going to her throat.

"I thought I heard you yammering on, Winnie," a male voice drawled behind them. "Hush and run along; the Master doesn't need you bending his ear."

Winnie dipped her head and backed away under command from the blood bond.

"Genevieve. What rarified company you're keeping.' Oxley stepped out of the shadows wearing striped trousers and an evening coat, the picture of a man-about-town. He was Winnie's master and the only one who could command her to stop talking —with his will. He was an obsequious little toad, and it was awful to have one's tongue leashed or to be puppeted like a doll, as sometimes took his fancy with Winnie. But there were worse vampires. Much worse.

"Be careful, sire; the stench down here is monstrous difficult to remove from one's clothes."

"Then I wonder at your presence," Kendrick said. "What is your name?"

"My name? Gerald Oxley." The vampire puffed up with the attention. Genevieve wondered why he couldn't sense Kendrick's displeasure. "I understand you're doing a little survey of your kingdom, with Genevieve's help. Did you ask Laurent first, Genevieve?"

Though she tried not to, she flinched.

"Do not address the lady so familiarly," Kendrick growled. What a puling, maggoty pustule of a vampire. Exactly the sort of grub one found hiding under a log that tried to wriggle away when exposed. And who was *Laurent*? He had not missed Miss Dryden's recoil at the name.

"I-I meant no disrespect, sire! My liege! Only I've known Ge —er, the lady a long time and—"

Kendrick was certain the man could not come up with Genevieve's last name even if thumbscrews were applied. Because he had never bothered to learn it.

"Do you make your home in the Ossuary?"

"Lud, no!" The man straightened his cuffs. "The linen would never stay clean."

"Then what is your purpose here?" Kendrick pressed, advancing on him.

"Ch-Checking on them—my girls and others. Letting their makers know how they get on."

"Spying and telling tales," Genevieve corrected, voice hard.

"You've turned vampires and abandoned them to fend for themselves?" Kendrick said dangerously.

"N-Not abandoned—"

"Neglected, left, forsaken?" Kendrick suggested, advancing on Oxley as he retreated.

"I say!"

"*I* say that you are not welcome here."

"I've the right to look in on—"

"You've no rights at all, and I'll make sure of it." Kendrick's hand moved towards the hilt of his sword, and Oxley bolted. He'd never seen a vampire move so fast in such tight trousers.

"Is that the sort of thing you guard against on your rounds, Miss Dryden?"

"Yes, some of it. Thank you," she said. "Winnie isn't my favorite person, but no one should have their autonomy removed." Her face was still shadowed, however.

"What is that look for?"

"You've bought yourself more trouble. He is a born and bred sycophant, and telling tales to those stronger than him will increase their dislike of you. More knives in the dark."

Kendrick smiled. "Then we'd better continue building more goodwill. And if you hear of more assassination plots, you can tell me directly now. Can't you?"

"Who cleans the rooms down here? Changes the sheets, refreshes the water, things like that." Kendrick gazed around the small portion of the Ossuary that boasted actual rooms with amenities. Someone had to trim the wicks and refill the oil in the few passages lit. "No one has done anything to the rooms, but someone must maintain the lights."

Genevieve shook her head. "I always assumed the vampires who stayed here just ordered someone to do it. That or someone angling to improve their prospects took initiative."

"Not paid for their labor, then."

"No. Not that I've ever heard."

"Hmm. The persistent Ossuary problem, as you've pointed out."

"It's a problem of personal dignity," Genevieve said, lifting her chin.

"No, you're right. To move from nothing to remembering that they are a voice-bearer takes effort and support."

She nodded like a governess approving an apt pupil, and he couldn't help but smile. "What would you do about the problem, Miss Dryden?"

She thought for a moment. "I'd make sure I knew how much was in the coffers and how much we could spend. I'd invest some of it the way humans do and purchase property with the rest. Earn more money through careful investing and provide housing to those without it. Perhaps there is some kind of industry we could contribute to. We all have skills if we can be reminded of them. We're not just husks driven by hunger." Her voice dropped to a whisper.

"That's very well thought out." Why hadn't he considered that? Genevieve Dryden had vision. And when she spoke from the heart, she glowed as brightly as a lamp. She was not content for the status quo, even though so many of the vampires she wanted to help could not fancy any other way for the Ossuary to function. How had she held on to such a picture? Was it just her circumstances, living in the Ossuary? Her relative youth as a vampire? Or was it something else?

"I've had a long time to think about it. Why do you smile at me so?" she asked warily.

Had he been smiling? He tilted his head to the side as understanding washed over him. That window in his mind, the one with cheery company and a good fire that he couldn't turn away from—Genevieve Dryden sat inside. And he wanted to press his hand to the window, ask her how she had found the door to come in from the cold. It was her tale he wanted to hear, her story he wanted to unravel. That was why he spoke so rashly. "Possibly because I find myself wanting you, Miss Dryden."

Chapter Thirteen

F ar away in a London townhouse, trouble was brewing.

"What do you mean, Gisela shot you down?" Laurent stared at Horace, who quailed under the onslaught of his hard stare and his glittering, red eyes.

"Sh-She said we needed a d-different approach," Horace stammered. "Because the last attempts didn't work."

"They didn't work because those vampires were too *cowardly* to do what needs to be done." Laurent slammed the decanter onto the table hard enough that he heard a little crunch of glass. "Are you *also* too lily-livered to challenge Kendrick? Don't you want him to answer for his crimes? He wants to destroy our traditions, dismantle our very way of life. He killed Rupert and Bacchus and so many others. He can't be allowed to live. Are you or are you not willing to avenge them?"

"Err, yes," Horace said uneasily. "But I think she had a point that we should pick a new strategy—"

"You *think*?"

Horace dodged the decanter. It shattered on the fireplace behind him, raining glass and spirits. The fire belched, and Horace jumped violently. All vampires had a horror of fire.

"You don't *think*," Laurent said, pointing at him. "You aren't here to *think*. *I* think, and then you do as I say, or I disembowel you and stake you out for the dawn. Is that clear, Horace?"

"Y-Yes, Laurent." Horace went paler, if that were possible.

Laurent yanked on the bell pull of the townhouse for a restorative. Afterwards, they could clean up the mess. But the person through the door wasn't a maid.

"Laurent! Have you heard?" Oxley demanded, his eyes shining red. The door rebounded back against the wall and nearly clipped him.

"Have I heard what?" Laurent ground out.

"Well, you see, I was down in the Ossuary because I felt it was my duty to check on my progeny, and monstrous rank it was, too—"

"Get to the point, Oxley." The man was a born and bred bootlicker, and Laurent would've stricken him from his circle years ago if he did not possess an uncanny ability to find himself in the middle of gossip.

"Kendrick was down there—"

"Don't tell me you tried to put a knife in his back?" Laurent laughed. The very idea was ridiculous. Oxley had the backbone of jelly.

Oxley turned the shade of bleached parchment. "Lud, no!"

"Pity. I might've been rid of the both of you." Laurent turned away.

"He was with Genevieve!"

"He *what?*" Laurent swung on Oxley and seized him by the lapels.

"S-She was leading him around, s-showing him the Ossuary rabble...demmed near swung that monstrous sword at me when all I was doing was checking on my vassals!"

Laurent released his hold.

Oxley scuttled backwards and brushed ineffectually at his

coat. "A fellow tries to tell a friend the news and gets treated like this..." he muttered.

Laurent held up a hand for silence and Oxley nearly swallowed his tongue. Gnashing his fangs in thought, Laurent turned the problem over in his mind.

Genevieve, his longtime plaything, was attempting to influence the new master. He had enjoyed toying with her over the years, forced as she was to obey him. How she had hated that! He had gained the sweetest pleasure from commanding her and watching her writhe under the weight of his metaphorical boot. So much more entertaining than puppeteering vampires of his own blood, like her little friend.

Genevieve and Elspeth had slipped his mind, focused on Kendrick as he had been. But now... his lip curled. Genevieve had not slunk off into the dark when her leash to Bacchus had been cut. She was still here, whispering in Kendrick's ear. He could only imagine what she had to say—she was always entirely too mouthy for her own good, and she had a puritanical, do-gooder spirit. She was probably wheedling her way into his good graces to make him *care* for the rabble.

Laurent recalled the pathetic times she had tried to defy him or protect others from his displeasure, and the satisfaction he had gotten from punishing her for it. Though... she had been the only one to ever attempt defiance. He sneered.

She wouldn't succeed in her little quest, of course...but it would be wise to have eyes on the situation. She must not be left to her own devices, especially if she was still trying to stand up to him. He'd show her, and Kendrick, what he did with those who got above themselves.

"I think I must question my dear, dear girl Elspeth," Laurent mused to Horace and Oxley. "It's been...far too long. But in the meantime, this is what I want you to do about our new *master*..."

Chapter Fourteen

"Ah! MacPherson, just the man I was looking for," Kendrick called the next evening.

Robbie MacPherson's brows shot up in surprise. He stepped away from the huddle of men to whom he had been speaking and bowed.

"Are you sure you know what it is you do?" Etienne murmured beside Kendrick.

"No, but I know it needs to be done," he said as they made their way towards the Scotsman. "MacPherson, you know Etienne?"

"Aye," Robbie said as the two shook hands companionably. "Good evening to you both."

"And you as well," Kendrick said. "MacPherson, was Miss Dryden correct when she said you knew everyone in the Ossuary?"

"A fair number, sir," he acknowledged.

"I could use your help. Rupert had a house, a grand place in Mayfair, that I understand he inherited from the previous master. It follows that the thing is mine now, but it needs a thorough cleaning and sprucing, top to bottom. Would you know people who would do good work and want to be paid for it?" Kendrick named the sum.

Robbie's eyes widened a little. "Aye, sir, I can think of a fair few who would. Would you like me to spread the word?"

"I would—but I hoped you might be interested in overseeing the logistics."

Robbie's eyebrows shot up, but he hesitated. "Not Joseph? He was the previous master's majordomo."

"I haven't ascertained if he wants to continue in the position," Kendrick said. "I'd like his help. He knows the house's history. But I got the impression he was not eager to return—at least in his prior function. But you know the people. If you'll get a preliminary work force together, I'll ask him if he'd like to assist. If not, you'll work with Etienne."

Etienne shot him a longsuffering look but didn't comment.

Kendrick added, "And let me know if anyone gives those you recruit a difficult time of it."

"Aye, sir. When would you like us to begin?"

"Whenever your interested work force can start. Etienne has the expenses for cleaning supplies and other items." He had not found the banking records for the Ossuary's funds, but he had accounts of his own, accrued over the centuries. Until now, he had had little need to dip into them for more than new clothes and travel expenses. Kendrick clapped them both on the shoulder. "Thank you both." Then he strode off to find Joseph.

He had not felt so electrified and purposeful in years. Speaking with Genevieve had lit a fire in him—enough that he had spoken without thought when he had realized that he was attracted to her. *Like some green lad*, Kendrick thought ruefully. It was no wonder that she had stiffened up and retreated. Gentlemen didn't speak to ladies of wanting them.

"I don't know why you'd say such an extraordinary thing," she had said stiffly, after staring at him like he had sprouted another head.

"Forgive me for putting it that way," he had said by way of apology. "I have never been truly civilized. But believe me that I meant it. And it is extraordinary—to me. It's been decades since I've found myself wanting anything. I find myself surprised...and delighted, Jenny."

He took some heart that the disturbed look on her face seemed to have more to do with the nickname he had bestowed upon her than by his declaration.

But all of it was true. Genevieve Dryden was a riddle of passion and hurts, fervent convictions and stubborn will that he wanted to unravel, one ribbon at a time. And Kendrick believed the best way to go about showing that he was sincere, as well as proving that he had listened to her and he believed she was correct in her assertions, was to put some of what they had spoken of into practice. Which was why he had approached Robbie MacPherson and was now looking for the former master's majordomo.

Joseph was a harder character to find. He had to inquire of several people—and they were not as helpful as Robbie, though Kendrick made a point to be persuasive and nonthreatening. But finally, he ran Joseph to ground on the streets above, outside a music hall teeming with life as performers wearing loud, colorful clothes danced and observers called encouragement and heckled in equal number.

"Listening again?" Kendrick asked, stopping beside the other vampire and gazing around at the crowd. Men and women milled around, bundled in all sorts of clothes and layers, skin colors blending from the browns of Africa and Hindustan to swarthy Mediterranean shades and up to pale, sickly Englishmen.

"And if I were?" Joseph murmured.

"I would say this is an ideal place to do it, but I marvel that you have not gone deaf by now," Kendrick said as another burst of laughter echoed. In the snatches of conversation and shouted comments in various languages and cants, he could even hear phrases of Mandarin.

"I assume you came looking for me for a reason. I have not found any more law books, though I have an appointment to meet with Dominic and go over the ones we have in hand later this week."

"I wondered how much you enjoyed the job you did for Rupert."

"Not at all," Joseph said with a grim smile.

"So, you would not be interested in assisting with a project that involves the house?"

He frowned. "What sort of project?"

Kendrick explained his plan to offer at least a small portion of those living in the Ossuary a wage to clean out the house, and Robbie's willingness to find people interested. "You are most familiar with it, but I understand if you would rather cut ties."

"Did you know that for all the years I spent on the fringes of Rupert's court, I never drew a wage?" Joseph tilted his head to the side, his eyes unfocused. "I was repaid with 'status' and 'power.'"

"So, you really stayed for the less fortunate who intersected with his circles."

"Yes. Those who drew his ire, who fell out of favor...those they wanted to make an example of. Or play with." His mouth twisted. "But I can help. Truth be told, I would enjoy seeing it scoured free of the past. And money talks."

Kendrick nodded. "I am hoping Miss Dryden's suggestions to improve the fare of the Ossuary dwellers will bear fruit."

"Miss Dryden?" Joseph shot him an odd look.

"You know her?" Kendrick questioned.

"Oh, yes. I know her. If she has given you suggestions, I am sure that they are good ones. Shall we go?" Joseph gestured away from the music hall.

Kendrick broke a trail through the crowd and wondered just *how* Joseph knew Genevieve—and how well.

When the insidious pull seized her, Elspeth dropped the piece of lace she was nearly finished tatting. Her throat closed.

She knew what that tug meant: Attend me. *Now.*

Laurent had decided to remember that she existed. And he was angry.

Dread cramping her stomach, Elspeth set aside her work with trembling hands and blew out the candle before the insistent call drew her out of their bolt hole. She hurried along the stone and shored up passageways of the Ossuary; the tug dictated her direction. Resistance would only bring pain and more ire when she finally appeared before Laurent.

She found herself at the Mayfair gate.

"I am called by my maker," she forced past her lips in explanation to the gate guards even as the tug redoubled into an insistent banging behind her eyes. *Now. Now. Now.* She flinched and pressed a hand to her temple, avoiding their gazes, but she knew her eyes were red.

"Name?"

"Elspeth Gibbins," she murmured.

They exchanged a glance and stepped aside. They could spot a blood bond being tugged. "Return through this gate before sunrise."

Elspeth slipped past them and emerged into a dark alleyway. She crept along until she reached the street. Then, obeying the direction of the tug, she hurried through thoroughfares and lanes until she found herself in a slightly less opulent neighborhood, in front of a modest townhouse she vaguely recognized, embellished with a raven above the door.

As Elspeth mounted the steps, the door flew open. Oxley, a vampire dandy, stared down at her narrow-eyed. "He's been waiting, girl, and not happy about the delay."

"It was a far walk," she whispered, her eyes on her toes. The headache was still banging away inside her skull.

The vampire scoffed, dusting off his lace cuffs. "Could have gotten a hackney, girl."

With what money, and what address? "He will be further irritated if you impede me," she pointed out.

The dandy jumped aside comically, and she entered.

The inside of the townhouse smelled like dust and blood. Stale, thankfully. She had been called to awful scenes in the past, simply because Bacchus and Laurent liked an audience. Bacchus, who had drawn the most glee from ordering her about, was dust and ash now, thanks be to a merciful God, but Laurent was the one who held her chains.

"My dear, dear Elspeth." Laurent descended the staircase slowly because he liked a dramatic entrance. Elspeth stood with her head down and face schooled to the carefully blank expression she had perfected over almost two decades, waiting for him to finally reach the parquet floor.

"It's been too long," Laurent said, gripping her chin with his long, cold fingers and raising her head. He was a long, boney man, with a face that could have been considered handsome in the pale English aristocratic way, but the skin clung a little too close to the bones of his skull in death now. In shadows, he maintained his appearance of striking attraction; in daylight, he would have appeared hideous and macabre.

He would also ignite in daylight, which would make the way he looked moot.

"Tell me, Elspeth, what is this I'm hearing about Genevieve? Oxley tells me she's been rather *friendly* with our new master."

"I don't know." Truth. She didn't know what he'd heard. She always made it a careful practice to lie by omission to her maker.

"You don't know? You, bosom friends with Genevieve, don't know?" Laurent's grip on her chin increased to a painful degree.

"He—He's been meeting people in the Ossuary? Perhaps they

ran into each other?" *Please let it not occur to him to command me*, Elspeth prayed.

"Oxley said Genevieve was bear-leading him."

"Sh-She made the introductions—"

"Genevieve, poking her long nose into things that are none of her concern." Laurent let her go and turned away, pacing up and down the black-and-white floor in thought. "And no one to keep her in check now."

Elspeth stayed very still.

"Well, we'll have to do something about that," Laurent mused. "Elspeth, my dear—I release you of the command to stay close to the Ossuary except for feeding."

Her dizzy rush of relief only lasted a second before he turned to her with a bright, fanged smile. He reached out and smoothed her hair away from her face, tucking it behind what remained of her right ear after he and Bacchus had cut it off. He put his lips directly against her mutilated flesh and murmured, "Listen carefully, now. You will keep an eye on Genevieve for me. You'll remember what she says, whom she meets, and where she goes, and you'll report back to me whenever there is aught to relate about the master and his plans for the Ossuary. I command you to do this, Elspeth."

Her throat closed in dread.

Laurent smiled. "Now run along and listen for any pieces of choice news to bring me. And you'll tell no one," he added idly. "No one is to know what you're doing for me. This is going to be *our secret*."

Elspeth hurried down the Ossuary corridor, patting her hair carefully to make sure she had hidden her ears once more. She had always been used as a weapon against Genevieve. In the beginning, Bacchus and Laurent had delighted in "punishing"

Genevieve for her infractions, but it was only when they had cut off Elspeth's ear that Genevieve had stopped rebelling against them so openly. She couldn't bear to be the cause of Elspeth's hurt.

Now I fear I will be forced to wound her far worse than anything they did to me, Elspeth thought in despair.

But how could she stop it?

She had barely made it to their shared bolt hole entrance before Robbie found her. "Did you go and feed, lass?" he asked, approaching nimbly on his crutch, even on the uneven surface of the tunnel.

"Yes." She nodded, the lie heavy on her tongue like a scold's bridle. "Were you looking for me?"

"Kendrick wants help to clean out Rupert's house. He has put me in charge, and he's going to pay, Elspeth! I wanted your opinion—and he'll pay you, too, if you want to help." He took her hand. "First step to independence."

Robbie MacPherson was the best man she knew, good and patient and careful as only a man who had known war and pain could be. He had been steady and constant, never pressing her, always there. But she had always known that she could never love him—not when she was still chained. And especially not now, when she was a knife in the dark, to be wielded against any she considered a friend.

Elspeth bit the inside of her cheek, hard. *Which is worse—to wound a lover or betray a friend?*

"What is it? Your eyes are glittering," he asked, leaning closer as his brogue strengthened. "This is the turning point, you'll see. There are better days ahead for us, lass."

She smiled even as guilt and Laurent's hateful mandates threatened to choke her. "I'm sure you're right," she said, in a voice she did not recognize. "Lead the way."

Chapter Fifteen

Genevieve blessed the quiet of the London streets as she left Sally Blevins's home. She had had a full complement of children tonight, and their mothers had come home later than usual, and all the children had been fractious, and one of the babies had been teething. August and June had not appeared, though, and Genevieve had been too busy trying to keep the peace to go knock on their door.

She had also been too busy to pick apart the previous night's interaction with Kendrick—in theory. It had intruded, unasked for, in between the squabbles and the crying babies and letter quizzing.

"I find myself wanting you, Miss Dryden."

"I have never been truly civilized."

"It's been decades since I've found myself wanting anything."

And then he had called her "Jenny." No one had called her "Jenny" since...

She shook her head. But it was all foolishness. He, who looked like he stepped from a heroic lay or poem of yore, wanting her? A spinster who flinched at unexpected touch? Ridiculous. The only sensible thing to do was to dismiss it as a passing fancy. An unwary thought. And she should certainly feel nothing at all one way or the other over the fact that he had not appeared out of the shadows this night.

Genevieve sighed as thunder rumbled ominously far off. She'd welcome the rain to wash away some of the street grime if the rain wouldn't drizzle for days on end, turning the whole world dreary and gray. On her way home, she kept an eye out for Fletcher. He had sounded like he had the sniffles the last time she had seen him. It wasn't like him to stay away so long. He liked having a routine.

Genevieve stopped at a street corner and bit her lip. Things happened to street children and dossers and the London poor all the time.

She recalled one of her father's turns of phrase from his spotty translation of *Beowulf*:

> *"All were endangered, both elder and younger,*
> *pursued by a killer, a shadow of death.*
> *He trod every night then the mist-covered moor-fens;*
> *men know not the wanderings of reavers from hell."*

Sometimes the *things* that happened to people were bloodsuckers like her.

Please be safe, Fletcher, she thought, wrapping her talent around her like a shroud as she approached the Ossuary entrance. Passing through the doors behind another vampire, Genevieve descended into the dark and walked unseen through the corridors, half-listening to the snatches of conversation around her, half lost in her thoughts.

Too many things pressed in on her mind. Fletcher's wellbeing as well as that of the other children, her friends' safety and comfort, and Kendrick.

Her body flinched away from the idea of someone wanting her—but her mind kept turning over and over. A man who had seen so many things—so many places and people lost to time.

He said that he meant it, her traitorous mind reminded her.

Her father had teased her when she'd been in her early twenties and finding no man who had caught her eye, saying that she would not be satisfied with a modern man when she had cut her teeth on knights and heroes. She had huffed and declared it poppycock; she had been perfectly content keeping house and assisting with his work and had not been mooning after some fictional romantic hero.

But I lied, Genevieve confessed. *I just didn't know it until the object of all my secret longings stepped off a page and into reality.*

She heard a voice say, "But what if Kendrick gets wind of—"

"Keep quiet and he won't," another hissed. "Laurent wants it done. Tomorrow."

Genevieve froze at the turn of the passage and listened hard.

❧

"You are late tonight," Sparrow commented, bent over her piecework.

"And I shall be later still," Genevieve said, setting down her reticule in their bolt hole. "I must find Kendrick. I went by the furnished rooms, but he was not there. Where is Elspeth?"

"Robbie wanted her opinion on the state of some linens and curtains," Sparrow said, knotting her thread. "Kendrick asked him to lead the cleanout of the late master's townhouse—perhaps he is there as well."

"Oh, thank you." Genevieve breathed in relief.

"What do you want Kendrick for?" Sparrow asked curiously.

Good question, Genevieve thought. Aloud, she said, "I've heard more mutterings. I think he ought to know about them right away." *Especially because they're from Laurent.*

"All this in just one night?" Kendrick marveled at the marked improvement. Two men cleaned the main chandelier, while several other people scrubbed and waxed every other surface, carting away rugs to beat them in the small garden behind the house. Already, fixtures and floors gleamed.

"Amazing what folk will do when motivated properly." Robbie leaned on his crutch and grinned proudly at the industry in the house's main foyer.

"We found more curtains," Miss Gibbins said triumphantly, descending the stairs with another woman carrying huge trunks.

Kendrick moved to the stairs and took the trunk from her. "Where do they go?"

"The main parlor for now. We'll replace the curtains room by room for safety, but the ones now are so dingy and dusty..." She shuddered.

Etienne appeared at his elbow to take the other from her helper.

Kendrick, Dominic, and Etienne had been in Dominic's townhome taking notes on all the old laws, dooms, and codices left behind from centuries of vampiric rule. Godfrey had finally made an appearance, looking wasted and sickly. But he'd spent the few minutes in Kendrick's company lecturing them all that their society should be entirely separate from humans in order to stay safe.

"And how does he imagine that we will feed ourselves?" Etienne had murmured.

"Salem managed it," Kendrick had pointed out.

Both Etienne's eyebrows had flown up. "Can you picture Godfrey gnawing on a sheep, *mon ami*?"

Kendrick had had to hide laughter, but he had hoped that pulling Dominic from that atmosphere would restore some animation to his friend, who had become faded and distant with each word his maker issued. So, he had pulled the three of them out to go see the progress Robbie and Joseph had wrought on the house.

"It's a marked difference already," Kendrick said, letting his voice carry. "Thank you all."

The women ducked their heads and smiled. The men grinned and pulled their forelocks.

An insistent knocking began tapping out a rhythm on the front door.

With a furtive glance about, one of the men eased towards the door and opened it. "Yes?"

"I need to speak to Etienne," the person on the other side of the door said. "Let me in."

"*Addie?*" Etienne exclaimed, nearly dropping his pince-nez.

The impromptu footman swung the door open.

"Addie, darling, what are you doing here?" Etienne stretched his hands out to her.

Addie beamed, throwing her arms around him. "Silly, you know I can always find you when I want you." That was her newly discovered talent.

"Dangerous, that," Dominic said dryly.

"You should be at home; dawn is not far off!" Etienne set her down. "You took a risk, darling!"

"I know, but I was careful. I have to tell you something important!" Addie said earnestly, clutching at his coat.

"What is it, dearest?"

"Did you know French vampires can be killed with baguettes?"

Etienne stared at her.

Addie continued. "The only problem is, the effort of driving baguettes into a heart is very *pain-staking!*"

Kendrick burst into laughter. Miraculously, so did Dominic.

Addie beamed.

Etienne slowly closed his eyes, looking like a man desperately clinging to the fringes of his sanity.

This only made Kendrick laugh harder.

"Did you get my joke?" Addie asked sweetly.

"Very clever, Addie, my love," Etienne said in a choked voice. "Did you come up with it yourself?"

"Well, you've been teaching me French, and I often like to sit outside the French bakery shop around the corner before dawn because they begin baking the bread and it smells so wonderful, even though I can't eat it, and listening to them speak is like practicing, which you said I need to do, and so when they were talking about the bread—"

"I see."

"It just came to me!" Addie said proudly.

Dominic had to brace his hands on his knees to stop chuckling.

Kendrick walked up and kissed Addie on the cheek. "What a marvelous end to a night, Addie. Masterful work." *You've made Dominic laugh. How long has it been since he's done that?*

Joseph emerged from the servants' green door, wiping his hands on a cloth. His sleeves were rolled up to his elbows. "My liege, you have a caller at the tunnel entrance."

"Practically inundated with visitors tonight." Kendrick raised an eyebrow. "Who is it?"

Joseph half-smiled. "Miss Dryden."

"Oh, you missed my joke," Addie said.

Kendrick patted her shoulder. "I'm sure Joseph and Etienne would love for you to tell it again." He excused himself and hurried down the servants' passages to the cellar door. Down here, it smelled so much more salubrious already, though more work was necessary. Inside, the tunnel entrance had been unbolted and stood open.

"Miss Dryden?" Kendrick said, stepping through.

For a moment, the tunnel was empty of occupants. The next, Genevieve appeared in the shadows.

The rush of delight at her presence had not dimmed. If

anything, it had grown stronger. "An impressive talent, Miss Dryden," Kendrick said. "I tip my hat to you. What brings you here?" *You've sought me out, Genevieve. You've not done that before.*

"I need to tell you something, but without anyone overhearing. There's been too much of that already." Her eyes looked shadowed, like she was pressed down under a weight of cares.

"Will you come up into the house? We are cleaning it presently, but I believe the library is unoccupied." He gestured for her to move ahead of him into the house. *Tell me what's the matter, Jenny. Tell me how I can help.*

⚜

The dusty library had not yet been touched by the industrious cleaning crew outside. Kendrick shut the door firmly behind them, which seemed to signal to the work crews to move farther away, and the hubbub faded in volume a bit. The room had also been designed for quietude and study by the hands that had built it. Few books adorned the shelves—Genevieve did not think Rupert had had any interest in reading—and the room on the whole seemed threadbare and forlorn. There was, however, a camelback trunk in the middle of the floor, old and much scarred.

Genevieve twisted her hands together and tried to think of how to begin.

Kendrick moved to the trunk and opened it, taking out some of the objects and setting them on the main library table. "These are mine; I left them behind with Dominic while I visited the Continent. They'll make a start on filling these shelves, I think. *Northanger Abbey*! My favorite of the Austens." He brushed the book off and set it on the table. "Do you like to read, Miss Dryden? I would think so, if you are a lady who knows her *Beowulf.*"

"Yes. My father read to me all the time as a child," she whispered.

Kendrick set another book on the table. "What is it you needed to tell me?"

"I have heard another whispered plot."

"Yes? Who is it this time?"

"This isn't a joke," she said, stung by his inattention.

Kendrick straightened to look at her. "I know that, Genevieve. I didn't expect them to stop after one benevolent gesture. Vampires don't like to change their thoughts or their behaviors."

"That's not an excuse."

"For their behavior, or my nonchalance? No, don't answer—I shudder to think what you will say. You could fatally wound my *amour-propre*." He smiled. "Tell me what you heard."

"Someone will move against you tomorrow night. I don't know who."

He nodded. "Forewarned is forearmed. I thank you."

"Be wary," she insisted. "The person driving this plot—he is craftier and more devious than most."

Kendrick's gaze sharpened. "You know who it is?"

"I heard a name," she hedged.

"And you know the name."

Reluctantly, she nodded. "Laurent." She stared down at the rugless floors, scuffed and dusty from years of neglect.

"I don't recall a vampire named Laurent. Unless he has taken a different name to the one I knew."

"He was good friends with my deceased maker. Bacchus."

"Ah. The one who was once Cuthbert." Kendrick's eyes narrowed dangerously. "I always thought of them as Cuthbert and Crony. I don't think I ever bothered to learn his real name. Still extant, is he?" He drummed his fingers on the library table.

"He will not be the one to try for you tomorrow, if you were thinking of changing that."

"No, it would be just like him to use another for his dirty work," Kendrick agreed. His eyes sharpened on her. "Oxley mentioned him. He said you should have asked Laurent before assisting me. But Laurent was not your maker."

"I told you they were good friends. They did nearly everything together," she reluctantly said. "I was commanded to obey him. He did not like it when I tried to protect Elspeth." *What an understatement.* "He is *her* maker."

Kendrick asked softly, "And what did he do to Elspeth? To you?"

"He hurt me," she said flatly. "But he can't anymore. The command to obey broke with Bacchus's death, and I am free of him. But please don't speak of this to Elspeth. Or Robbie," she added as an afterthought. "I will tell her myself. Laurent is just a symptom of the larger problem."

"We are making progress," Kendrick said, gesturing to the industry she could still faintly hear, even though dawn had to be nearly upon them.

"Not quickly enough."

"Everything must be done immediately, is that it?"

"As soon as it can be accomplished! You never know how close a soul is to the brink. Why do you think so many snap and go mad down in the dark?"

Kendrick urged, "Won't you help me, Genevieve? I could accomplish much more with your assistance."

She sobered, her shoulders slumping. "I can't help you."

"Why not?"

She laughed and heard the bitterness in her voice. "You think those vampires will let a woman be in charge? Not the ones grateful for your coin, but the ones who think might makes right. Who think their power gives them the ability to rule over vampires and humans alike."

"This age is so backward. In my time, women had more rights and protections. They could even divorce a husband if they needed to."

"The Dooms of Æthelberht," she murmured. Even dry law code could sound like magic when her father read it in the original tongue. Genevieve shook her head, shoving aside the grief. "Sadly, all these vampires share this unenlightened perspective. If I tried to do anything on your authority, everyone would think I was your—your leman."

Kendrick raised an eyebrow. "So?"

"It would erode any respect I tried to build! Gisela—Rupert's woman—and the previous master's leman liked the power that came with the position enough to make any who slighted them regret it through fear and pain. To say nothing of what the Master would have done. But no one respected them, and I heard all the resentment and hatred that was muttered behind their backs. I can't become the target of such distaste."

Kendrick crossed his arms. "Because you think I won't support you?"

Genevieve threw up her hands. "Ugh, men! No. Because it would destroy any trust I tried to build with the rest of the Ossuary."

"What if you *were* my woman?"

She snorted and turned away, staring at the empty shelves. What a metaphor for her life. "No, thank you."

"Not like how you're thinking. If you were my wife."

Her eyes flew wide.

From behind her, Kendrick said, "Queens hold power in their own right. If I am ruler of the Ossuary—lord, king, what have you —then you would be queen. And no one would have a reason to resent you for getting above yourself or enacting change."

Genevieve said shakily, "Vampires don't get married."

"Vampires don't *bother* to get married. There is no reason that we can't."

She turned around and examined his face. "You're serious?"

His eyes flared gold in the dark. "Yes."

She swallowed and lifted her chin. "Why? Why marry me?"

Kendrick took a step towards her. "I need your vision for what could be. It's very hard to see the way to anything different when you are as old as I am. I know things need to change, but you can see how with new possibilities. I need your hope. And a covenant between us would protect you and give you the respect and power to enact your own change without bringing the matters to me."

Genevieve clenched her hands in her skirts. "And you're willing to go through a farce of a marriage to get it?"

He moved closer and tilted his head to the side. "It wouldn't be a farce."

"What?" she breathed.

"Everyone would need to believe we were truly married to accept my authority conveyed to you."

"Yes, but no one would need to know it is a—a marriage of convenience."

He tilted his head, watching her closely. "They would be able to tell."

"H-How?"

"Through scent. Have you never noticed?"

"Oh," she breathed. Genevieve suddenly realized why she associated some vampires together in her mind, even though they did not lodge together. Scent. "How...?"

"Vampires in intimate relationships—that is, ones beyond casual coupling—exchange blood as well."

She flinched and looked away. The ghost of the past she could not remember rose up. She whispered, "I don't know that I can do that."

"Not handsome enough for you, am I?"

Her head snapped up.

Only a step away now, Kendrick grinned at her. "You watch me when you think I don't notice, Jenny."

Her stomach swooped and decided to take roost in her throat.

He chuckled. "It's all right. I watch you when I know you don't notice, so fair's fair."

Vampires didn't blush, so why was her face so hot? "Kendrick, I can't marry you."

"Will you think about my suggestion? That's all I ask. And— here. It's no bride gift, but I think you appreciate a good tale." He sorted through the piles of books on the table and plucked one free. "This is one of my favorites, in the vein of Sir Walter Scott's books. I think you would enjoy it."

Genevieve took the book and stared down at the faded, green-cloth cover, worn at the corners like it had been much thumbed. She could still read the title in gold text: *Wynnflaed's Knight*, by E.D. Saxon.

With shaking hands, she opened the cover to touch the dedication.

To My Daughter Jenny,
  Who has always believed there is nothing a heroine cannot do.

Genevieve burst into tears.

Every sob she had held in the cage of her ribs for the last month escaped at once as she clutched the book to her chest. Her vision blurred, hot liquid spilling down her cheeks in a red river.

"Genevieve," Kendrick said in helpless alarm, his arms encircling her. She pressed her face into his shirtfront to try to muffle the keening wail clawing its way out of her throat. But she couldn't stop it. The wave of grief was crashing over her, pulling her into the undertow.

Her knees gave way.

Genevieve never hit the ground. Kendrick scooped her up, and for a second, she was airborne. Then she came to rest in a lap, still held in his embrace.

"Ah, Jenny," he murmured in her ear, his hand coming up to cradle the back of her neck. "I never meant to make you weep."

"It's my book," she gasped brokenly. "How did you know it was my book?"

"*Your* book?"

She clutched it tighter, curling around the book like it might disappear. The grief tore into her like a wild thing. "My father wrote it for me."

Chapter Sixteen

Genevieve's father, Ezra Dryden, had been a man set on a life of scholarship. He had had a passion for history and the Old English language, and he'd set out to Oxford to earn his degree and enter the world of academia. He would translate old, moldering documents and write treatises and teach young men how to mind their þs and ðs.

Then he'd met Constance Thorne at a small chapel in Oxford and the course of his life had shifted.

She had been the only woman for him, and they'd fallen in love like lightning, like thunderbolts, as her father had declaimed to a young Genevieve many a night, narrating their love story. But he could not become an Oxford fellow if he'd followed his heart—Oxford professors were not allowed to marry. Dreams of recognition and success, or love?

Setting aside his dreams of research and scholarship, Ezra had taken up tutoring young men looking to enter Oxford or attending school and struggling with their studies, and had married Constance, though he'd made only enough for them to scrape by on the fringes of respectability. After a few years, when they realized that they had a child on the way—"*Me!*" a young

Genevieve had always exclaimed—Ezra had taken a risk and used his background in history and language and his love of story to write a novel.

And it had sold.

Thanks to the burgeoning love of novels and the popularity of Sir Walter Scott's *Ivanhoe* in particular, Ezra's novels, full of romance and daring set in a pre-Norman Britain during the rise of Saxon kingdoms and the Viking invasions, had allowed the Drydens to live in relative comfort as he'd tutored young men in language and history during the day, sneaking in his own research during the sessions, and he'd written at night under the penname E.D. Saxon. Much of the passion, romance, and heroism in the books had been due to Constance, who had urged less emphasis on dry, political-focused plots and what the era would have been exactly like, and more artistic freedom to allow the characters to follow the spirit of adventure. Ezra had often worked out details of the novels in Genevieve's bedtime stories or by discussing the tales with Constance.

After her mother had died when Genevieve had been seventeen, her father had lost some of the heart for the historical novels. He had penned a series of short satirical works while focusing on translating Old English texts with some philology associates. He'd retreated into his books and into the past. While Genevieve had assisted with copying out his translations and proofreading his satires as she'd kept house and looked after him, she had urged him to return to the sweeping, romantic historical tales she had loved so much as a child, since he had told her many tales he had not yet developed into novels—but he had not made much progress on those stories.

And then she'd been taken, and it had been too late for anything.

Genevieve couldn't tell how long she sobbed against Kendrick's chest. She was no rational being, just pain and anguish, only held together by his arms around her.

By the time she'd managed to sob herself spent, her eyes throbbed and her throat ached. She felt like she had been pounded by relentless waves of sorrow.

"I'm sorry," she whispered, her voice a thread.

Kendrick's hands tightened around her. "Don't apologize for your grief, Jenny. Not to me."

"My father always called me Jenny. How did you know that?"

Kendrick's hand stroked her neck. "It's him you wear the black for, is it not?"

She sniffed and nodded. "When the blood bond broke, I ran before anyone could stop me. I had tried so many times before to go home, but I had never made it out of the city. I went to Oxford by train, fighting to stay awake during the day, trying to find safe places to wait until dark. But he wasn't there. Someone else lived in our house. I couldn't find any of his colleagues. Finally, I looked in the cemetery." She clenched her hand in his shirt, but all her tears had run dry. Her head dropped to Kendrick's shoulder. "He died last year," she said tonelessly. "I was too late. By one year. I didn't—couldn't—"

She sucked in a gasping breath to brace against the pain. "Afterwards, I came back here. Because I didn't have anywhere else. And there was Elspeth, and Sparrow. A-And this is why we have to make the Ossuary better." She sniffed. "Because this is all I have now, and I can't accept this being all there is with no change for eternity." Her voice dropped into a whisper.

Kendrick's comforting voice was almost an embrace on its own. "Jenny, I don't believe that a man who writes with such touching sincerity and warmth didn't let you know he loved you."

"I know he loved me. I just hate thinking that he believed *I* would abandon *him*."

Her position curled in his lap dawned on her. She cleared her throat and sat up straighter. "Oh—I've gotten your shirtfront all bloody—" She raised a hand and then checked herself. How would she wipe her face or his shirt without staining her gloves? She had given away her handkerchief.

"I am no stranger to a bit of blood. It will wash out." Kendrick stilled her hands' fluttering and wiped her face with his handkerchief, one finger under her chin to hold it steady.

Genevieve looked into his gold eyes and wet her lips. "You really like his books?"

"Really. He writes adventure in such a way that the blood sings, and you can smell the heather and the scent of the sea. Some of the history is pure invention, but he was able to get so much of the spirit of the time correct." He smiled crookedly. "Even the invented aspects carry the right spirit."

"He—He would have l-loved to know that." She gulped. "He loved history and language. He would read to me from Old English texts so I might fall asleep. I had no idea what he was saying, but it was the way he said it that captivated me. Why is *Wynnflaed* your favorite?" she murmured. "Everyone always remarks upon *The Wife of Weland* and *Finwold Law* as being his best works."

"It has the best romance," Kendrick said, his eyes sparkling. "But I have all of them, or very nearly."

"You do?" Genevieve moved to stand, and Kendrick lifted her from his lap and steadied her as she found her balance once more. Unsettled, she ducked her head and slapped ineffectually at her skirts before making for the book table.

"Oh, goodness—*Wolfhead Tree, Sigestan of Emberlost*—even *The Broken Spear*! That was his first one, you know, and most people didn't know what to make of it, though it sold well. You really do have all of them."

"I think I am missing the second volume of *The Banished*, but it might be in a different trunk."

"You do have a lot of books," she noted.

He laughed. "Not compared to a friend of mine's hoard, but a few. I have always liked a good tale. They contain possibility. They paint not just how the world is or was, but how it could've been. How it could be."

Her gloved fingers lingered over the worn cover of *Wynnflaed's Knight*.

"You do that, too," he murmured. "Will you give me the chance to build that better world you can see so clearly, Genevieve? Not just for you...but with you?"

⁂

"You were in there quite a while," Etienne murmured as Robbie escorted Genevieve and Elspeth to the tunnels below. If Kendrick could read a man—and he thought he could, after so many centuries—he'd put money on the Scotsman walking them all the way back to their abode, based upon the many times he turned towards Miss Gibbins to ask for her opinion tonight. Kendrick had wanted to be the one to get them home safe, but he'd thought better of it when Robbie had offered. Genevieve needed some time to process his offer.

But she had taken the book with her.

"And *mademoiselle* came out looking discomposed."

"Hmm?" Kendrick said absently, watching the rest of the vampires pack up the cleaning supplies and file below before dawn broke above the horizon and sent them to sleep.

"And there's blood all over your shirt," Etienne continued, sounding a little irritated now.

"Is there?" He looked down. "Imagine that."

Etienne made a wordless exclamation.

Kendrick turned and grinned. Winding up Etienne was too easy. "What?"

Addie sighed and rested her chin on Etienne's shoulder. "You're so nosy."

"I was merely inquiring about the lady's welfare," Etienne forced out through gritted teeth.

"Oh, was there an interrogative in there? I didn't hear one." Kendrick laughed. "The lady is all right. She had an...emotional moment. There's apparently going to be another attempt on my life soon; make a note, will you?"

"'Someone will try to kill Kendrick in the near future.' Will it be I or someone else?" Etienne muttered, pretending to scribble in the air.

"Is that all?" Addie asked. "She couldn't have been weeping all over you about assassination attempts. I don't know her well, but I believe Miss Dryden to be very sensible."

"Well, I proposed, but she wasn't crying about that."

"*Quoi?*" Etienne exclaimed.

"You *proposed?*" Addie squealed at the same time.

"You mean *marriage?*" Etienne pushed his pince-nez further up his nose, magnifying his eyes. "But why?"

Addie smacked him in the arm. "What do you mean, *why?*"

"I thought he would ask her about improvements for the Ossuary, not plight his troth. But *marriage...*"

Addie planted her fists on her hips. "*We're* getting married."

Etienne pulled Addie into his arms and rubbed his nose against hers. "Yes, but that is different, *mon chaton.*" Etienne shot Kendrick a narrow look. "You didn't know who Miss Dryden was a week ago."

"Not very romantic of you, Etienne." Kendrick smirked.

"Yes, Kendrick can fall in love if he wants!" Addie insisted.

Kendrick stilled. *Love?*

"When are you getting married, Kendrick? Oh! We could have a double wedding."

"Or, we could not," Etienne said. Kendrick correctly read *that* response as, *"Get your own damn wedding."*

"I only put the question to her tonight, Addie; Miss Dryden must think about it. She may refuse me," Kendrick said gently.

Addie frowned at him. "Good grief, why?"

Kendrick laughed. "Thank you for your vote of confidence."

She rubbed her eyes and yawned. "Maybe if you didn't walk around in bloody shirts..."

"Time for bed," Etienne said, steering Addie towards the tunnels. "With your leave, Kendrick, we shall make use of the rooms below instead of venturing out. I believe dawn is in a few minutes."

"Feel free. And if you can spot who maintains the rooms, let me know," Kendrick said. Before retiring himself, he picked up his second-favorite E.D. Saxon novel, *Eardwulf of the Vale*, from the table in the library. It, too, contained a shocking proposal of marriage—but in this tale, it had been the plucky girl from the Highlands offering a handfast ceremony to the stranger come among them in return for his protection.

Why had he suggested marriage? He smiled ruefully down at the book in his hand. It had seemed like the logical choice at the time to give Genevieve what she wanted most and give the Ossuary what it needed. But would she accept it? Would she accept *him*?

It would depend on how offended she was that he had acted like a barbarian instead of a gentleman and mentioned marital relations. He hadn't missed how her face had frozen. But it had been true, and something they would need to consider. No vampire worth their fangs would miss what was or was not being exchanged. A relationship could be disguised without one or the other, but not both. Blood left a stamp on a body. That was why vampires—most, anyway—did not regularly drink from opium eaters, or any constantly inebriated humans, or those with blood sicknesses. Beyond taste, it left a miasma on a body, even second-hand. Regular blood drinking from the same person forged a scent connection.

She may well say no, the pessimist in him prodded as he carried the book with him to his rest. *She is under no obligation to trot out her demons on your say-so.*

The thought unaccountably depressed Kendrick. He had found himself willing to slay any number of demons and foes for her upon seeing her tears.

Brought low by a woman's weeping. He was not too proud to admit it. He could not think of a time in the last century he had felt so helpless.

Kendrick shut the door to his room and lay down on his bed as the sun crept above the horizon. Thumbing through the pages of the book, Kendrick contemplated what kind of man the author had been, to pen such stories that reached out through time to touch a man who had walked similar roads. What kind of woman was Genevieve, to have been raised on such tales?

Maybe that was what had drawn him to her. She seemed to breathe a different kind of air than the rest of the Ossuary—when they had to breathe. When he looked at Genevieve, he could smell the morning mist and picture the way the sun glinted off the dewy heather. He could picture the landscape the way it had been long, long ago.

Ossuary rulers, to his memory, had never shared power. A Master's consort might have supported him in exchange for status and prestige—but they had never been equals.

Maybe they could re-learn a lesson from humanity. What better start could there be for the vampires of London?

As long as Genevieve did not find him too bad a bargain, of course.

❧

"I don't know what to do," Genevieve whispered, having bared all to Elspeth in the privacy of their bolt hole. Sparrow was already asleep. "Elspeth, he wants it to be a real marriage."

Elspeth's eyes flicked up from the lace she was attempting to tat by one struggling candle in the few minutes before dawn. "You know that if every man was like Bacchus and Laurent, no woman would marry," she said carefully. "But they do, all the time."

"Is it all men, or all vampires?" Genevieve muttered.

Elspeth hummed in the back of her throat.

Genevieve pensively twisted a short lock of hair around one finger. "No, you're right. I'm being silly. Nothing in his character has shown that Kendrick would hurt me."

"It's not silly," Elspeth said gently.

"I have attacks of panic. Nightmares. I flinch when people touch me. How could I handle marriage and all the intimacy that entails?"

"You've really never..." Elspeth asked hesitantly. "Not since?"

Genevieve shook her head.

Twenty years as a vampire had gleaned her an insight into how human societal rules loosened in the dark. While some, like Gisela, sought a partner for power and status, others only wanted comfort and companionship amidst the pain, whether it be a brief liaison or a more long-standing relationship.

But Genevieve had survived by going unnoticed.

"It would be an obstacle," Elspeth said carefully. "But I thought you liked him."

Genevieve buried her head in her hands. "That's the other part of the problem."

"Well, he is right about one thing," Elspeth said. "You would have real power to make a difference."

"Because a man gave it to me."

"Because he is inviting you to be his equal in all things—which is something Rupert never did for Gisela, as much as she wanted it. Kendrick would give you that—and his protection."

Genevieve made a frustrated noise in the back of her throat. "*Protection.*"

Elspeth's mouth pursed in disapproval. "Genevieve, we both

would have given our fangs for protection five or ten years ago; don't deny it."

Genevieve couldn't. *I am safely free of Bacchus, but Elspeth is not free of her maker. It is not an unreasonable wish.* "No, of course you're right. I'm sorry."

"Do you think a man would talk down to you as the wife of... what are we calling him?"

"King of the Ossuary? That sounds pretentious." Genevieve gnawed at her lip. "He did offer to kill Bacchus, when we first met. And then looked very pleased he was already dead." *If I married him, I could extend the safety he grants me to others.*

"There you go." After a moment, Elspeth said, "Marriage is a contract, you know. Don't be afraid to lay down your own terms for him as well."

"What will he think about that?" she muttered. Think she was more of a scold than previously believed?

"Ask him and you'll find out," Elspeth said placidly. "He did not strike me as a man who was unreasonable."

As the pull of the day sent lethargy through their bones, Elspeth blew out the candle and they curled up in their cloaks to sleep the day away.

The allure of sleep's oblivion did not take Genevieve right away, however. She stared sightlessly up into the dark, fighting the pull.

Why *her*? There were others better suited for the consort of the Ossuary. Like—well, not Gisela, who had tried to kill him and liked power for its own sake. Definitely not someone like Winnie, who was too young and had too many selfish impulses. Elspeth would have been an ideal candidate, with her calm and rational listening ear, but she wanted Robbie. Which was good, because the thought of Kendrick and Elspeth was enough to make Genevieve's throat tighten with...something like envy.

Of every woman with whom he could have suggested an alliance, he had seen *her*.

He watches me when I don't notice.

She pulled her cloak over her head, recalling his quip: *"Not handsome enough to tempt you, am I?"*

That was not the issue. Not at all.

But that's all it is, she told herself firmly. Interest. Liking. An... attraction. *He doesn't love me. And I don't love him! But would a marriage with common goals be enough?*

A real marriage.

When contemplating a theoretical union, she had never imagined anything otherwise when she had been human. It was only after becoming a vampire, and after her body had begun to flinch without input from her conscious mind, that she had written off any such future.

If she agreed, she would have to tell him. No, untrue. Regardless of what she decided, in order to explain her reasoning, she would have to tell him. All that she remembered, at least.

But if she said *yes*, she could do all that she longed to do, without asking for permission or relaying her wishes through him and depending on Kendrick to implement her ideas. She could give others hope—what she had been denied.

And she'd be married to a man who sent shivers up her arms.

Genevieve wrapped the cloak tighter around herself, her head pillowed on her father's book about a heroine who ventured out into the wide world and gained a knight champion.

She had always wanted a hero. But heroes only lived between the pages of books, men larger than life who did what was right. Was she looking for something that did not exist?

As the inexorable pull of the sun drew her into slumber, it struck her at last what she had found so strange about their meeting in the library.

She had not flinched as he had held her and comforted her. Not once.

What terms would she ask for?

Chapter Seventeen

Kendrick, after an interruption that had required him to change his coat, had reached the imposing bank edifice just before closing and now left with a vast number of bank notes secreted about his person.

The gas streetlights illuminated the gold lettering above the door as he stepped out and merged with the foot traffic on the still-bustling street. He made his way down to Regent Street, where many goldsmiths and smelters plied their trade. He found the shop he wanted and knocked on the door.

"Is your forge banked?" he asked when the door opened.

"We're closed."

"Is it banked?" he repeated, narrowing his eyes.

"No," the man said, recoiling from whatever it was he saw in Kendrick's face.

Kendrick put bank notes in the man's hand. "Good. I would like to buy a portion of gold from you, and I'm renting your forge for the night."

That, plus the persuasion, was enough for the man to leave Kendrick alone with the fire and the anvil and the tools once more bank notes had changed hands for the gold and other necessary metals.

Fire was a vampire's natural enemy. They could die by fire or sunlight just as much as a sword to the neck. But Kendrick knew forges and bellows and hammers and tongs, and he had a healthy enough respect for flames to be wary about his business. He had observed and learned many crafts over the centuries, but smithing had always been one of his favorites. It took skill, strength, imagination—and for one such as he, a chance to face one of his last remaining fears.

He set his sword aside and doffed his coat, rolling up his sleeves before donning a smelter's apron. He reached for a gold bar and set it to heat.

Giver of rings, a king was.

He stoked the fire high.

This evening at Sally's, Hannah had been full of questions about Christmas. "Is it really coming? What do you do at Christmas? What is it about?"

What is it about? Genevieve wondered as baby Justin blew bubbles on her shoulder. Could a child get to this age and not know anything about the season? "Does your mother have a Bible, Hannah? If so, I could read you the story."

"Don't think so," Peter said. "But Augie's mum takes them to church. She might."

"Oh, is she home?"

Peter shrugged.

"I shall go and inquire." Genevieve carted the baby with her out of the room and up the stairs. She didn't need the number—she could follow the scent trails of the children to the second floor. She knocked on the door quietly.

The normal sounds of movement and quiet voices behind the door ceased. After a long silence, feet moved towards the door and someone carefully unlocked it. "Yes?"

The woman behind the door blinked bottle-green eyes at Genevieve. Blonde hair struggled out of the pins piling it on top of her head. The woman looked hollow-cheeked, as if she were not eating enough. Perhaps she was giving her portions to the children.

Genevieve smiled. "Good evening. My name is Genevieve Dryden. I watch children for Sally Blevins and others."

"Oh!" The woman's expression cleared. "Miss Dryden—thank you so much for helping June and August. I hate leaving them alone, but I—I had to go out suddenly." She swallowed. "I am pleased to meet you. I am Evangeline Hartshorne."

Genevieve shifted Justin to her other arm and shook hands with the woman whose name and accent marked her an outsider among the East End's inhabitants. "I was happy to. And if you ever need to, you can always bring the children by for a while. I try to do a short lesson on their letters or numbers. But I wondered if you had a Bible I might borrow. Hannah has asked about the Christmas story, and I thought I would read it to them."

"Oh, yes! One moment." Mrs. Hartshorne disappeared into the room and through the open door, Genevieve saw August playing with June on a threadbare quilt that covered the bare floor. He waved at her, the solemn tyke. Genevieve smiled and returned the motion. Then she helped Justin wave too before the baby shoved his hand back in his mouth.

"Here. What a wonderful idea, to read through the Christmas story," Mrs. Hartshorne said. "We have been reading the Old Testament stories lately, but switching to the Gospels for the season is very appropriate."

"Thank you so much," Genevieve said. "I shall return it before I leave."

On her way back to Sally's room, she wondered what sort of

past Evangeline Hartshorne had, to have begun her life some-where very different and ended up here.

But didn't we all, Genevieve thought. Except perhaps Fletcher. Worry roiled in her stomach, but there was nothing she could do about it until Sally came back.

With Hannah waiting expectantly around the wobbly table and Peter pretending indifference but still listening, Genevieve sat down and opened the book to the Gospel of Luke.

"'And in the sixth month the angel Gabriel was sent from God unto a city of Galilee, named Nazareth, to a virgin espoused to a man whose name was Joseph, of the house of David; and the virgin's name was Mary...'"

The story of the angel's arrival to Mary and his announcement that she would be the mother of the Most High rolled off her tongue in the small, squalid room, until she reached the next-to-last verse of the section. "'For—'"

Genevieve's throat closed. She cleared it. Cleared it again.

"'For with God, nothing shall be impossible.'"

She stared at the type on the page, faded as if another thumb had smoothed the words over and over, clinging to the promise. Genevieve swallowed hard. The words were not some ephemeral *maybe* or *perhaps*. They were declarative. Without equivocation.

"Nothing shall be impossible."

"Is there more?" Hannah broke in.

"This is just the start," Genevieve said, pushing aside the hurts the season held for her. "Christmas is the time of hope coming to fulfillment. The long-awaited Savior of the world being born to Mary." She took a deep breath and continued.

Once her bonnet was tied on and her cloak fastened, Genevieve delivered the Bible back to Mrs. Hartshorne. "Thank you for the loan," she whispered as Mrs. Hartshorne opened the door. She could hear the quiet breathing of the sleeping children.

Mrs. Hartshorne wrapped her shawl around her. "You're very welcome, Miss Dryden."

"Please call me Genevieve." She smiled. "Have a good night, Mrs. Hartshorne."

"Evangeline." The woman returned the smile. "You as well, Genevieve."

Pleasure bloomed when Genevieve found Kendrick waiting for her in the dark street. "You're here."

"That I am." He smiled, and it was as if some of the darkness rolled back when he caught her in his warm gaze.

"You didn't have anything better to do tonight besides wait for me to finish minding children?"

"Actually, I managed quite a lot this eve. Arranged for furnishings to be delivered, looked in on the cleanup efforts, stopped an assassination attempt—"

"Already?" she exclaimed, eyes widening.

"Not to worry," he assured her. "It was a vampire named Damon, and all he did was ruin my coat. Joseph and I stopped him—we even tried to take him alive, but when he saw which way the wind blew..." He shrugged. "But I am safe this night, fair lady." He bowed.

"Then why do you smell like smoke?" The scent of hot iron and burning coal hung about him in the air. Even the heat of the fire seemed to cling to him like a phantom.

"That was after I changed my coat." He offered her his arm.

Heaven help her, she took it.

She expected him to press her on her answer to his proposal, but he didn't, instead asking, "And how were the children tonight?"

"I read them the Christmas story—up to Bethlehem's star. I thought to save the Magi and the Flight into Egypt for another night. I thought I remembered the words by heart, but they surprised me again."

Kendrick lifted his face to the moon, visible this night as it waxed nearly full. "Christmas draws nigh. And what shall I give you, Miss Dryden?"

She blinked at him. "Me?"

He smiled. "For the twelve days of Christmas. What would you like?"

"I have no need of an abundance of birds," she said, smiling a little. "I don't even know what the original singer did with twelve days of birds."

"And lords and ladies dancing and leaping, with a smattering of musicians thrown in for good measure."

"They must have had a grand estate," Genevieve said.

"I do have gold rings, however. That is what I made this eve. In days long past, a king was a giver of rings to his nobles and those with whom he made oaths. I took what you said under advisement and decided that would be as good a way as any to forge new bonds with the people."

"I think that is—"

Genevieve halted at the street corner, slowly turning to breathe in the cold, fetid air. Under the stink of the street and the snap of the wind, she thought she had scented something.

"What is it?" Kendrick asked, his hand twitching towards his sword.

"I thought—there's a boy who sometimes walks me partway home. He lives on the streets. I haven't seen him in a few days, and I've been worried. Never mind." She bit her lip. She could have sworn she sensed him.

"No, trust your instincts. Which direction?"

When she would have demurred, he directed, "Close your eyes and reach out with your other senses."

Genevieve let her eyes flutter shut as she listened to the low murmur of voices in pubs and doss-houses, breathed in the air that carried the hint of snow coming on and something that reminded her of Fletcher. She hesitantly pointed. "But I don't—"

Kendrick pivoted, his eyes narrowing as he followed where she indicated. "Blood."

He swiftly made for an alley. Genevieve seized her skirts and hurried after him. They left the light. Only the moon guided them through the twisting, ramshackle passageways between buildings—Kendrick nearly had to turn sideways to fit a time or two. Finally, the narrow passage disgorged them before a building half-rotted.

"Stay here," Kendrick said, waving her back.

"What in there can hurt me? I'm a vampire," Genevieve objected.

"Keep close, then," Kendrick said before putting his shoulder to the door. It gave with little resistance, and Genevieve followed him in.

They found Fletcher in what passed for a cellar—he had been entering and exiting by a broken window. The boy huddled under a pile of rags, his breathing thick with phlegm and his face marred with bruises.

"Fletcher?" Genevieve breathed, touching his mottled cheek. It was blazing hot.

Something under his jacket squeaked.

Kendrick moved the fabric aside. They came face to face with a puppy, a small, skinny thing that barely looked old enough to be weaned and still had its milk teeth. It yelped and attempted a growl.

The noise roused the boy. He flinched away.

Kendrick yanked her back just as silver in his hand flashed. The object was not a shiv or a switchblade, but a silver-plated table knife.

"Get back," Fletcher forced out. He held the knife out in front of him warningly as he coughed. The rattle in his chest sounded horrible. "Get back, reavers, back..."

Genevieve pulled against Kendrick's hold. "Let go; he's not well. Fletcher, it's me. Miss Dryden. What happened?"

Kendrick released her and bent over, ridding Fletcher of the knife. "He's delirious." She heard the sizzle of the silver against his skin as he slid the knife into his pocket.

The puppy squeaked and flinched away, and that made Fletcher gasp and recoil.

"He's hurt; I have to help him!" Genevieve pulled back the rags and the boy's coat to find the gashes on his arms. "Dear God, what happened?"

"He's human."

"He's a child and my *friend*!" Genevieve spat. "I am not leaving this boy here." She moved to lift him.

Kendrick gently pressed her aside to lift the boy himself. "Carry the dog."

"Dogs don't like vampires." She eyed it dubiously.

"He fought for the thing; he will want to see it when he recovers."

"Will he recover?" she whispered, using some of the ragged blankets to tuck around the boy. She carefully used another to lift the squirming dog.

"We'll do our best."

"*We?*"

"Well, you're not taking him down to the Ossuary. Besides it being off limits to humans, it is probably the worst place for him. But as it happens, I have a nice, clean house." He nodded towards the rickety stairs they climbed down. "After you, Miss Dryden."

Chapter Eighteen

"Have any of the bedrooms been cleaned?" Kendrick asked as he came through the door, the injured boy rousing enough to twist in his hold. Genevieve hovered at his elbow, the puppy squirming unhappily in its swaddle, much like the boy.

Joseph looked up from conferring with one of the maids. His brows snapped down. "Only the master."

"That will do." Kendrick started for the stairs.

"What's toward?" Joseph met him at the base of the steps.

"L'go," the boy muttered, but then he coughed, the low, thick sound of his lungs fighting the sickness in them. "Le'go!"

"It's all right, Fletcher," Genevieve said, setting her hand on his head. "I'm here."

"The boy is sick and injured."

Joseph's eyes snapped to Kendrick's. "You won't—"

"No." Blood wouldn't do any good at this point. Vampire blood was not intended for true healing. It fixed at its own fixed rate and purpose—and sometimes the fix happened after death.

Joseph relaxed infinitesimally. "Would you like my help? I was a doctor—once."

Kendrick felt Genevieve still beside him. "Come, and welcome," he said, ascending the stairs.

In the cleaned and refreshed master bedroom, Kendrick set the boy on the bed and stepped back, taking the dog from Genevieve so she and Joseph could assess the patient. He held the quivering puppy under his arm as he set coal in the fireplace and lit the tinder. They'd need it warm in here to sweat the sickness out of him.

"I'll ask someone to heat water, shall I?" he said. "I doubt he's ever seen a tub."

"Please," Joseph said, rolling up his sleeves.

"What else will you need?"

Joseph hesitated and then rattled off a list of things. "For fever, for plasters, for disinfecting these cuts. An apothecary—pharmacist," he corrected himself, "will have them. Do you want me to write them down?"

"I'll remember." If he didn't, he'd wake up a doctor and ask him. Before Kendrick left, he acquired a box and rags from Robbie and set the puppy in it close to the room's fire. It would need a good wash, too, before reuniting with the boy. Then he relayed the request for hot water to the kitchens. They had plenty on hand because they had been scouring surfaces this eve.

Acquiring the rest of the items in the dead of night, short of breaking into shops and finding the right supplies in the dark, took some doing. Kendrick had to knock on the doors of a few shops before he found one where the proprietor lived in a flat above. Then he had to make the man agreeable to his will—not hard, but taking a little time if he didn't want to sublimate the man entirely. Then the pharmacist had to find all the items, and a few things he didn't have. But he was able to direct Kendrick to another shop that might, and then Kendrick had to ensure he wouldn't remember any of this before sending him back to bed. And then he repeated the process all over again at the next shop. And while he was out, he might as well get food for the boy as well, since they certainly didn't have any of that, and then he must stop a milkman and get milk for the boy and the dog.

By the time he was returning to Carmine House, the earliest wave of knocker-uppers had just taken to the streets with their long sticks and their peashooters, rousing factory workers and others who needed to rise before the sun. Kendrick passed them with a nod and kept on until the streets broadened and the thoroughfares became cleaner, though more carriages passed carrying the members of the *haute ton*, or whatever they called the London upper-class nowadays, home from parties and social events. A group of drunken gentlemen passed him singing a rousing chorus of "Here We Come A-wassailing."

"Sheason's greetingsh to you, shir," one of them called, doffing his hat in splendid flourish and nearly falling on his face before one of his friends hauled him back up.

Kendrick smiled as he went around the house to the kitchen door. How many days was it until Christmas? He had lost track.

Robbie met him at the door and relieved him of half his burden. "Joseph's been a regular martinet. Did you know he was a doctor?"

"No, but it doesn't surprise me that he is proficient in leechcraft." The look in his eyes—a man who had healing hands forced to dark deeds.

"He wants some of this boiled and steeped and whatnot, but he wants the rest of it on the double. Oh, food." He blinked in mild surprise. "Smart."

"The boy?"

Robbie shrugged. "Still breathing."

Kendrick found the boy tucked up into the bed—smelling much better, along with the dog. His eyes were bright and glassy, but he was lucid, based on the baleful glare he shot at Kendrick over Genevieve's shoulder.

"Wonderful, wonderful," Joseph said, taking Kendrick's burden from him before muttering to himself about dosages.

"How long, exactly, has it been since you were a doctor?" Kendrick asked in an undertone.

"I'm not going to bleed him, if that's what you're worried about," Joseph said tartly. "I've kept up with the scientific journals published."

"I am glad to hear it," Kendrick said sincerely before moving to Genevieve's side. "How is he?"

"Better. His fever's gone down." She sat on the edge of the bed and smoothed the hair back from the boy's face. "Fletcher, I never knew you were so handsome under that layer of dirt."

As small boys never find being handsome a virtue, he made a face. "Who's the cove?" Deep suspicion laced the words.

Genevieve opened her mouth and then hesitated. "Well, I think...I'm going to marry him?"

The boy's jaw dropped. "Coo!"

Kendrick was unprepared for the rush of delight and triumph that surged through him. Getting a hold of himself, Kendrick looked down at her and cocked an eyebrow. "Are you?"

She pressed her lips into a line. "I have stipulations, which we will get into later."

Kendrick laughed. "I look forward to it, sweetheart."

"I want you to drink this," Joseph said, holding a cup of tea under the boy's nose. "And have some every hour."

"Don't want none," the boy said sulkily. Then he coughed hard enough to shake his whole body.

"Fletcher, you must if you want to get better. Joseph is a doctor," Genevieve said, taking the cup and holding for him.

"No, he ain't. I know a reaver when I see one."

Illumination dawned for Kendrick.

"What is a reaver?" Genevieve said absently, her focus on the task at hand.

"We are," Kendrick said. He exchanged a look with Joseph.

Genevieve looked at them both and then back at the boy. "Fletcher?"

"I thought you wasn't for the longest, but you are. But you're a good one." The boy said, with some surprise, "I never saw a reaver who never went on a bender before."

"You knew?" Genevieve said in a small voice. "That I was..." The cup in her hand rattled against the saucer before she controlled her reaction. "Fletcher, none of us will hurt you. *I* will not hurt you."

"*You* won't. But all us know to scarper when we see reavers. They're barking; kill you soon as look at you." The boy coughed again, explosively, his skin flushing with the force of his lungs' exertion.

Kendrick slung the baldric from his shoulder and pulled the sword free of his sheath. "In days long ago, men were bound by the guest right. That is the right of protection and sanctuary to a guest who comes into a house by the house holder. In this case, this is my house, and you are the guest." He laid the sword on the bed and put his hand on the blade. "And I will swear to you that no harm will come to you under my roof. May my blade turn against me should I fail in this."

No doubt suitably impressed by the large weapon, the boy blinked owlishly.

"To seal the bond, put your hand on the blade and say that you accept my hospitality."

The boy extended a hand. One round of washing could not eradicate all the dirt under his nails. "Cor blimey," he said. "Right you are, guv'nor."

Good enough, Kendrick thought. "Now I am bound to protect you, Fletcher. No one will hurt you in my house."

"Or you'll stick them with that bleedin' great sword?" Fletcher demanded around a raspy cough.

"That's right. Now drink all of that tea Joseph has for you."

Genevieve stood and put the sword against the wall. "Weaponry does not belong in bed."

"I'll remember that for later," Kendrick said dryly.

She would ignore the double entendre for now in favor of larger matters. "Did you magic him?" she demanded under her breath. "Fletcher deserves to make decisions and feel safe as much as anybody."

"Not actively. I think it was a small boy's awe at weaponry more than anything." When she shot Kendrick a narrow look, he said, "I will keep a hold on it. And I mean what I said. He will be safe in this house."

"Good." She wrapped her arms around herself.

"How did you meet the child?"

"A year and a half ago, I noticed him in the streets as I went out to feed and began to recognize him as a regular face in the crowds. More so later when I approached Sally and some other women about childminding. I think I spoke to him once when he was sweeping a corner and gave him a penny. One of the first I earned on my own. He began to greet me when I came across him and then walk me to and from the East End. He's a very smart boy. Very curious. Also very proud and resistant to help. A few times, I suggested charitable organizations, places he could go, but he refused." She swallowed. "It was so hard to know he was alone on the streets, but he didn't want what help I could give him. I should've seen he was getting sick—"

"This is not your fault," Kendrick said firmly. "Has he told you what happened?"

"He developed a bad cough or cold. And then he came upon boys wanting to do mischief to the dog. He put himself between the dog and their knives and snatched it up, but he couldn't outrun them. They *kicked* him," she said. "Joseph had to wrap his ribs."

"He got away," he reminded her. "The boy is tough."

"Only because a copper came," she said darkly. "He managed to crawl back to that hidey hole and then everything got worse."

She worried at her lip. "I can't *do* anything for him except hold his hand. I can't make him better. I wish I could."

"With blood?" Kendrick said neutrally.

"What?" Genevieve recoiled. "No! He's a *child*; I would never turn anyone, but *especially* not a child!"

"Good," Kendrick said. "I wouldn't have let you."

She could practically feel steam boiling out of her ears. "Then why did you suggest it?" she hissed in a whisper.

"I didn't mean turning him. When an illness is not life-threatening, vampire blood *can* help humans recover. But it isn't wise. It is...not fast-acting. There is always a risk. If you had wanted to attempt to heal him, I would have advised against it."

Her eyebrows shot up. "I never knew that." Genevieve glanced over her shoulder at Fletcher. "They never told us that."

"Time was, kings or lords wanted one of us among them so they could cheat fate, but wyrd always finds a way in the end."

"Really? Humans have known about—vampires?"

Kendrick nodded, his face dark. "Men have always made use of monsters. I am not surprised the boy knew of us as night-stalkers. Rupert was incautious in his rule." Kendrick nudged her back towards the bed. "Don't be afraid. It isn't you he's wary of. You proved yourself to him before you knew you had to."

Genevieve turned back to Fletcher and helped Joseph with a plaster that he spread on his chest. Joseph instructed him to let them know if it burned or if he felt different and then went downstairs to prepare more brews.

"Smells rank," the boy muttered.

"That's the mustard. It will help you breathe."

"Don't go, miss," Fletcher said, his eyes fluttering shut.

Genevieve took his hand, still too hot. "I'm right here, Fletcher. You rest. I won't go anywhere. You're safe."

The puppy, washed, snuffled from beside the boy. "We shall have to find something for the both of you," she murmured.

"I bought food," Kendrick said, coming back in the room with a cot under his arm. She hadn't even heard him leave. "Let him sleep, and when he wakes again, we'll feed him."

"He's drunk water," Genevieve said distractedly. "What are you doing?"

"Sunrise is soon."

"Oh—but what shall we do? I can't leave him alone."

"The cot is for you, Genevieve," Kendrick said. "I'll stay up with the boy."

She stared at him in astonishment. "You can stay awake in daylight?"

"Enough to get him what he needs. Centuries of practice."

Genevieve murmured, "Rupert would not have allowed this. I don't know if anyone would've."

"He is important to you," Kendrick said simply, stacking the bedding on the cot. "So he is important to me."

Genevieve swallowed, a deep warmth spreading through her. She had not been warm in so long. "You know, if we do marry, there will be resistance. Change of any sort does not go over well with our kind."

"They really don't get a say," Kendrick said mildly. "But if you are worried, we can give them a fait accompli. They can be as unhappy as they like, but it will have no bearing on whatever lies between us." He paused and then added, "If that is your only impediment, I can arrange it all very quickly."

"Given it some thought, have you?" she said dryly.

"I confess I have." He smiled.

Genevieve twisted her free hand in her skirt. *It's not my* only *impediment, but if I am considering this, I had best lay out my stipulations, as Elspeth advised.* "I have conditions," she said, straightening her shoulders.

His eyes gleamed. "Lay them out."

"If we are to be married, it must be a true marriage. With vows, before God. I know it cannot be in a church—"

"Why can't it be in a church?" he asked, puzzled.

She stared back at him, equally puzzled. "We can't go in churches."

"Says who?"

Her mouth dropped open. "I..."

Bacchus, she realized. Bacchus had put that command on her, as well as a myriad of small, onerous dos and don'ts over the years. And she was free of all of them.

Kendrick's speculative gaze moved from her to the covered windows at the end of the room. "I've never encountered an impediment. Some may not be able to enter churches, but they're hindered by their own souls, I think. I have found nothing to fear in a church. If you wish to be married in one, we can accomplish that. You can even be written in the registry."

She blurted out, "Will that be legal?"

Kendrick looked back at her steadily.

"Oh. Silly question." She ducked her head. "I would like it to be in a church," she admitted slowly, "but then Elspeth could not attend. Her command is still in effect. Sparrow's might be as well." *And there is some part of me that is still afraid*, she admitted to herself.

A muscle in Kendrick's jaw ticked, but he nodded.

"What about banns, or a license? There might be questions without them..."

"We will not need the banns read. The priest will see it my way." He smiled. "What else?"

"Well, I'm Church of England, but we can discuss more particulars later." She swallowed. "As a real marriage, I expect fidelity."

"Genevieve, you have only known me a short time, and you have no reason to believe my word holds. But the only thing we emerge from the grave with intact is our word of honor. Too many vampires decide that power is a sufficient replacement. But that is not so. If I make a vow or swear an oath, I keep it. And is not marriage a vow?"

"It is—but you wouldn't know it based on some of the

behavior I've witnessed from human and vampire alike." She fisted her hands in her skirts.

Kendrick's keen eyes glinted. "You worry that I will find forever too long a time when not hemmed in by 'till death do us part'?"

"Vampires get bored. I've always thought that the main reason for the general aversion to marriage."

He smiled and ran a finger down the curve of her cheek. "Fools, all of them. Jenny, how could I ever grow bored with you?"

Genevieve stammered, "T-That's another thing. I do not... I am not sure..." She set Fletcher's hand down and crossed to the window. She couldn't say this.

She wiped her hands on her skirts. She had to say it.

She felt Kendrick follow her, though he didn't make noise on the floorboards missing their rugs. "What?"

"I know you wanted a real marriage, and—truly, I do not think that I would want a *sham* marriage, but—I don't do well with touch," she forced out. "Because of what my body remembers and my mind does not." Her throat closed, her body already flinching.

Gently, Kendrick said, "Genevieve, I noticed."

She clenched her hands so tightly that a seam in her glove burst. "It's foolish."

Kendrick set his hand over hers, a slow, quiet touch. "No, it isn't. Do you know if it's more to do with blood drinking, or physical intimacy?"

"I don't know," she admitted. "Likely...the latter."

"As long as we do one or the other, that's needed to convince the general populace. Don't worry about anything else."

"But you said it would have to be real," she pushed on doggedly. "That people would be able to tell. I can't promise I could...be a wife in the full sense of the word."

"Genevieve, we're vampires. We have nothing *but* time. The blood exchange will be enough to start. Everything else can come later, in the fulfillment of its own time. As long as *I* am not what holds you back. I don't want you to fear me."

"I don't," she said, surprised.

"But you don't trust me. Yet."

"But I want to," she whispered as a wave of exhaustion swept over. The sun. It was rising.

"I would make you promises, Genevieve," Kendrick said. "And pledge to stay true to you until the world's end, or mine." He took hold of her elbow and guided her to the cot. "Will you marry me, Genevieve?"

"Yes, please." Her eyes fluttered shut before she wrenched them open again. "Fletcher," she mumbled.

"Sleep, Jenny. I'll watch him for you."

He eased her down on the bedding and she succumbed to slumber.

Chapter Nineteen

Kendrick's eyes narrowed to slits, tracking the daylight as it moved across the floor in a faint line from beneath the curtains. Its path was not close enough to come anywhere near the room's inhabitants, but he traced it warily, anyway. A predator always kept its eyes on an equal threat.

When the small line of light was strongest, and Kendrick felt the pull of sleep the most, the boy stirred. Of course. Small humans were never considerate of elders.

Fletcher mumbled something and plucked at the counterpane over him.

"Are you thirsty?"

The boy froze, his still slightly glassy eyes darting around. "Who's that?" He fisted his hands in the blankets.

To Kendrick, everything in the room was visible just from the trickle of sunlight, but human frailties required a lamp. He slowly pushed himself out of the chair and moved to the table, striking a match.

The boy recoiled as the vampire lit the lamp and waved the match into nothingness, smoke dissipating up to the ceiling. "Where's the lady?"

"She's sleeping." Kendrick pointed to the cot. "You see?"

"Why's she sleeping? It's day, ain't it?" He glanced towards the windows before a cough overtook him, rattling his small chest. Once he had his breath back, he said, "Can't you open the curtains, guv?"

Kendrick shook his head. "No, I can't."

"Why?"

"I'll tell you after you drink this water and take your medicine."

The boy sipped at the water and then choked down what Joseph had left, his eyes on Kendrick the whole time. *Keeping his eyes on the threat*, Kendrick thought, darkly amused.

"Now, Fletcher—is that your name?"

The boy nodded. "Older boys used to call me 'Fetch,' but she changed it."

Kendrick raised an eyebrow. "Why?"

"Because she said it sounded like calling a dog or one of them fairy things and both weren't true. Right angry when I told her, she was. So she said I could be Fletcher 'cause I'm sharp as an arrow."

"That you are," Kendrick acknowledged. "It's because you're so sharp that I'm going to tell you this, Fletcher. I must go below to get you food and a new plaster for your chest." Kendrick rubbed at his eyes. "I'm going to tell you why you shouldn't open the curtains."

"Why?" the boy said reluctantly.

"You know what I am. What Genevieve is. You call us 'reavers.' A not-inaccurate word. But mostly we call ourselves 'vampires.'"

Fletcher swallowed.

"I have promised you safety, and I will hold my promise. Now you must promise me this. Most vampires sleep during the day, and that is because sunlight burns us. If you opened the curtains and the sunlight touched Genevieve, she'd burst into flame."

The boy's eyes rounded. "Cor!"

"I don't think you want that to happen," Kendrick said. "Will you promise me that you'll watch over her while I am gone? Keep her from harm?"

The boy's jaw worked, and then he nodded. "Right you are, guv. Want me to put my hand on the blade again?"

"How about we shake on it, like men?" Kendrick held out his hand.

The boy eyed it for a long moment and then put out his own. They shook.

I can see why Genevieve likes the boy, Kendrick thought as he descended to the kitchens. He *was* as sharp as an arrow, and stubborn too. And clearly had spirit.

Kendrick roused Joseph briefly to get instructions on how to mix the plaster. The other vampire tried to help, but he couldn't stay awake. "Don't worry," Kendrick said. "I can do it." He made the plaster and heated the pot of soup left on the hob, then found a tray and carried it all up, stopping for a moment by the library on his way.

He found Fletcher sitting up and coughing, a frustrated and embarrassed look on his face.

"You shouldn't be up," Kendrick said. "You hurt your ribs."

"But I need—" The boy broke off, flushing, and coughed again.

Ah, the pressing necessities of humanity. "I'll help you."

"Lor' lumme, guv, not with a lady in the room," the boy said, horrified.

"She won't wake until dusk," Kendrick said, hiding his smile. "I'll shield you, in any case." He helped the boy with his business in the extremely dusty chamber pot below the bed—how long had it been since the vessel had been used for its intended purpose?—and then got him back under the covers. The endeavor had clearly tired the boy out, so much that he could barely hold the spoon, but Kendrick insisted he eat at least half the bowl of soup. At the end, it was Kendrick holding the spoon for the boy.

"I'm full, guv," Fletcher insisted. "You keep pokin' the spoon in my gullet, I'll think you're fattenin' me up." He glared balefully over the spoon in front of his mouth.

Kendrick laughed. "All right." He sat the bowl on the table and sat back in the chair, moving the sword that had slipped since he had first roused himself.

"Is that your pig sticker?" Fletcher's eyes stared at the sword.

Kendrick lifted it and set it in his lap, unsheathing the blade. "It was given to me by a friend a few weeks ago. Before that, it hung over her fireplace, the broadsword of her ancestor." He turned the blade so the boy could see it.

"You duel with it, like toffs used to?"

"A light, fast sword is best for dueling. Advance and retreat, very quick. A broadsword like this is used for hacking. You want to take the enemy down in one blow." Kendrick lifted the sword and demonstrated the swing.

Fletcher followed the movement, eyes wide. "You killed a body with that?"

Kendrick judged this simple youthful interest. "A few. But they were vampires."

The boy made a face. "You killed any *people*?"

"Not in a few centuries."

The boy's jaw dropped. "You're *that* bleedin' old?"

"Older," Kendrick said wryly. "I have a book here that is set close to when I lived. Would you like to hear it?" Kendrick lifted *Sigestan of Emberlost*. "It is an adventure about a wanderer, what you might call a knight-errant before the arrival of the Normans."

"Here in England?"

"Yes."

"It's got fights? With swords?"

"Many."

"All right," the boy allowed. His eyes were growing heavy.

Kendrick thumbed the pages to the opening chapter. "'In the far north of England, many years before King Harold forfeited his crown to William of Normandy on the field of Hastings, along the sea cliffs of the North York moors, where tiny becks wear their way to the sea, and storms rage, and the roaring waves beat upon the rocks and pull sailors down to drown among the selkie maidens and the mer-lasses of the deep, a small stone house-place had been reinforced against the elements, and that was where Sigestan was born one winter eve...'"

❧

After breaking half the furniture in his sitting room and nearly ripping off the arm of the toady who had brought the news that the attempt against Kendrick had failed, *again*, Laurent stormed out into the streets still full of humans going about their business, oblivious that death walked among them.

Foiled! Again! Was the man a cat, that he had nine lives? Were the vampires he sent so incompetent? How hard was it to kill *one vampire*?

"I do hate to say I told you so," Gisela had said, when she'd arrived on his doorstep minutes after the little birdy who'd broken the news, "but I would be remiss if I let you continue in this crackbrained manner. Stop your ill-conceived attacks against Kendrick. They are doing us no good."

"Disloyal wench," Laurent had growled. "You would just give up? Roll over beneath this new master? A very easy posture for you."

"It is not disloyalty to recognize when one is outmatched," she had snarled. "And trying the same thing over and over isn't wisdom. It's stupidity. I worry for you, Laurent," she'd gone on in a venomously sweet tone. "You spent too many years letting Bacchus do your thinking for you, and now I believe you find it hard to take up again."

She had turned on her heel and stalked out, smoothly dodging the marble bust he had sent flying at her head.

Laurent made his way to the East End, where humans did not care about the poor disappearing. After slaking his thirst and relieving some of his fury on a dosser, he left the body behind in a dark alley and straightened his clothing, ensuring no blood speckled his waistcoat. As he dabbed his handkerchief against his lips, he caught a thread of scent on the air, and he froze.

Genevieve.

Hunting the scent, he stepped out into the street and scanned the crowds. No Genevieve to be seen. So why did he smell her? It was there, mixed in with the smell of the unwashed and coal and food cooking poorly and sewage in the streets.

His gaze settled on the pinched face of a woman, eyes down, walking past him.

Her.

He trailed her for two blocks until a convenient patch of darkness and alley mouth coincided. Then Laurent seized her.

"Shhh," he said, hand over her mouth as she tried to scream.

He held her in place as she tried to fight him with her paltry strength, and he searched her. She smelled like Genevieve—why? Had she supped from this woman recently? Given her something? What?

He found the culprit in her pocket, a worn handkerchief spotted with dried human blood not yet laundered, but with the faded initials *GD*.

"Where did you get this?" he asked, perfectly pleasant. He dangled the handkerchief in front of her. "Where did a human like you run into Genevieve? You can speak," he added, belatedly moving his hand from her mouth to her throat. It was pathetically easy to abort her struggling escape attempt. Humans were no match for a vampire.

The woman's eyes were so wide, he could see the whites all

around the lovely, green irises. Fear rolled off her, but she didn't open her mouth.

Laurent's mouth pursed. "I will pay you for the information." He jingled the coin in his purse. He wouldn't; he never paid humans if he could help it, but she wouldn't know that. "Simply tell me where you acquired this handkerchief and why. Perhaps you do not know her name; she is a woman with cropped, dark hair and a mouth full of upstart opinions. Pointed little nose and chin, pale. Only comes out at night."

She could not hide the spark of recognition. She swallowed but still said nothing.

Laurent's lips thinned. "Cat got your tongue?"

Genevieve was a do-gooder and a bleeding heart. She was trying to twist her way into Kendrick's confidence, to get her fingers into the Ossuary. She had run into this woman at some point, and she had given her a handkerchief to staunch blood.

There was a connection here, and every connection was a leverage point of weakness.

He leaned closer to the woman and smiled. "You and I are going to become acquainted. And you'll tell me what I want to know...eventually."

That loosened her tongue. "No, please," she begged, futilely fighting as he dragged her away.

"Too late." He would find out what he wanted to know, and he would hurt Genevieve at the same time. Revenge did taste sweet.

Sweet like blood.

Chapter Twenty

Genevieve pulled herself out of the dark to the sound of Kendrick's voice.

"'And so the good lady spake and said, 'Bold wanderer, I bid you welcome to this hall, and offer you a cup of mead in hospitality. All I ask is that you tell me all you know of Sigestan, once my childhood companion and now gone from this place to gain glory and honor among men...'"

Genevieve slowly sat up and removed her bonnet, pulling her fingers through her disarranged hair.

"Miss! You're awake!" The exclamation ended in a cough.

Kendrick paused in his reading.

Genevieve smiled at Fletcher and stood. "I am. Are you feeling better?"

"Still full of snot," the boy said disgustedly.

She felt his forehead. "Your fever is lower, though. What have you been listening to?"

"There's a bloke what's named Si—Sig—"

"Sigestan," Kendrick said.

"And he's not allowed to marry the girl he's in love with, so he's going 'round doing lots of great deeds."

Genevieve nodded. "I was fond of Sigestan, though he has a little too much pride for my taste."

"We're only on chapter three," Kendrick said. "The lad keeps falling asleep." To prove his point, Fletcher yawned.

"Have you taken your medicine?" Genevieve asked.

"Tastes blinking awful," the boy mumbled.

"He has. If you want to keep reading, I'll get Joseph to come look at him before he falls asleep again." Kendrick stood and handed the book over to her, pointing to where they had stopped.

Genevieve took his place and picked up the narrative until Joseph came in. "Good evening, Fletcher. My name is Joseph. I'm a doctor. We met yesterday, but you were very sick. I am glad to see you doing better."

"Can't I eat something besides soup?" Fletcher complained. "I'm starving to death, I am."

"Tomorrow," Joseph promised. He checked him over quickly and praised him for the medicine he had taken with only mild to moderate complaining. "Kendrick said he had a few things to see to, and he would be back later. Let me know if you need me. Robbie and I are overseeing deliveries for the house."

"What deliveries?" Genevieve asked.

"Furniture, mostly, but other amenities too, to replace what's missing. He said to let me know if there was anything in particular you wanted for the house."

"I can't think of anything," she said honestly. "We'll be all right, won't we, Fletcher? We've got a chapter to finish."

She read until the end of the chapter when Fletcher drifted off into a dreamless sleep, different from his restless, muttering fever-fueled slumber of the previous night. She remained sitting by him, the book in her lap, as she thought about what she had agreed to.

"Will you marry me, Genevieve?"

"Yes, please."

Yes, please? As if he had offered a choice of different colored ribbons? Gracious. She pressed a hand to her face. And he hadn't said a word about it when she'd woken. And now he was *gone—*

Stop it, she scolded herself. *There is no point to this hen-wittedness.* No point in wishing she had been a little more sophisticated when accepting her marriage proposal.

He had offered and she had accepted, and that was all that mattered. They would be stepping forward into the unknown, trying to forge a new path for the Ossuary. But they'd do it together.

She reached for the fringes of her talent. It was an automatic impulse to gather it about herself and disappear until she had gathered her composure. But strangely, it took far more effort to accomplish than normal.

Genevieve swallowed and dropped the intangible cloak of invisibility, repeating the action several times. Where once drawing her talent about her had been as easy as breathing, she now fumbled for it. Was she out of practice? Ordinarily, she used her talent every night. How long had it been since she had felt the need? She had never heard of a vampire's talent growing rusty.

She swallowed back the unease, even as part of her mind reminded her, *Your talent was born from fear. Kendrick's promised you won't have to be afraid anymore.*

She clung to that thought.

A little past midnight, Elspeth entered the room with a quiet knock on the door. "Genevieve? This came for you."

"For me?" She turned—and stared at the pile of boxes Elspeth carried. "What on earth...?"

"They're from Kendrick." Elspeth piled the boxes of all different sizes and types on the side table and handed her the note.

Jenny,
If you are agreeable, we can be married before

dawn. I have made all the arrangements. Be ready an hour before daylight. Here are some things I hoped you might like. I will see you then.

K

Genevieve blew out an incredulous breath. How high-handed of him. But—efficient.

Will I really get married? Tonight? she thought a bit wildly.

But logic and reason intruded. *As Kendrick said, why wait? Change requires it. And he understood your reservations. Kendrick won't push you into things you aren't ready for.*

Genevieve crossed to the boxes and lifted the lids. A stylish hat, in blue. A dress in the fashions of this year, in blue as well. All the underpinnings such a dress would need. A new pair of soft kid boots. And—

"Gloves," Genevieve said, swallowing. Several pairs of gloves in silk and cotton, white and black and dyed to match the dress.

"He has a good eye," Elspeth said softly. "The clothes will fit like a dream. And there are boxes for Sparrow and me, too. That was kind of him." Her voice had a strange note to it.

Genevieve's eyes flew up to meet hers. "I said *yes*, Elspeth."

Elspeth took her hand. "If there's one thing I'll say for the man, once he sets his mind to something, he moves fast."

"What on earth shall I do?" Genevieve asked a little helplessly.

"Well, first, I think you should put the dress on."

"It's blue." Genevieve swept her hands over her streaked, black skirts.

"A dark blue, one you'll look lovely in. And every woman should look well at her wedding." Elspeth hugged her. "I'll sit with the boy. Go on."

"You're bringing *that*?"

Kendrick raised an eyebrow and left off adjusting the sword baldric over the cut of his morning coat. "Why not?"

"Your prospective bride might not want the bridegroom bringing a sword to the wedding," Etienne said, adjusting his cuffs.

"I'll ask her, then. Are you ready, Dominic?"

"Explain to me again how you managed this," Dominic said, smoothing his cravat. He had pulled out his best embroidered silk coat and hose for the occasion. Etienne had kept his comments about the anachronism to himself so far, but Kendrick could tell it was a struggle. Etienne hated being seen as a man out of time.

"I'm charming and people like me," Kendrick said.

"Not the arrangements with the vicar. With the woman."

"I'm charming and Genevieve likes me."

"No accounting for taste," Etienne said dryly as a knock came on the door.

"Are you all decent? Moonset is not far off," Addie warned.

Kendrick had sent a note to Etienne and Addie as well as Dominic before he had left on his rounds, warning of his intentions and his timetable, and asked if they would stand up with him. They had gathered at Fernside, Dominic's home, to get ready. "All dressed. *Decent* is debatable," Kendrick called.

Addie laughed and opened the door. "Are you ready to go? You don't want your bride to think you've forgotten her."

"Not possible," Kendrick said. How could he? She was never far from his thoughts.

In the early morning, London was as still as it ever was. The air was cold, but the wind had stilled. It took no time at all to walk from Dominic's house to what Kendrick must start thinking of *his* house.

Joseph opened the door and admitted them. "They're nearly ready," he said.

"Thank you." He shook Joseph's hand and Robbie's. "Not just

for this. You've done a wonderful job on this house. It barely looks like the same building."

Everything shone, lit by candles and lamps. Floors had been scrubbed, new wallpaper hung, bannisters polished, and furniture dusted. New life had been breathed into it.

"There's more to do," Robbie said modestly. "But it's a start."

A rustle of fabric caught Kendrick's attention. He lifted his gaze to the top of the stair.

A vision in blue.

Gone were the mourning blacks. Genevieve wore the blue gown he had found with its straight skirt and bustle, long-sleeved, as were most dresses for the season, a smart and attractive hat pinned to her head. Her brown locks had been arranged around her face and the strands brushed her neck. She clutched the stair rail with a white-gloved hand and worried at her lip as she slowly descended.

Kendrick went to meet her at the base of the stairs, taking her hand gloved in new silk. He pressed his lips to the back of her hand, tasting the silk. "You look beautiful, Genevieve."

He didn't think there would be anything better than seeing the light kindle in her eyes at his words. "Thank you," she whispered.

"Are you ready?"

She lifted her chin, and that was answer enough.

Chapter Twenty-One

The church was no St. George's, but it was an attractive if small building. Genevieve clung to Kendrick's arm in the shadow of its edifice. Behind them, Etienne, Addie, Dominic, Robbie, Elspeth, and Sparrow waited. Next to the church, the parsonage had a light burning in the window.

"The vicar should be waiting for us. I was specific about the time," Kendrick murmured.

Genevieve chewed on her lip.

"Trust me?" he said quietly.

"I do," she said.

He knocked on the parsonage door and it swung open, revealing the sleepy and somewhat glassy-eyed human vicar. "Come in, come in," he said, ushering the group of vampires into his sitting room, a cozy enough space with overflowing bookshelves and a fire burning down to embers on the hearth. He asked no questions, merely directed them to join hands.

Genevieve held on to Kendrick like a lifeline. The vicar opened his prayer book and began. "Dearly Beloved."

The ceremony went quickly and without issue until the giving of rings. Dominic placed a gold band in Kendrick's hand. It was made of many strands intertwined in a complex braid pattern. She knew instinctively that it was not something he had seen in a shop window.

He had made it himself. A giver of rings. But a special one just for her.

Her long-dead heart wanted to thump. It wanted to leap. The back of her throat ached.

Genevieve stared down at her gloves. She needed to take them off to put the ring on. The ring would not fit over her glove.

You can do this. You have *to do this.* She fumbled at the buttons, but she couldn't make the loops come free. Her hands shook. A second more and she would tear the silk.

Kendrick stilled her trembling fingers. "May I?"

Miserably, wretchedly, she nodded.

Carefully, he undid the buttons at her wrist and slid the left glove free.

Genevieve stared down at her hand, the long fingers all fish-belly pale...and the ruined nailbeds on all fingers save the smallest. The empty places where nails used to be made her curl her hand into a fist. Shame crawled up her throat. How strange it was that this, after all that had happened to her, was what she was most desperate to hide.

Kendrick took her hand with his own strong, calloused one, with its own nicks and scars. He gently uncurled her fist before slipping the gold ring onto her fourth finger. "With this ring, I thee wed, with my body, I thee worship, and with all my worldly goods, I thee endow in the name of the Father, and of the Son, and of the Holy Ghost. Amen."

The vicar said, "Let us pray."

And then they were married. And before Kendrick dipped his head to kiss her lips, he lifted their entwined hands and kissed her fingertips first—every ruined one of them.

Elspeth and Sparrow embraced her on the steps of the parsonage, squeezing Genevieve tightly. "I'm so happy for you," Sparrow said in a thick voice, looking beautiful in a claret-colored gown.

"Don't worry about the boy today," Elspeth assured her, her smile lopsided. A rose-colored hat had been pinned carefully to her hair. "I will look after him, and so will Robbie and Joseph."

"What do you mean?"

Her friends exchanged an amused glance. "Genevieve, every bride deserves a honeymoon, even a short one."

A hand rested on the small of her back. Kendrick's.

"What have you all conspired on?" Genevieve asked, even as her heart thumped at the contact.

"We have a reservation at the Langham before sunrise."

"The *Langham?*" It was the largest and most modern hotel in the city—she heard it had electric light in some portions now. "But the risk—" *The expense*, she added internally.

"Don't worry." Kendrick took her hand—he had helped put her gloves back on after the ceremony—and tucked it in the curve of his elbow. "I've taken care of everything."

❧

He assisted her out of the hansom cab as the sky was greying in the east. The entrance to the Langham shone bright and yellow; she could hear the hum from the light bulbs that illuminated the portico. Bellboys dashed forward to accept the luggage from the cab driver as Kendrick escorted her through the entrance and over the plush carpet to the front desk. A large tree festooned with ribbon and baubles took center stage in the lobby, one of the Queen's fads that had gained popularity. Elsewhere in the hotel, greenery and holly had been artfully placed for the Christmas season.

"Welcome, sir, madam," the night concierge said, a small furrow between his brows at a guest's arrival at six in the morning.

His eyes widened at the sight of the sword hilt over Kendrick's shoulder.

"We have a reservation, under Kendrick," Kendrick rumbled, catching the man's eye and holding it.

"Ah—yes, here it is." His face smoothed out into a smile as he produced the information in the reservation book. "Fuller will show you up." He indicated the waiting gentleman. "Your luggage will be delivered momentarily. Will you require a maid or valet's service?"

"No," Kendrick said. "And we request not to be disturbed. Should we need anything, we will ring."

"Very good, sir," the concierge said. "We strive to accommodate all our guests."

As she and her new husband followed Fuller up the grand staircase, Genevieve whispered, "Did you magic *him*?"

"I'm tired. I wanted to stop answering questions," Kendrick replied in an undertone.

"Hmph."

When he opened the door to the room, Kendrick immediately did a circuit through the suite, making sure all the window curtains were closed. Genevieve waited in the main room, after glancing into the bedroom at the massive, four-poster bed. The luggage arrived momentarily, and after refusing help to unpack, Kendrick kindly sent the man away with a tip.

"Did I tell you that you looked beautiful this morning, Genevieve?" he asked, propping the sword against the bed and divesting himself of his coat.

"You did," she said, swallowing. "But it's nice to hear."

"It's true. I think there ought to be a nightgown in the luggage. I told Elspeth to pack one. Do you want to change before the sun comes up?"

"Are we not going to...?"

"Have a wedding breakfast? Not if you're not hungry."

She stared at him blankly.

"The breakfast is me, Genevieve. And there's no rush. Let me know if you need help."

She opened the trunk and found the white, silk gown and matching robe inside, carefully packed with a small note from Elspeth: *"Enjoy it."* Genevieve disappeared behind the screen with it.

Unpinning her hat and doffing her gloves, Genevieve started unbuttoning her dress. She hadn't worn a nightgown in twenty years. This one was beautiful, if filmy. The silk was thin enough that she could pull it through her wedding ring.

She stared at the ring that glinted on her ruined finger.

Once she had taken off her new gown and corset, she removed her shift and pulled the nightgown over her head. Belting on the robe, she emerged from the screen and said, "Did you really make this?" She held out her hand.

Asking about the ring had been a conscious decision to leave off the gloves. He had already seen the left hand. There was no point in hiding the right, with its missing three nails and a deep gouge in her thumb.

"Yes." Kendrick had stripped to his shirtsleeves, his braces hanging loose from his trouser waist, and had removed his shoes and socks. He unbuttoned the collar of his shirt. She could see the line of his neck, and she remembered his comment about a wedding breakfast. She swallowed.

"Do you like it?"

He's talking about the ring, Genevieve. "Yes." Her gaze dropped back down to the braided gold. "You were planning on me saying *yes* even before we found Fletcher? That was when you made it, wasn't it?"

"Planning, no. Just hoping. And I did make plain rings to give away." He took her hand in his and chuckled. "After working in that heat, I felt like I had absorbed enough to be a great wyrm belching forth fire. It was enough to wish I could sweat again."

"You're no dragon," she said. "A lion, maybe, but no dragon."

He smiled. "Lion?"

She nodded as a wave of exhaustion washed over her. He steadied her when she swayed. "All golden mane and roar," she murmured.

He ran his thumb over her cheek. "You're tired. Come."

"But what about—" she mumbled as he led her to the bed and pulled back the coverlet.

"It will keep, Genevieve. We have all the time in the world. You really have no patience, do you?"

That roused her enough that she frowned up into his face. "It isn't about time. It's about importance, and making sure important things are not forgotten."

"I won't forget," he promised. "Go to sleep."

"You need to sleep, too," she said, sinking into the soft mattress.

"I was planning on it. Scoot over."

The last thing she remembered was resting her head on his shoulder instead of the pillow. It felt...good. And she didn't flinch.

As light appeared and strengthened around the edges of the curtains at the far end of the room, Kendrick listened to the sounds of the hotel and London at large waking to greet the day. Cabs ran to and fro, maids entered rooms to make the beds, guests prepared to check out or embark on their daily excursions. The rhythms of the city that they had no part in.

As he lay there, sometimes slumbering, sometimes waking, the weight on his arm was unfamiliar but welcome—because it was Genevieve. His wife.

He was married.

New experiences, after so long. He ran his fingers through Genevieve's hair, the soft strands a lovely sensation on his fingers.

Life can still surprise you, he told himself. *There is still wonder to be found in the world.*

Genevieve curled her face further against his shoulder. "Don't," she mumbled.

"Hmm?" He paused his motion.

"My hair," she whispered, drugged with sleep. "Too short."

"I think you look beautiful with short hair, sweetheart."

One eye cracked open. "Really?"

"Yes. Your hair frames your face, and it's soft. I like watching it move." He ran his fingers through it again. "And it's nothing to be ashamed of."

"'M not ashamed. People just... think poorly of it."

"Were you ill, Jenny?" he asked.

She shook her head. "No. I sold it."

"There's a story there," he murmured.

She opened one eye again.

"I like a good tale."

"My friend Hetty," she said. "She had the loveliest red hair. And then one day, it was all gone. She didn't tell anyone why, but anyone who bothered to pause half a minute to think could realize. And then...the next Sunday, our vicar preaches on a woman's hair being her glory and covering." She growled in the back of her throat. "If I could have, I would have slain him on the spot. I went after her and got the story out of her. That her family was close to ruin and desperate, and she had sold it to the wigmaker for only a few coins. I marched her back to the wigmaker's and demanded he pay her a fair sum, and then I cut mine, too, and gave her the money."

She sighed. The words seemed to have exhausted her. "It was just hair."

Kendrick tightened his arm around her and pressed a kiss to her beautiful hair. "People will think what they like, but you gave your hair to help a friend. There is nothing nobler. And you were right to be angry." He snorted. "By that vicar's estimation, I should cut my hair."

"Don't you dare," Genevieve said darkly.

"Oh? Why not?"

"Cut your hair and I'll get an annulment," she muttered.

He burst out laughing, his whole body shaking with the force of it, so much so that she shot him an irritated look, like a sleepy cat annoyed at being disturbed. *Now the truth comes out*, he thought. He got himself under control and assured her, "Never fear, sweetheart." He stroked his hand over her head again. "All of it is yours."

"Feels nice. Your hand," she said, her lips against his chest. She gave more of her weight to his side and relaxed into sleep again.

Kendrick kept up the motion. She was a precious thing, fierce and intelligent and starchy, but full of love and care and belief. Some part of him felt like he knew her already, but maybe that was because her father had penned those novels Kendrick had loved so well, windows to a past he could no longer reach. He and Genevieve shared that common bond. But another part of him thought he could spend the next hundred years discovering new things about Genevieve Dryden.

Not Dryden, he reminded himself. He didn't know what she would like to use as married name. As changing centuries and shifting language had modified his name, he simply kept both versions and used them as given and surname interchangeably when required. She might not like that.

Perhaps she'd like to pick a new one for them both. A new start. He would not go so far as styling himself setting up a dynasty.

But a new start. That had promise. It might be just the thing for a new direction for the Ossuary, and vampires at large.

Chapter Twenty-Two

"Genevieve."

The voice pulled her out of the nightmare of darkness and blood. She flinched away from the hand on her shoulder before she placed the voice. "Kendrick?"

"Yes. Bad dream?"

"Old nightmare." One that broke into intangible shadows upon waking. Sometimes not remembering proved more frightening than the dream itself. An intangible spectre of fear, lurking just out of reach. Genevieve unclenched her hands from the bedclothes. "I'm sorry."

"What have you to apologize for?" he asked. The question must have been rhetorical, because he continued. "May I touch you?"

She nodded, and as his hand stroked down her back, the tension drained away. "Is it still daylight?" she murmured without opening her eyes. Even through the terror the nightmare had conjured, she still felt exhausted and lethargic.

"Midafternoon, by my reckoning," Kendrick said, his voice low and raspy.

"We're married."

"Mm-hmm." The sound carried amusement in it.

"Will you tell me your story? About yourself?" she whispered, opening her eyes a sliver. She found his face in the darkness, so close to hers. Maybe it would chase away the lingering shadows. "I like a good tale, too. Are you Saxon? Briton? Celt? Where do you hail from?"

His gaze turned inward. "My name is—was—Cyneric. Old English, they call it now. I have no Norsemen in my line that I know of, though I speak it the way it used to be. You could call me Saxon, I believe, though mayhap there was Briton in my blood. The particulars—the peoples, the year, the region—I don't remember. They come and go in snatches and images in my mind, sometimes so vivid, I think I could find the spot where the dun in which I grew to manhood used to be. But so much has changed... Thirty-odd years under the sun is a blink compared to centuries in the dark."

Her hand seized compulsively in the fabric of his shirt.

"As to how I was turned, there was a battle," he said slowly, as if he had to pull the memory out of deep sleep. "I was no one of consequence, but I had trained as a fighter. It seemed important at the time, and very fraught. A man came to our king and offered him soldiers who would fall and rise again, a sure bulwark against the threat that harried our borders. Those who were true and loyal in their purpose would get back up and fight on, no matter their injuries."

"Codswallop," she murmured.

The corner of his mouth turned up. "The greatest fighters drank a bloody brew and went out to do what we did best: vanquish enemies. Many did fall, and we did rise and turn the tide. At least I think we did." He sighed. "But we were no longer a part of that sunlit world. Our new master commanded us to come away with him—an indomitable force for hire. We were forced to abandon home and kin to their fate. But mayhap we spared them monsters in their midst. I don't know. But our new master had overreached himself; there were too many of us for him to control. It wasn't long before one of us killed him. Then I began to wander from hearth fire to hearth fire. I like a good tale." He smiled.

"Who was he? Another vampire?"

"I can't remember. I think not. I remember his blood being hot when it spilled. Some magician, perhaps, who delved too far into what should never have been."

"And you were alone?"

"Not always, but many of those from the same warrior band got themselves killed," Kendrick said. "It was...hard, in those days. You were either killed or cast out of human settlements when they discovered what you were, and there were few refuges from the daylight. Or you were used by those who wanted your powers. But it was a long time ago."

"Nearly a thousand years," she whispered.

"Or longer. Before the coming of the conqueror. I remember that," he said, with a quick, flashing smile. "But after the Romans. I did not learn Latin until I learned to read."

"And when was that?"

"At an abbey."

"What were you doing at an abbey?"

He thought about it. "I helped defend it. They needed help fending off attacks."

"From Norsemen?"

"I assume." He was silent for a moment. "Sometimes I believe it has all disappeared, but then with a turn of phrase or a standing stone, my memory flickers to life with fragments and images, and all the words come pouring back to me. Put a sword in my grasp and my hand remembers, even though which battles I fought in or commanders I fought under has faded with time." The corner of his mouth turned up. "But stories—stories I've heard repeated over the centuries—those, I remember. Those linger in my mind like a bell rung, the sound echoing through the years."

"And you still read new stories," Genevieve realized.

"Mmm. I like to read. Even when life begins to wear on me, something new still exists within the pages."

"And the stories are about humans."

"Well, I have read a book about a scientist's monster, and a fairy tale about a mermaid, but by and large, yes," Kendrick said, the corners of his mouth turning up.

"They're written by humans, I mean. Told by humans." She pushed herself up on an elbow so she could look Kendrick in the face. Her sleep-drugged brain was trying to make connections. She wet her lips and tried to explain. "Vampires do not paint because all the colors we see are via candle flame and moonlight. We do not make music because we hide ourselves away in shadows and silence. We tell stories, but not often, and we do not invent new ones. We are divorced from humanity. The breach of death is between us."

Kendrick nodded.

She continued. "But those who listen to music, to stories, and who see the art that others create—I believe it helps us cling to who we were, to our humanity. When we stop recalling our past, stop listening to human living voices, that is when vampires begin to lose themselves to the rot of cruelty or base instinct."

"And Rupert started forcibly isolating the bulk of the London vampire population twenty years ago," Kendrick murmured. "Along with his laissez-faire method of policing the actions of the cruel. And recidivism has mounted among the young. You may have stumbled upon something, Genevieve." He ran his hand through her hair. "That's brilliant."

"Otherwise, how would you be fine, and vampires under a hundred are losing their grip and killing indiscriminately?" she pointed out.

"Among other things, poor impulse control around craving blood. But you are right."

Tiredness tried to swamp her, but she yawned determinedly. "How do you fix that?"

"Feeding regularly so the craving doesn't outpace your ability to control, mixed with carefully monitored periods of fasting so you learn what you can endure and increase your tolerance. Do you need to sleep more, my heart's gleam?"

She shook her head. "I tried to feed as often as I could because I was around the children, but I always hated it, and I hated having to do it."

"Why?"

She mumbled into his shirt, "Stealing from people. Being a parasite."

His hand stroked through her hair. "Then come to me when you are hungry, Jenny. I'll feed you."

She lifted her heavy head. "How will that work?"

"If I've fed recently enough, you'll receive sustenance just like from any other." He stroked a hand up and down her back. "I won't mind."

She protested, "It doesn't solve the larger problem. What do others do?"

"You assume others have the same inhibitions," he pointed out. "It's something you get used to."

"What if they don't?" she said mulishly.

He grinned at her. "So impatient. We don't have to eat the whole elephant at once. Be content with small bites. We will get there eventually. Ideally, your maker would teach you all this when you are turned, but I don't think any of you young ones have had good teachers in anything."

"No. Not at all. No one ever taught me," she whispered. "They only hobbled me."

Kendrick's gaze darkened. His eyes flickered from her hand on his chest to her face, but to her relief, he did not ask. He simply said, "You know I would end your tormentor in a moment if you wished it."

"We're trying to start a new way for the Ossuary. As much as I would like to see Laurent dead, that wouldn't be wise. He's not the problem, really. It's the blood bond that's the problem."

He raised an eyebrow. "How so?"

"Well, so many vampires are still chained by their blood bonds, like Elspeth. It still exists, for all that he isn't ordering her around by it right now. He still could, and all his previous loathsome edicts stand. Is there a way to break it?"

"Time, or making a vampire yourself."

"That's all?" she mumbled, dropping her head to his shoulder again.

"All that I have heard." His thumb rubbed down her arm comfortingly. "Sleep a bit, my dear heart. You're not used to being awake."

"I used to love the late afternoon," she murmured, her gaze moving to the small ribbons of light that the curtains could not fully block. "The way the world looked with a patina of gold. I'd come home from school and do lessons at the table in my father's study as he spoke to university students and grilled them on their vocabulary." The days had been full of light and language, and the nights full of stories. Stories and love.

Her eyes fluttered closed.

"They only hobbled me."

"I always hated it and hated having to do it."

The words rang in Kendrick's head long after Genevieve had subsided into a doze again, and he realized that what he saw as two separate things—her hatred of drinking blood, the only thing that could sustain them, and her traumatic and painful beginning as a vampire—were probably linked far more closely than he would have liked.

Whatever it was, her body remembered, and her mind did

not. He recalled the way she had frozen when he had first confronted her outside his Ossuary rooms. An unexpected, unseen hold had sent her into a panic.

You've been entrusted with a treasure, he told himself. *And now you must prove worthy of it. Don't damage it at the first opportunity.*

When the sunlight under the curtains dimmed and the sun had set nearly level with the horizon, Genevieve woke again, blinking eyes that flashed ruby.

"Hungry, love?" Kendrick asked, running a hand over her cheek.

She opened her mouth and then checked herself. "We need to complete the blood bond, don't we?"

"That's not what I asked. Are you hungry?"

She shot him a narrow look. "I suppose."

"Do you always wake so grumpy, or are those the hunger pangs talking?"

Her mouth dropped open in wordless outrage, and so she did not react when he sat up in bed and pulled her along with him. "Drink from me," he said.

She tried to put distance between them.

"Can you tell me what you are afraid of?"

She stared at him apprehensively and then shook her head. "I don't know," she said honestly.

"All right. Try this." He rolled up his right cuff and bit into his wrist. The sharp fangs tore the skin and nicked the vein. Blood welled up in a crimson stream. He held his wrist out to her.

She stared at him. "What are you doing?"

"Is my starchy bluestocking going to take me to task or is she going to have a meal before I ruin the sheets?" he asked.

"It just feels—a little intimate," she forced out.

He said gently, "We're married, and you spent all day with your face pressed to my shoulder. Your cheek has my shirt creases imprinted in it."

Narrowing her eyes to slits, she took hold of his wrist, and with a slight twist to her mouth, licked the blood off.

Hot zings of sensation traveled from his wrists up his arm.

"Oh," she said, in a puzzled but not-disgusted tone.

"What?"

"It's not awful."

"Is it usually?" he asked, voice gravely.

"Metallic and coppery. This is..." She took a longer sip from his wrist, her eyes flashing ruby once more. "Like a warm honey. With a sting of fire to it. I wonder if that is what a bee tastes?" She licked the blood from her lips.

"You don't have to worry about hurting me, Jenny," Kendrick said. "Take your fill."

She met his eyes, a spark of wonder dawning. Then she lifted his wrist to her mouth and drank, fully absorbed. Her teeth in his skin sent a shock down his spine. Her eyes met his, and he smiled, pleased.

❧

Genevieve had forgotten what it had felt like to be hungry, and to be fed.

She had forced herself to feed regularly, militantly, and always from those who could spare it. But she had never fed for pleasure from the tacky, metallic taste. She had never drunk *joyfully*.

Why did Kendrick taste like all the sweetness of honey and all the spice of a Christmas wine? And why did she like it so much?

Her stomach felt pleasantly full, and she reluctantly let go of his wrist, licking the blood from her lips. She held out her wrist to him.

"I'm not hungry," he said gently, misreading her gesture.

"No," she said, "we need to complete the blood exchange." *Even if there's a part of me that shakes for reasons I can't remember.*

"Are you sure?"

She pursed her lips and narrowed her eyes at him. "Do you think I don't know my own mind?"

"I would never presume that, Jenny," he said with a smile before taking her hand in his.

If she'd had a beating heart, it would have pounded. As it was, all was silent as he lifted her wrist to his mouth. *Mirroring what he did for me...?* Her swallow lodged halfway down her throat.

She barely felt his teeth break the skin on the inside of her wrist. But she felt him drink. His mouth was cool on her skin, but sparks traveled up her arm to flood her body. Her lungs had forgotten she didn't need to breathe; they were a mite unsteady. Kendrick didn't take his fill from her—she hadn't had a proper meal in longer than he—but he took several long pulls, his eyes flashing gold as he met her gaze over her wrist.

If the touch of his mouth was like embers, the feel of his gaze was like lightning.

For the first time in years, she felt warm enough to flush.

After half a minute, he pulled back from her wrist and licked her skin clean of the blood. His wrist was nearly healed, and hers had begun to knit itself back together. "Are you well?"

"Well?" she whispered. With that thrumming inside her? The fire that had not banked itself since he had given her his blood? "Yes. I am well."

"Good." He leaned towards her again. "Forgive me for going about this a little backwards."

"Backwards?"

"I didn't even give you a good evening kiss upon waking."

She blinked at him. Kiss? She had not even thought of it. He had kissed her at the conclusion of the wedding ceremony, but it had been a feather-light touch of lips on hers, gossamer in its sweetness. The kisses to her ruined fingers had felt far more momentous.

"Allow me to remedy it?" he murmured. He cupped her face in his hand.

Genevieve stared at his mouth and managed a nod.

His lips slanted over hers. Her eyes fluttered closed.

She breathed him in, tasting the honey and spice as he nibbled at her mouth. Her hands buried themselves in his hair of their own accord as she deepened the kiss, dragging her lips across his. The feeling of his beard against her skin was novel and fascinating. She felt him smile against her mouth before his lips wandered down her jaw to her earlobe, where he gently set his teeth. The sensation set off a flock of butterflies in her stomach. But when he dipped his head as if to kiss her neck, she stiffened.

He moved his head to kiss her cheek, her nose, her eyebrow as his hands stroked her back soothingly. "All right?" he murmured.

"Yes."

"Good." He dropped his head and rubbed his nose against hers. "I can't swear to being a perfect husband, but I'll never knowingly hurt you, Genevieve. Do you believe me?"

Her eyes flicked up to meet his. "I do." Then she stretched up and brushed a kiss of her own against his mouth and was gratified to see his eyes glow gold.

Chapter Twenty-Three

Kendrick held out his hand to help Genevieve, his *wife*, disembark the hackney in front of Carmine House. That was the gentlemanly thing to do. Grabbing your woman by the waist and swinging her down into your embrace was probably not, even on a dark street.

Much as he wanted to.

Married life has things to recommend it, he thought as she placed her hand in his and stepped down.

The door at the top of the steps opened, and Robbie directed a young man in a footman's uniform to get the trunk from the driver. "Welcome back, sir," Robbie said when they'd reached him, but the smile was tight on his face.

Kendrick came to alertness. "What's toward?"

"Joseph will tell you," Robbie said. "Danny, you take the luggage up."

"It's not Fletcher, is it?" Genevieve asked anxiously, unpinning her hat.

"No, no." Elspeth appeared at her elbow and took the hat from her. "He's all right. Just cross because I wouldn't let him get up and roam about. He'll be glad to see you."

"Go on," Kendrick said. He could tell she was barely keeping herself from rushing up to check on the boy. 'I'll find out what Joseph wants."

Genevieve hurried up the steps—but she turned to cast a glance back at him at the top of the stairs. Kendrick knew because he was looking over his shoulder at her too.

Yes, he thought, descending to the cellar and the Ossuary entrance, *I could get used to this*.

Joseph nearly collided with him in the passage. "Ah, good." Without preamble, he waved Kendrick on. "We've got another one."

"An assassin?"

"No. Mad," he said bluntly. "Just after dusk today."

Kendrick reflexively reached for the hilt over his shoulder. "Who've they killed?"

"No one. Yet. Marshall Cutter found her."

Marshall Cutter? He knew that name. Kendrick thought a moment, and the image of the vampire he'd met on the street when he'd been searching for Genevieve flashed before him.

"Found her doing what?"

"He can tell it better than I can. We have her in one of the audience rooms off the main chamber." Joseph led him around the labyrinth of tunnels in the Ossuary before they emerged into the main room. At the side of what Rupert had considered a dais, an archway led to a slightly smaller utilitarian chamber. Joseph entered and stepped to the side.

Kendrick ducked beneath the archway and took in the scene. Several guards held a small, plain woman in chains on the floor. Her eyes were red, and she hissed at all assembled. Kendrick could see no reason behind her gaze.

Marshall Cutter, in the attire of a city clerk or office worker, barely took his eyes off the woman. He swallowed hard, Adam's apple bobbing.

"Mr. Cutter?" Kendrick held out his hand. "I wish we were meeting again under better circumstances."

"Aye, sir." Cutter murmured.

"Tell me what happened," Kendrick said.

His normally deep-brown complexion paled a few shades. "Sir, I would ask for clemency for her."

"You know her?"

He hesitated and then nodded. "I know of her. Her name is Lily Pendleton. She was one of Julius's vassals. I saw her once or twice after her maker...well, you know. She didn't look well, but I thought it had to do with the change, fear from upheaval, that sort of thing. But tonight, I saw her on the street, and she didn't know me." He hurried to add, "We never spoke much—her maker didn't like that—but she always would acknowledge me when she saw me, or when I passed her on the street. Tonight, she looked right past me. Not like she was ignoring me—like she didn't see me at all. It worried me, so I followed her. I thought she was just going to feed, but—it wasn't normal feeding. She fair fell on her victim, and if I hadn't stopped her, she would've ripped that human girl's throat out."

"She lives, this girl?"

He nodded. "I knocked her out so I could bring Lily below—and that took some doing—but I sent one of the door guards to play human and raise a hue and cry that they found her. I didn't want her to come to some harm from another human."

"Good man," Kendrick said.

"What is going to happen to Lily?" Marshall asked.

"That may depend on Miss Pendleton." Current Ossuary policy was that any lost to the madness or those who had killed in a rampage were to be put to death, to safeguard vampiric existence. Lily hadn't killed, but she still was lost to the madness and the bloodlust. Kendrick could guess what had happened. No one had taught her control or how to craft her own fetters for the urges. Her maker had been the one to control her, and now he was dead, and she was unmoored.

Come back out of the dark, lass, he thought.

"Call her," he told Marshall.

"What?"

"You knew her. Speak to her. Use her name. See if she is too lost in her urges, or if there is a way back for her."

Marshall swallowed and then stepped forward to where the woman was struggling against her silver fetters. "Lily," Marshall said. "It's Marshall. Lily, I'm sorry I didn't see you were struggling. I didn't think to—to reach out to you. But I am now. I'm right here, Lily. It's not too late."

He took another step forward, trying to catch the woman's attention. "Can you look at me? This isn't all you are. You're a flower in spring, and that's one of the best scents I can think of. Do you remember that scent? Easter Sunday, and the whole world smelling of lilies?"

Lily blinked red eyes, her frantic movements slowing.

Go on, Kendrick thought. *Come back to us, lass.*

Marshall kept speaking in a low, soothing voice. "I know you're hurting. Those early days—I had forgotten how hard it seemed, to do any little thing. To be anything other than desire and a pit of despair. But we're still people, Lily. You're still you. Don't give that up."

She stilled. She was listening.

Marshall reached out to her. "Will you take my hand, Lily? If you can hear me, take my hand. If you do, I swear I won't let go."

His hand waited in space for an eternity.

Then a trembling hand slipped into his, and he clasped it tightly.

The woman's eyes were still red, and she shook like a human in the throes of the drink, but she held tightly to the hand offered to her.

"My God," Joseph whispered. Kendrick had forgotten he and the guards were still in the room.

"Marshall, do you know where Lily stays? For that matter, where do *you* stay?"

Marshall blinked. "H-Here in the Ossuary, I think. I do, too—but with two or three other fellows."

In a hole or a cave or some such. Like where Genevieve and her friends had lodged.

"Take one of the furnished rooms," Kendrick said. "Make her comfortable and see if you can bring her back to reason enough to remove her bonds." He nodded at the guards to make it so. "Joseph—your ear a moment."

He pulled Joseph aside. "I need to speak to everyone assembled—the whole Ossuary, and as many vampires in London as we can find. I have left it too long. Can we notify enough by the early hours?"

Joseph thought a moment. "If you wish to speak, say, two hours before dawn? Yes. I know where the prominent vampires live and will send others to spread the word." At Kendrick's look, Joseph said, "I was the majordomo, remember?"

"Good. I thank you. I need to make a change, and this seems as good an omen as any."

"I'd never dreamed it possible for someone to come back from the madness," Joseph said.

It could have been a near thing had Marshall not stopped her from killing. Lily's case served as a hope and a warning. Things *must* change—if they were to stop any further cases from progressing so far. "How old is Lily, do you think?"

"Forty, if that," Joseph said. They shared a long, thoughtful look.

"Really married?" Fletcher pressed. "A ring and everything?" He was sitting up in bed and looking very well. The puppy, freshly washed and sleepy, hid under the covers at his side. After one brave growl at Genevieve, it had decided discretion was the better part of valor. Once she had delivered Fletcher's improving bill of health, Elspeth had left the room to fetch the boy's supper.

Genevieve described the scene in the rectory's parlor for the boy. "Kendrick made the ring," she added.

"Made it, his own self?" Fletcher said from the bed, his gaze dropping to her gloved hand. "Can I have a gander, mum?"

He couldn't see the beautiful ring under her lovely glove, just the imprint where it lay. Her hand trembled a moment, and then Genevieve deliberately unfastened the buttons of her glove. "Here. Isn't it lovely?" she said, extending her bare hand to the boy so he could see the beautiful, braided strands of gold.

Fletcher dutifully examined the ring, but his gaze kept returning to her ruined fingernails. "What happened?" he finally asked.

Genevieve considered several responses and finally decided to tell the truth. "I was punished for disobedience. Several times."

"By who?" the boy demanded furiously, sitting up straighter in bed.

"A bad man. But he is dead now."

"Any hand raised against a body in my protection will find his cut off," Fletcher said.

Genevieve gaped at him. It was a poorly paraphrased line from *Sigestan of Emberlost*: *"Any hand raised against one of the souls under my protection will be severed. Protection is my duty and my vocation, to the Lady Eawyn and her vassals most of all."*

"You remembered that, Fletcher?" she asked, voice thick.

"It's a crackin' good story, mum. Means the cove will have his guts for garters."

"It does, indeed." *Did you hear that, Papa? "A cracking good story." And my husband reads him the book.*

Hands settled carefully on her shoulders, but she was proud that she didn't flinch. She knew their touch and had recognized the near-silent tread of his feet.

"Is all well?" she asked in a low voice.

"Yes, it will be. I have asked Joseph to gather everyone two hours before dawn in the Ossuary. Do you think Elspeth or one of your other friends would be content to sit with Fletcher? I would like to introduce you as my wife."

"I think I can prevail upon Elspeth again," Genevieve murmured.

"Thank you."

"Is that all right with you, Fletcher?" she asked.

"Suppose so." The boy eyed Kendrick. "What are you doin'?"

"We're going to be making a change to the way reavers behave in London," Kendrick said. "Making a change to many things. I'll find you when it's time, Jenny. You have plenty of time to make friends with the dog." So, he hadn't missed the lump under the covers. "Has it a name?" he asked Fletcher.

"Wulfric. Out o' the book."

Kendrick chuckled. Genevieve broke into a wide smile at the thought of the faithful friend of Sigestan living on in a dog, also a faithful friend. "What a wonderful thought, Fletcher. If you learned your letters, you could read all manner of stories in time," Genevieve coaxed, reaching for the book on the bedside table. "Shall I show you a few and then read another chapter?"

"Suppose that would be all right, missus," he said, his eager eyes belying his blasé words. "What am I to call you now?"

Genevieve looked up at Kendrick. "Well, we haven't really discussed it. But I don't think it would be too improper for you to call me Miss Genevieve for now."

"And you're all right with watching him?" Genevieve asked Elspeth again as the time drew close for the assembly Kendrick wished to hold.

"Yes, of course," Elspeth said. "He's asleep, anyway. And you'll be back before dawn—at least I expect so."

"That is the plan."

"What is Kendrick going to say?" Elspeth asked.

"Truth be told, I'm not entirely sure," Genevieve said. "I will give you a full report when we return. Or I'm sure Robbie will as well."

"He volunteered to keep me company, but I told him to go and hear the news in person," Elspeth said, a lopsided smile on her face.

"That was sweet of him." Genevieve studied her face. "Is everything all right, Elspeth?"

Her friend looked up from the lacework in her lap. "Yes, of course. Why?"

"I... I suppose it feels like things are moving so quickly, and... we've spent the last two decades together, for the most part. I wasn't sure if you felt similarly strange."

Elspeth's mouth trembled for a second, but then her smile steadied. "It *is* strange, and change is hard, but I am happy for you, truly."

"And I spoke to Kendrick—he offered rooms for you and Sparrow here, once we have more of the house furnished. There are floors and floors of them, after all. You don't have to return to the Ossuary." Genevieve raised her eyebrows at her friend. "I believe he's planning to offer residence to Robbie and Joseph as well."

Elspeth licked her lips. "How kind. And just think—we won't have to bother with packing."

When Kendrick came looking for her, he found them holding on to each other, trying to muffle their laughter, lest they wake Fletcher and the dog.

Looking out at the sea of vampires squeezed into the main room of the Ossuary, Genevieve realized just how many vampires there were in London, and just how many were trapped underground. "Is this everyone?" she whispered to Etienne, who waited beside her.

"It's everyone we could pinpoint as crucial or influential, and then everyone else we could get word to. Some of us will be appointed to carry the word and make sure everyone hears in the coming days."

"And...do you know exactly what we are to hear?" Kendrick had asked her to come and stand with him when she heard her cue. But he had neglected to mention what that cue *was*.

"Exactly? *Non*. But I have an idea."

Kendrick looked at their knot of people—Etienne, Addie, Joseph, Robbie, Dominic, and a few other vampires she did not recognize—at the head of the room. He nodded to them and then ascended the dais. The crowd, which had been murmuring and humming with tension and speculation, hushed. She could have heard an inhaled breath. But they were all vampires, and they did not breathe.

Kendrick looked out upon the sea of assembled vampires, studying their faces. Finally, he spoke.

"My name is Kendrick. I was born sometime between the Romans leaving Britain's shores and the Normans arriving. I lived under the sun thirty-odd years before dwelling in the dark until now. I killed Rupert, and so I gained his position and property, and by precedent, that made me Master of the Ossuary. But I don't wish to be your master. You are not my serfs or slaves. You are my people, and I would rule justly, for the betterment of all.

"Kings, in days long past, did not just receive tribute from vassals. They exchanged oaths with those under them. In return for oaths of loyalty and service, kings vowed to provide security, justice, help in need. If kings broke those oaths, it would absolve their vassals of their oaths as well."

He turned to glance at Genevieve, and she stared at him, breathless. He swung the sword from his shoulder and ran the blade along his arm, wetting the blade with his blood. He set his hand on it.

"This oath I make to you now, as your lord: I will provide security and protection for all vampires under my rule. I forbid all wrongful deeds of murder, robbery, and abuse, no matter their station, and will forswear those who commit them. And I will provide justice and mercy in all judgments...so that, when we are given our final judgment at the end of the world, we may acquit ourselves honorably." He looked over at Genevieve once more.

A shiver ran down her spine. She nodded a little and gathered her skirts to ascend the dais. She was glad she had let Elspeth talk her into the second fine dress, green and glowing in the lamplight, which only had elbow-length sleeves.

"Do you vow the same, my wife?" Kendrick asked in a carrying voice.

A susurrus of whispers swept the crowd.

Genevieve unbuttoned her glove and let it drop before copying his motion to wet the sword with her blood. She set her hand on the blade. "This I vow to the inhabitants of the Ossuary: to speak and advocate for those who cannot speak for themselves, to protect the lowly, to make a better life for all vampires so we may enjoy true peace, that the gracious and compassionate God who lives and reigns may grant us all His everlasting mercy."

"Have I not chosen well?" Kendrick said, eyes still on hers. "Your queen has future vision for her people, even in the dark."

Genevieve smiled.

"Hail Kendrick and Genevieve, first King and Queen of the Ossuary!" Etienne called in a loud voice. "Hail!" Joseph and Robbie took up the call, and soon much of the room was chanting it. Genevieve leaned against Kendrick's side to hide her trembling.

He held up his hand. "Who will exchange oaths with me?"

Joseph stepped forward and knelt, slicing his hand and laying it on the outstretched blade. He spoke in a voice that carried to the far corners of the room: "I will to Kendrick be faithful and true, loving all that he loves and shunning all that he shuns, according to the law of God and the custom of the world; and never by will or by force, in word or in deed, will I do anything that is hateful to him; on condition that he will hold me as I deserve and will furnish all that was agreed between us when I bowed myself before him and submitted to his will."

"Kings in my time were known as givers of rings," Kendrick said, reaching for the pouch at his waist. "Take this ring as a sealing of the oaths between us." He proffered the gold band in his free hand. Joseph took it and slipped it on his bloody finger.

"Who else will exchange oaths with me?" Kendrick called.

The cavern echoed with the cries. "I!"

"I will swear!"

"I!"

"You should've seen it, Elspeth," Genevieve whispered. "I know it wasn't everyone, but a good number—so much so that blood started to pool from where it dripped off the sword. He gave out nearly all the rings he had forged. He's going to make more, for the future," she added. "And afterwards, he set out the main dooms for the Ossuary: that anyone who kills a fellow vampire or a human shall be punished with death, but those who go mad and have not killed shall be offered a chance to regain their sanity. That those who have been abused can petition us for protection and aid, and they can bring their abusers to justice. And he has promised to improve the living conditions of the Ossuary.

Kendrick and Joseph are meeting to discuss opportunities for the Ossuary to employ people and give them support." She shook her head. "It's more than I dreamed. And I can do all of that on my own, just as he promised."

"No one objected, as you feared?" Elspeth asked.

"We heard reports of mutterings afterwards, which I expected, but no one openly challenged it." Genevieve lifted her head. "I think this really is the start of true change."

"I can scarcely believe it," her friend whispered.

Genevieve squeezed her hand. "It's nearly dawn. Thank you for all your help these past days. I'll keep watch over Fletcher. Why don't you pick out a room for your own?"

Elspeth returned the press and slipped out of the room.

She sat there for a while, soothing the puppy when it roused to wakefulness and watching the boy breathe. He was bouncing back at a quick pace; the blessing of youth, Joseph had said. But he was still thin and undernourished. She started her mental list.

New clothes for Fletcher, and teaching him to read to keep him from mischief.

Furniture for the empty rooms.

A place to begin receiving guests and hearing petitions.

Meeting more of the vampires who did not live in the Ossuary. She didn't know many of them. How many did Kendrick know? They would need to call on them and make sure that they knew they were not exempt from the new laws. Perhaps a census?

Settling those who were alone or without defenders into families or support networks to look out for each other.

They would need some way to handle daylight deliveries and callers, Genevieve knew. She wasn't sure how others managed that.

And she'd need to inform Sally that she wouldn't be able to look after the children anymore. Genevieve's pang of regret was stronger than she'd expected. She would miss them greatly, and it would certainly put a strain on Sally and the other women.

Tomorrow, she'd have to speak with her and perhaps find another solution beyond just tendering her resignation.

"Still awake?" Kendrick murmured from the doorway.

"Just thinking. There's such a lot to do," she said, looking at him over her shoulder.

"Are you going to stay up with the boy?"

"I had thought to," she admitted.

"You won't fall asleep?"

She peeked through her lashes at him. "Not if someone were with me."

Kendrick pulled up a chair beside her and took her hand, raising it to his lips. "Thank you for tonight."

"I didn't do so very much."

"You gave me the eyes to see, and the hope for something better. I think whatever light may dawn upon us is all due to you, my wife."

Chapter Twenty-Four

Through a fog of drowsiness, Genevieve heard Kendrick order, "Back in bed."

"I already spent more time abed than a body can, guv," Fletcher protested. "I'm going barmy!"

Genevieve pried open her eyes in time to see Kendrick pick the boy up bodily and place him back in the bed. "You'll go nowhere until the doctor gives you a clean bill of health, my lad. This is the third time you've tried to slip out today."

"Fletcher!" Genevieve straightened in her chair, surprised and injured at this turn of events. "You'd leave without a word? And what of Wulfric—you'd leave him behind?" She cast a glance at the puppy in his blanket-lined basket beside the fire.

The boy rubbed his eyes and protested, "Ain't no reason to stay abed. I been sicker than this before! I need to check on the nippers! I promised I'd look in on them..."

Genevieve reached out and stroked the hair back from his forehead. "You may be feeling better, but I know you're not at full strength, dear. Whom do you look in on? Peter and Hannah? August and June?"

"Yes," Fletcher said, looking very small in the middle of the vast bed. Sometimes, she forgot he was only around ten; he acted so much older than his age. "I keep an eye on them when their mum can't."

"Very noble of you," Kendrick said. "But we can do that easily, if you'll deputize us in your stead."

"Eh?" Fletcher blinked.

Genevieve looked over at him in surprise and gratitude. "What a good idea. I had meant to speak to Sally this evening as well. I can go—"

"We," Kendrick said.

It was Genevieve's turn to blink.

"A queen should have an escort, should she not?"

"That was clever of you, to distract Fletcher with notions of queen and kingship and describe what that meant," Genevieve remarked as she and Kendrick made their way into the East End. She'd donned her old dress, and Kendrick had put on his yeoman garb so they did not stick out like sore thumbs in the street.

"He's clever. He could learn his letters in no time."

"If he makes the effort."

"I think your father's books have sunk their teeth into him. They won't let him go so easily." Kendrick smiled down at her.

Genevieve warmed. "It is something, isn't it? That his words endure, even now."

"Men in my time believed great deeds and lauded reputations were the only hope for lasting glory, and even now, I believe it to be so. Many things pass away—monuments, monarchs, even mountains—but stories remain."

On a street corner, a small girl sang in a high, piping voice, "Christmas is coming, the goose is getting fat, please put a penny in the old man's hat," while a boy crouched by the ragged cap on the pavement. Kendrick flicked a coin in a perfect arc into the hat, which made the boy stare open-mouthed.

Genevieve's smile trembled. She was leaving Hannah and Peter before Christmas. But perhaps she could think of something, a gift that wouldn't be too much, to give them, one that Sally would not be too proud to accept.

As they approached Sally's house, a clamor of noise broke over her—one that no one else on the street could hear. "What is that?"

Kendrick's brows drew down over his eyes "It's coming from your friend's house."

Genevieve seized hold of her skirts and hurried as fast as was she dared.

On the main stair of the house, she found Sally and several other lodgers lobbing complaints and insults at a florid-faced man in an overly flashy waistcoat and jacket. "They haven't paid the rent, so they'll be out on the morrow!" he bellowed back at the crowd.

"Shame on you!" a woman called.

"If they can't pay, they must be out!" he demanded.

Sally glared at him, her large arms crossed over her chest, then caught sight of Genevieve and Kendrick. "Glory be, Miss Dryden," she burst out.

Genevieve could not place the reason for such an exclamation. "Sally? Whatever is the matter?"

"He thinks he's gonna turf out the Hartshornes in the morn," Sally said, her eyes still wide.

"What? You, sir—explain yourself!" Genevieve demanded, advancing on the man. "What is the meaning of this? To put a family out on the street because they are in arrears—how badly?"

The florid-faced man cast a dismissive glance at her—and then recoiled, his gaze lifting as Kendrick's solid presence made itself known at her back.

Oh, Genevieve thought. *That's what had Sally so discombobulated.*

"Two days late on the rent," the man said. "Won't open the door. Tried my key, but they've got something in front of the door. In the morning, I'll come back with a locksmith and take the door off its hinges if we have to."

Through the name-calling and muttering of the people on the landings spectating at the confrontation, Genevieve heard crying. "Then take yourself away, sir, and stop disturbing these good people's evenings. I am sure you have many other tasks that demand your attention. Like kicking puppies."

"As my wife said," Kendrick rumbled in a voice that silenced the jeers and made the man pale. "Get you gone."

"Coo," one woman muttered. "Ain't that voice blooming marvelous?"

The man attempted to tug at his waistcoat and cuffs, but Kendrick's gaze on him made sweat bead at his hairline. "Tomorrow morning. Eight sharp!" he repeated in a voice no doubt intended to be firm, but it came out querulous. Then he quit the premises with haste.

"When did you get a leg shackle, Miss Dryden?" Sally asked in the wake of the man's departure. "Or have you always had him?"

"No, it's a fairly recent acquirement, Sally," Genevieve said, distracted. "What on earth did he mean? Has Mrs. Hartshorne barricaded her family in their rooms?"

Sally looked grave. "She ain't there, missus."

Genevieve gasped. "What?"

"If we told old Morehouse, he'd pack them both off to the poor house or an orphan asylum. We kept hoping she'd come home, but no one knows what's happened to her."

Her words struck Genevieve to the heart. "You mean August and June are in there alone?"

Sally nodded. "And when Morehouse started making a fuss about the rent, I think the boy blocked the door."

Genevieve looked up at Kendrick, biting her lip.

He met her gaze steadily. "Which door is theirs?"

Genevieve led the way to the second floor. She could hear them better now. The baby was crying, and though he made little sound, she thought she could hear the boy sniffle.

"August?" she said, pressing her forehead to the door. "Sweetheart, it's Miss Dryden. We've sent the bad man away. Please don't be afraid. We're here to help. Can you open the door?"

A long silence, before a voice thick with tears said, "The chair's stuck."

Kendrick set his hand on the door and gave her a nod.

Genevieve called, "That's all right. We're going to open the door. Make sure you and June are standing far back."

Kendrick tilted his head, listening, and then nodded again. With one shove, he pushed the door inward, and a wooden chair cracked and tumbled over.

Genevieve stepped over the chair and into the cold room that smelled of unwashed napkins overflowing the rubbish pail and burnt food. August held the weakly crying child wrapped in a quilt. Genevieve crouched down in front of him and wrapped her arms around them both. "It's all right," she whispered. "Tell me what's happened."

"Mama left," August whispered, and her heart seized. But he immediately continued. "She said she'd be home soon. She always comes home soon. But she didn't. I waited and waited. June got hungry, and I burned the food, and June didn't want any more sugar water, and the coal ran low—" He hiccupped, valiantly trying to hold back tears. "It's been two days. Has something happened to Mama?"

"I don't know," Genevieve said, even as her stomach sank. Evangeline Hartshorne had not struck her as a woman to abandon her children. "I certainly hope not, August."

"Then where is she?" the little boy whispered.

Kendrick crouched down next to them. The boy recoiled as he realized there was someone besides Genevieve in the room.

"It's all right," she hurriedly said. "This is my husband, Kendrick. Kendrick, this is August and June Hartshorne."

Kendrick stretched out his hand and touched August's head. "You are safe. I promise you." August's shoulders slumped.

Eyeing them, Genevieve would swear to the fact that Kendrick was not doing anything to influence the boy. But there was just something about Kendrick that you couldn't help but believe. The sincerity, more than anything, was what persuaded you.

Genevieve held out her hands. "May I hold June? Does she need changing?"

"She's hungry," August whispered.

"She still nurses?"

He nodded. "She eats a little food, but I couldn't make it right. She didn't like it," he said, shamefaced. He swiped away the tear tracks on his cheeks with the back of his hand.

"Then the first thing we need to do is get some food for June," Genevieve said, lifting the baby into her arms. But where would they find a wet nurse? And what would the children do after that? Sally couldn't take them, not if June still needed milk, and she couldn't afford to support two more children.

Is this my fault? Genevieve wondered. *Should I have done more for Mrs. Hartshorne? Checked in on her more?* She hadn't realized how responsible she had felt for those her life touched until now. First Fletcher, now the children...

"We can't leave them here," she breathed, glancing desperately at her husband.

"I know where we can find someone nursing," Kendrick said suddenly.

Genevieve stared at him in astonishment. "You do?"

"Yes." He offered August his hand. "Help me gather your things, and we'll go. And then we will search for your mother."

Kendrick rang the bell at Dominic's house with his free hand, the other holding the boy in his arm. They had taken the little family's important belongings—not enough to fill two carpetbags—and what other clothing and supplies were necessary from their small room and caught a hackney. Kendrick could piece out the separate scent trails of the boy and the baby and identify the scent of the woman on the clothes left behind.

He would get the family settled and then go hunting.

Seeing Genevieve with the children and her friend Sally had made him understand that his wife's human tribe was just as important to her as the vampires in the Ossuary. She cared for them, felt responsibility for them. And he hadn't missed the way her face had frozen when Sally had reported no one knew what had happened to Mrs. Hartshorne.

Her father hadn't known what had happened to Genevieve, either.

So he would hunt the missing human woman, even though it might have been more politically expedient to solidify the Ossuary's laws and their political position. Because these were Genevieve's people, too, and she needed to know that they were all right.

Dominic answered the door and stared at their group in astonishment. "Kendrick? What's toward?"

"There is someone in your house with a babe, is there not?" Kendrick asked. "We seek a wet nurse for the child." He indicated the baby in Genevieve's arms, too resigned to hunger to do more than whimper anymore.

"Kate," Dominic said, understanding passing over his face. "Come in, come in. I'll fetch her."

He saw them settled in the parlor before disappearing. Genevieve turned to Kendrick with a narrow stare. "He has humans in this house?"

"Yes. Can't you smell them?"

Her eyes became distant. "Maybe. But you mean that they're his—" She shot a look at August.

"They primarily manage the house and take care of all the human things that occur during the light."

"They're family," Dominic said, reappearing with a sleepy-eyed woman in a nightdress and robe. "This is Kate. She has milk to spare and is happy to help the child."

"Poor little mite," Kate said, peering at June. "I can take her to the kitchen and have a cup of tea while she has dinner, missus," she offered.

"Thank you," Genevieve said, bemused. "Her name is June."

"Pretty." Kate asked August, "And you're her brother? I'll bring her back sharp-like. Or would you like to come and have a ginger biscuit?"

August looked up at Kendrick.

"Go on," he said gently, setting him down. "You and June will be safe here. He may need more than a biscuit," he told the girl.

"Hungry? I know how that is." She took June from Genevieve and reached out a hand for August. "Let's see if we can get you both set before my Benny wakes up."

The door closed behind them. "Where on earth did you acquire two human children?" Dominic asked.

"Where did you 'acquire' Kate?" Genevieve asked sweetly, but her eyes flashed.

"Kate was a street girl dressing as a boy and working for a cracksman to steal objects and jewelry. She climbed down one of our chimneys and got stuck. I had to pull half the bricks out to get her lose." Dominic smiled. "Then I ate the man who had forced her to do it. By that time, our cook had taken a liking to her, and she stayed."

"You have a cook?"

"We have a whole staff. Many are descended from those who were staff at the time of my turning, and a few even from Godfrey's. They're family." He smiled thinly. "Do they donate a pint of blood every week or so? Yes. Are they also given full access to the house, fed, clothed, paid handsomely, and allowed to marry and raise families here, something not afforded to many of the London serving class? Yes. We value loyalty. Something sadly unappreciated by this generation of vampires."

"How many vampire households function this way?" Kendrick questioned, his gaze flicking to Dominic. "Cohabiting while humans manage their daylight affairs?"

"That is how it was often done," Dominic said.

Genevieve pressed her hands to her stomach. "They are not—harmed? Or imprisoned?"

She must've heard from Elspeth or Robbie how they'd found the master's townhome. Kendrick shook his head. "They shouldn't be. That wouldn't engender loyalty." Something niggled in his mind, about humans and vampires coexisting, but he couldn't pull the thought free. He made a note to come back to it later.

Dominic concurred. "If you have to fetter your retainers while you sleep, they're not retainers; they're slaves. Now, to return to the more pressing matter: did you just pick two children off the street?"

"No." Genevieve briefly explained her tutoring and child-minding role and ended with, "Their mother has been missing for two days. May the children stay here, since Kate seems willing to care for the child, while we search for their mother?"

"Yes, of course." Dominic met Kendrick's eyes. "Do you need help?"

In one of the East End's twisted and narrow thoroughfares, Kendrick ripped the threadbare shift left behind by Evangeline Hartshorne in three pieces to follow her scent. He passed the pieces to Genevieve and Dominic and said, "We'll search block by block and meet back at Mrs. Hartshorne's home if we find nothing."

Genevieve nodded decisively and melded into the stream of people.

"You really think this woman is still alive?" Dominic asked. "After two days? Assuming she didn't just abandon her children."

"Genevieve says abandonment is unlikely. And do you want to be the one to tell the boy you gave up?" Kendrick asked. *Do I want to be the one to tell Genevieve the same?* "We hope until we find evidence to the contrary."

Dominic turned the cloth over in his hands, then lifted it to his nose and inhaled.

Kendrick strode off among the warren of streets, listening to crying children and cockney shouts and calls as tiny pubs teemed with humans. Horse and dog droppings fouled all the scent trails for humans who went to and fro by foot every day. He closed his eyes and searched.

Tracking was no easy thing. Humans traced their paths over and over through the days. Scent trails doubled back on each other and took patience and time to find. They layered, aged, and disappeared under the weight of worse or overpowering smells or were washed away by the rain and snow.

It took time for Kendrick to find one of her scent trails, and it took time to trace. He learned her patterns, where her daily tasks and needs took her in the streets around her home, wandering paths and straggling circles making up the pattern of her small world. Sometimes she walked with the children, sometimes not. But Kendrick kept to the traces sans children, doggedly following the paths wherever they led—and then, partway through the night, he found the site of an encounter full of fear and decay.

Kendrick did not know the scent of the vampire with her. But he did not scent blood—not here. He marked the place and left, now hunting for Dominic and his wife. He found Dominic first.

"Come with me," he said. "I've found something, but I can't recognize the scent."

Dominic followed him to the place and paused. His face turned cold and hard as a rumble of thunder echoed, drawing closer.

"Do you know who it is?"

Dominic's hand clenched around the cloth he held. "You won't like this."

Behind them, Genevieve gasped.

Kendrick turned to see her in the mouth of the alley, her face stark white. He crossed to her immediately and took her hands. "Genevieve?"

She stared up at him with eyes rimmed red. "It's Laurent."

❧

Genevieve stepped over the threshold of the house in a rush, her skirts clenched in her hands. Kendrick squeezed her shoulder as he called for Robbie and Joseph. "Send a message looking for volunteers," he commanded. "We're hunting a vampire, and time is of the essence."

Genevieve lifted her chin and hurried up the stairs to find Fletcher and Elspeth. "Fletcher, dear—would you like to come with me? August and June—" her voice wavered. "August and June's mother is missing, and they need a friend. Would you like a little change of scenery?"

"What happened to their mum?" Fletcher demanded. "I can help. I know some places to look."

"We don't know yet. We shall be glad of places to send the searchers, but I think the best thing you could do is be a friend to them. We've moved them to a home where a nice lady named Kate can help with June, but I'm sure August would like to see a familiar face so he isn't afraid. Do you need help getting dressed?"

"Naw," he said scornfully, throwing back the covers. "What about Wulfric?"

"He'll be all right here; he's napping in his basket and Robbie will look in on him. Are you sure you don't need—"

"I can do it, missus!"

Genevieve and Elspeth left the room. "What's happened?" Elspeth whispered as they waited on the other side of the door. She peered closer at Genevieve. "There's something you're not saying."

"Oh, Elspeth." Her shoulders slumped, the jitters and shakes from pent-up anxious energy draining away into despair. "Their mother was taken. By Laurent."

Elspeth froze, her hand clasped against her chest.

"I'm going to take Fletcher to Dominic Penrose's home and then join the search. Kendrick is organizing it. We must hurry—rain is coming on. I'm so sorry. This must be so upsetting—"

"No!" Elspeth shook her head. "He—the one we should concern ourselves with is their mother. Don't worry about me."

The door latch lifted. Fletcher stepped out in new, clean clothes.

"Are you ready?" Genevieve asked, extending her hand. Fletcher seized it without hesitation, which made Genevieve's throat tighten.

"I'll try to think where *he* might be and help with the search's organizing from here," Elspeth whispered.

"Thank you," Genevieve said gratefully. She hurried down the stairs with Fletcher to the waiting hackney. Thunder rolled, advancing on the city. *Do not rain*, she commanded the skies sternly. *Do not rain*.

Chapter Twenty-Five

The scent of blood and pain turned her stomach and roused old ghosts, but Elspeth steeled her resolve and followed Laurent's underling into the hideout north of New Oxford Street. The new thoroughfare had pushed much of the poverty and the Rookery south towards Seven Dials, providing much convenient hunting ground for Laurent and his ilk, but Laurent was too lofty to lodge among them.

"Elspeth," Laurent said, wiping his lips free of blood in the sparse interior. "I was not expecting you." He advanced on her with the gait of a predator.

"You commanded me to report on Genevieve's doings, master," Elspeth said, heart in her mouth.

He seized her jaw and squeezed. "Mmm, I did. So why did I hear about her *marriage* and elevation to *queen* from Oxley?" Laurent smiled. It was not a happy expression.

"I th-thought it would be more suspicious were I to try to leave at a time she wanted me close," Elspeth mumbled through his hold. "But I've come now to warn you now, master!"

Laurent paused. "Warn me?"

Elspeth kept her gaze away from the prone figure behind him, the blonde hair so like her own strewn across the dirty, bare floor. She could hear the woman breathe—for now. "They are searching for the missing woman. Kendrick caught your scent in the surrounding streets. They are hunting you—all the volunteers Kendrick could muster."

"Hunting *me*? With no proof?" Laurent raged. He threw a chair across the room and swore.

Elspeth stared at the floor. *You did do it, though.*

"What do they care for some human woman? I have pressed her for her connection to Genevieve for hours upon hours—she says nothing! What is she to Genevieve that she would set a witch hunt on me?" Laurent gnashed his teeth.

A mother, Elspeth thought. *One who knows she stands between you and her children.*

Oxley said anxiously, "Laurent, my place ain't all that secret; soon they'll find someone who knows you frequent it, y'know. And the new master—he's a dab hand at that pig sticker."

"He is *not* the master," Laurent snarled. He turned his gaze on the crumpled form in the corner. "So, Genevieve cares so much about one measly human woman she'd have her new attack dog hurt me? She's taking to power quite well." He drummed his fingers on his thigh. "Well, I suppose I should leave her a present. A gift, to celebrate her queenship, as it were." He smiled. "Elspeth, come here."

Elspeth's throat closed.

Laurent clamped his fingers in her hair and dragged her eyes up to meet his. He looked from her to the woman crumpled on the ground. "I command you to kill her."

The command fell on Elspeth like the sword of Damocles, cleaving through her marrow.

"Oxley and I will go to Chelsea. You will follow when the deed is done and the body is found." He smiled. "I would like to hear what they think of my gift. Come, Oxley."

"Chelsea?" Oxley complained. "Can't get a decent meal in Chelsea."

"Offer one more opinion on my plans, Oxley," Laurent said, his voice fading as they felt the room, "and I'll rip out your tongue, so you'll moo just like your namesake."

Then they were gone. Silence fell.

Elspeth dropped to her knees like a cut marionette. The compulsion sank its teeth into her, beginning its insistent staccato that would only build until she had completed her master's bidding.

If only it were dawn, she thought frantically. But it was only half past two. There was no way she could hold out until dawn.

"Please," the woman whispered. Evangeline. "I have—children." She had heard all.

Elspeth pressed her hands to her mouth to stifle her sobs. "I'm sorry," she gasped. "I'm so sorry." Hot, red tears ran down her cheeks. "I c-c-can't defy him."

Kill her. Kill her. Kill her.

The repetitive command built until it was a hammer in her brain.

She crawled to Evangeline and turned her over. She was in a bad way. Cut and bruised and bitten on her neck and face and arms. Maybe some broken bones. But not on her last breath. Not yet.

Elspeth closed her eyes against the flashbacks of memory.

"I wanted to die when they were hurting me...but my children. They're alone," Evangeline whispered.

"No," Elspeth gulped. "No, Genevieve found them. They're safe. She'll keep them safe."

Evangeline let out a sudden breath and relaxed against the floor.

Kill her. Kill her.

Elspeth pressed her hands to her temples, trying to keep out the drumming. Thunder growled overhead, adding to the insistent clamor.

The past she had pushed away for twenty years was melding with the present. In that maelstrom of horror, a thought struck her like lightning. "I c-can't gainsay this. I c-can't, but—d-did he make you drink his blood?" She shook Evangeline so that the woman would look at her. "Did you feel close to death and then get better?"

Bottle-green eyes blinked slowly. "Yes."

Not again. *Not again.* "D-Drink mine." Elspeth ripped into her wrist and let the blood flow. "D-Drink mine or you'll be his slave past even death. You'll never be free of him. *Hurry.*"

She pressed her wrist on Evangeline and held it to her lips as long as she could, until Elspeth's whole body shook and blood dripped from her ears and nose from holding off Laurent's order.

The bites on Evangeline's face and neck were closing.

"I'm sorry," Elspeth whispered. "Please forgive me."

Then she snapped Evangeline's neck.

❧

Raindrops had begun to spatter the cobblestones on New Oxford Street when Dominic called, "Here! His trail leads here!"

They had traced Laurent's scent out of the East End and through London to St. Giles. The skies were opening. If they lost the trail...

Kendrick ran after him, but by the time he had made it to the vacant house, Dominic had already forced open the door. They rushed inside.

The house was empty, its inhabitants fled—except for the body of a woman lying on the floor. Kendrick swore once, bitterly. He could hear no heartbeat, no breath.

Scanning the room, he could identify Laurent's scent, as well as that of Oxley, the lackey he had encountered in the Ossuary—and one more presence.

Elspeth Gibbins.

"Laurent is Elspeth's master," Kendrick muttered. *Damn*. He hadn't seen it.

Dominic crouched over the body. "Elspeth's scent is here," he said.

Kendrick stared around the room. The patter of raindrops would increase into a downpour in another minute. "Leave the body. Let's follow their scents as far as we can—"

"No!" Dominic burst out, his eyes flashing red.

His objection startled them both.

"She is not dead," Dominic continued in a rough voice.

"Dominic," Kendrick began, not sure if this had reopened his friend's wound of grief.

"There is blood here," he said harshly. "Elspeth's blood. And the woman's neck is broken. If I had to guess—Laurent has been manipulating Elspeth through the blood bond."

"And ordered Evangeline's death?" Kendrick crouched to examine the scene and mulled that over. "And in a fit of defiance—"

"We won't know until Evangeline wakes," Dominic said, turning back to the woman and carefully gathering her in his arms. He made sure to tuck her head into the curve of his neck.

"Are you sure she will?"

"What was it you said?" Dominic said, raising a sardonic eyebrow. "'We hope until we find evidence to the contrary'?"

The rain drummed on the roof and found its way between loose and missing shingles to drip down into the house. The trickle had become a deluge, and the trail likely diluted or washed away altogether now.

Kendrick nodded. "Let us go, then. I shall pass the word to the searchers to be on the lookout for Elspeth, if they cannot find

Laurent's trail." This would hurt Genevieve—badly. His face set in grim lines, he pushed himself to his full height.

"We'll go to my house," Dominic said, standing with his limp burden in his arms. He held her close, a protective stance.

Kendrick watched him closely but said nothing as they stepped out into the freezing rain that washed away the muck of London and any hope of finding Laurent that night.

Genevieve dragged herself up the stairs of Fernside, her cloak waterlogged and freezing rivulets of water sliding down her collar as the rain continued to fall. She felt like a drowned rat. If the temperature dropped any lower, the downpour would turn to icy sleet, and she'd be a frozen rat. Genevieve had hunted over much of the East End that night with Joseph as her searching partner, searching for Laurent's scent trails, going to any locations she recalled him frequenting. But they had found neither hide nor hair of Laurent or any of his cronies, and now, just before dawn, she felt bedraggled and discouraged.

What was she to tell August and June? Dominic's butler opened the door and ushered Joseph and her inside, taking their miserably soaked outer garments.

"Madam, your husband requested I alert him when you arrived," the butler said quietly.

"He's back already?" Genevieve asked, surprise pulling her from her blue-deviled humors. "Where is he?"

"He is below in the cellars with Mr. Penrose. May the staff and I offer a hot brick or a change of clothes—"

"No, no, that can wait," Genevieve said. "I'll go down, if you'll point me towards the door? Oh—how are the children?"

"Asleep upstairs, all three. Kate is with them."

"I wouldn't say no to a change of clothes," Joseph said, pulling at his soaked woolens.

"If you'll follow me, sir," the butler said, after indicating the way to Genevieve.

She hurried through the far green door and in the servants' portion of the house, locating the door to the cellars. "Kendrick?" she called at the top of the stairs.

"Genevieve?" Her husband came into view at the foot of the stairs. "You're soaked!"

"You're not," she said, puzzled.

"Yes." His face turned grave. "We have news."

She stopped halfway down the stairs. "Oh, please don't tell me..."

Kendrick met her there and wrapped his strong arms around her, pulling her tight against him.

"I'll get your clothes all wet," she said in a thick voice.

"What's a little rain?" he murmured. "Here it is—we found Evangeline. Her neck was broken. But Dominic believes there is a chance she may rise. We have brought her body back, and he is keeping vigil."

Genevieve fisted her hand in his coat. "Dead?" she whispered. "No..."

"We must wait and see."

She pressed her face into his neck to try to stem the tears that wanted to flow. "Laurent—Laurent and Bacchus both liked tormenting their victims. Hurting and then bringing them back from the brink so they didn't lose their playthings before they were ready. Does Dominic think..." She trailed off, couldn't say it.

"Here." With no effort at all, Kendrick lifted her and carried her down the stairs into the glow of lamplight. Where one might have expected racks of wine and other choice vintages like in other fine homes, Dominic's cellar was partitioned off into small rooms, protected from the light for their kind. Kendrick brought her to a small room with a table and an overstuffed armchair next to a bed. He sat in the armchair and held her in his lap, much as he had when she had broken down about her father's books.

"The other thing we discovered," he said, continuing, "was that we could scent Elspeth in the room…and on the body."

Genevieve blinked, shook her head. "But…that's… No, no I left Elspeth at Carmine House. How would she…?" The truth sank in. "Oh, no."

"It's possible that she might have—"

"Been used. Ordered. I never thought—I'm so stupid," she whispered. "I didn't see it. Elspeth—I'll have to break the news to Robbie." She pressed her hand to her mouth. "Where is she? Do you know?"

Kendrick's hands stroked over her back. "She wasn't present in the house where we found the body, and the rain started right after."

Her eyes stung, her stomach cramping from shame. "She was suffering, and I didn't see it. Who knows how long he's been ordering her about. He must've ordered her to keep silent…" Grief, worry, and fury warred for dominance within her. "Can we revisit you killing him?"

"Absolutely," Kendrick growled. "I'd like to get within skewering distance of him."

"And you really think there's a chance for Evangeline?"

"Dominic is very insistent," Kendrick said wryly. "We won't say anything to any of the others until tomorrow eve. That's probably when we'll know for sure."

But what would happen when she woke and found herself tied to Laurent even in death? Genevieve sighed, her shoulders slumping.

"Let's get you out of these wet things," Kendrick said, lifting her up and beginning to undo her buttons. "Dawn comes soon."

Genevieve was too tired and heartsick to protest. And in all honestly, she didn't want to.

Chapter Twenty-Six

As soon as the sun had set, Genevieve gathered with Kendrick and Dominic around Evangeline's still form, lying on a bed in the largest room of the cellar. Her face was still and gray with the pallor of death. They could all smell that rigor mortis was passing, the stiffness of the body's limbs relaxing.

Genevieve sat in a chair against the wall, her hands tightly clasped. Kendrick stood with his hand on her shoulder. Dominic waited by the bedside, his eyes curiously bright.

As time ticked by with no sign, Genevieve's stomach sank. She licked her lips and looked away. *I am going to have to break it to the children that she is not coming home*, she thought. *But at least we have a body to bury. There is some relief in* knowing, *at the very least...* She swallowed and wiped her eyes, her own unquiet grief that she had thought she had set aside rioting within her.

"Do you think we should lay her out for the children to see, or should we find a coffin first?" she whispered to Kendrick. "I don't want them to think—"

"*Wait*," Dominic barked harshly.

Genevieve and Kendrick both swung towards him. Dominic hovered by the bed, his gaze fixed on the body.

The room was still. None of them moved.

Evangeline Hartshorne's head twitched.

She jerked upright with a gasp, her eyes flying open. She stared around the room in a confused panic, her eyes flaring ruby red.

Dominic was by her side in a moment, but she shrank away from him.

"W-Who are you?" she forced out, coughing as her throat muscles fought to work. "W-Where *am I*—"

"Evangeline." Genevieve approached the bed, extending a hand to the frightened woman. "You are safe. Do you remember me?"

Evangeline stared at her, and recognition slowly dawned. "Miss Dryden. My children—?"

Dominic said, "They are safe. They are upstairs, in my house, and you can see them soon."

She shrank away from him. "Who are you?"

"This is Dominic Penrose," Genevieve said hastily. "And this is my husband, Kendrick." She indicated the men. "He is correct. August and June are well. They are upstairs."

"What happened? I thought—" Evangeline wet her lips. Her hand crept up to her neck. "I was sure..." Her fingers trembled. She pressed a fluttering hand to her chest but did not find what she sought. She looked between them, searching for answers.

Genevieve sat carefully on the edge of the bed. "I'm so sorry. Let me explain..."

❧

Elspeth huddled in the corner of the house in Chelsea where Laurent had gone to ground. In the middle of a bustling artist community, no one paid much attention to nocturnal comings and goings. The terraced house was sparsely furnished, with thick shutters over the windows. Oxley still snored in his chair, though the sun had gone down and vampires had no need of breath. Some habits were too ingrained to break, it seemed.

Laurent had gone out to feed as soon as dusk had fallen, but he had commanded her to stay and wait for his return. He felt secure and confident in venturing out, since it had rained all night and day. They had seen no sign of their pursuers.

Elspeth scrubbed at her chest as Oxley rolled over and snorted, coming awake. With much smacking of lips and muttering, he fought to a sitting position.

"What are you looking at?" he asked, catching sight of her. "Where the devil's Laurent?"

"Gone out," Elspeth said curtly.

"*Out*? With searchers out looking for him? Is he completely—"

"What? Off his rocker? Mad? Stark-raving?" Laurent loomed in the doorway.

Oxley jumped. "O-Of course not. I only thought—"

"I've spoken to you about thinking before, Oxley," Laurent drawled. "Elspeth, find some water for washing," he added casually.

Elspeth waited for the command to bang against her eyelids and force her to her feet. Instead, there was a curious ripping sensation in her chest, as if old, rotten threads had parted ways from their stitching. She touched her fingers to her gown's neckline, as if perhaps some of the stitching *had* ripped and that was what she had felt.

"Well?" Laurent demanded. "What are you waiting for?"

Elspeth got to her feet jerkily, nodded, and walked out the door. In the hallway, she paused, touched her breastbone, waited for the compulsion.

It didn't come.

Not daring to breathe, Elspeth walked to the house's door and stepped out into the freezing drizzle. She looked both ways down the street and then began to walk, slowly at first, and then faster. When no invisible leash pulled her back, her rapid walk turned into a run.

Streets flashed by in a blur as Elspeth dodged horse-drawn carts and pedestrians. She splashed through puddles and evaded dirty sprays of water thrown up by carriage wheels. She had no idea where she was going. She just wanted to get as far away as she possibly could.

Only when her vision blurred with tears did she stumble to a stop and cover her face with her hands on the corner of Bond Street.

Is this freedom? she thought, sobs pouring out in a paroxysm of giddy disbelief. Could she be rid of Laurent at last?

Her reprieve did not last long. "I have killed a human," she whispered between her fingers.

Chapter Twenty-Seven

The rain continued, foiling their efforts. Kendrick turned up his collar and pulled his hat low as he left Fernside to coordinate with the searchers still on the hunt in other areas. Most of the search teams had relocated to Fernside as a base of operations, but a few had gone to ground during daylight elsewhere. They were still hunting for Laurent, though much hope that they would find him soon, or at all, had passed. He had gone several blocks and had just turned north on Regent Street when a figure stepped out of the shadows.

He checked the motion to reach for his sword when the figure fell to their knees, trembling.

"F-Forgive me, sire. I have k-killed a human. I submit myself to the king's justice," Elspeth forced out through chattering teeth.

"Elspeth," Kendrick said. She flinched but steeled herself when he advanced on her.

"I h-have left Laurent," she continued. 'He made me inform him of what Genevieve was doing, but I tried—I tried not to tell him anything important! I can tell you where he bides—there is a house in Chelsea—"

She swallowed the rest of her sentence when Kendrick went

to one knee in front of her and placed his hands on her shoulders. "Are you well?" he asked. She looked wet to the skin.

She blinked at him uncomprehendingly. Kendrick could still see the brown trails where the rain had not managed to mop away old tears. "I have come t-to confess and place myself under the king's justice. I have c-conspired with your enemy. Killing a human m-means death."

"Are you sure you wouldn't rather submit yourself to the king's mercy?"

She gaped at him.

Kendrick gentled his voice. "You were commanded and manipulated against your well, Elspeth. While it is true that you did unlawfully kill and turn a human, you enabled Evangeline to come back to her family, unfettered by evil. I pardon you."

"I-It *worked?*" she whispered. "She's woken up?"

"Yes."

She hiccupped. "I just didn't want what happened to me to happen to her... and then this evening... I don't understand what happened. Laurent ordered me to do something, and there was no force behind it. No pain. I didn't have to do it. So I ran."

"What you did freed you both," Kendrick assured her. "And I believe you will be far more cognizant of the responsibility you hold. Here is my sentence—you will come back with me to Fernside to teach, guide, and help Evangeline navigate this new world. Will you do it?"

Elspeth nodded, pressing a fist to her mouth. "Yes, of course, my liege."

Kendrick stood and extended his hand. Trembling, Elspeth took it, and Kendrick lifted her to her feet. Then he kissed her on both cheeks. "You are a brave and honorable woman, Elspeth Gibbins." He handed his handkerchief, and she wiped her tears away.

Elspeth walked back to Fernside beside Kendrick in silence, still reeling. A reprieve. Acquitted of the sin she had committed. And free—gloriously *free!*—of Laurent. The persistent drizzle was like a cleansing rain straight from heaven for her soul.

The whole world felt changed, turned upside down. She did not know when it would turn aright. Did she even want it to?

As she and Kendrick approached Fernside, Elspeth looked up apprehensively at the door. But she did not have long to fret.

The front door flew open, a figure in a kilt backlit in the doorway.

Elspeth shrank back, shame and guilt strangling her. What must Robbie think of her? They all had to have heard what she had done. She reached up to pat her hair reflexively and realized her bonnet was gone. She had lost it somewhere between Chelsea and Mayfair. And her sodden hair was half tumbled down her back.

Kendrick whispered, "Courage."

In the next moment, Robbie MacPherson leapt down all eight steps and landed agilely on his one leg. Elspeth gasped.

His crutch clattered to the pavement as he seized her by the shoulders, his eyes scanning her wildly. Then he crushed her into his embrace. Elspeth stared over his shoulder in shock as he clutched her to him. "Robbie...?"

"Elspeth, please forgive me for not seeing your suffering," Robbie whispered. "I'm so sorry."

The tension in her frame drained away. "You don't hate me?" she said in a small voice.

"Hate you?" Robbie repeated, incredulous. He pulled back to face her. "I *love* you, silly lass."

Elspeth trembled. "But I lied to you, and I—"

"None of that, now," Robbie commanded. "I know very well what it's like for a master to forge your chains of obedience." He lifted his hands to cup her face, spearing his fingers through her wet hair.

"Oh, don't—" Elspeth blurted out, raising her hands instinctively.

Robbie gave her an all-too-knowing look. "You don't have to hide your scars from me. Isn't that what you told me about my leg?" He cradled the sides of her head, purposefully cupping her mutilated ears. "That scars are just part of who we are and what we survived?"

Tears blurred Elspeth's eyes. She pressed her face into his steady hands.

"I said that?" she managed to say. "Are you sure?"

"I recall it so clearly because it was the moment I lost my head over the wisest and loveliest woman I've ever known," Robbie said. "Come inside, Elspeth."

Elspeth came on trembling legs, clutching the arm Robbie did not use for his crutch. She had only just stepped inside the door when Genevieve flew through the green servants' door at the end of the hall and came running towards her, her skirts hoisted nearly to her knees. "Elspeth!" she called.

Oh, but I'm not ready, Elspeth thought. She hadn't rehearsed her apology yet! "Genevieve—"

Genevieve hit her at nearly full speed, wrapping her arms around her. "Are you all right?" she demanded. "You're not hurt?"

"I'm sorry, Genevieve," Elspeth said, sniffing hard. "He wanted me to tell him secrets, things about you and Kendrick—but I tried so hard not to betray you. Please believe me."

"Of *course* I do," Genevieve said, sniffing herself. "*I'm* the one who's sorry. I should have seen the signs. I should have known Laurent would have—" Genevieve's voice cracked. "I've been a poor friend."

Elspeth shook her head. "That's never been true yet in the twenty years I've known you." Genevieve had been the one who had held them all together by the skin of her teeth down in the dark. She had survived torture and grief and the howling madness of solitude because of Genevieve. "And to repay you this way, after everything..."

"Let there be no talk of payment between you and me." Genevieve squeezed her again and then turned to Kendrick. "You won't hold what happened against her, will you?"

"Did I not promise you equal parts justice and mercy?" Kendrick murmured, brushing some of her hair behind her ear.

Genevieve smiled up at him. "Yes. And I know you for a man who keeps his word."

"Be wary of Laurent, Genevieve," Elspeth urged. "He's unreasonable about you."

"With any luck, he does not have many days left on the earth," Kendrick rumbled. "Searchers, to me! We have a location."

❧

Elspeth clung hard to Genevieve's hand as they ventured down to the cellar. She was hard-pressed to say whether or not approaching Kendrick expecting death had been worse than this. Entering the small, lantern-lit room, Elspeth met the gaze of the woman sitting with unnatural stillness on the bed as Dominic Penrose hovered protectively. Evangeline Hartshorne's once-green eyes had faded to the typical vampire colorless gaze, and no sound emerged from her chest. She had awakened, true enough, but had firmly passed the boundary from life to death.

Even though she had been given mercy for her crime, Elspeth knew she still had to acknowledge the wrong. "I have to say I'm sorry." Elspeth spoke up, before anyone else said anything. "No matter the outcome, I still—I still killed you. I have to—beg your forgiveness. I turned you. I can't express how I wish—how I wish I could have made a different choice. I know what it's like to have your life—stolen. To be ripped away from the human world, sundered—"

"But all that would have happened to me, anyway," Evangeline

Hartshorne said with a strange preternatural calm, holding her gaze.

Elspeth pulled up sharply as her ears rang. "What?"

Evangeline Hartshorne smiled a little. "Don't you remember? That man—Laurent. He had given me his blood. I believe he always intended to kill me. Based on what Mr. Penrose has told me," she said, her eyes flicking to Dominic, "by giving me your blood, you snatched me out of his clutches, Miss Gibbins."

Elspeth worked her mouth, trying to speak. But it felt full of cotton. Genevieve's hands steadied her as she swayed.

She had forgotten.

That was how the bond had broken tonight. That was how she had escaped.

She had broken her own chains.

But I have forged another set, she realized with cold dread.

Evangeline continued. "He told you to kill me, but he meant for the act to wound *you*. Please believe me—you don't have to carry the guilt of an act that was meant to hurt you."

"You ought to hate me," Elspeth burst out. "I—I'm your *maker* now." The realization filled her with a newfound horror and revulsion. "I c-could make you do *h-horrible* things."

Turn against friends. Stop her mouth. Turn her into a living puppet. Reduce her down to a frantic wild thing, trapped in her own body, not able to even scream. Elspeth pressed her clenched fist to her mouth.

"No, you won't," Genevieve said, putting her arms about Elspeth. "Because we won't allow what was done to us to happen to anyone else. The blood bond can be so easily abused, as we know. Newly created vampires ought to have protections and resources that we never did."

"And makers must be taught how to help their children," Dominic said firmly.

"Children?" Elspeth said faintly. She had never seen a vampire blood bond in even vaguely familial terms.

"Children," Dominic repeated. "We will never have natural progeny. The vampires we make are our only legacy, our only bloodline. I have *never* understood how those we make can be abandoned—or abused and manipulated—so shamefully. I will help you both as you navigate this new world," he promised, looking down at Evangeline and then back to Elspeth.

"We can write a new way forward," Genevieve said. "Mentors. Teachers. Social workers, for those who may be in precarious or dangerous blood bond relationships. You both are not alone."

Elspeth stared hopefully at her friend, blinking her blurry vision clear. Her enthusiasm was nearly a tangible thing. That was Genevieve's best trait—she enabled those around her to hope.

"Speaking of children," Evangeline said, lacing her fingers together in her lap. A spark of yearning lit in her eyes, belying her collected poise. "Can I see August and June?" Deep longing and fear reverberated in her voice. "I won't hurt them, will I? I—I drank earlier, but I can't help but worry—"

Dominic set his hand on her shoulder. "I will be right there with you. I will not let you hurt them. I promise."

Evangeline looked up at him and slowly nodded.

❦

Genevieve followed the small procession up the stairs, Evangeline wobbling like a newborn foal as she grew used to the new rhythms of her body, Dominic steadying her when she paused. Genevieve watched with quiet fascination. Dominic had shown intense interest in the family, so much so that earlier, Kendrick and Genevieve had exchanged speculative looks.

"Shall I bring the children down to the parlor?" Genevieve asked once they'd passed the green door.

Dominic nodded. "I think that will be best. But she'll be just fine."

Genevieve hurried upstairs to the nursery where Kate held

June and showed her a rattle as a nursery maid held a little boy with very curly hair. August sat on the rug surrounded by toy soldiers, but he hugged his knees, his eyes on the door. "August, would you and June like to come down to the parlor?" Genevieve asked, smiling brilliantly. "I think someone would like to see you."

August's eyes flew wide, and he jumped to his feet.

"Want to go see who it is, lovey?" Kate asked, standing with June. "Nancy, you'll look after Ben a moment?"

They all hurried downstairs, August's hand clasped tightly on Genevieve's until they reached the open parlor door. Then August caught sight of Evangeline sitting on the sofa, and he ran into her arms. June strained towards her mother in Kate's hold, shrieking.

Dominic and Elspeth hovered close by, watching carefully.

Genevieve bit her lip as her heart swelled with emotion from the exclaiming, wildly excited but also sobbing children and their mother.

Still—something was missing. She frowned and glanced around her.

Kendrick, in the hallway dispatching the last team of searchers, caught her eye and came towards her. "What is it?"

"Where is Fletcher?"

Chapter Twenty-Eight

Kendrick found the boy preparing to slip out Fernside's back door with just the clothes on his back and a wholly inadequate coat.

"Fletcher!" Genevieve exclaimed in a voice full of surprise and hurt. "Where are you going?"

It was clear where the boy was going. He had a cap pulled low over his head and a cloth of indeterminate origin wrapped around his neck as a scarf. To top it off, he clenched his jaw to still the quivering of his chin.

"It's night and raining still," Genevieve continued, confused and upset. "And what about Wulfric? Were you going to leave him?"

"A man doesn't sneak off without a word. He bids his friends adieu when he takes his leave," Kendrick said.

"Ain't no reason for me to stay among reavers," the boy said, jutting his chin out.

"Fletcher, are you calling my word into question?" Kendrick asked mildly.

To his credit, the boy's eyes widened in surprise. "No, guv."

"Good, because I might have to challenge you to a duel."

"*Kendrick*!" Genevieve exclaimed.

"Coo!" Fletcher burst out. "You off your head, guv?"

"No, Fletcher, I'm very serious." Kendrick opened the door to the butler's pantry and gestured. "Let's discuss it together, shall we?" He set a calming hand on Genevieve's arm when she would have opened her mouth to protest. *Trust me*, he said with his eyes.

Even though her expression was drawn and worried, Genevieve bit her lip and nodded.

It was as if the floorboards under him had shifted, throwing him off-balance. His *wife* was willing to put her trust in him. Kendrick swallowed, determined to prove himself worthy of it.

Genevieve wanted the boy safe. But safety was not what Fletcher wanted most. So they would have to meet him where he was.

To Fletcher, Kendrick said, "If you want to have this conversation in front of the kitchen staff, we can, but I thought you'd want a bit of privacy."

Fletcher stuck out his chin and stalked into the room. Kendrick and Genevieve followed him in. Shutting the door, Kendrick took a seat in one of the threadbare armchairs and set his hands on his knees. "Tell us why you want to leave," he said simply, watching the boy's pride war with a yearning he likely had no name for.

"I'm better, and the tykes have their mum back. There ain't no reason for me to stick around, guv," Fletcher declared. His voice was firm and full of cockney bluster, but he wouldn't meet their eyes.

"Our invitation isn't enough?" Genevieve asked, clasping her hands together in her lap. Her knuckles were very white.

"Ain't taking charity, mum."

"You need to earn your keep? Pull your weight?" Kendrick asked. "What if I told you I had a reason for you to stay?"

Genevieve turned a confused gaze on him.

"Like what?" Fletcher said, grudgingly curious.

"We need you."

"Nobody never needed me, guv," the boy said in tones of deep scorn. "Most tried to get me to scarper double quick."

"To their own detriment," Kendrick said seriously. "For you are a clever, loyal lad. But it is true. I suspect we need you."

"What do you mean?" Genevieve asked, looking from Kendrick to Fletcher.

Kendrick leaned back in the chair and said to her, "I think we need a connection to humanity more than we admit to ourselves. I don't think it's a coincidence that episodes of madness have occurred in younger and younger vampires confined to the Ossuary, but I have maintained my equilibrium."

"I lived in the Ossuary and never had a problem," Genevieve said, working through his thoughts.

"But you could get out...and you had the children and Fletcher."

Genevieve's eyes lit up in understanding.

"If we lose the tether to humanity, we lose everything. One of the ways to do that is to maintain connections to the human world—and human people." Kendrick turned to the boy, who had followed his exchange with a frown. "Fletcher, we need you. You helped Genevieve stay sane these last few years."

"I ain't saying I won't visit," Fletcher offered uneasily. "But these houses ain't for the likes of me. I'm no toff."

Genevieve leaned forward, the lines of her body tense. "Fletcher, do you think they're for me?"

"'Course."

"I grew up in a far humbler home than Carmine House. And for the last few years, I walked into the East End to mind children and wore a badly dyed dress twenty years out of style because I could not afford a new one—you *know* that," Genevieve urged. "I lived in a hole underground with nothing but what I kept in my pockets to my name. We are not all that different. If our house is not for you, then it can't be for me."

"Don't be fooled by a grand façade," Kendrick said. "The truth is that for years, the house that is now mine was an unwholesome pit of despair. *It* is the thing that is unworthy of my wife and of you, Fletcher. But we are in the midst of a great work to mend what is now in ruins."

Fletcher shook his head, his gaze darting around the room. "Still—"

Kendrick pressed, "But if I tell you that beyond our need, beyond any apparent worthiness, that we *want* you to stay with us—"

"You don't want me, guv!" Fletcher blurted out.

Kendrick saw the tremble in Fletcher's lower lip that he tried so hard to stiffen. The bravado had cracked. Just a little, but enough.

"*Fletcher*," Genevieve said, her voice anguished. "Yes, we do! We do!"

He reddened but stiffened his shoulders. "You do, but he don't! I ain't his son."

There it is, Kendrick thought. He propped his chin on his fist, staring at Fletcher intently. "What does that have to do with anything?"

"You—you don't want a cove who ain't your blood—who don't even know who his people are—"

"Don't tell me what I want," Kendrick said flatly. "You think you're unworthy because you're not our blood? Are only sons of the blood allowed to lodge with us? If so, Genevieve and I will have a very empty house. Didn't I make you promises, Fletcher? Didn't I swear to lodge and protect you? Perhaps I imagined you accepting my hospitality in return."

Fletcher swallowed hard, his shoulders hunched. "You only did that 'cause she asked."

"Be very careful," Kendrick said, leaning forward. "You come perilously close to calling me a liar, Fletcher. A man's honor and reputation are the most important things he possesses. Tell me what I have done, in word or deed, that led you to believe I don't want you."

Fletcher's mouth opened and closed, finally at a loss for words.

"You think I don't want a superfluous child underfoot, perhaps taking Genevieve's attention? Let me tell you something, Fletcher. In days long ago, a lord would send his son to be fostered, raised by a tenant or another lord, and would take in another man's son and raise him in order to strengthen the bond of kinship and alliances between them. Families are not forged by bonds of blood alone."

"Are you having me on?" Fletcher demanded.

"My father wrote about it in his book *The Banished*," Genevieve said. Her eyes were shining with emotion.

"I'll show you when we get home tonight if you are still calling my honor into question." Kendrick sharpened his eyes on Fletcher and waited.

It did not take long. Fletcher's chin trembled. "You don't know what I done," Fletcher burst out. "I nicked from coster-mongers. I stood lookout for cracksmen. I told off mutton shunters, picked pockets, piked off—"

"You walked Genevieve back from the East End for months in the dark. You looked out for children who weren't as canny as you when you were only a little older than they were. You survived hell on your own. But you don't have to anymore. Don't you know you're our boy? We want you to stay with us, Fletcher. If pride demands you be useful, fine. But we want to be your home."

A gamut of emotions passed over Fletcher's face as he blinked hard, fiercely trying to keep tears away.

Kendrick stood and gentled his voice. "You'll always be able to choose, but a hard-hearted man it is who turns his back on a warm hearth to walk back out into a storm. Come inside, Fletcher."

Fletcher swallowed. "You're not witching me? You really want me to stay?"

"I'll never lie to you, Fletcher, and if I were 'witching' you, you'd be in front of the fire with a cup for wassail already," Kendrick said dryly.

The last of Fletcher's defenses broke. With a sob, he threw himself at Kendrick.

He wrapped his arms around the small scrap of vital humanity and held him tightly.

❧

Genevieve had had to hold herself back as Kendrick had spoken to Fletcher. Her mind had been thrown into a spiral at the idea of the boy going back to his itinerant and uncertain existence. Fletcher couldn't go, he just *couldn't*. It had been different when she had had to leave him to return to her own precarious and dangerous existence.

But she had a home now. A safe place to land. A guarantee from Kendrick that vampire households would be protected and safeguarded. How could Fletcher want to go back? And to leave his dog?

It was fear, she realized halfway through the conversation with herself. Fletcher was just as afraid as she was. But she was afraid of losing him. He was afraid to hope.

She knew all about that sort of fear.

So she knew that she could not hold tight to him to keep him from leaving. Fletcher had to decide to stay of his own free will.

So she had let Kendrick talk.

That was his gift, after all.

And hadn't he been the one to free her from her own fear?

When Fletcher broke and threw his arms around Kendrick, Genevieve could not hold back her own tears. She opened her arms and wrapped them around them both, the human boy who had stuck to her like a shadow and the man who had given her back her hope.

"Thank you," Genevieve breathed, pressing her head against his shoulder.

Kendrick's arm wrapped around her tightly. He had heard.

"Cor, you're like to squish me to death. Let a body breathe," Fletcher complained. "Blimey, missus, is that *blood* leakin' out your eyes?"

Genevieve sniffed and dabbed at her cheeks. "Don't be alarmed. I'm just a little teary." She brushed Fletcher's hair out of his face. It was too long and managed to get into the most ridiculous tangles now that the grime was no longer weighing down the thick waves. "Let's go home, shall we? We'll have to get you your own room," she said with a trembling laugh. "Once we have the furniture. Oh, I didn't think I could be happier tonight." She shared a glowing look with Kendrick, who smiled.

"Gonna have to hire a cook if I'm to stay with you, missus, or send out to a chophouse. Meals ain't your strong point," Fletcher said with a quick grin. "It's been soup, soup, soup."

Unable to resist, Genevieve brushed a hand over his hair again. "That's because you were sick."

"But nobody at your house eats."

"That's true. We will need a cook for you—but we'll need other people as well." If Kendrick was indeed right that vampires held on to their sanity and maintained an even equilibrium for far longer when they interacted with humans, it would make sense to set up a household similar to Fernside, with humans for staff to handle the daylight business. "Perhaps a housekeeper, a footman, and a maid for the daytime, though I think we would have willing staff for the evenings..."

Fletcher tilted his head. "What about Sally?"

Genevieve sighed. "I've been meaning to go back and explain that I can't look after the children anymore...'

Fletcher shook his head. "Naw. I mean, for that housekeeping job."

Genevieve's gaze shot to Kendrick as the idea blossomed in

her mind. "Fletcher. You are brilliant. What would we do without you?"

Just then, a commotion at the front door carried down into the kitchens.

Fletcher's eyes widened. "Maybe they have news about the bad cove."

Hand in hand, the three of them hurried towards the din. As they reached the upper hallways, the occupants of the parlor also spilled out into the hall.

The searchers entered Fernside, much grime-covered and annoyed, and recounted the events for all assembled. When they had reached the terrace house in Chelsea, they'd found it abandoned. Further, parts of it had been sabotaged to collapse and *had* collapsed, leading to their bedraggled state. Thankfully, no one had been harmed beyond what vampirism could repair.

Joseph accepted Genevieve's offered handkerchief and wiped his face. "Laurent must have realized that Elspeth had bypassed his control over her and fled ahead of us."

Genevieve's shoulders slumped in discouragement. "So what do we do?"

"We keep looking," Kendrick said grimly.

Etienne, looking as annoyed as a wet cat, pulled off his pince-nez as his blond hair dripped down his nose. "How? The rain continues. We will not find a trace of him easily, if at all."

"He can't hide forever," Kendrick growled.

"Why don't we do what the humans do?" Joseph suggested.

Etienne and Genevieve stared at him blankly, but his meaning dawned on Kendrick. He nodded slowly.

"Offer a reward."

Chapter Twenty-Nine

enevieve was trapped in the dark. She panted, panicked, as her heart thundered in her ears. Elspeth wasn't in the dark— she couldn't find her, couldn't see even the faintest glimmer of light. She fumbled over the dirt floor, felt along rough brick for any egress. There was a door, a door—but no knob. She scrabbled at the closed door, trying to wedge her fingers into any crack to pry it open, tearing her gloves.

It hurt to swallow. The sides of her neck, her wrists, her shoulders throbbed.

Choking back a sob, she renewed her struggle as her arms trembled with effort.

She had to get the door open. She had to get out.

Then, from the dark—

"I do admire your tenacity, Genevieve. You never give up, do you?"

Hands seized her shoulders.

Sheer terror stopped her heart.

Genevieve tried to tear herself away from the grip, away from the fangs in her neck—

"Genevieve. Wake, dear heart."

She opened her eyes with a violent start, recoiling away from the voice that called her.

Fear electrified her—so much so that she thought she felt the phantom hammering of her long-still heart.

Light bloomed. Kendrick replaced the glass on the lamp and sat back against the headboard.

Genevieve pressed a hand to her chest. There was no sound there.

She was not trapped in a grimy, lightless hole with her captor. She was here, with Kendrick. Her husband. She swallowed and pressed her hands to her face.

"Another nightmare?" Kendrick asked quietly.

She nodded. "It's as though now I am finally allowing myself to be frightened of all that happened."

"I don't think it's all that surprising that bad memories are surfacing, given Evangeline's similar experience," Kendrick said carefully.

Genevieve swallowed. "That must be it." Apologetically, she said, "It feels so silly once I wake."

"No, it isn't." Kendrick gathered her into his arms, holding her against his chest. She rested her head against his chest and sighed.

It had been nearly a week since they had circulated a five-thousand-pound reward among the inhabitants of the London Ossuary and its environs, asking for the location of or information related to the capture of Laurent. While all remained alert, the active search had been put on hold for more important matters—solidifying their new rulership in the Ossuary and addressing the Ossuary's long-ignored issues.

"No one is trying to kill you anymore," Genevieve pointed out. "We're winning people over with our works projects to clean out, furnish, and make the Ossuary livable. Those who dislike our changes aren't resorting to Laurent's brand of malice. He's not a threat."

"He's not a *political* threat," Kendrick corrected her. "He's not smart enough to hold the position of Ossuary rulership for himself. But he *is* a threat to vampires with less power than he, and to humans he encounters, because he covets the latitude to exert control over others with impunity. That's what he liked so much about Rupert. And he obtains that control through pain and fear and meanness. So yes. He is a threat. And we will find him and deal with him as he deserves."

Genevieve held back a shudder, remembering the terror. "I've never understood how anyone could revel in callousness to such an extent."

"Grendel hated the sound of harps."

Genevieve lifted her head from his shoulder. "What?"

"Grendel attacked the Hall of Heorot because he hated the sound of the harps."

Genevieve nodded in understanding. Laurent would lash out in a whirlwind of fury, simply because what they stood for enraged him.

She just wished the dreams and the scraps of memory from her time before her death would stop. Her grip tightened on Kendrick.

"Would a kiss help?" he asked in a voice like smoke.

She looked up at him through her lashes. "I don't think it would hurt."

His smile made the room take on a glow, just like the lamp. He lowered his head and pressed his mouth to hers, sweetly. A shiver traveled through Genevieve, but not one of fear this time. Of delight. She reveled in the feeling of his beard against her cheek and against her palm, which she brought up to cup his jaw.

She had not realized how much she would like kissing. She had grown quite fond of it over the last week.

His hands traveled down her back and then lifted her into his lap. "This is better," he said in a low voice.

"For what?" she asked, her voice thready.

"This." He kissed her, his lips stroking across her own, coaxing them open. "Mmm."

Mmm, Genevieve thought in return as he sipped at her lips, keeping the slow, drugging kisses sweet. Her toes curled in response.

Since their wedding, they had shared a bed and blood, but nothing more. Genevieve liked the closeness of falling into dreams beside him—wanted it, in fact, because he made her feel brave enough to fall into dreams where she might meet some of her worst fears, and safe enough to go into his arms upon waking. After the second such dream, Kendrick had offered to give her a knife to put under her pillow if it would make her feel more secure.

"Then I might stab you!" she had objected.

"Not unless your aim is much better than everyone else who has tried," he had said, unconcerned.

"Oh, don't tease!"

He never pressured her—only inquired if she was hungry at the close of the evening. He always made it a point to feed while he was out, so she could feed from him. He had said nothing more of them making their bond a real marriage. But sometimes she thought about what it might be like, like tonight when tingles traveled all the way down to her toes and to other places. She liked his strong arms about her. Liked his kisses more.

His kisses eventually relaxed her enough that the pull of the sun overhead, outside their darkened and protected bedchamber, was enough to make her drowsy once more.

"Sleepy?" he murmured in a rough voice.

"Mm-hmm."

He blew out the lamp and slid them both under the coverlet again, her head on his shoulder. He stroked her hair, careful of her neck, which still made her start if he touched it without warning.

They lay in the dark for a time before Genevieve lifted her head and asked, "Do you think having a group of vampires making lace will undercut human lacemakers?"

Silence.

"Is that what you were thinking about all this time?" he asked, sounding highly amused. "And here I thought I might have put some other thoughts in your head."

"Well, I was worrying about it before we fell asleep. It seemed like a good way for some of the women in the Ossuary to earn a living if we provide them with the materials, like I did with Elspeth. But will we be undercutting the human market by selling less expensive lace?"

"Not if you're inventing your own patterns. And you're keeping humans from losing their eyesight to the lace."

"All right. Thank you." Genevieve relaxed and set her head back on his shoulder. After a moment, she added, "And you *did* put some other thoughts in my head. I'm...contemplating."

"Mull those thoughts over as long as you like, my heart's gleam," Kendrick said. She could feel him smiling against her hair. "I'm just glad to know they're there."

❧

Kendrick smiled in the dark as Genevieve relaxed into sleep. Being married agreed with him more than he'd ever imagined.

Every night before *uhta*, just before sunrise, they would return to Carmine House after their long night's work and, after assuring themselves of the household's comfort and safety, they would go to bed. Nothing had happened in their bed yet except kissing, but every night, Genevieve fed from him before they surrendered to slumber. Kendrick did not think any other pleasure could compare to knowing his wife was safe and well-fed and happy.

Kendrick stroked his hand over her hair again. She *was* happy now that she could finally throw herself into the changes for which she had longed for years, but she also pushed herself too hard. She needed her rest.

Genevieve had taken the bit in her teeth this week, beginning a census of the vampire population, evaluating who still had an active master bond and what was the health of the relationship.

Her rationale was that this would then allow them to set up committees for training young, newly turned vampires to control their urges, as well as connect makers with mentors and oversight. Dominic had volunteered to provide some names he thought would be interested in mentoring, and Elspeth had begun working with Evangeline, making notes of what she and Genevieve had had to learn on their own.

Knowing where people resided would also be crucial if portions of the Ossuary were deemed unsafe and the inhabitants would need to be rehoused. It would also allow them to take the temperature, as it were, of the vampires in London and which of them were dancing a little too close to the line of madness. Kendrick had lifted the restrictions on the comings and goings of those who resided in the Ossuary and was brainstorming with Etienne what kind of focused efforts could be enacted to bring people back.

Every evening at dusk, they woke and dressed, taking some time to meet with the human members of Carmine House—of which there were more besides just Fletcher now. Kendrick and Genevieve had gone to her friend Sally Blevins and offered her the housekeeper position at Carmine House, a paid position with rooms for herself and her children.

When Genevieve had hesitantly said that there were a few key conditions of the employment, Sally had said, "Miss Dryden—you could be holding bloomin' orgies in the back garden, and I'd come keep house for you."

"We are *not* going to be doing anything of the sort," Genevieve had said firmly. "But it is rather...troublesome." She had taken a deep breath and explained.

Kendrick had watched the woman's face as Genevieve had laid the situation before her, and he had been inwardly impressed at how well she'd taken the news.

"Glory be," Sally muttered. "Well, I always knew there was something a mite odd that a woman like you would be willing to look after the wee ones, but only after dark." She sat and thought a moment. "So I'd run the house during the daylight?"

"Yes, and we are in the process of finding someone to manage the nights, so you would have all your evenings free. We would also ensure that Peter and Hannah had their own rooms and provide the food and clothing and salary for the human members of the household," Genevieve said. "Actually, one of our friends was a cook in her former life, and she is thrilled for the chance to make food people will actually eat again. Your position will be housekeeper, and you will be compensated accordingly. There have been...bad practices in the past. We want no one tempted to fall into old patterns. This is going to be a new start for everyone, and we begin as we mean to go on."

Kendrick stirred. "And we have promised to keep you and the children safe. You have my word on it, ma'am. If at any point you feel unsafe or pestered by anyone, human or vampire, you have only to tell us, and we will take care of the matter."

"Coo," Sally said, blinking rapidly at Kendrick. "I can see why you married *him*, missus." She had even blushed as Kendrick had smiled.

In the end, Sally had accepted the position, and they had moved her and the children into Carmine House without delay. Fletcher had been delighted to have the younger children follow him and Wulfric around like ducklings, and Genevieve had informed Sally if she knew of anyone who would like a daytime maid or footman position who could be trusted, they would consider interviewing them, but until that time, Fletcher was ready and more than willing to run errands or do any small tasks that she might need.

Watching Genevieve interact with the humans, Kendrick believed his supposition about vampires and humans was right. Genevieve did need her human circle just as much as she needed to make the Ossuary habitable. He noticed it especially when vampires arrived at the cellar door, hat in hand for a petition or a hearing from their rulers, and they ushered them through the kitchen—which had quickly become the heart of the human portion of the house—on the way to the library to hear their requests.

And he could not deny that it made the house feel like a home, to have children's footraces in the long back hallways and the smell of cookery in the kitchen.

So, every sunset when they woke, Genevieve listened to the children relay the goings-on of their day and spoke with Sally about the running of the house. Often the children would request a chapter of *Sigestan* as they ate their dinner.

He was always happy to oblige.

Houses becoming homes. The solitary settled into families. Small changes—but more to come. To show the Ossuary a better way to be.

Chapter Thirty

The next evening, after meeting with Dominic on the potential vampires to lead their new mentorship program, Kendrick exited the library and nearly ran into Genevieve. She was wearing one of her new frocks and looked very fetching, even as she frowned at the card in her hand. "We have callers," she said, handing him the card.

"Montmorency." He fingered the card in thought. "I know him, I think."

"A good knowing or a bad knowing?"

"His name was on Etienne's list." Kendrick exchanged a look with Genevieve. "Where are they?"

"Mr. MacPherson's put him and his wife in the newly furnished receiving room."

"What a good thing we've acquired new furniture." He offered Genevieve his arm and they proceeded into the receiving room.

Mr. Weston Montmorency was a tall, angular man in perhaps his mid-sixties. His hair and beard had been blond once but now had lightened to almost gray, and his face was lined with age. Sharp and canny eyes combined with the prominent set of his nose gave him the appearance of a raptor scanning for prey.

Mrs. Montmorency, on the other hand, was a small, plump young woman with a pretty face and curling strawberry-blond ringlets. She looked like a young girl about to have her first season. She seemed like a highly incongruous mate for such a gentleman unless the union had been founded on money and land.

But of course, it hadn't been, for they were both vampires.

"I am so pleased to meet you, Your Majesty." Mrs. Montmorency twinkled at Genevieve.

Genevieve smiled politely, probably aware that this woman would not have given her a greeting on the street a month ago. "How do you, Mrs. Montmorency?"

"We wanted to pay a call to offer our congratulations on your newlywed status," Mrs. Montmorency said, settling onto the divan with a rustle of skirts. She glanced at the door and back again.

"How kind," Genevieve murmured.

Her husband squared his shoulders. "And also to inquire as to the changes you are making among the Ossuary rabble, Kendrick. It isn't wise to give them a very long rope, you know."

"Oh? Why is that?" Kendrick asked, sounding bored.

"They might get above themselves. They are lower class."

"I have always wondered where that perception comes from," Genevieve said conversationally. "Human society is built upon the rock of wealth and family. Vampire society seems to be built upon age and deception."

"*Deception?*" Montmorency echoed, with a sharp look between Kendrick and Genevieve. Kendrick merely sat back in his chair and smiled a little.

Genevieve explained, "If you've only lived a handful of years as a vampire, everyone remembers who turned you and where you came from. You start with nothing, ripped from your human bonds. It's only when those older die off or you outlive your peers that you gain respectability and class. Because now you are older than those you deem 'rabble.'"

"You cannot *age* into respectability." Montmorency shot another look at Kendrick. "Is that what all this surveying has been about? I've been presented with a *bill*," he said, producing the offensive document and rattling the sheet.

Kendrick raised an eyebrow. "You don't believe it's accurate?"

"It's a damned disgrace! What have *I* got to do with 'Ossuary upkeep'?" He scoffed.

"You don't believe makers are responsible for their dependents?"

"*What?*" Montmorency said, his eyes popping.

"According to those we've surveyed so far, we've found seven vampires who were turned by you or your wife, sir," Kendrick said. "Three with an active blood bond. We've calculated what you owe them."

"Owe? *Owe?*"

"What my husband means to say," Mrs. Montmorency said hurriedly, "is that shouldn't they make their own way in the world? How will doling out handouts encourage them to abandon their shiftless nature?"

"How does turning them and abandoning them to their own devices serve them?" Genevieve said tightly. "Leaving them penned up in the Ossuary, leashed by your commands—"

Montmorency looked from her to Kendrick. "Think what sort of a precedent you are setting," he warned, shaking his finger warningly. "You may find support waning if you institute these policies."

"Is that a threat?" Kendrick asked mildly.

The Montmorencys paused. The wife stepped into the breach. "Sire," she said in a particularly sweet tone. Only those with a good ear could hear the venom under it. "Please pardon my husband. The pressures of this age weigh on him. It was concern for the future that made him speak out of turn."

"Madam, I understand fear of change. But staying in a broken system is its own kind of death."

Genevieve said firmly, "Vampires cannot be allowed to turn and abandon humans with impunity. That is why we have instituted a turning ban and have put oversight of blood bonds into place."

Montmorency opened his mouth, but Kendrick drawled, "My wife is quite right, Montmorency." His eyes glittered. "For one thing, it looks suspicious."

Silence descended on the room.

In the stillness, Kendrick stood and planted himself in front of the fireplace, holding his hands out to the fire in the grate, though he did not need the flame to warm him. "After all, you went out of your way to turn them." He spun around and nailed the other vampire with his gaze. "It makes us question whether or not you obtained their consent. Whether or not you applied to the ruler of the Ossuary for consent."

"The Draugodrottin did not require it," Mrs. Montmorency said in her tinkly voice.

Kendrick smiled at her, all teeth. "We do. It also makes us question your goal in turning them, if not to bring them into your own household. I'm curious."

She didn't move a muscle.

"It's something we like to mull over. A little thought exercise, positing different vampire motivations. Perhaps you are thinking of setting up your own little kingdom in the Ossuary. Your own power base, if you will. But that, of course, would be akin to a contestation of rulership." He fingered the sword that was never far from his side, even now. "Wouldn't it?"

They did not have any response to that.

Genevieve spread her hands. "Mr. Montmorency, if you don't wish to make restitution to your dependents, we have a very simple solution to make sure everyone contributes fairly to what you term 'Ossuary upkeep.'"

"What is that?" Montmorency said, drumming his fingers on his knee.

"Taxes."

As the Montmorencys recoiled, Genevieve raised an eyebrow. "Well, we clearly can't depend on good Christian charity, can we? Either way, we will not turn a blind eye to the less fortunate among us anymore."

Kendrick just smiled. "What you may not understand about my wife, Montmorency, is that she was one of the Ossuary 'rabble,' and a more industrious woman I have never met."

Mrs. Montmorency jumped into the breach. "How romantic," she breathed, "that you met in such a way."

"I think so, since she saved my life," Kendrick said. He turned his head and met Genevieve's wide eyes.

The Montmorencys pulled up abruptly.

"Genevieve was the one to warn me of the assassination attempts against me. A true heroine." Kendrick smiled. "How could I not be captivated?"

"Assassination attempts," Montmorency said, attempting to regain control of the conversation. "You see, the rabble are not to be trusted!"

"Most of the attempts came from Rupert's power group, who were very much not rabble. Joseph has confirmed which had dependents and which did not and has seized their unclaimed assets. They were in truth very well off in vampire terms. Stupidity is not limited by class." Kendrick smiled again, but this time it was all teeth.

❧

Once they had bidden the Montmorencys a firm adieu, Kendrick wrapped his arm around Genevieve's shoulders. "Well, I think that went well."

"It was certainly interesting," Genevieve admitted.

"I thought we'd get some 'helpful' visits sooner or later. He just couldn't help himself, could he?" Kendrick mused.

"What on earth was she doing? Her neck was on a swivel, did you notice that? Who did she expect to come through the door?"

"Refreshments," Kendrick said dryly.

"But we don't—" Genevieve broke off, arrested. "She expected *human* refreshments?"

"I would put money on it."

"She really expected a human to walk through the door and let her bite them? Or perhaps bleed into a teacup to be a bit more proper?" Genevieve's tone wavered between outraged and flabbergasted.

"I think they are the type of vampires to maintain a connection to the human world in order to puppeteer people and events to their liking," Kendrick said. "But they certainly don't view humans as beings of worth."

"Goodness, there are *more* like them?" She sounded only half-joking.

"I'm sure."

They exchanged a look.

"You want to do something about that, don't you?" Kendrick smiled.

"Well, we will need to check on any humans who are a part of their households. I don't know how to do that yet, but..."

"You will," he assured her.

Genevieve bit her lip. "Thank you for what you said. About me being a...heroine."

"It was true," he said, taking her hand. "My wife is an astoundingly capable woman, and I am blessed to be married to her." He bent his head and kissed her, laving his tongue over the lip she had been worrying, soothing away the hurt.

Genevieve wrapped her arms around his neck and kissed him back. "I like it when you call me your wife," she whispered in his ear. Kendrick could feel her smile against his cheek.

"I am thankful that it is true."

Chapter Thirty-One

J ust as Genevieve was setting the new hat that had arrived at Carmine House during the day on her head—a smart article in blue with cloth flowers adorning the brim, resembling nothing so much as an upside-down flowerpot —someone knocked at her door.

"Come," she called, picking up her reticule.

Elspeth opened the door and poked her head in. "Oh, good, you're ready. What an interesting hat."

"Kendrick ordered it, as a surprise," Genevieve said. "Does it look all right?"

Elspeth stepped in the room and adjusted the position of the hat a touch. "Perfect. How romantic of him."

"He buys things and then has Fletcher present them to me like it's a great mystery whom they're from," Genevieve murmured, picking up her reticule. "I believe he bought it because it wouldn't require a hatpin like some styles, though in the note for this one, he said that the milliner assured him the style would be all the rage soon."

Elspeth smiled. "It looks very well on you."

"How is Evangeline?" Genevieve asked as they descended the stairs and made their way to the Ossuary's entrance in the cellar. "And how are you doing?"

"Evangeline is doing well. She worries about her control around the children, but it also motivates her to learn control. Mr. Penrose helps as well."

"And you?" Genevieve asked again, touching her arm.

Elspeth sighed. "I feel like the worst sort of jailer."

"How so?"

"Mr. Penrose insisted we learn to locate and understand what the blood bond is like between us—what if there is some sort of pressure in these early days that causes Evangeline to lash out, and I must order her to desist? And she must also understand what it feels like to be commanded in order to divine the difference between her own will and mine. Which I understand. A weapon we don't know how to wield will end up cutting us both. And Evangeline gave her consent before we began. I just *hate* it," Elspeth said in a low, fervent voice. "I feel like the monster we always thought our makers were."

"You are nothing like them," Genevieve told her.

"I hope not. But I don't believe it is the natural order of things for one being to hold such sway over another."

"I don't believe we could describe vampirism as 'natural,'" Genevieve said dryly.

"Exactly. I've had several conversations with Sparrow about this. None of us really know how vampires came to be, but she thinks that it's a twisting, a corruption of humanity. I'm inclined to believe her."

"Some sort of attempt to preserve life gone horribly wrong?"

"Or a rejection of what lies after death. I don't know. But do we bear the burden of that rejection? Do we carry that sin?"

Genevieve's throat closed.

"I'm going to introduce Sparrow to Evangeline," Elspeth continued. "I think they'd have some interesting conversations."

"Good idea," Genevieve managed.

When they made their way to the area that they had converted into a distribution point for the goods and services they were trying to disperse about the underground, they found Sparrow already there behind a long, wooden table used to set out goods, in a heated discussion with a man Genevieve recognized but whose name she didn't know. He wore a patched coat and a belligerent expression as he used his height to loom over Sparrow. Five similarly dressed toughs backed him up as waiting vampires watched warily from the sidelines.

He was one of many underground. Every few months, an enterprising soul would chafe against their maker's and the Ossuary's restrictions and, in an effort to kick against the pricks, would form a gang to provide protection and exert influence on all the other vampires penned up by their makers. It would inevitably decline as their behavior devolved into bullying and the underlings rebelled or a rival gang formed. Eventually, two opposing forces would confront each other and leave each other bloody or dead. Or their makers would step in and lay commands on all involved.

Genevieve had always made it a priority to stay out of the way of those types. Often she had used her talent to advise those in harm's way to relocate out of a particular area of "turf" or to be wary of a particular vampire. She felt a moment's urge to go unseen, instinct in the face of danger. But she squared her shoulders instead and approached with Elspeth at her side.

"What is all this?"

The man spun around to face her, hands on his hips. A scuffed bowler covered his head, pulled low over his eyes. Based on the scowl on his craggy face, he looked like what Fletcher would have described as a "hard man."

That, or "bent as a nine-bob note."

"This gentleman believes he should have a larger share of goods than anyone else," Sparrow said, mouth pursed.

"And why is that, Mister...?"

"Name's Barrett," the man said, scowling in Genevieve's direction. "This here's my patch. I'm collecting for those what live on my patch. And what's with holding the rest of the goods in reserve, missy? That's a load of bollocks. Ain't we good enough to warrant it?" He puffed himself up like a bantam.

A hiss from the onlookers. "That's the *lady*, that is," someone said.

Genevieve held up a hand. "I do understand the trouble, Mr. Barrett. We have not precisely nailed down the new titles for the rulers of the Ossuary. However." Her voice dropped into frigid territory. "I have never been, nor will I ever be, a 'missy.'"

His lip curled. "Missus, then. I still need the shares for those on my patch. A hundred of 'em." He stabbed a thick finger into the top of the table.

"And their names?" Genevieve said.

He reared back. "Names?"

"Yes, names," she said, enunciating sharply. "All one hundred of them."

"Don't have to give you their names."

"If you claimed them as dependents, you absolutely would, Mr. Barrett, but as it stands, you cannot request a portion for a dependent. They must come themselves and put down their name to receive a share, as these good people are prepared to do." She continued, "Everyone receives one bedroll and a certain amount in cash to purchase clothing at a secondhand shop or to hire one of our new tailors. All other goods are in reserve for those who wish to set up a business and have a proposal for said business. There are no 'patches' in the Ossuary anymore."

Mr. Barrett bared his fangs at her and took a step forward. "You don't want to cross me."

"No, Mr. Barrett," Genevieve said, eyes flashing. "You don't want to cross *me*. The Ossuary is changing. Bullies who engage in petty turf wars no longer hold sway." Aware of the eyes on her, she let her voice carry as she said, "We are very interested when we hear reports of exploitation, and those reports will be investigated, and they will be judged. Do not test me, Mr. Barrett."

Barrett and his cronies looked around, weighing their odds. After all, there were six of them against three women. But the vampire onlookers were an unknown—and they were drifting away from them, leaving a conspicuous empty space around the toughs.

Genevieve narrowed her eyes. "I'll give you a choice, Mr. Barrett. You can abide by the old way or the new way. According to the new way, you abide by the laws, you reside in harmony with your neighbors, you refrain from killing or turning humans, and we endeavor to make everyone's existence fulfilling and profitable."

He sneered. "And according to the old way?"

"According to the old way, you insult my wife, and I cut your head off, and no one blinks an eye," Kendrick said. He appeared behind the knot of men, his sword slung over his shoulder and a stony look on his face.

The men jumped, pivoting to face him. He eyed them all with his yellow gaze. "Choose carefully." He gestured between himself and Genevieve.

Barrett licked his lips. His eyes flicked back and forth, like a rat looking for an exit.

The slow stream of workers coming up behind Kendrick carrying building materials and tools turned the tide.

Barrett scowled and spat, abandoning the table and distribution point entirely. He stalked away with his bully boys hurrying after him.

"Good choice," Kendrick rumbled. "If anyone would like to earn a night's wages, we're going to be shoring up sections of the Ossuary. If you're interested, sign up with Marshall Cutter and follow me."

As he passed by Genevieve, he shot her a quick smile.

"'And it came to pass in those days, that there went out a decree from Caesar Augustus that all the world should be taxed,'" Genevieve murmured to herself towards the end of the night. She and Sparrow had decided to bring their census to the eastern warrens of the Ossuary, which were farthest from the social center and probably had received the least information regarding their changes.

Sparrow shifted the basket on her arm. "'And Joseph also went up from Galilee, out of the city of Nazareth into Judea, to the city of David, which is called Bethlehem: because he was of the house and family of David, to be enrolled with Mary, his espoused wife, who was with child.'"

Genevieve smiled fleetingly, a bittersweet melancholy in its wake.

There were so many more people pressed into the alcoves and corners of the underground tunnels than was healthy or safe. They had been sharing small comforts like candles and mending kits and spreading news of the available goods one could acquire as part of the census, as well as the industries vampires could apply for.

Some vampires they spoke to were overawed and shocked at the barest extension of kindness. Others scoffed and sneered like Mr. Barrett and his ilk. All the things Genevieve had feared—but no one offered them blatant disrespect. For every scoffer, there was someone else to rebuke the naysayer and tip their hats or curtsey to her and Sparrow.

"It is nearly four," Sparrow pointed out, checking the pocket watch pinned to her waist.

"We can check another corridor," Genevieve said. "We still have a few bundles left."

"Rome wasn't built in a day, you know," Sparrow told her gently.

"I know. But I keep thinking, what if the person around the next corner is in dire need, and I turned around before I reached them?"

"That may be true, but if you sacrifice yourself in reaching them, what will the rest of the Ossuary do?" she pointed out.

Genevieve took a deep breath and sighed. "All right. But let's go back a different route so we can speak to different people?"

Sparrow acknowledged that as fair.

On the return trip, after speaking to two vampires taking shelter in a sliver of rock all too reminiscent of a tomb, Genevieve remembered, *There are yet all those who dwell in the cemeteries to survey.* She winced. Perhaps Sparrow had been right to tell her to pace herself.

"Genevieve?"

She turned to see Winnie coming down the passage towards her. Sparrow stiffened slightly, but Genevieve put a hand on her arm. "Good evening, Winnie."

Winnie did not look as self-composed as she usually did. Her haughty demeanor had faded into apprehension and a bit of a sullen pout. Belatedly, she curtseyed. "Congratulations on your marriage."

"Thank you." Genevieve waited.

Winnie shifted. "I heard that you were offering jobs to people, and I thought...well, because we were friends and all, that I might be considered."

Genevieve tilted her head and regarded Winnie. "Well, we have several positions for maids as well as a restoration crew, those willing to clean and rebuild sections of the Ossuary."

Winnie's face soured. "I thought there were seamstress positions."

"You had never seemed very interested in piecework or sewing before. I didn't think you'd be interested."

"Well, it's better than *scrubbing*," Winnie said.

"I'm afraid we're reserving those positions for people with a passion for the work. So I would say it's cleaning or nothing."

Winnie's jaw dropped.

"No?" Genevieve asked.

"Is this because of what I said before?" Winnie burst out. "I'm sorry."

"For what?"

"For...being rude. And...pushy."

She certainly appeared remorseful, but remorse did not always equal repentance. Anyway, in Genevieve's mind, Winnie's sins had a quite different root.

"You know, Winnie, I think there *is* something we need help with," Genevieve said after a moment's thought. She could not say whether this was a good idea or a bad one. "Why don't you come with me? Sparrow, I'll see you tomorrow night."

"Of course. Have a good evening," Sparrow said, her eyes alight with curiosity.

☙❧

Genevieve and Winnie found Joseph in Carmine House's cellar, going through some of the supplies he had collected from various sources.

"How goes it, Joseph?" Genevieve asked.

"If worse comes to worst and the endeavor fails, we would at least be able to make money as an apothecary," Joseph said, dusting off his hands and inclining his head to the two of them. "Joseph, meet Winnie. Winnie, Joseph is a doctor."

"Was," he said.

"Is," Genevieve said firmly. "You finished that anatomy book in three days, and you helped Fletcher heal. You are still a doctor." To Winnie, she said, "Joseph was previously Carmine House's caretaker, but now he wishes to pursue other interests. Joseph will receive a monthly stipend for supplies and resources and will go and treat the needy at no cost. He could use an assistant and nurse on his rounds."

"Treat?" Winnie repeated. "*Humans?*" Her nose scrunched up in evident baffled disdain.

"Yes, humans. The people who keep us sanguine and tethered to this mortal coil." Joseph crossed his arms. "But if you don't want the job, then——"

"No! I——" Winnie broke off, looking uncertainly from Joseph to Genevieve.

"Joseph will pay his assistant from the stipend, so you must decide if you will suit," Genevieve said.

"I would like the position," Winnie said, swallowing.

Joseph looked up her up and down, blonde curls and the dress full of flounces. "I'll take you on a trial basis," he said finally, reluctance written all over him. "Meet me here tomorrow evening and wear something less...fluffy."

"The Ossuary will provide a uniform," Genevieve murmured, since Winnie probably did not possess anything less fluffy.

"If you can't do what's needed..." Joseph warned.

Winnie stubbornly lifted her chin. "I can do it."

"Then be here tomorrow. Six sharp."

"My lady," Joseph said wearily when Winnie had gone, "what were you thinking? I've seen hundreds of her type. Hedonistic, selfish, with no thought for tomorrow..."

"I was thinking maybe she isn't too far gone, and the opportunity should not be squandered. She's smart and thinks fast, and she has the needed control over her bloodlust, if I'm right that she can keep her presence of mind to empty pockets while feeding. It's merely a lack of vision. I hope that going on rounds will help her relearn how to see humanity again and realize what she might leave behind. But I meant what I said—you are the doctor and have the final word on your nursing staff. If problems arise or if she does not suit after the trial, that is your affair. She must prove herself to your satisfaction."

Joseph shrugged. "On your head be it," he said, and rolled another bandage.

Chapter Thirty-Two

Kendrick lifted the pile of timbers and carried them down the tunnel. He had taken on responsibility for the maintenance of the Ossuary, which had badly declined in the last few decades. After recruiting groups of cleaners and teams of builders who knew their architecture and masonry, he had sought out cartographers who could map exactly what was above certain portions of the Ossuary and say whether or not expansion was possible.

This night, he was engaged in shoring up sections of the Ossuary, and this section in particular needed fortification because it was not stone or clay bricks, but plain earth. It had been a late addition to the Ossuary and expanded without much of the proper safety measures. Comparatively short, it connected two of the main stone tunnels and was regularly used as a short-cut. Now it frequently grew damp when it rained. Somewhere, moisture was getting in.

Kendrick and his volunteer workers waited while Marshall Cutter, who turned out to have an architecture background, examined the earthworks. "We'll start here." Marshall finally decided, indicating the section, and he went on to explain the process to set the timbers and wood planks in place to support the tunnel walls and roof. "Wood first, temporarily. But stone is best."

"We'll have stone. Let's just make sure we don't have this come down on our heads first," Kendrick said.

The men and women set to work under Marshall's direction, hammering timbers into place and lifting beams. They all grew grimy, working in London's chalky soil.

"Not much clay in this spot," Marshall said, scooping up a handful of dirt in his hand and working through it. "Part of the problem. And it's getting wetter, too."

"Shall we call it off for the night?" one worker asked.

"I think—"

Above them came not so much a rumble, but a groan.

"Move," Kendrick barked as earth started to crumble.

All the workers scrambled for the shored-up entrance of the tunnel. Kendrick seized a vampire bodily and pulled them along when they would have tried to rescue tools scattered along the tunnel. "Go!"

The vampires were fast enough to escape the falling edge of the dirt that came piling in—all except Marshall, who was the last out.

The dirt swallowed him in a deluge before the fall slowed and stopped.

Kendrick commanded, "Get those timbers and shovels!"

Marshall was a vampire and could not die from lack of air, but it would be one of the more frightening things to have happen to you, Kendrick thought, digging with a will as the others came behind, trying to make the dirt stable. Trapped under the weight of earth, buried alive, just as imprisoned as any human would have been.

Finally, he moved enough earth to see some of it twitch, and he switched to his hands, scooping the earth away and reaching for the vampire. Kendrick found a hand and seized it, pulling hard. Marshall came forth, wheezing after being freed from the crushing pressure, and the vampires quickly made sure that no more of the tunnel would come down.

"All right?" Kendrick asked, a hand on Marshall's shoulder as the vampire wiped his face and coughed.

"All right," Marshall said, wiping some of the grime from his face and looking down at himself. "Ugh. Lily is going to kill me."

"How is Miss Pendleton doing?"

"Better," Marshall admitted. "I stick by her when we leave the Ossuary, and I try to do more aboveground than just feed. I took her to a pantomime yesterday, since it's nearly Christmas. She enjoyed that. She still has moments of...distance, but she's improving."

"I don't think she'll be very distant when she learns what happened." Kendrick grinned. "It means she cares enough to worry and take you to task for it." He wiped a hand down his own shirt and shook off some of the grime. "I'm looking forward to seeing that myself."

❧

"I just wanted to thank you again for letting me cook," Addie said cheerfully in the kitchen of Carmine House, a huge apron wrapped around her and a smudge of flour on her cheek.

"You're very welcome. We ought to be thanking *you* for stepping in until we have an official cook for the human staff. What did you make tonight?"

"I baked some bread to see if I could match the smells of the bakery near our house and then made some biscuits for the children." Addie smiled. "Do you think the staff would enjoy brisket of beef for dinner tonight or a mutton roast? Etienne bought me a new cookbook, but I can't decide what to make!" She cast a glance at Etienne, who was writing up a report for Kendrick at the kitchen table. "And *he*'s no help. Any recipe that isn't French is suspect."

"*Mon ange de beauté et d'amour*, all I meant was that I never sampled the English cuisine and so cannot tell you what would be best. I will purchase you a French cookbook next, and then I shall have an opinion," Etienne murmured, staring over his pince-nez at the papers spread out before him.

"Sally should be awake shortly. You can ask her what she'd prefer. Fletcher will be more than happy to do the marketing for you if you leave a list of what you need." Fletcher had settled into the household rhythm, but he still had a burning need to be useful.

"Oh, good idea," Addie agreed happily, filling a tin with the cooled biscuits. "Oh! And Christmas is soon! I could roast a goose or make oyster soup—and cranberry sauce! Plum pudding!" Her face glowed with the possibilities.

Genevieve resisted the urge to worry at her fingernails. She had been leaving her gloves off purposefully more and more, trying to be at ease with her hands, but the knowledge that Christmas was so close made her antsy. "You make whatever the staff would like, Addie, though you certainly don't have to."

"Oh, but I want to," Addie assured her as Sally entered the kitchen, her apron fresh and clean and her hair swept up in a knot.

"Want to what, ducks?" Sally asked. She had taken on something of a maternal countenance towards Addie because she appeared so young. Addie didn't mind.

She beamed. "Cook a Christmas feast! Would you rather a goose, or perhaps a turkey?"

They set to a spirited discussion of possible Christmas menus. Genevieve had just stood to excuse herself quietly when the dirtiest person Genevieve had ever seen emerged from the Ossuary's lower entrance.

It took her a long moment for her to recognize her husband. "Kendrick! What happened?!" she exclaimed, flying to his side.

"Lor' lumme, I ain't never seen any cove so dirty." Sally blinked rapidly as she took in Kendrick's appearance. "Except maybe for one night soil man who accidentally fell in."

"I don't smell *that* bad." He laughed, a bright smile flashing through the grime. "But don't embrace me unless you're resigned to throwing away that gown," he warned Genevieve.

"Hang the gown!" Genevieve said, seizing him by the shoulders. "Are you all right?"

His eyes twinkled at her. "Yes, I'm fine. We had a little problem in the tunnels, but no one is hurt."

"What is *a little problem*?"

"A little cave-in, I should say, but only a small tunnel that probably should not have been there in the first place. We had to dig Marshall Cutter out, but he was remarkably phlegmatic about the whole thing. I'll meet with the architecture team again tomorrow to determine whether or not we're going to try to dig it out again or reinforce it and fill it in." Kendrick looked down at himself thoughtfully. "Could do with a bath, though."

"I should say so!" Genevieve exclaimed.

"You take him on upstairs, missus; I'll have one of the girls start heating water," Sally said, waving them on.

❧

Genevieve sat by the fire in their bedroom and paged through *Wynnflaed's Knight*, waiting for the door to open. The sun was nearly up, and she was becoming drowsy, but Kendrick was *still* washing. The procession of buckets up and down the stairs had been daunting. He had looked like a mud monster when he had come through the door, after all.

She settled deeper into the armchair as she reached the chapter in the book where Wynnflaed and her wounded stranger had a discussion on names and what she should call him, as he would not reveal his true name to her. He rejected Wynnflaed's suggestions of Æthelweard, "noble guardian," and Sæwine, "sea friend," before finally accepting Wærmund, which meant "cautious protection." It was telling that he had rejected the two names that seemed lofty or open in favor of the one that alluded to the secrets and reasons that he had come to be in Wynnflaed's home, wounded and alone.

In a lot of ways, it reminded her of the passage in Ruth where Naomi declared to her friends to call her "Mara," which meant bitter, after the loss of all her menfolk. The text never referred to her that way, though—it was always "Naomi."

She was still pondering names when Kendrick came into the room in a scarlet dressing gown, scrubbed clean of mud and dirt with his hair wet around his shoulders. "What are you thinking about with such a serious look on your face?" he asked, pulling up another chair beside the fire. He ran his fingers through his hair and winced when he hit a snarl.

"Names, and what they mean." Genevieve got up and fetched a comb from her dressing table. "Here—I'll do it," she said, when Kendrick reached for the comb.

"I knew you married me for my hair," he murmured, his eyes full of wicked humor.

Just for that, she rapped him on the head with the comb before tackling the knots, which made him laugh. "Are you going to smack my knuckles with a ruler next?"

"You'll have to see, won't you?" She slowly pulled the comb through his hair, carding through the strands to remove the tangles and dry it.

"What sorts of names?" he asked after a moment.

"The passage in *Wynnflaed* where the warrior won't speak his name, and she names him. He decides based on the name's meaning, and he doesn't accept the more noble suggestions. I was just considering how names can inform character. Certainly, they do in the Ossuary, where people can put on a new name like a different coat."

"Would you like a new name? A surname," Kendrick amended, looking up at her. "I like Genevieve too much to change it. But a new family name."

"For both of us?"

He nodded. "I had the thought during our honeymoon that it might be something you'd like. A signal of the change for the Ossuary, a direction for the people."

"It would have to be the right name," she said.

"That's right. You'll have to think about it."

She put her hands on her hips. "*Me?*"

"You're good at that sort of thing," he said. "Thinking of the future and what direction to head from here. Far better than I."

"I don't know about that," she hedged.

Kendrick roared with laughter. "Genevieve, how quickly we forget how you harangued me on the poor job I was doing at the start of the month. It was a needful harangue, and a helpful one. I would be lost if you began *yes, dear*-ing me now. Promise you'll never stop chiding me when I go wrong."

She smiled, pleased, and dropped a brief kiss on his lips. "Most men would hate that, you know. Master of their household and all that."

"Even masters have counselors. What good are yea-sayers when the lord is wrong, and the wolves are at the door?" Kendrick sobered. "The truth is, Jenny...when thinking of the future—or just thinking of humanity in general, it feels like the world is a warmly lit room full of light and life, and I and all the rest of us vampires are outside, consigned to the dark."

Genevieve put her hand on his shoulder and squeezed. "But you said that the madness had to do with the proximity to humanity. Could that be it? You interact with humans, you allow humanity's stories to change you."

His hand came up to cover hers, rubbing the gold ring on her finger. "Yes, that tether to humanity may decide which vampires turn their backs and walk into the outer darkness. But there's a difference between staving off madness at the window and stepping into the room to join in concert with life.

"I don't know what makes the second possible, but, Jenny—you're in the room. One of the few vampires I've met who've accomplished that task."

Genevieve stared down at him in wordless surprise.

He smiled up at her. "I told you. I enjoy mysteries. Come to bed."

Chapter Thirty-Three

"We should have a ball," she told Kendrick the next night.

"A ball?"

"Or at the very least, a party," she said. "There's nothing people like more than a party. It could be a New Year's ball!"

Kendrick watched her carefully. "Not a Christmas ball?"

Genevieve swallowed, and a brief flash of pain crossed her face.

So, he had not been imagining things. Although she had been forging ahead with her plans and changes, his wife had grown quieter and more pensive as the month had progressed, averting her eyes from carolers on street corners and holiday shop window decorations.

Kendrick added, "Though you're right, a New Year's ball would signal a new start for all of us."

She nodded. "It would be a fine thing to do—we could invite everyone, not just people of a certain set. And it would continue the Ossuary improvements—give custom to the seamstresses and tailors. I'm sure there are people with musical talents—we could find them instruments, pay them to perform."

"That sounds grand."

"We don't need refreshments—of any kind," she said darkly. "I heard about some of Rupert's entertainments. We can make it clear that this will be different. We could even invite people who are farther away, who might not have heard your proclamations, like your friends in Ireland. We could include it in the invitations!"

Kendrick doubted Salem would come, but he acknowledged that it was possible.

After some further discussion about the ball, he asked gently, "What would you like for Christmas?"

Genevieve's eyes flicked away from his. "This is enough. This is more than I ever hoped for."

"This is all things you wanted for the Ossuary. What do *you*, my wife, want for Christmas? It can be anything."

"What I want I can't have," she finally said.

"Tell me, anyway," he prompted.

She pleated her skirts. "I had thought I knew how my life would go. I was content to be a spinster, once I realized what was happening. I was all right with it. I wanted to look after my father. I wanted to be there, even though I feared him aging, feared watching it happen and being unable to do anything about it. And then I was denied both things, after all," she whispered. "I never closed that chapter of my life. I never got to say goodbye of my own volition. And there isn't anything I have from it—none of my mother's teacups or samplers, none of my father's letter openers—not even a single pen wiper. Nothing, save your books."

Kendrick said, "You may have all of them. Whichever is missing, I'll buy you."

"Thank you," she said, looking up at him. "It means so much. But there is a lack there—in my past. I suppose that's why I have such—trouble with Christmas."

Inwardly, he thought, *How long has it been since you have had a Christmas, Genevieve? And how can I, old fool that I am, see that it comes for you?* But all he said was, "Would you like to do some small things, then? For the children?"

She bit her lip. "Oh, yes, we can purchase presents for the children. They might never have had gifts before." She thought about it. "Maybe a little greenery?"

"We can manage a little greenery," he assured her. *We can manage so much more, if you'll only let me, Genevieve.* But he had to remind himself to go slow. Healing came slowly and at its own pace.

But they'd have a little Christmas in the meantime.

❧

The two older women watched Genevieve and Kendrick with birdlike intensity from their chairs beside the fire. Both gray-haired and thin, one knitted while the other embroidered on an embroidery hoop. Otherwise, they looked exactly the same. Twins. They were draped with several shawls, as if to keep off the night's winter chill.

But they did not need them. They were vampires, after all.

"It's about time," Miss Dolores Connors said over her knitting. "We've been waiting this age for a visit from the new master." She cast a speculative glance at Genevieve. "And you, my girl? Who are your people?"

"I'm from Oxford originally—"

"No, no. Your bloodline."

Genevieve's mouth thinned. "Cuthbert."

"Oh, yes, we knew him." Miss Hattie Connors chortled. "He was from Preminger, was he not?"

"Quite so, quite so."

"Too much wildness in the blood in that line. You're not wild, though, are you?" It was a rhetorical question. "But you do the proper thing. Rupert, that upstart, never did the proper thing. We *told* Gisela she was backing the wrong horse, but did she listen?"

The two sisters wagged their heads solemnly. "She should have set her cap for that other lad—Salem, wasn't it?"

Beside Genevieve, Kendrick stirred. To Genevieve's practiced eye, he looked like he was trying not to laugh. "How is Gisela related to you, ma'am?"

The old woman cackled. "In more ways than one!" She rang the bell on the side table and the human woman who had admitted Genevieve and Kendrick to the small terrace house reappeared. She looked about forty, with hair beginning to show a few strands of silver, but she kept herself well.

The other Miss Connors said, "Ana, do ask Gisela to join us if she is in the house."

The woman replied, "Yes, Aunt Hattie," and withdrew.

"*Are* you her aunt?" Kendrick asked.

"Many times great-aunt, but a lady never tells her age." Hattie Connors wagged her finger at him slyly. "We are the family's godmothers and benefactors! We invested in the 'Change, you see! Right at the start!"

"Ana and Gisela are sisters, you know," Miss Dolores said, her needles pausing their comforting click-clack. "We erred with Gisela." She and her twin sister shared a commiserating look. "She was so beautiful as a little girl. She begged us to turn her so she could be young and beautiful forever. We forgot that with age comes maturity."

Genevieve tried to turn the subject. "You didn't approve of the previous master?"

Miss Hattie snorted. "He was younger than us! But liked to pretend he was older. Gathered a bunch of claptrap around him as treasures of a bygone era and surrounded himself with toadies. He liked being fawned over, not getting his hands dirty. And the master before him was ineffectual—it was all that woman, what was her name?"

"Renata," Kendrick supplied.

"Yes, yes. Yet he kept power so long because he recognized

that she was intelligent and smart, and he used his might to enforce what she dictated. Unfortunate that so much of what she decreed was regrettable and in support of her own desires. They kept power for quite some time—longer than we've been extant. All and all, it's been quite a while since the Ossuary has seen true change."

Miss Dolores sniffed. "Gisela thought she could steer that ship, and perhaps she did, but what good is a rudder when your ship has no oars or sails?"

She broke off as the door opened. Gisela stepped into the room, looking cool and svelte in a day dress of icy blue. When she saw Genevieve and Kendrick, she froze. Kendrick stood as she entered, and she curtseyed belatedly.

"Gisela, have you met the new master?" Miss Dolores inquired, making the introductions.

"Not in his new capacity," Gisela said in an arid voice. "How do you do?"

Genevieve tried to get a hold of her temper. She did not want to be civil to the woman who had tried to *kill* Kendrick—or had at least plotted to do so. *But that is the point of this night's visit*, she thought. *We have won over all our friends. It is now time to treat with our enemies.*

And of course she was thankful that Kendrick was the sort of person who cared to build bridges. She was thankful he was willing to pursue other avenues to find Laurent and his ilk rather than just waiting for them to poke their heads out of their hidey-holes and hurt someone else. She was grateful that he agreed with her that they needed to make a strong stand against despicable behavior in order for the Ossuary to be healthy.

She just didn't like that his strategy included the woman who had orchestrated several knives aimed at his back.

Kendrick nodded. "We do very well, all things considered. Ladies, I wonder if you would mind if my wife and I have a private conversation with Miss Gisela. It will not take long."

The two birdlike gazes sharpened into the eyes of a couple of falcons, but they said all that was correct and vacated the parlor room with the ease of women decades younger. They would still be able to hear perfectly well if they chose to eavesdrop, but Genevieve had mentioned to Kendrick that this approach might be best, to give Gisela the veneer of privacy.

"Well," Gisela said, taking one of the seats the women had vacated. "I'm honored, I'm sure. What brings you to our little corner of London? You would not have come all this way to speak to me." The neighborhood was well off, but nothing like the vast townhouses and squares of Mayfair.

"Actually," Genevieve said, setting her gloved hands in her lap, "we are visiting influential vampires within the confines of London to share our progress with the Ossuary and explain further our plans for the future. For instance, we have completed nearly seventy-five percent of the Ossuary's census and will soon begin on the aboveground residents of London. We have also begun several industries within the Ossuary."

"How nice."

"It is," Genevieve said, keeping a hold of her temper. "Very nice when we can give people something to live for."

"Well, it is kind of you to think of me and pay a call, but I'm afraid I do not qualify as 'influential.'" She smiled tightly. "Not anymore."

Kendrick said, "We think you do."

How did he look so at ease? All Genevieve's concentration was put towards not glaring at Gisela. She had insisted to Kendrick when he had broached the idea, "But she tried to kill you! Multiple times!"

"I believe you, but it does need to be said that the instance where you heard her plotting, she was advocating for a different approach," Kendrick had pointed out.

"A different approach to *killing* you," Genevieve had groused.

"Fair," Kendrick had admitted. "But it demonstrates that

Gisela has intelligence enough to see which way the wind is blowing. If we can get her on our side, or at least ensure that she has no more involvement with plots, we could sway a distinct amount of the undecided among the Ossuary in our favor."

Genevieve had agreed to the meeting, still inwardly doubtful.

Now Gisela raised one disbelieving eyebrow. "Then why did you choose to share these notable accomplishments in private, instead of in front of my aunts? If it was in an effort to spare salting my wounds, it was very diplomatic of you, I'm sure, but everyone knows what happened in Yorkshire."

Genevieve did her best not to clench her teeth. "No, you're absolutely right, Miss Connors."

Gisela smiled thinly.

Kendrick pinned the other woman with a hard stare. "The truth is, Miss Connors, I know you were one of the masterminds behind some of the attempts on my life."

Gisela stilled. Her gaze flickered from Kendrick to the scabbard behind his chair. "You've no proof of that."

"Do I need proof, when I heard it from your own lips?" Genevieve said, tilting her head to the side.

Gisela's expression turned as cold as marble. She could not call the lady of the Ossuary a liar—not to her face. "And so, the reason for this visit becomes clear. Must I submit myself to the Ossuary's justice?"

Kendrick watched her closely. "No, but you may have to humble yourself and receive the Ossuary's mercy."

She glanced between them, something flickering behind her eyes. "I don't understand."

Kendrick drummed his fingers on the arm of the chair. "You're a smart and clever woman. You survived as a vampire and reached one of the highest positions of power available to you. And you weren't hotheaded enough to come at me with a knife yourself. Now, whether you should answer for the men and women you sent to their deaths is a different question."

"Allegedly," Gisela said, voice flat. "Unless you have evidence besides your unsupported word."

Kendrick acknowledged that with a nod. "But we have noted a distinct downturn in the number of assassination attempts."

She folded her hands deliberately in her lap. "Only fools try the same thing over and over. Perhaps your would-be conspirators have decided not to be fools."

"I do believe you are no one's fool, Miss Connors. But Laurent is," Genevieve pointed out.

Gisela's gaze snapped to her. "Is this what this meeting is about? Laurent?"

Kendrick said, "He is the other side of this coin. Laurent has not only plotted against me, but also has abused his privilege over those he turns and killed a human by proxy. His crimes go too far, and I believe that unless he is found, he will not show the good sense to stop, as you have."

"I don't know where he is."

"But you know those who might," Genevieve said.

The corners of her mouth turned down. "And in return for... what? Whispering in ears, I get to live?"

"You get to live either way," Genevieve said flatly. "Much to my disappointment."

Kendrick laid a hand over Genevieve's. "What my wife means is, Miss Connors—we present you with two alternate futures. The direction we would like to take the Ossuary: the improvements and care for all its citizens, and the capacity of mercy that was so lacking in years past. And the direction Laurent would like to drag the Ossuary, which is exactly nowhere."

"Or in whatever direction best serves his changing desires," Genevieve said.

Kendrick told Gisela, "I believe what we have said. You are a very intelligent and capable woman, one who probably chafed surrounded by men with grasping, self-serving ambitions. And probably many in the Ossuary realized that. Whatever direction you decide to support—or not support, as it happens—we simply ask that you let that decision be known." He stood and bowed.

"All the vampire members of your household are also invited to our New Year's ball," Genevieve said, dipping her hand into her reticule and handing Gisela the invitation. "There will not be refreshments, but an evening of conversation and dancing and entertainment. I hope you will all be able to come. Everyone in the Ossuary is welcome."

✦

"Do you think anything will come of it?" Genevieve asked as she and Kendrick took their leave of the Connors household and stepped out onto the dark street, a few cabs and a carriage passing in front of the house.

"All we can do is plant seeds and see," Kendrick said. "Thank you for coming with me."

"I wasn't going to let you step into the lion's den alone," she said tartly, tucking her hand into the crook of his arm. In an altogether different tone, she added, "But you were right. Holding a grudge against Gisela will not be helpful for the Ossuary."

"I do have productive ideas every so often." He smirked.

"You didn't even use your talent on her."

"No. I think she is the sort who is hypersensitive to that sort of thing, like you. I had to rely on words alone."

"Poor you." Genevieve smiled. "I don't *really* hate Gisela. I just take exception to people who try to kill you."

He set his hand over hers and squeezed. "Since that brought your path to cross with mine in the first place, I'll never cease being grateful for it, Jenny."

Chapter Thirty-Four

Kendrick returned home one evening covered in whitewash from Ossuary improvements to find Genevieve pacing stiff-armed outside the ballroom, a pinched look on her face as loud voices echoed behind the door. "What's toward?" he asked. Ball preparations had consumed Genevieve the last two nights.

"Nothing dire," she said with a sigh. "Merely a conflict between some of the musicians. The conductor is entirely fixed on the 'correct' way an orchestra should perform. But we have two performers who are insistent the only instruments they know how to play—though I think it should be *willing* to play—are the hurdy-gurdy and psaltery." As voices rose once again behind the door, she winced. "Perhaps letting them work it out themselves was not the best idea, but I don't think I can go back in now. We hired Monsieur Dupont as maestro, and to go back in now and sort it out would diminish his authority."

"Wise of you. What else is causing that frown?"

"Oh," she sighed. "It's Fletcher. His sleep is entirely disordered from being in a household that is always active, and I feel a bit guilty about it. He doesn't seem to mind being awake at two in the morning, though."

"As long as he *is* sleeping, I don't see it harming him. Part of it is the newness. The other part is that he likely was used to it even before—he walked you back from Sally's consistently late at night, and we don't know what he did after that. He will settle into a rhythm."

"I think he is, but I don't know," Genevieve admitted.

"I was planning to join Dominic at the fencing club after I wash. I'll bring him along." When Genevieve bit her lip, Kendrick said, "He will enjoy it, and a boy ought to have weapons training. I learned the spear at his age, or even younger."

"Not in this era," Genevieve said with a bit of fond exasperation.

"Any era. And it will tire him out." Kendrick leaned to kiss Genevieve carefully on the mouth without touching her elsewhere. "I will content myself with this so I do not mar your gown with whitewash. We'll be back before dawn."

❦

A scrubbed Kendrick and eager Fletcher, who showed no signs of flagging even though it was past midnight, met Dominic at the fencing academy.

Kendrick's friend had continued to lodge Evangeline and her children because of the convenience of a wet nurse. He was also a comfort to Evangeline, who continued to worry she might harm the children on accident. Dominic thought it highly unlikely, but he was more than happy for them to remain at Fernside. He had determined to assist Evangeline in handling her transition from human to vampire, along with Elspeth. However, it created a lot of anger in him for Laurent, Elspeth had confided to Kendrick one night.

Kendrick had made the appointment thinking that beating on

each other with swords a sufficient outlet for feeling helpless. All in all, though, he was feeling quite cheerful about Dominic. What better way to pull someone back to the land of the living than to care for another?

Kendrick spent the first half hour instructing Fletcher on how to hold the blunted training sword and how to do a few simple thrusts and parries, recruiting Dominic for demonstrations.

"This is a weapon and not a toy, for all that it is a training weapon," Kendrick told Fletcher seriously. "You respect it similarly."

"Right you are, guv," Fletcher said, taking hold of the training foil with reverence. "Bloomin' great pig sticker, ain't it?"

"However, if you're ever attacked by a vampire, you need silver."

"I know that, guv. Reavers are scared of silver."

"We aren't scared," Kendrick corrected him. "It burns us, like thrusting your hand into fire would sear you. To take down a vampire, you need silver, and you aim for the heart." He demonstrated the strike. "In a real fight, you may not get a second chance."

"Need a pretty wicked knife for that," Fletcher observed.

"You would." Kendrick made himself a note to commission silver-plated daggers for the human members of their household. He had sworn oaths of protection. To his mind, that included giving his dependents the tools to protect themselves.

"You must do something about his elocution," Dominic said as they watched the boy practice his lunges and return to the ready position. The boy was small but quick; he could be a swordsman if he wanted to be. And who knew? With regular meals and safety, he might have some growth in him yet.

"First Genevieve has to get him to agree to learn to read," Kendrick said dryly. "Are you ready?"

"Ready to trounce you? Of course," Dominic said, laying aside his coat.

"One of these days, I really must find another broadsword."

"Oh, no. You're just disappointed the attacks against you have dwindled down. You're not about to cleave *me* open if you get a little too enthusiastic."

"What if I found wooden practice broadswords?" Kendrick suggested with a longsuffering sigh.

"*Maybe*. A very conditional maybe. *En garde.*"

The men spent a very companionable time slashing at each other with swords. Partway through their duel, Fletcher wandered over to watch. However, when he started to yawn, even with the rapid, thrilling moves they were performing, Kendrick called a halt.

"Bed for you," he informed Fletcher.

"Naw," Fletcher said, but he spoiled it by yawning so hugely, Kendrick could see his tonsils.

Kendrick laughed and scooped the boy up as Dominic set the room to rights and extinguished the lights.

"Here, put me down, guv! I ain't no parcel to be toted about!" Fletcher said in dismay.

"Neither is Genevieve. I carry her all the time," Kendrick said. The boy's weight was negligible for Kendrick's strength. "Climb on my back if you'd rather."

The boy agreed to this, resting his chin on the shoulder that did not sport the hilt of Kendrick's sword, his arms around Kendrick's neck. They only walked a block before he felt Fletcher's body relax.

"The stubbornness of youth," Dominic murmured. "I have enjoyed having August and June in my house. Children say the most astounding things."

"They do. Their power of absorption rivals the sponge. I'm glad that the housing situation has turned out so well," Kendrick added. "I had hoped it would benefit everyone for the family to remain at Fernside."

"It's the most curious thing, Kendrick," Dominic said, stopping at the street where they would part ways. "It feels as though something in me is waking up again." He rubbed a hand absently over his chest before bidding Kendrick a good evening.

Kendrick smiled a little as he turned towards Carmine House, Fletcher snoring quietly on his back and exhaling little puffs of steam into the air.

⚜

The next night, Genevieve arrived at the Ossuary's new dressmaker's station just in time to see Sparrow unearth the bolts of fabric purchased to outfit London's vampires in ball finery. Miss Singh and Miss Doyle, who had been hired on as dressmakers to assist in crafting everyone's ball attire, exclaimed over the bounty.

"Oh, I've longed to see the new dress patterns." Miss Doyle sighed, smoothing her hands over the new bolts of fabric. "And the colors! So vibrant." Her own gown's fabric was faded to an indeterminate shade of gray the same shade of her hair. Her pale skin was nearly translucent in the lamplight, and she sported fine lines at the corners of her eyes.

Miss Singh, a taller, visibly younger woman with a dark completion and very large eyes, though colorless, as was typical of vampires, reviewed the pattern books avidly. "How glad I am that hoops and crinoline have decreased. But what shall we do about the tail that the gowns now require?"

"Certainly, some people will not wish a dramatic bustle," Miss Doyle said, glancing anxiously at Sparrow and Genevieve. "Perhaps simply a pad of some sort, to give the correct shape?"

"I'm sure that would serve very well," Genevieve said. "If there is a high demand for bustles that we can't supply before the ball, I'm sure we could order whatever we lack."

Both dressmakers froze.

"From...a human establishment?" Miss Doyle ventured tentatively.

Miss Singh huffed. "No, from a djinn. Of course human, Margaret." However, her expression remained dubious.

Genevieve exchanged a look with Sparrow. "Would that be a problem?"

"Oh, no!" Miss Doyle exclaimed hurriedly, a waxen smile stretching across her face. "No, no. Of course not. We would never dream of questioning..." She swallowed.

"I should have phrased that better," Genevieve amended. "I should have said, 'I would like to know your thoughts on the subject.'"

Sparrow sent her a subtle nod.

Miss Doyle worried at her lower lip.

Miss Singh sighed and said, "We have always been instructed by our maker that vampires and humans shouldn't mix."

"I see," Genevieve said.

Certain vampires—such as Godfrey, Dominic's maker—thought vampires should maintain a separate existence from human society. They never took into account how feasible that actually was with vampires' need to feed. Or how such beliefs conflicted with their actual lifestyles, such as in Godfrey's case, with a human household that supported them.

However, that was only one outlook. There were those like Dominic, who understood humans were necessary to their survival and functioning in a household, and subsequently took care of those who took care of them. There were those like Laurent and Cuthbert, who loved causing chaos and pain and viewed humans only as playthings and food. Then there were the puppeteers who wished to move other vampires and humans according to their whims like pieces on a chess board. Genevieve had acquired a much closer acquaintance with the first and last groups since she and Kendrick had begun to make what she privately thought as "lord and lady of the manor" trips to all the known large vampiric households in London.

Though she privately wondered, *Where do you think all the fabric came from?* she did not say that. The women could very well have been subject to their makers' opinions and foibles, just as she and Elspeth had been. Disobeying could have resulted in their punishment—and still could, she noted cautiously. Tart rejoinders would not serve here. Instead, she gathered her thoughts and said, "There are many opinions on the subject, but I do believe that interacting with humans is healthful and, in many cases, necessary to maintain control over one's urges. When we stop seeing humans as people, we lose our way and can give in to the madness."

"Was it a command from your maker to avoid mixing with humans?" Sparrow asked gently.

"*No*, no, not a command," Miss Doyle said hurriedly. "Not...as such."

"Rest assured that if we need to purchase foundation garments from humans, the expense will be part of the Ossuary's budget, and Sparrow will facilitate the purchase," Genevieve said. "However, if you do ever find yourself encountering...trouble because of a lingering command from your maker, we are always available to mediate those issues."

"Thank you," Miss Singh said quietly, her eyes flicking up and away.

Genevieve nodded and turned the conversation towards the seamstresses' workspace and upcoming fittings, but she exchanged a subtle glance with Sparrow.

Sparrow nodded, making a note on her writing tablet to have one of their newly selected mentors check on the women and their relationship with their maker.

After checking on the other Ossuary projects in progress, Genevieve hurried home along the corridors that led to Carmine House's cellar. As she approached, the cellar door swung open with some force, banging into the wall.

Genevieve froze.

Someone carrying a stack of hatboxes higher than their head walked through the doorway. As the figure turned and awkwardly reached for the door to shut it, Genevieve realized it was Elspeth.

Her held breath escaped in a choked gurgle.

Elspeth looked up. "Oh! Genevieve. I didn't see you."

"How could you, with all those boxes?" Genevieve said faintly.

"These hats were supposed to go to the millinery station, but they got left behind. I'm just delivering them to the hatters."

"Do you need help?"

"No, no," Elspeth assured her. "After I drop them off, I'll be turning in for the dawn. Have a good rest!" She smiled and hurried along the passage.

Genevieve stood a moment and then slumped against the wall, passing a hand over her face as she tried to get her churning emotions under control.

The door slamming against the wall—it had thrown her body into a panic. So she had frozen reflexively. She understood that.

But she had also reached for her talent on instinct, attempting to go unseen.

And she hadn't managed it.

Genevieve pressed a hand to her chest. How was that possible? She had never heard of any vampire *losing* a talent.

You might've been too alarmed. Might not have had time, she tried to tell herself, even though she had been able to go unseen between one breath and the next for years before now. That was how she had survived. How she had gleaned the knowledge for all their continued survival.

She closed her eyes and tried to find the vestiges of her talent to wrap around herself and disappear in the shadows.

But she stayed right where she was, stubbornly visible.

❧

"Did you have a good evening, dear heart?" Kendrick asked, entering their bedroom and crossing to where she sat at the vanity fiddling with her hairbrush. It was almost dawn.

"Well enough," Genevieve said, looking up at him.

He tilted his head to the side and took the brush from her hand. "Yes?" He slowly pulled the brush through her hair, even though it rarely tangled because of its length.

"You don't have to do that," she murmured.

"I'll brush your hair and then you can brush mine," he said with a smile. "What made the night simply well enough?"

"I was able to check on progress for the dressmakers and tailors," Genevieve said slowly. "But something happened on my way home that worried me."

Kendrick came alert behind her. "What was that?"

"The cellar door banged open and it...startled me. It was fine. Elspeth was leaving and had pushed the door so it would swing wide for what she was carrying. But...I reached for my talent, and I couldn't go unseen. Have you ever heard of that happening before? Someone...losing their talent?"

Kendrick pondered the question, resuming the brushstrokes through her hair. "I can't say that I have. You could speak to Joseph if you're concerned," he offered.

"Joseph?"

"He's a doctor." Kendrick shrugged wryly. "I don't know who else would be knowledgeable, considering vampires typically have no need of leechcraft. It's not something I have ever heard of." He set the brush down. "Have you considered that...perhaps you don't need it anymore?"

Genevieve jerked with surprise. "Don't *need* it?"

"Don't need to hide anymore," he clarified. "You probably developed your talent as a protective measure. A way to escape notice. But I don't believe Genevieve Dryden's natural state was meekness." He tucked a strand of hair behind her ear, his eyes warm and understanding.

"No, it wasn't," she murmured. Meekness had been adopted as a defense mechanism, as all of her objections and protests had gained her pain and humiliation, her spirit smashed, those she cared for like Elspeth used as weapons against her. She stared at her bare hands on the vanity, at the missing nails. A momentary pain, but a bone-deep despair once she'd realized that they would not grow back now that she was a vampire. That anything Cuthbert and Laurent did to her and her friends, their bodies would repair enough for them to be functional, but they would never be fully restored.

Never fully healed.

"I don't want you to have to hide," Kendrick said, taking her hand and kissing it. "You should never feel like you have to disappear, or I'm not doing my job as your husband."

But it was never for me, Genevieve thought as Kendrick unbuttoned his cuffs and began disrobing to sleep. *Not really. I hid in the shadows to protect others. To protect* you.

How will I protect those I care for now?

She stood and turned down the coverlet on the bed. *We have a new way to protect people now*, she reminded herself. *We are trying to instruct the Ossuary in a new way. We will need new tools. Maybe he is right, that it is something I won't need anymore.*

But something still felt disquieted in her soul.

Genevieve pondered Kendrick as he emerged from behind the screen and reached for the book they had been reading before their rest the past few mornings. He had seen it in a shop window and bought it because he'd thought she'd like it. He was continually doing that. Giving her gifts.

She bit her lip. *What would he like for Christmas?*

She could not ignore that the holiday was only a week away. Regardless of how she viewed the day, surely a wife should give her husband something for the occasion. He did so much for her. Fulfilling her requests and sometimes anticipating her needs, or acting on a whim to present her with a token just because he'd thought it would bring her joy.

It all seemed—unbalanced, somehow, that she should have so much benefit from their marriage and him so little.

They still did not live together as true man and wife, though they did share a bed. Sometimes she didn't even wake from bad dreams anymore.

What does he want? Genevieve wondered as Kendrick passed in front of the window to make sure the drapes were secured.

His words came back to her, about being on the outside of life, looking in.

He wants to come in from the cold, she thought, much struck.

How could she bring him in?

Chapter Thirty-Five

"Since we're lifting the travel ban Rupert put in place," Kendrick told Genevieve a few days before Christmas as she sat at her vanity, "I've decided to deliver some of the ball invitations in person to residences in the London country-side, to allay any fears about coming."

"Should we go together? A united front?" Genevieve asked, pausing in her hair brushing.

"I thought of that, but you and Sparrow are in the midst of your preparations helping everyone here ready themselves—that's more important. It should only take a few evenings. Will you be all right without me?"

"Of course," Genevieve said. "We haven't heard a peep from Laurent or his ilk in days. When will you leave?"

"At dusk. Do you need anything? Any requests from my travels?"

She turned, shooting him a slightly exasperated glance. "You've already given me gifts."

Kendrick smiled. "A husband can't buy things for his wife?" Though what he had given her so far had been mere tokens: a pair of gloves, a hat, a soft scarf, a new book he'd thought she might enjoy. Just signs he'd been thinking about her. That he cared about her.

She rose and pulled back the covers on their bed. "I don't need anything, truly. Will you wake me when you go?"

"I will." Kendrick stripped off his clothes down to his smalls and got into bed beside her. She hadn't had a nightmare for the last three nights. Kendrick dropped a kiss on Genevieve's lips. "Good night, Wife."

"Good night," she whispered, laying her head on his arm.

When the sun had journeyed across the sky and begun to set, he slipped out of her embrace and rose. Dressing, he secured the invitations in the pocket of his coat and settled his sword on his back.

"Travel safe," Genevieve murmured, still mostly asleep. "And return soon."

Her dark hair fanned across her cheek and the pillow, the sight enchanting to him. *Will you miss me, Genevieve?* "Always." He bent and kissed her forehead before he slipped out of the room.

He was telling the truth. The first night, he did go around to the vampire households around London and deliver the invitations personally, visiting with the inhabitants and assuring them of his promises to the vampire citizenry of London, if they had not yet heard of his oaths.

But the second night, he boarded at Paddington Station for the train to Oxford. In the baggage car, he pushed aside some trunks and a gentleman's portmanteau and crossed his arms. *Christmas*, Kendrick thought. Christmas, and Genevieve. She did not want a Christmas ball, but a New Year's ball she would have. He had even dashed an invitation off for Salem, though Kendrick doubted that he would come.

But what about Christmas?

Twenty years ago, Jenny was turned just before Christmas, and last year her father had died before Christmas. She had admitted that that chapter of her life did not feel closed. Her journey to Oxford in the wake of her broken blood bond had been panicked and she had returned in the grip of grief. There might have been possibilities she'd overlooked, colleagues of her father's whom Kendrick could coax to speak, neighbors he could question. He hadn't wanted to mention the possibility to her in case he raised her hopes.

His were already high enough.

He disembarked the train at Botley Road and stepped out into the old cathedral city that was home to pillars of knowledge and learning. He had asked Elspeth for the direction of Genevieve's former home, as that seemed like the most logical place to begin, and she had told him the street. He wended his way through the old city that always felt strangely comfortable to him, surrounded as he was by every style of building and architecture he could remember.

Making his way to the little side street, he stared up at the cozy and comfortable house with a light glowing in the window and the sound of sleepy children's voices behind the doors. Kendrick waited until the small voices dropped off into slumber before he knocked on the door.

The man who answered the door was plain and unassuming, with thinning, brown hair and spectacles on his nose. "May I help you?"

"I hope so," Kendrick said with a smile. "Is this the home of Ezra Dryden?"

"Yes, it was, but I'm sorry—Ezra passed away a year ago." The man frowned at the sword hilt over Kendrick's shoulder. "What's this about, Mister...?"

"I'm looking for anyone who may have known him." Kendrick used a little of his persuasion. "My name is Kendrick. May I come in?"

The frown smoothed away from the man's forehead. "Oh! Yes, come in." He held the door open and ushered Kendrick across the threshold. "Pleased to meet you, Mr. Kendrick. I am Arthur Cooper. Ezra—" He stopped and cleared his throat. "Ezra is greatly missed."

"You knew him, then," Kendrick said.

"Yes, we—"

"Dear, who is it?" A woman about forty stepped out of a sitting room and eyed Kendrick in puzzlement. Some threads of silver wended through her red hair, but it still glowed like flame in the lamplight.

"This is Mr. Kendrick; he's come asking about Ezra."

"I'm looking for anyone who may have known Mr. Dryden and his daughter," Kendrick said.

"Genevieve?" the woman exclaimed. "What about Genevieve?"

Kendrick paused, taking in her hair and the expression on her face. The way her heart had skipped a beat. "Forgive me, ma'am... but is your Christian name Hetty?"

She recoiled, her lips parting.

"Genevieve said that you were her friend," Kendrick said.

The woman paled and swayed. Her husband was by her side at an instant to steady her. That was a yes, then.

"Perhaps we had best sit down," Kendrick said soothingly.

In the sitting room, the Coopers sat beside each other on the settee, their hands clasped. Kendrick sat in a much-loved armchair across from them and propped his sword on its side. They barely gave it a distracted glance.

"Can you tell me about Genevieve and her father? How did you know her?" Kendrick asked, letting his gaze and his voice do their work.

"I never met her," Mr. Cooper said. "Hetty was her friend, though." He squeezed his wife's hand.

"Yes," Mrs. Cooper whispered, her eyes far away. "She was a

friend to me, though she was several years older. She and her father were one of the few families who still associated with us after we slid into dire straits. My father had died far sooner than anyone expected, you see," she explained, "and left behind my mother and sisters and my little brother, who had years yet to reach his majority. There was trouble with the will—it was outdated, and the money tied up by awful legalisms until my brother came of age. So, we were forced to genteel poverty, scrimping and stretching everything and trying to pretend like nothing was wrong. My mother would fly into the boughs whenever I brought up seeking what employment was available to an unwed young lady. In her mind, all we had to do was wait the years out, and then all would be well again. I would not have minded being a shop girl or something of the like. But shame was stronger than hunger—for a time. But eventually, it got so bad, we were only drinking weak tea and stretching the gruel and bread throughout the day."

She lifted her face to Kendrick. "I decided to sell my hair. I didn't know what else to do. But then the wigmaker looked down his nose at me, and I got so little for it, and the next Sunday, the vicar preached on"—her voice trembled, even years after the event—"on a woman's hair being her glory. And it seemed as though he were looking right at me. I ran out of the service crying, but Genevieve came after me and got the whole story out of me. She marched me back to the wigmakers and pounded on the doors—on a Sunday!—until the proprietor opened them, and then she took her bonnet off and demanded to know what he would give her for her hair. And it was long, far past her waist. She browbeat the man until she had talked him up from that paltry sum, and then she demanded to know why I had received so little in payment for mine. She bullied him into paying me the difference, and then she said, 'Don't put your moneybox away just yet, sir. Hand me your shears.'"

She bit her lip, shaking her head in amazement. "She sold her hair for me. It was the bravest, most selfless thing I had ever seen. I really think she saved my life a little," she told Kendrick earnestly. "It certainly felt that way at the time."

She swallowed. "It was only a few days later she disappeared. I was so shocked. She never would have left her father," she assured him. "Not without a word like that. And because— because I wanted to be like her, and be brave and think of others, I looked in on him those first few days. Making sure he was eating, giving him a distraction from the worry. He didn't have any other family. And then Mr. Dryden offered me a job. I could keep house for him and live in, to take some burden off my family and earn an income—more generous than it warranted. And though they were horrified about me taking employment, I did it because I realized I was needed, and I was smart enough to learn what I didn't know, and I could be brave in the face of adversity."

"And it was for the best," she said, with a warm glance at her husband. "When the vicar preached a few too many sermons about souls who wandered from God's path, and a woman's place, Ezra took himself to the Methodist church. And that's where Arthur struck up an acquaintance with Ezra, who brought him to dinner. And that's how we met." Her husband squeezed her hand.

Kendrick asked, "And you remained with Mr. Dryden?"

Mrs. Cooper nodded. "At first, he wanted me there in case she came home and—needed someone. A woman's help. Something like that." She bit her lip. "And then it was the company. We didn't like the idea of leaving him on his own after we married, and then he said hang convention, we were part of his family, so we started married life here. The children thought of him as their grandfather, and they miss him still. But I think—it really was a double-edged sword. Every time he heard my foot on the stair, there was a split second where he hoped it was her." She lifted her handkerchief and dabbed at her eyes again.

"And he left you this house?"

Mr. Cooper nodded. "In his will, and the rest of his belongings and money given to women's charities."

"Even personal effects? You see..." Kendrick deepened his talent's influence. "I know Genevieve."

Mrs. Cooper gasped. "She's *alive*? She's all right?"

"Yes," he assured her, letting a wave of calm flood the words. "She is all right now. She is my wife. But I know it would mean a lot to her if she had something of her father's. Is there some trinket, or a book of his that you might part with?"

The husband blinked. "There's the trunk."

Kendrick raised an inquiring eyebrow.

"He left a trunk," Mrs. Cooper said, leaning forward eagerly. "He always hoped she would come home, but he knew we needed the room when the children started coming. So, we packed up all her personal things, and later everything he wanted her to have, and put it in a trunk. It's in the attic. Dearest, will you—"

"No need," Kendrick said, lifting a hand. "I will bring it down if you point me to it."

Kendrick followed the husband up the narrow stairs to the attic to unearth the dusty camelback trunk with "ESD" stamped on the cover. He wiped some of the grime off the brass plate and touched the keyhole.

"Hetty has the key," Mr. Cooper assured him.

Kendrick carried the trunk down the stairs to where Mrs. Cooper waited. She held out the small, brass key. "Will you tell her—" She faltered. "We named our son for him—Ezra. And our oldest girl is Jenny. I never forgot what she did for me."

Kendrick pocketed the key. "She hasn't forgotten, either. I will tell her that you acted in her stead where she could not, and that you loved her father well." He let his talent reach out as he caught the eyes of the husband and wife. "I am most grateful to you both. You will not remember much of tonight. But know that she is well and taken care of, and you have discharged this duty. Thank you."

A puzzled expression crossed both their faces as his persuasion did its work, but they nodded and smiled, Mrs. Cooper with tears in her eyes.

Kendrick left the small, cozy house with the mysterious trunk over his shoulder. *Maybe this will be cause for Christmas, after all, Genevieve.*

Chapter Thirty-Six

Genevieve had spent the last few days sleeping badly and feeling guilty. The first day without Kendrick beside her, she had woken from a nightmare. She had reached for him instinctively and when she had not found his comforting presence, she had plunged into melancholy. To top it all off, every shop was full of evergreen garlands and every person on the street seemed to exude good cheer, and Fletcher had returned at dusk from visiting the children at Dominic's house to report that "a ruddy great tree" had been installed in the family parlor. The children had excitedly decorated it and hung stockings upon the fireplace. Carmine House had not a garland or festive bow to be seen.

"We going to get some of them gewgaws?" Fletcher wanted to know. "Peter and Hannah could decorate." He had eyed Genevieve pointedly, which meant he would like to decorate too.

How miserly of her, to deny the children the delight of a fully bedecked Christmas, all because she could not reckon with her feelings towards the season. *Scrooge-like*, she thought morosely. *How ghastly*.

She finally squared her shoulders against her—what was it,

pride or fear?—and asked Robbie to get them a tree and some greenery, since Kendrick was away.

The tree arrived the next night, so large, it nearly didn't fit through the door. The three burly human deliverymen had to shove it through the doorway.

"Criffins, watch where you're going!" Robbie commanded as it nearly careened into a wall. "Here, this way."

"You gave in, did you?" Elspeth murmured over Genevieve's shoulder.

"I did." Genevieve sighed. "Fletcher recruited help."

"Hannah has very effective soulful eyes."

"That she does. Let us just hope that Wulfric does not get confused with other trees he prefers to water in the garden."

"A kissing bough, even," Elspeth said in an intrigued voice.

"A *kissing* bough?" Genevieve repeated, her eyebrows flying up. "I said nothing about a kissing bough!"

"Robbie must've taking the initiative, then." Elspeth smiled. "I'll just tell him where to put it, shall I?"

They had gathered the children and were busily engaged in cutting out paper ornaments and stringing popcorn, a welcome respite from ball preparation, when a voice said, "I'm away for two days and you decide to redecorate?"

The smile that broke across Genevieve's face at the sound of Kendrick's voice could not be stifled. Kendrick stood in the doorway, freshly scrubbed of travel dust, watching the goings-on with amused interest.

Genevieve got from the floor to the doorway in a twinkling and wrapped her arms around him.

"Did you miss me?" he murmured in her ear.

"I think I did," she said in a thick voice. "Oh—a letter came for you yesterday. Let me find it."

"I have something for you as well," he said.

"I told you not to get me anything."

"I didn't—precisely. And you may decide whether you would like it now or wait until Christmas for it."

"Now, if you're so determined on it," her traitorous heart wanted to say, still afraid of what fraught feelings the day might invoke. But she heard herself say, "I'll wait until Christmas."

Kendrick followed her into the hall, where she handed him the missive that had arrived the day before. His eyes flew up at the return address. He broke it open and scanned its contents before laughing. "You will have to add another two to the guest list, sweetheart," he said, handing it to her. She read it curiously.

Dear Kendrick,

What do you mean, <u>MARRIED</u>? Good God, man, it's not even been two months since we last saw you. Who on earth could you have met? What, did Etienne tell you, "Thou art sad; get thee a wife, get thee a wife"?

<u>Ophelia and I</u> aren't even married yet, though we will be by the time you read this. We have been in Ireland, Ophelia learning much from the Ossory werewolves. Ophelia has come to terms with raw meat on the full moon and getting furrier than she would like, though she still has moments that take her aback. However, she wishes to spend Christmas with her human friend Marie-Claire in Yorkshire and marry there. So, your letter arrived at precisely the right time.

When you receive this, we shall be en route to Yorkshire—or Ophelia and the menagerie will. I will be packed away with a book in a very large steamer trunk, counting the minutes. Time goes on crutches till love hath all his rites. But Ophelia was delighted to hear that you have married, and she wishes to be at Addie and Etienne's ceremony in a few weeks, anyway, so we will hie to London for the new year after the holidays. Thank you for the invitation.

And I mean that sincerely. Receiving your letter made me realize what a lot of baggage I was holding on to concerning London and the Ossuary. I will never regret turning down any sort of leadership—I do not have the temperament for that—but I am impressed and

gladder than I can say that you are righting the ship. And I think
Ophelia will be glad to know more female friends besides Addie.
We will arrive in London on the 28th if the trains run on time. Or
Ophelia will. I will be safely ensconced in the aforementioned trunk.
Your friend,
Salem

"These are the friends you told me about. Our first proper houseguests," Genevieve said with some surprise. "What menagerie does he speak of?"

"Ophelia has a dog and three cats that I assume she'll be bringing."

"Oh. And they don't mind vampires?"

"They're warming to them."

"Well, Wulfric will have some company. Perhaps it will keep him from being naughty. Sally was very cross with him for besmirching the dining room rug. Let me tell Sally that we will need a room cleaned—preferably one fully furnished—"

"That can wait a bit. For right now..." He trailed off.

Genevieve asked, "What is it?"

"You're under the kissing bough, mum!" Hannah exclaimed, clapping her hands.

Genevieve turned to find the children in the doorway, flanked by Sally and Elspeth, all with mischievous smiles on their faces. She looked up. Sure enough, there was a sprig of mistletoe hanging above them in the archway.

"When did that get there?" she asked.

"Never mind that; you've got to kiss—those are the rules!" Elspeth smirked.

"How do you know?"

"Robbie and I tested it. It's ironclad," she said virtuously.

"Mysterious are the ways of the kissing bough," Kendrick said, his eyes twinkling.

"And you love a mystery," Genevieve said.

He grinned down at her as he pulled her close. "That I do."

As he pressed a kiss to her mouth, all the children cheered, and Genevieve remembered what it was like to be warm.

Christmas was planned as a "family" holiday. Vampire staff would be given the holiday of both Christmas Eve and Christmas Day. Human staff would receive Christmas Day and Boxing Day off, though they would be having their own meals and celebration at the house. Addie would be cooking and baking in the evenings.

The staff gift had been a bonus in advance of Christmas so they might buy themselves whatever they liked, since many had never had ready money of their own. Genevieve and Kendrick would exchange gifts on Christmas Eve, since Genevieve had gifts for Fletcher and Hannah and Peter. Nothing else was planned.

Except, as the carolers went door to door on the evenings before Christmas Eve and the church bells rang out in the clear night air, Genevieve kept thinking of her wedding night. Or rather, wedding morning. How she had wanted to be married in a church. And how she longed to believe that she could step freely over the threshold without fear of retribution or condemnation.

"I have found nothing to fear in a church," Kendrick had said.

Genevieve laughed suddenly to herself, covering her face with her hand. How strange, to long for something so much yet equally shrink back from it! To wish for the comfort and familiarity of the church building yet shrink back from the holiest of days it upheld!

Goose, she castigated herself, and she went to find Kendrick.

He was in the library, rolling his eyes over another "helpful note" from one of the better-off vampire households. "One more page to add to the kindling," he said, handing the letter to her, one written in a spidery hand full of caution and woes that may betide they who change ancient vampiric traditions.

"If the ancient vampire does not give a jot for the traditions, you'd think that would give them some pause," Genevieve remarked.

"I'll have you know I'm not a year past a thousand," Kendrick said. "Maybe."

"Still, it gives us insight into the portion of the Ossuary that is still hidebound and resistant to change." Genevieve set the missive down on the desk. "Don't burn it just yet."

"I commend your forethought." Kendrick lifted an eyebrow. "Did you need me, Genevieve?"

Staring into his gold eyes, she knew that the answer was *yes*. "I think I would like to attend a Christmas Eve service," she admitted in a small voice. "But I'm afraid."

He didn't ask why. He didn't say there was nothing to be afraid of. All he said was, "Would you like me to go with you?"

She nodded.

"I believe St. Alban's is holding one. I shall be pleased to escort you, ma'am." He stood and bowed over her hand. "You find yourself in possession of a willing knight-errant."

"Thank you," she murmured.

"Tonight, then."

Tonight! She stared at the clock on the desk. It was past midnight. Christmas Eve had officially begun.

❧

It pleased Kendrick to see Genevieve wearing one of her fine dresses and a matching cloak. He had told her to order a ballgown and whatever other finery she liked from the new seamstresses they had set up in the Ossuary, and this was in a lovely shade of rose. It made her glow, and the fashionable hat—carefully secured, since she did not have a pile of hair in which to anchor a formidable hat pin—was offset to give her face a bit of a gamine look. He had put aside his everyday wear and put on a suit of superfine wool. He left the sword in their bedchamber.

At the door, he donned a hat and handed her a pretty fur muff. She stared down at it and then up at him with wide eyes.

"I know you don't need it, Jenny, but it completes your outfit nicely," he said. He offered her his arm.

The street was dark, but the night was clear; horses' harnesses jingled with bells and an air of festive cheer was in the air. It was a short walk to the church, and they joined the other parishioners who filed in and found places in the pews. They garnered some stares, as neighborhood churches knew most of their attendees, but Kendrick turned away the most avid looks with a quick flick of his eyes.

Genevieve paid no attention to the humans around them. Her face was entirely concerned with the threshold, as if she were on a hunter and it was a particularly tricky jump. He was unaccountably proud of her when she stepped forward into the church with only a slight hesitation.

It was not a particularly remarkable church building—rather rundown, in fact, not much noticed or attended by any of the finer inhabitants of the neighborhood. But the vicar had a good voice and stepped into the pulpit with a smile to wish his congregants a joyous yuletide. The altar boasted a wooden nativity scene, perhaps carved by one of the parishioners. As they rose to sing a hymn, Kendrick held the hymn book for Genevieve. He was not sure she heard more than one word in three that the vicar had uttered so far, but he hoped this was what she needed.

How very humbling, he thought ruefully. *The man who has lived so long and done so many things has finally found one thing he cannot accomplish through persuasion or reason or sheer force of will: heal the hurts of the heart.*

The church smelled of evergreens and flowers, candlewax and stone. *Christmas*. It had been so long.

She sat in the pew, her hands tightly clasped. The vicar's words came to her through a roaring in her ears. Her heart did not beat, which was the only reason it was not hammering out of her chest.

Only Kendrick's hand under her elbow helped her stand, and even then, she stared unseeing at the hymnal until the words finally penetrated her mind:

> *O holy night, the stars are brightly shining;*
> *It is the night of the dear Saviour's birth.*
> *Long lay the world in sin and error pining,*
> *Till He appeared and the soul felt its worth.*

As the music swelled, sung by cheerful men and women slightly off-key and just behind tempo as the church organist struggled to keep pace, Genevieve's throat closed.

She hadn't realized she had been so afraid to step into the ordinary holiness.

For years, she had firmly believed the lie that she—that all vampires—were banned from all of this. She had carried bitterness in her heart because of it. How could a good God bar her from Himself, who had come to redeem all the hurts of the world? Was she trapped in an existence too far from what He'd intended with His creation? Did that make her hurts too deep, too blighted for His work? Was she and all those like her too far away for His grace to reach?

But no. That had been a lie, like so many others. Had Paul not said, "For I am persuaded that neither death, nor life, nor angels, nor principalities, nor powers, nor things present, nor things to come, nor height, nor depth, nor any other creature, shall be able to separate us from the love of God, which is in Christ Jesus our Lord"?

Even if she was undead?

Even if that creature was a vampire?

Nothing kept her from stepping forward now except her own bitterness.

And in the candlelight, assailed by the peace of the season, what place did that bitterness have now?

I have believed a lie, and I doubted what I knew of the Lord, she admitted. *The flaw was in me, and not in Him.*

Lord, have mercy on me, a sinner.

Kendrick set one solid hand over hers, and she clung to it and closed her eyes as the second verse washed over her.

The King of kings lay thus in lowly manger,
In all our trials born to be our friend.
He knows our need, to our weakness no stranger.
Behold your King, before Him lowly bend!
Behold your King, your King, before Him lowly bend!

At the close of the song, the vicar stood and read the Annunciation from Luke, the same verses she had read for Hannah and Peter weeks before. *"For with God, nothing shall be impossible."*

In the ruins of her shattered hopes and grieving heart, she hadn't known what lay ahead. Genevieve hadn't believed this kind of change had been possible for the Ossuary. She hadn't even believed her heart could warm so quickly. But it had.

She straightened and turned to Kendrick. He met her eyes and raised an eyebrow in inquiry. She bit her lip and tightened her hand around his.

At the close of the service, Genevieve stepped out of the church in a daze. She felt curiously light. Around her, people exclaimed in delight.

"Look. It's snowing," Kendrick said, pointing with his free hand to the flakes softly falling, settling on the street and the houses all around, dusting everything in a coating of white.

"Snow on Christmas?" a woman exclaimed in surprise. "Unheard of!"

"Nothing is impossible, it seems," Genevieve murmured.

◈

"It's snowing, mum!" Fletcher crowed as Kendrick and Genevieve returned, handing their snow-dusted capes and hats to Robbie, who was manning the door. "D'you think it will be there tomorrow?" he asked wistfully.

"If it falls steadily, it should be," Kendrick said. "You will have to make snow angels and snowmen in the park, where we can see them at dusk."

Fletcher bit his lip. "Wish you and missus could be there, guv."

Kendrick reached out and ruffled his hair. "We'll have a snowball fight at dusk. How about that?"

Fletcher brightened. "I think the nippers would like that. We can build fortifications, like against the Vikings!" He dashed off to the family parlor to impart the news.

Genevieve shot Kendrick a look. "Have you been telling him more stories?"

"It was a tangent from *Sigestan*."

"You've been reading? Without me?" she teased.

"We can't resist a good tale." He smiled and led her into the parlor.

Sally had set a fire in the fireplace and lit the candles placed on the tree—with a handy bucket of water nearby, Genevieve noted. The children's cut-out ornaments and strung popcorn and paper chains festooned the tree, which smelled strongly of evergreen. Much like the church.

"Is it time for presents?" Hannah whispered.

"I think Kendrick and I would like to see you open the presents from us," Genevieve said with a smile.

"Mum's presents are tomorrow," Peter said, looking very serious with his hair slicked down over his brow.

"How wonderful, to have Christmas twice!" Elspeth said, alighting on a small stool. Robbie followed her into the room and put his free hand on her shoulder.

"Peter, would you like to hand out the gifts?" Kendrick asked.

The boy obediently handed colorfully wrapped packages to Hannah and Fletcher and his mother, ending with one in front of him. Genevieve nearly beamed with pride watching how he hadn't hesitated over the letters.

At a nod from Kendrick, the children pulled the paper free from their gifts. Hannah gasped at the porcelain doll in a silk dress. Peter exclaimed over a set of toy soldiers and immediately began setting them up on the rug, and they chorused 'thank you' when prompted by their mother. Wulfric was very interested in the pitched battle that soon began over the floral rosettes in the rug.

Fletcher looked up from unwrapping his long and skinny gift in wonder. "A real sword?" he breathed.

"It's a practice foil, so it isn't sharp," Genevieve hastened to say. She had stipulated that it not be sharp when Kendrick had suggested the idea of giving the boy his own sword. "And you'll have to learn when it is appropriate to use and when not."

"A real sword," Fletcher repeated. He hadn't heard a word, eyes eating up the practice foil and sword belt with sheaths for both the foil and the silvered knife that Kendrick had passed to all the human members of the household a few days before. Most regarded the bequest with puzzlement. Fletcher was the only one who wished to keep his knife on his person. Genevieve chose to regard that as a quirk of his history rather than an indictment of their household.

Kendrick set his hand over Fletcher's. "The first thing a man learns is how to respect that he holds a weapon and not a toy. This isn't for chasing someone through hallways or hacking at innocent bannisters. But if you promise to use it well, I will teach you how to fence with it."

"I promise, guv," Fletcher swore fervently.

"Good lad."

"He's still going to do those things," Genevieve murmured at a register Fletcher wouldn't be able to hear.

"He will," Kendrick acknowledged. "But now he will do them less often."

"Now you, Mummy," Hannah said, stroking her doll's hair.

"I already had my gift, missus. You didn't need to get me anything else," Sally said, flushing at the package Peter pushed towards her.

"This is more a joint gift from Elspeth and me," Genevieve assured her. "You run the house for half the day, Sally. That's no small task, and we appreciate you looking after it. After us," she amended.

Sally unwrapped the paper and exclaimed over the fine lace collar that Genevieve had commissioned Elspeth to make. "I've never had anything so fine! Thank you." She showed it to her children, and Hannah reached out a hand to stroke the tiny stitches.

Looking up from the enchanted daze his foil and its accompanying sword belt had put him in, Fletcher stood up and bowed to Genevieve and Kendrick. "I didn't have anything to get you, missus, but I reckon if you're still wanting to teach me to read... that would be all right."

Genevieve beamed. "I would *love* to teach you, Fletcher. What a wonderful Christmas this is."

"And you haven't even gotten to the end of your presents yet," Kendrick said, smirking. He set a small, flat box in her lap. "And before you tell me I didn't need to give you anything—it gives me pleasure to see you happy."

Genevieve opened the box and breathed out a shaky breath, staring down at the circular, golden brooch with the raised figure of a fox head surrounded by ivy leaves. "Is it...?"

"As near an approximation I could find," Kendrick said.

Genevieve lifted it out of the plush satin and cradled it in her hands. "I won't say you shouldn't have," she murmured, "because I love it."

He smiled and took it to pin at the neck of her gown.

"This is from my very favorite of my father's books," she explained to the children. "*Wynnflaed's Knight*. Her lover gives her a brooch very much like this, though that brocch was used as a cloak pin and fastened at the shoulder. Thank you," she told Kendrick, and kissed him on the cheek. "My gift to you is twofold. Fletcher, will you hand me the last package?"

Fletcher handed over the squarish package to Kendrick.

"This is the first part," she said, feeling unaccountably nervous as he unwrapped the gift.

"*Phantastes* by George MacDonald," he read, his eyes sparking at the title.

"I remember it being enjoyable—a bit like *The Faerie Queene*, a bit like... well, nothing I can think of." She laughed. "I did not see it in our library."

"No, I have not read it. Thank you," he said, turning it over in his hands. "I did not think there was much myth-making in this era."

She cleared her throat. "The second part isn't something I could wrap, but... you did say I could pick the name. Our name," she said as his gaze sharpened. "To usher in a new era for all of us."

"What did you pick?"

"Well... what would you think of Stewart? To emblematize what we want to accomplish for the Ossuary as a whole."

He smiled. "House Guardian. I think that will do very well, Mrs. Stewart."

Chapter Thirty-Seven

❧

"Did you have a good Christmas?" Genevieve asked hesitantly as they sat in front of the fire, watching the embers burn low. Dawn was not far away.

"I did. My first true Christmas in this era was very memorable."

Genevieve sat up, arrested. "Your first—! You should have said something! We would have—" She broke off. He hadn't said anything because of her.

"I remember Christmas," he told her. "But I have not celebrated it the way we do now—certainly not with trees and kissing boughs."

"But you enjoyed it?"

"I did." He kissed her hand. "I have something else for you— though that isn't precisely true. It is a gift, but not mine. I hoped it would make you happy, but I don't know."

"*More?* My goodness, what is it?" Genevieve asked, mystified.

"It's upstairs. Come and see."

He led her to their rooms and said, "Wait a moment," before disappearing. Genevieve reached for the buttons on her shoes and had nearly all of them undone by the time Kendrick returned with a large trunk on his shoulder. He softly closed the door and set it on the floor.

She straightened in confusion. "You got me an old trunk?"

Kendrick pressed a small, brass key into her hand. "Your friend Hetty kept it for you."

She looked at the key in her hand. She seemed to hear the words from far away. "Hetty?" she whispered. "You—You went to Oxford?"

"Yes. When I told you I was delivering the invitations, I was— but I took a little detour. Your friend Hetty kept house for your father until he died, and she and her husband inherited the house. They have several children, two named Ezra and Jenny."

Her knees went out from under her, but she barely noticed Kendrick scooping her up and placing her on the bed. "Hetty?" she said again, helplessly.

Her husband put an arm around her. "Yes. She has never forgotten what you did for her. I went to see if I could find anything of your father's that you might have as a keepsake because you had said you felt so unsettled in that part of your life. But I got luckier than I expected."

"These are...*my* things?"

"I don't know. I didn't open the trunk. But it is everything your father kept for you and wanted you to have. They told me so."

Genevieve closed her hand around the key, feeling the metal cut into her hand. She couldn't speak for a long time. The burn of tears stung her eyes and throat, but none fell.

"Did I overstep, sweetheart?"

She shook her head. "Why are you so good to me?"

"Am I not supposed to be? I thought a man treasured that which was most precious to him."

I think I love this man, Genevieve thought, staring up at him through a haze of tears. How was he everything she had hoped and dreamed of all those long years ago? "Will you open it?" she croaked, handing him the key.

He took it and knelt on the rug to turn the key in the lock.

Genevieve sank to the floor by his side, and because of his steady presence found the courage to open the lid.

Pushing aside layers of tissue and sachets to keep the contents fresh, Genevieve peered into the trunk, recognizing the jewelry box she had been given as a child—not that she had had many jewels, but it had been a convenient place to keep her trinkets and a few necklaces and bracelets that she'd owned. And below that was the lovely cedar box that had been her mother's. Her father had given it to her upon her mother's passing, but she'd always kept the contents separate. The next layer consisted of clothing— her favorites, though now sadly out of date, and other personal belongings. A few pieces of embroidery, stitched for Genevieve's one-day trousseau. A shawl she remembered had been her mother's. And then below that—

"Oh," Genevieve whispered. "Books." She lifted them out. They were all her father's works—her personal copies, worn and thumbed, but a few appeared new. She looked closer.

The Adventures of Dunstan, an Anglo-Saxon Boy. Bold Amice, Wise Amice. The Dragon of Langsey Isle. The Chapel at Canterbury, Or, In the Days of King Harold.

They were all attributed as Mr. Anglesy's Stories for Children.

"I know these stories," she whispered, thumbing through *Bold Amice, Wise Amice.* "He told them to me at night, but after Mother died, he never made them into novels...but he finished them? They're children's books?" She turned to the dedication pages.

For Jenny, be brave and bold and never give up.
For Jenny, nowhere in the wide world is too far to come home.
For Jenny, you are my most precious work.
For Jenny, for no other reason than I love you.

Genevieve covered her face with her hands and just breathed. *He did not hate me. He did not resent me.*

Kendrick pressed a handkerchief into her hand.

After sniffing into the handkerchief, she stacked the books carefully. She looked around for her favorite, *Wynnflaed's Knight.* As she picked it up, she saw the edge of an envelope sticking out above the pages.

The book fell open to the place where the envelope lay. Inscribed in her father's scholar handwriting that she would know anywhere, it read, "Jenny."

Oh, God, she thought.

Everything she had begged for. Everything she feared.

Kendrick's arm wrapped around her shoulders as she, with horribly shaking hands, freed the sheets of paper from the envelope.

My dearest, best beloved, only daughter Jenny,

It is hard to believe I have not laid eyes on you for nearly nineteen years. The year turns colder, and my chest once again battles every cough and sniffle the winter provokes. I ask the Lord for what I have requested every Christmas—that I will see you again—but I write this letter to leave with Hetty and Arthur in case the Lord in His wisdom allows me to see your mother again first.

People have tried to tell me you eloped with some man, or left for parts unknown, or worse—been shamed somehow and do not want to return. I have never believed them. You had opportunities to marry— I would not have minded, Jenny—but you insisted on staying and running the house. You believed I needed looking after. You always wanted to look after people, Jenny. I never believed you would have left without a word. I cling to the belief that something kept you from coming home. You knew that there was nothing you could do that would have ever made me turn you away.

I look to Anglo-Saxon quotes for the familiar comfort they have always afforded me, but they had no hope in death. "Unknown to them was the Wielder of Glory, High King of the World," as the Beowulf poet says. And maybe that is why I have loved them so—they see so imperfectly through a glass darkly, but we who have hope can see the glimmer of what is more, both in their tales, as the Beowulf poet draws out, and in our own stories.

I will admit to the temptation of Job, when his so-called friends told him to curse God and die. But what will that profit me? Then I am like the Geats, who believed death was the end, that only men's glory and great deeds would endure after one surrendered to the dark.

No, I will not. God has shown Himself to be ever present in my grief. He brought your friend Hetty to keep house for me, and I felt pleased I could help her support her family, and she reminded me of you. And then I found kinship with Arthur, a Methodist and another scholar at heart, and he began taking dinner with me for company—and to flirt with Hetty. Blessings in the midst of sorrow.

No, I will not be cursing God. I increasingly turn to His words in these years. And what I lean on as the years have crept forward is that no word from God will ever fail. And has He not said, "I am the resurrection, and the life: he that believeth in me, though he were dead, yet shall he live: and whosoever liveth and believeth in me shall never die"?

Whether you have departed this life—or if one day I will see you again in the land of the living—or if you will read this letter after I am gone, I hold to this. Whether you have gone before me to see your mother, or whether I will meet her before you—I believe that no word from God will ever fail.

I will see you again, Jenny.

Your loving Papa

The letter crumpled in her hands as she pressed her face to Kendrick's shoulder and cried.

Through bloody tears, Genevieve reread the words in her father's hand again.

And again.

And again.

The most amazing, unlooked-for Christmas gift, full of hope that one day she would read these words. Even as they smote her heart, they found all the hopes smashed by Laurent and Cuthbert and twenty years of darkness and held them up to the light.

This night had begun to put all her broken pieces back together.

And Kendrick had done this for her?

"How did you know where to go?" she asked, pulling off her gloves and wiping her face with them.

"Elspeth told me your address."

"And you saw Hetty? You really went all that way?"

"I did. She misses you. Maybe at some point, we can go and see her again in a way that won't jeopardize the Ossuary's secrets."

Genevieve pressed her lips together to keep them from trembling. "But you couldn't have known..."

"No, I didn't, but I hoped there would be something left behind I could bring back to you."

"Why?" she whispered, looking up at him through the blood crusting on her lashes.

He reached out and wiped the tears away with his thumbs. "I wanted you to have a good Christmas."

Genevieve ran her bare fingers over the letter, straightening out the crease she'd made in the paper. She carefully slipped it into the book. Her voice cracked. "How can I ever repay you for this?"

Kendrick frowned in confusion. "There is no ledger between you and me. You are my wife, Jenny. If I was able, why shouldn't I have done it? What is too much for the woman to whom I have pledged myself?"

I do not deserve this man who gives me so much, she thought. The events of the night felt as though they had cracked her heart right open, freeing all that she had been holding on to for twenty years. She reached up to touch his face. "No one has ever loved me like this."

Kendrick went still under her hand.

"You don't think the word fits?" she asked, throat suddenly tight.

"No, it does fit." He clasped her hands and kissed them. "You woke me up, Genevieve, when I didn't even know I was walking through this world asleep. You are my wife. My home. My only love. But I declared myself through actions rather than words because of your hurts—your fears."

All the worries and fears she had stored up inside melted away under the joy of his declaration. She recalled what he had said in the weeks before, about standing before a window on a dark street, watching those inside participate in the rhythms of life. And she had wondered how she could usher him in.

The answer had been before her all the time. "For the first time in twenty years, I'm not scared anymore. Because I love you." She opened her arms to him. "I love you. Come in from the cold, Kendrick."

He dipped his head and kissed her, and Genevieve was finally home.

Chapter Thirty-Eight

Rats. He could hear rats in the walls.

Laurent's lip curled in a sneer as he woke in the rundown accommodations by the water. He could hear their squeaking and their feet scurrying. He could picture their beady little eyes, their disagreeable expressions as they filched what they could from a larder.

It made him sick to think he had fallen so low.

He had had to keep moving ahead of Kendrick's well-ordered patrols, abandoning comfortable hideouts and advancing into less and less salubrious neighborhoods. Ones that stank of unemptied privies, full of pests and parasites. Wharf rats, that was what they were. Plague-filled vermin. Just like the unwashed who walked to and fro in the narrow, smoke-filled streets outside. To think that he was forced to rub shoulders with those he supped on!

He shuddered and rose. He had partaken of a fairly robust factory worker the night before, so his hunger was still assuaged, but his irritation rose as laughter and a rousing chorus of "Deck the hall with boughs of holly" filtered in through the closed shutters.

What right did they have to humor and cheer, while he was here suffering?

He stalked out of the room to the squalid parlor, where Oxley and a few others of his followers waited, murmuring in low voices.

"One of you make yourselves useful and go kill those carolers," he snarled. "I can't stand the din."

They exchanged glances among themselves, making his ire rise all the more. What call did they have to question his orders? If he demanded something of them, they ought to fall over themselves to carry out his commands!

The knocker on the front door of the house rang out.

"I'll get it," Oxley said, sounding far too chipper. He hurried away and returned a moment later, escorting a woman in a black, voluminous coat.

The woman pulled the hood away from her face and shook out her dark hair; she stared around at the assembled vampires with a coldly bored expression.

"Ah, Gisela, good," Laurent said, smiling widely. "I'm glad you're here. I've thought of another way to strike at the new master and his unblushing bride." Laurent sneered.

"Then you'd best forget it," she said flatly.

Laurent pulled up short. "What?"

"I've come to tell you to leave off this foolishness. They're entrenched now. It's too late. They've got too much support."

He leaned forward like a striking snake. "You're giving up?!"

She sniffed disdainfully. "I'm not fool enough to keep digging a hole for myself. Do I like them? No. But the truth of it is, they don't want power for power's sake. They're actually doing things to improve the Ossuary, and they might even succeed. I'm willing to let them try. It will either work, or they'll have enough rope to hang themselves."

"You're going to let Rupert's murderer keep the power *he stole*? It ought to be yours be rights!"

"You mean *yours?*" Gisela leveled a cool look at Laurent.

"Don't play the innocent with me. I know the moment I would have reached for the throne, you would have done your best to strike me down as well. You couldn't stand to see a woman in power in the Ossuary, and that's a good amount of your problem with Genevieve."

Laurent advanced on her. "You conniving *hetaera*—"

"So, you *do* remember something from your long-ago education. You keep back," she warned, a sharp dagger appearing in her hand. "I'm not letting pride and hate get me killed, Laurent. You're welcome to your schemes. But keep me out of it. There is no profit in them." She turned on her heel to leave.

Laurent picked up a chair and threw it at her.

Gisela neatly dodged. It shattered against the wall.

"That's the sort of thing I mean," she said, staring down her nose at the wreckage of the chair. "Tantrums that come to nothing. You all watch yourselves," she warned the room at large. "Or he'll shatter you against the rocks of his insurmountable ambitions without a thought."

"Coward!" Laurent screamed after her. "*Tantrums?* I'll show you tantrums! I'll kill Genevieve and Kendrick, and I'll take the power for myself, and then we'll see! You'd better watch yourself then, Gisela! You frigid—"

He broke off, noticing Oxley edging away from him. "What? Are you scared, worm?"

"No need to be nasty, Laurent," Oxley said, having the gall to look injured. "But are you sure this is—"

"You're questioning me? *Me?*"

"I just thought, since it's Christmas and all, we might leave the revenge for a few days. Spirit of the season and all—"

"You think I care about *Christmas?*" In a blink, Laurent had Oxley by the throat, his other hand ready and poised to rip out his larynx or his heart, whatever the haze of rage found easiest. But someone grabbed hold of his arm, and another vampire seized him by the shoulder, hauling him away from Oxley.

Oxley wheezed, staring at him with wounded eyes. "There was no call for that!" he rasped.

"Let go of me, or I'll—"

A short and stocky vampire countered, "What? You'll try to off us like Oxley? Like the Master?"

Laurent didn't know that vampire's name and didn't care to. "He is *not* the Master, and I'll kill every single one of you pigeon-livered fools if I like!"

"Laurent!" Oxley objected.

"Pigeon-livered, are we?" the vampire said. "Well, you're a fly-by-night windbag and a sapskull. I might like a dry place to lay my head at night, and a little ready coin in my pocket."

Another man added, "Following you, on the other hand? About as fruitful as pissing in the wind."

"I'm willing to give Kendrick a chance," the stocky vampire said. "Come on, lads."

The hands released Laurent, and he staggered back as the rest of the assembled vampires left the room. Last was Oxley, who appeared torn as he glanced back—but left all the same.

"Go on!" Laurent screamed. "When I'm sitting on the Ossuary's throne, I'll remember this! I'll call each one of you to account, you traitors! I'll kill you all!"

Inside the walls, the rats squeaked and ran.

Chapter Thirty-Nine

Genevieve realized that she had built the woman who had bestowed upon Kendrick his sword into some mythic, beloved figure. So much so that she had regarded her coming with a bit of apprehension.

All that was dashed when upon their meeting, she tried to curtsey to Genevieve.

"It's a great pleasure to meet you, my lady," Ophelia began. She was not more than twenty if Genevieve had to guess, with auburn hair and hazel eyes and a limp to her stride that the long skirts could not fully disguise.

"Oh, please!" Genevieve said, disregarding everything she had been about to say. "None of that. I am the one pleased to meet *you*. And after having been the spinster daughter of an Old English scholar, this *my lady*-ing is quite strange some nights. I am Genevieve." She held out her hands.

After a moment's hesitation, the woman clasped Genevieve's hands, a warm press. Her heartbeat was the only sound in the room. "I am Ophelia, then." She smiled suddenly. "I know what you mean. It is quite strange for porters and cabmen to address me as 'Mrs.' now." She pinked a little. "I am grateful for you housing us for our visit, and for being understanding about the animals. Addie and Etienne offered, but they are unencumbered by the basic needs of life, and, well..." She laughed. "You have a working kitchen."

Genevieve smiled. "I have seen proof that it *does* work, and Addie often bakes in it when she has an urge to create. And one dog and three cats are hardly a menagerie, especially when we are housing one dog already. Fletcher is over the moon about a dog that will do tricks. I am sure he is planning to teach his puppy all manner of commands."

Indeed, the boy had immediately appointed himself chief dog wrangler. The cats wrangled themselves, apparently. He and Sally's children had disappeared into the back garden with Blaze and Wulfric at dusk, leaving the adults to the parlor. "We are happy to have all of you. Isn't that right?" she asked over her shoulder, sensing the menfolk drawing nearer after they had completed their backslapping and ribbing, a crucial part of any male greeting.

"Certainly," Kendrick said. His hand was a comforting weight at her back. "And Salem has said he'll get his hands dirty and help me with the drainage problem in the southwest corner."

"I said I would *advise*, you fiend. Where did you get this mania for dirt?" Salem had the appearance of a tall, thin young man with slightly overlong dark hair that brushed his collar. He smiled with all his teeth.

Kendrick snorted. "Etienne rubbing off on you? Bold words coming from the one who lived in a hole in the ground by choice."

"Built by whose people?" Salem countered.

"I'm sure you'll have a grand time," Ophelia said dryly. "I volunteer to help with preparations for the ball—if you need the help?" She bit her lip. "I've never attended a real ball before."

"I would love that," Genevieve assured her. "Addie will be arriving shortly to help with the decorations."

Ophelia lit up. "Oh, I can't wait to show her my ring." She

lifted her hand. The gold had been cunningly worked into loops and curlicues around an oval moonstone.

"How lovely!" Genevieve said.

"Salem picked it out. A bit of a joke, and apparently, moonstone...helps." Ophelia glanced from Salem to Genevieve. "There won't be a problem on that front, either," she murmured. "The full moon isn't till the fifteenth, and we plan to be in the countryside then, visiting our...*friend* Faelad."

"If you wanted to extend your visit, we would accommodate you," Kendrick said. "It is no imposition when friends arrive. Speaking of..."

Addie burst into the parlor with Etienne hard on her heels. "Ophelia!" she exclaimed, throwing her arms around her friend.

"And what about me?" Salem muttered good-naturedly.

Etienne shook his hand. "Brothers never get the same reaction as female friends."

❦

"As hanging and wiving goes by destiny, I think you've been dealt a great hand of fate, my friend," Salem said as he, Etienne, Dominic, and Kendrick decamped from Carmine House and the frighteningly competent industry of womenfolk to find a bite and then survey the earthworks in the Ossuary.

Dominic had brought over Evangeline and her son to socialize, and the hen party had turned into a delighted coo over Blaze the dog. In a delightful turn of events, Elspeth had discovered he was quite willing to be petted by any sort of person, no matter their extant status.

"We both have," Kendrick acknowledged.

"You didn't say how pretty she was in your letter," Salem said slyly.

"Was it relevant?"

"'Dear Salem,'" his friend quoted, turning around and walking backwards to face all of them, "'I realize you're rusticating in Ireland and probably turning into a mushroom, but I have married, and my wife is throwing a ball on New Year's Eve. You're invited.' You failed to state why, or that your wife was uncommonly lovely." He smirked. "So what happened?"

"He took one look at her and lost his head," Etienne said.

Kendrick opened his mouth and then paused. "Not...entirely inaccurate." To this day, he remained shocked that Genevieve had spent so long unnoticed among the inhabitants of the Ossuary. Though that had partly been by design on her part. He added, in no small amount of wonder, "She makes me feel alive."

Salem sobered. "That is not an insignificant thing. How did you meet her?"

Kendrick shrugged. "I met her in the Ossuary."

"There must be a story there."

"And what a story it is." Etienne smirked. "Shall you tell him, or shall I?"

"You're all a gossipy bunch of henwives. I'll tell you after dinner," Kendrick said, rolling his eyes.

❧

Once they were all pleasantly full and had gathered in a human pub with pints of bad beer that none of them would drink, Kendrick explained how he had met Genevieve, and how the marriage had come about. "I married her to steal a march on the other bachelors," Kendrick said, with a sidelong look at Dominic. He was studying his pint glass intently and did not look up.

"A wise and calculated move," Salem said, "with so lovely a lady."

Kendrick said, "She's like a book I will never tire of reading, with new chapters to discover every night."

Salem's smirk morphed into genuine pleasure. "I am happy for you, my friend."

"She's the one you should credit with the changes in the Ossuary. She can see what needs doing in a way I never could."

Salem nodded in understanding. "And the human boy?"

"He's ours." Kendrick caught Dominic's eye as he finally looked up. "Children don't have to be blood to be kin."

"Dominic's taken in two children as well," Etienne said, following Kendrick's gaze.

"Filled with a benevolent spirit, are you?" Salem questioned.

"Nothing quite so simple," Etienne said. They explained to Salem the saga of Laurent and his perfidies.

Salem drummed his fingers on the table. "So are we killing him, or...?"

"He's found a hole to hide in, unfortunately. But we hope that enough people will turn from him that he will reveal himself, or a former comrade will tell us where he bides. We hope the ball brings more goodwill on that front," Kendrick added. "If you all could be on the watch for any potential problems that night, we would appreciate it."

His friends agreed happily.

"I should collect Evangeline and get home." Dominic smiled. "June is cutting a tooth, and Evangeline will want to check on her."

"So unbelievably domestic, all of you," Salem drawled.

"Says the dog father," Etienne replied, adjusting his pince-nez.

"I'll own that one."

⚜

"Ireland was beautiful," Ophelia said as they all sat around a large table, working to construct the paper lanterns that Genevieve and Elspeth had decided on for part of the ball décor. "Cold, of course, and rainy. But we were in the country, and I've never seen a greener place. After Faelad vouched for us, the locals were very hospitable and kind. It was a rather difficult adjustment, getting used to heightened senses and the discomfort that comes with a change," Ophelia admitted. "But Faelad was able to explain most of what to expect, and the other werewolf was in residence to help me when I was...not myself."

"*Other* werewolf?" Evangeline questioned, her hands pausing in her work.

"Yes, there are only two Ossory werewolves, you see. It is a condition passed on from one to another. Only ever two," Ophelia explained. "I got the impression that we were not the only two people in the world who become wolves, but that this... strain...is a little different." She shifted in her chair. "I can't say any more without violating the promise I made to keep their secrets."

"Of course not," Elspeth assured her.

"Oh, but surely, you can tell us what it's like to run around as a wolf?" Addie asked, her eyes shining with hope.

"It's not something that is easy to put into words. There's a lot of smelling involved, more than I ever expected. And very few words. Lots of ear movement and tail flicking for communication. But oh..." Ophelia sighed. "I have never felt like such a singer as when we howled. It felt like... Well, it felt like the music of the spheres because we howled to the moon. We spent the majority of the two months in Ireland and then traveled back to Yorkshire. Salem and I could have married in Ireland, but I wanted Marie-Claire to be there. It was a lovely ceremony, even if it was in her parlor at evening." She blushed, and the rest of the table smiled knowingly. "And soon she will have her baby. She's threatened to make Salem and me godparents." A little smile played at the corner of her mouth.

"How lovely," Genevieve said quietly.

Ophelia looked up and met her eyes in a moment of understanding. For who knew what werewolves were capable of, but Ophelia had married a vampire, and there would be no children for such a union. No children for any of them.

But it was not quite true, was it? Because what was Fletcher if not her boy? She stared at the half-complete paper lantern in her hands. She had an endless life, unless someone put a period to her existence, or the Lord came again to bring everything to completion. And there were so many children who needed a home.

She tucked that thought away for further reflection with Kendrick.

"Speaking of marriage, how should we address you?" Addie asked.

Ophelia laughed. "I don't know. Salem has told me what his name was before, but he does not want to go back to that. And it isn't very flattering, to be honest. I don't really relish remaining a Shaw, though."

"No, you get to set that aside! No more of that."

"Faelad offered his name, which was sweet of him," Ophelia said. "But I think he mostly did it to see the look on Salem's face. I've never seen such a mixture of chagrin and outrage." She chuckled.

"It is a conundrum," observed Genevieve. "Kendrick said I could choose a new name for us going forward. I picked Stewart. Perhaps you could discuss something similar."

"What would it be for us, though?" Ophelia frowned.

"Well, I wanted something symbolic," Genevieve said apologetically. "Stewart comes from the roots 'stig,' which means house, and 'weard,' which means guard. And it had the added benefit of signaling a shift in how we were ruling the Ossuary. Not cruel overlords, but stewards. Poor Elspeth was subjected to all my choices beforehand. You, however, could simply choose something that you both liked."

"Isn't it so funny how some vampires are perfectly content using the names they were born with," Evangeline said quietly, "yet others reinvent themselves totally? Dominic finds the practice quite ridiculous."

"Many do it to puff themselves up," Addie said. "But I know

Salem did it because he felt he had become so changed from the person he had been before, he needed a new name."

"Due to trauma," Ophelia murmured.

"Exactly so," Genevieve said, thinking of Sparrow. "A name change of any sort is quite normal—we have just said that even human women do it to signal a change of identity. It's far more important what that change is. Who you are becoming."

And who have we become, by taking on the mantle of Mr. and Mrs. Stewart? she thought. *People to be proud of, I hope. A name to wear with honor.*

Just before sunrise, after she and Kendrick had said good morning to the human staff and were readying for bed, Genevieve remarked, "You know, I like Salem and Ophelia so much."

"I thought you would." Kendrick picked up *The Dragon of Langsey Isle*. They had decided to savor the experience of reading one of Genevieve's father's books for the very first time together. They were about to start chapter five.

"We all fussed over Blaze," Genevieve said, marveling. "He didn't mind it a bit. Wulfric was by turns growling and wagging his tail. It was so funny to see." She pulled the covers back and got into bed. "I'm so glad they came."

"I am too. I hadn't much hope for their coming. It was an unlooked-for boon." Kendrick took her hand and kissed it, meeting her eyes. "You were right to invite them, Wife. You always are."

"I don't know about that," Genevieve said, demurring. "The ball is nearly upon us, and I'm not sure all will be ready. Or if anyone will come." She twisted the covers in her hands.

Kendrick laid a hand over hers. "All will be well," he assured her.

She sat up straight and quickly pecked him on the lips. "Thank you for your faith in me. It's a comfort."

"Love, you never have to thank me for that," Kendrick murmured, capturing her lips in a longer, deeper kiss that sent sparks flowing through her. He rubbed his nose against hers before opening the book and beginning to read.

Chapter Forty

On the night of the ball, Genevieve woke up calm and quiet, knowing that she had done all she could to ready the house and the servers for the event. She went downstairs to make sure the last preparations had been taken care of and greeted Sally and the children in the kitchen.

"But everyone will look so beautiful," Hannah said wistfully over her supper. "Can't we stay up to see the dresses, Mrs. Stewart?"

"I'm afraid not, Hannah," Genevieve said kindly but firmly. "This is a new venture, you know, and I think it will be best if all the human occupants of the house are well away from the ballroom by the time guests start arriving. Not that you will be unsafe, dear," she said, her eyes darting up to meet Sally's. "But to make sure everyone behaves. Perhaps, if you get ready for bed promptly, Elspeth and I will come and show you our finery before we go down to play hostess."

Hannah's eyes lit up. "Oh! Really?"

"Yes, really." Genevieve laughed.

"What d'you say, love?" Sally prompted.

"Thank you," Hannah said, smiling.

"Perhaps Ophelia too, if she is ready in time. I will ask her when I fetch her tray."

"You don't have to fetch it, ma'am," Sally protested. "Me or one of the girls can do it."

"Nonsense. It will be on my way, and you have been on your feet all day. Thank you for all the work you have put in," she added, raising her voice to address the table. "We appreciate it very much."

"Wish you were having a fencing match instead of a ball," Fletcher mumbled. "That would be more fun by half."

Genevieve smiled. "What a good idea, Fletcher! An exhibition of all manner of skills! How interesting and educational. I shall mention it to Kendrick."

"Educational," Fletcher muttered, dragging his hands down his face. He was quick and sharp with his letters and numbers, but the chore of sitting still at a table in front of a book wore on him.

"Wouldn't you like to learn smithing or navigation in addition to fighting techniques? I think there might be a wealth of hidden talents among our people."

Fletcher squinted up at her. "Smithing? Like a blacksmith?"

"Yes, like a blacksmith, but smith-craft is also used to make coins and rings and jewelry."

"Like how the guv made your ring."

"Exactly so."

Fletcher considered. "I might like that," he conceded before chewing his bread roll with an open mouth.

Genevieve made a mental note for a lesson in table manners at another time.

❧

Later, surveying her fancy gown, Genevieve realized she had a problem. The sumptuous dress, made of amethyst watered silk, required several petticoats over the bustle, and then an underskirt, an overskirt, and the bodice. She had gotten her corset and bustle on over her chemise without issue, having become used to the updated underpinnings of this decade. But now she surveyed the petticoats and skirt with trepidation.

"This is why ladies engage lady's maids," she said aloud. The human staff would be finishing preparations for the ball or taking their rest. And everyone else would be busy dressing themselves.

There was no help for it. Genevieve struggled into the two petticoats and tied them on, fluffing and jumping up and down a little to get them to lay correctly. Then on went the underskirt, with the same problem. The overskirt was a bit easier, attaching with tapes and hooks and settling over her hips easily. But then came the bodice.

Genevieve muttered under her breath, attempting to fix the tiny hooks up and down her spine when she couldn't see them. The bodice, off the shoulder and very tight fitting, was not accommodating.

"Do you need help?" Kendrick rumbled from the other side of the screen.

She peered over the top. He was inserting the cufflinks into his cuffs and buttoning his waistcoat. "Are you volunteering?"

"What do you need?"

"I can't fasten this," she said, frustrated. "Please don't let me walk out of here with my hooks done up wrong."

"Of course, my love." Kendrick walked around the screen. His eyes widened as he spied her. "You look beautiful."

Genevieve pivoted to face the full-length mirror. "I'll have to take your word for it," she joked, as neither of them appeared in the reflection. "Why do we have this, anyway?"

Kendrick stepped behind her—or as close as he could get with her skirts in the way—and carefully did up the tiny hooks along her spine one by one. "Trust me," he said. "You are one of the fairest women I have ever beheld, Genevieve."

It was a beautiful dress—beyond the silk, it was more decadent than any she had ever worn, and it had a good deal of bead-work that caught the light, as well as an elegant drape that gave the impression of a train without actually dragging on the floor. But the rest... "Not *the* fairest?" she said with a smile, thinking of the fairytale rhyme.

"If I said, 'the fairest,' you wouldn't believe me." He turned her around gently and cupped her face, smiling. "Your beauty is from within. You glow, the brightest star in the dark, my heart's gleam. It doesn't matter what you wear. Though this dress suits you," he added.

"My fingers can't seem to stop twitching," she admitted, lacing the offending digits together.

Kendrick wrapped his hands around hers. "Everything will be fine."

"But what if—"

"Our friends are here to help us handle it. But it may surprise you. I think you have put together something to be proud of."

"And what's that?" she said with a little laugh.

"A real community. Belonging. Hope."

She smiled. "A kind thing to say."

"A true thing. You gave me hope when I was lacking it."

"Kendrick, no, that's—"

"Oh, yes, you did."

"If we've made any kind of change, we did it together."

"See, that's why I love you. You argue with me, and you challenge me, and you've found a way to see through the dark. You're a wonder, Genevieve. I hope you saved the first dance for me, even if it isn't done."

"We're creating new traditions, aren't me? You may have the first, the last. All the ones in between." She set her hand on his jaw and kissed him with all the love that was in her heart.

His arms came around her and held her tightly. "Much as I'd like to continue with this," he said against her lips, "if we don't stop now, we'll never go downstairs."

"If we don't stop now, you'll crush my dress," Genevieve said, laughing.

Kendrick let her go. "It's going to be a new year and a new era for all of us."

"That, it will," Genevieve said, checking that the headband to which she had affixed her hair ornaments was still in place. She picked up the gloves dyed the same color as her gown and slid them on past her elbows.

"What do you think of the Ossuary being located somewhere other than London?" Kendrick asked suddenly as he pulled on his evening coat. "Or at least us having another place that isn't this house?"

"I hadn't thought of it. Why?"

"I wondered if hunting for a location with a bit more healthful air would be worth it, if we keep acquiring humans this way. London is not the most wholesome place. And beyond it being one of the largest cities and ample hunting grounds, I don't see another reason to demand vampires stay within its city limits. Once we have instilled better habits and ensure that the laws are being followed, I see no reason why we couldn't live elsewhere. Or have a second residence, the way the wealthy class do."

"I wouldn't mind a place with fewer ghosts," Genevieve admitted. They shared a smile.

Then Ophelia knocked on the door, and it was time to visit the children before guests began to arrive.

⚜

Peter was unimpressed. Fletcher wanted to know how women sat with "that big ol' tail." Hannah was in raptures.

Ophelia smiled and happily turned in a slow circle so Hannah could have the full effect. She wore a green-and-gold gown that set off her auburn hair to a dramatic effect.

"Am I too late?" Elspeth asked, poking her head in the door.

Her blonde hair had been curled and piled artfully around her head, and she wore a pale-rose gown with lace and ruffles.

"Pink is my favorite color," Hannah declared upon seeing the full effect.

"You look beautiful," Genevieve assured her friend.

"So do you! Purple—so inspired!" When Genevieve just blinked at her, Elspeth laughed. "Is there finally something I know that you don't? Purple—the color of royalty."

"I hadn't even thought about that," Genevieve admitted. "I just loved the color."

"Well, clearly, it's perfect." Elspeth clasped her hand.

"I heard there was a fashion parade happening," Evangeline said shyly from the hallway.

"Oh, yes, come in, come in!" Ophelia exclaimed.

Evangeline's gown of burgundy made her look striking, and Hannah said, "No, *red* is my favorite color!"

The women laughed. With four ladies and their bustles, the small nursery had become a bit crowded. Ophelia and Elspeth filed out as Genevieve bid Hannah and Peter good night.

"Augie didn't come?" Hannah said a bit sadly.

"No, he wanted to stay with June," Evangeline explained. "There would have been no playing, you know. You're to go right to sleep." She smoothed Hannah's hair back over her forehead with a hand that trembled imperceptively.

"Good night, Fletcher," Genevieve said. "You'll stay in bed, won't you?"

"Yes, mum," he said, rolling his eyes.

"We'll have another chapter of *Sigestan* tomorrow," she promised.

"You look fine as a fivepence," Fletcher admitted.

"Thank you," Genevieve said, her heart warming. She risked mussing her dress to bend down and peck a kiss on his head.

"Steady," Kendrick said, holding Genevieve's hand tucked in his.

Her eyes rolled around to fix on him. "I'm not a horse."

"I know that."

"Next you'll be telling me, 'Whoa, girl.'"

"I would never," he said around a laugh.

"Only because you don't remember what it's like to handle horses," she murmured, and then the first guests were upon them in the receiving line.

Guests could enter by the front door, or by the cellar if they were coming from the Ossuary. Both guests would pass by the cloak room and the retiring room, if anyone needed to repair a flounce or re-pin their hair, and then come up to the open ballroom on the first floor in the receiving line. Genevieve had never presided over so large a social gathering, in this life or in her previous one, but she had been to a few assemblies and parties when she was alive and had watched those hostesses.

Welcome everyone, she reminded herself. *Smile. Find partners for those without when the dancing starts. Be civil, be kind, and be firm when you need to be.*

Beyond her and Kendrick, Dominic and Evangeline were passing out dance cards to the ladies. The orchestra was warming up—she could hear the distinct creak-groan of the hurdy-gurdy; wouldn't that be a fun addition?—and the ballroom shone with its newly polished floor and the mirrors and beeswax candles set around the perimeter to reflect the light.

"Thank you so much for coming," she said, meeting all the colorless eyes that came her way—some direct and arrogant, some lifted up from under eyelashes, some wary, some hopeful. "We're so glad you're here."

⁂

"It's a crush!" Elspeth declared as the windows at the far end of the ballroom were flung open to try to relieve the sound in the ballroom. It would have been suffocatingly hot if they'd had pulses, but Ophelia's heart was the only one that beat within the ballroom.

"And the dancing hasn't even started yet," Genevieve marveled.

"It won't start until we open the dancing," Kendrick said, offering his hand to her.

"Oh, dear," she said, but she followed him out onto the floor.

He nodded to the orchestra and smiled reassuringly down at her. "I promise I won't say *whoa*."

Genevieve set her gloved hand in his. Waltz strains wound about them as the vampiric grace allowed them to nearly float over the ballroom—or perhaps that was just how she felt in his arms. Lighter than air.

"I think it's safe to say your ball is a success," Kendrick rumbled.

"Don't tempt fate so early in the night," she begged, half-laughing.

"No chance of that. Shall we sing 'Auld Lang Syne' at midnight? It is Hogmanay, though MacPherson is guarding the door like a bulldog to make certain we get no first-footers he does not approve of."

"Perhaps the orchestra can play it."

"How are they doing?"

"Quite well. I think Monsieur Dupont came to a compromise with the more eccentric instruments. We'll have a few minuets, waltzes, and quadrilles and then move to country dances and some older styles, such as galliards and allemandes."

"You dance very well, Genevieve," Kendrick said, his eyes shining.

"So do you. When have you had the opportunity to waltz?"

"Not often in recent years, but Elspeth helped me brush up."

"Kendrick," Genevieve said in a whisper. "You're sweet."

"Our secret," he said, dipping his head to brush her nose with his.

❦

Later, as Genevieve was speaking civilly with the Montmorencys, Winnie appeared in the doorway of the ballroom, her gaze sweeping the room. When she spotted Genevieve, she froze—but then set out across the room.

Genevieve gracefully extricated herself from the conversation and met Winnie halfway across the floor. "Winnie—welcome. I'm glad you came." She stretched out her hands and Winnie placed hers in Genevieve's.

"Thank you for the invitation," Winnie said. "Is it all right if— could we speak for a moment?"

"Of course." Genevieve led her onto the ballroom's terrace over the back garden. "You look lovely, by the way." Winnie wore a yellow gown that complemented her skin and was reminiscent of a daffodil.

Winnie wrung her gloves. "Joseph bought it. Commissioned it, rather. From the dressmakers. It was very kind of him."

Genevieve made a noncommittal noise and waited.

"I—I wanted to apologize," Winnie finally said, gazing over the back garden. "Not just for one thing. For...oh, for the last several years I've known you, Genevieve. I've been a selfish brat, with a sneering attitude. It's a wonder you didn't slap me silly any number of times."

"What brought on this change of heart?"

Winnie looked up at her in some surprise. "Yes, that's what it was, exactly: a change of heart. I had...purposefully hardened my heart to people. But I started going on Joseph's rounds with him, offering medicine and aid to those in the slums, and I had to really look at the people who were suffering. Not just assess who would make a convenient meal. I had wrapped myself in my own anger and hurt and let it numb me. The height of selfishness. But on those long nights, I either had to wrap myself in my pretension to keep my distance or let the façade crack. It cracked."

Genevieve reached for her hand, squeezing it. "I'm glad, Winnie. We need soft hearts to connect us to the world."

Winnie cleared her throat, her eyes glittering with a wet sheen. "It was just easier to make the world my enemy when I was hurting."

"I know."

"Did you know what would happen when you sent me to Joseph?" she asked.

"No. But I hoped."

All the windows of Carmine House glowed with bright candlelight. Laughter echoed through the walls. The musical strains of the orchestra flowed from the house, filling the street.

It infuriated Laurent. He stood in the dark, watching the house, gnashing his teeth. All those traitors who had turned away from him...! And Genevieve, that instigator of it all. She wanted to see him crawl. She wanted to see him suffer.

Well, he wouldn't have it. He'd show her. He'd make her see that all this...could be brought to nothing.

Chapter Forty-One

K endrick moved around the ballroom with Genevieve's hand tucked in his, greeting vampires of all physical ages and nationalities. Some had come in up-to-date costumes, and some had clearly pulled out favored clothing from days gone by. *How that must set Etienne's teeth on edge*, Kendrick thought, hiding a smile.

"Genevieve, have you met Marshall Cutter? I have been assisting him with the Ossuary's rebuilding project."

"No, I have not. It's a pleasure to meet you, Mr. Cutter." Genevieve's eyes sparkled. "I have noticed a lack of whitewash and brick dust when Kendrick returns from your endeavors of late. The repairs are going well?"

"A pleasure, ma'am," Marshall said, bowing. "Yes, we hope to be finished with the major rebuilding by the end of January. May I present my friend Miss Pendleton?"

Miss Pendleton was quite changed from how she'd appeared the last time Kendrick had seen her. No longer wild and red-eyed, she wore a white gown reminiscent of her name, and lilies were pinned to her collar and in her hair. "How do you do?" she whispered, holding tight to Marshall's arm.

"You look lovely, Miss Pendleton," Kendrick said.

Her shy eyes darted to him and a small smile crept over her face. "Thank you, sir."

A few minutes later, Kendrick was pulled into another circle of vampires. "I hadn't thought you'd do it," one of the louder naysayers was saying to him, "but there are more vampires here than in all the prior years' assemblies, and those were mandatory! Ha ha!"

"All the credit is due to my wife," Kendrick said, squeezing Genevieve's hand.

"Ah, yes. Heard you were married. Can't quite credit it," the blowhard said.

Kendrick narrowed his eyes in warning. "You must believe it, for I have snatched the best treasure from among you for myself."

The vampire's lady companion, appearing as a stout matron in chartreuse, clearly had no trouble believing it. She tittered and rapped Kendrick playfully with her fan. "You devil."

Kendrick glanced at Genevieve and raised an inquiring eyebrow, as if to say, *Am I a devil?*

She made a face behind her fan at him.

Just then, a susurrus passed through the ballroom. People pulled away from the doorway, staring with wide eyes.

"What is it?" Genevieve asked.

"Gisela is here." He exchanged a look with her.

"Oh, good." Genevieve set her shoulders and strode towards Gisela, Kendrick in perfect time with her.

By the time they'd reached the ballroom door, a semicircle of emptiness had formed around Gisela and her aunts.

"Miss Gisela! How wonderful you look," Genevieve said, taking her hand and admiring the wine-red gown. "And Miss Hattie and Miss Connors, you both look exceedingly well." Gisela's aunts wore matronly gowns of dark blue and brown. "How glad we are that you could attend."

"Thank you," Gisela said, a cynical quirk at the corner of her mouth. "You've garnered quite a crush. What a good thing no one needs to breathe."

A genuine smile spread over Genevieve's face. "I believe the Roger de Coverley is beginning in a few minutes. Do you—"

"Gisela." Salem strolled up, Ophelia on his arm. "How interesting to see you."

"Salem. How do you do?"

"Quite well. I'm married now."

Gisela favored Ophelia with a nod. "Congratulations."

"Thank you," Ophelia said.

Salem heaved a sigh. "I suppose you have not been engaged for this number, Gisela? Would you care to dance?" He held out a hand.

After a second of hesitation, Gisela curtseyed regally and took his hand as he led her out onto the floor. Wide-eyed, the crowd stared and milled about before the dance took form and the orchestra struck up the first bars.

"Did you and he…?" Genevieve murmured to Ophelia.

"We talked about it. He agreed to be civil. I still don't like her," Ophelia said through her teeth.

Etienne and Addie walked up. Etienne goggled. "*Bon Dieu*, is that *Gisela*?"

"How daring of her to wear the shade of blood," Addie said. She was wearing gold silk.

"Provocative," Ophelia said.

"Shall we join them?" Kendrick asked, offering his hand to Ophelia.

"Actually, my knee is beginning to hurt," Ophelia demurred. "I'd rather rest it than continue bounding about."

"Shall we sit?" Genevieve offered. "I have not had a chance to sit down yet this night!"

"Abandoned at every turn. In that case, will you favor me with a dance, Addie?" Kendrick asked. Addie accepted with every sign of pleasure.

"Better?" Genevieve asked, as she and Ophelia took a seat around the perimeter of the room.

"Yes, much."

"Oh—do you need a drink? Something to eat?"

Ophelia shook her head. "Salem brought me a snack and a cup of punch from the kitchens just a little while ago, but thank you. I did get some odd looks as I ate a plate of sandwiches." She smiled.

"You haven't been bothered, I hope?"

"Salem has a very ferocious glare that he wields well. Truly, I've been having a lovely time. This is my first true ball. I used to think I couldn't ever go to balls because of my leg, but Salem practiced with me enough that I can manage slow dances just fine." She beamed. "And I danced with several gentlemen." She glanced out at the floor. "Gisela looks like she's sucking on a lemon, doesn't she?"

"She might be suffering just as much as Salem," Genevieve said. "But it was good of him to offer."

"Mending fences is important. Finding people willing to mend them with you is also important." A shadow passed over her face.

"There is still much lingering reluctance and those hesitant to change, but I am glad that the Ossuary is warming to transformation. We need it so badly. Vampires have such trouble with the future. I don't know if you realized that," Genevieve added dryly. "There is so much looking back at the past, at what was lost, and so little towards what could be."

"You're teaching them how to hope after they've forgotten how," Ophelia said. "I think that, more than anything, is what people crave."

Later, as Kendrick returned to her side and they were approached by people with congratulations or questions or those who just wanted to speak to them for a moment, the sentiment stuck with Genevieve as she looked these people in the face—young, old, men, women, frozen in time, exiled from the normal flow of humanity.

They all took to the floor for the last waltz, a slow revolution around the floor. Genevieve laid her head on Kendrick's shoulder.

That's all they want. A little hope, to bear the march of time, she thought, holding on to Kendrick.

Maybe we can show them where to find it.

Chapter Forty-Two

"Best get to bed, Mr. MacPherson," Genevieve said with a half-smile. "Jeremy comes on duty in a moment. I can smell the breakfast cooking."

Robbie bowed from his place by the front door. "It was a marvelous ball, ma'am. Faith, I think every vampire in London came through the doors at one time or another."

Not everyone, thankfully. "Any trouble?"

"A few humans, young bucks if you ken the type, tried to slip in here and there, but I gave them the boot," Robbie said with a smile. "No other problems. Everyone departed in their carriages in good order ahead of the sun."

"Thank you," Genevieve said. Day would soon be upon them, and because of it, they had ended the ball much sooner than many human affairs that brought around carriages at dawn to cart away the partygoers. The teeming house was now quiet and still, save for the muffled voices from the billiards room. Kendrick and Salem were still awake and talking.

Ophelia had begged off early in the morning, saying she was still unused to nocturnal activities and had never been used to parties extending so far into the night. She was asleep, almost certainly. The human staff members were just waking up. And Genevieve was feeling warm and fuzzy, slowing as the sun rose closer to the horizon, still in her ballgown.

Ascending the stair to the now-deserted ballroom, she surveyed the scene with an air of surprised propriety. The chalk designs on the ballroom floor had been blurred and trampled beyond recognition, but that was how it should be. The floor had been packed with dancers, and though there had been no "refreshments," she had received compliments on the décor, the gaming rooms set up with all manner of activities, and the music selection.

Monsieur Dupont had succeeded admirably as maestro and had played a wide variety of selections from various decades, which made even the starchiest and most disapproving vampires get up and dance when they recognized songs from their era. It had been a fascinating thing to see the Montmorencys take to the floor with an agility and lightness that a casual observer would have found unbelievable.

She smiled in the silence and went around to make sure all the windows and drapes had been securely closed.

❦

"Don't think I didn't notice you disappear after Ophelia went to bed," Kendrick told Salem, who was rolling an abandoned cigar contemplatively between his fingers.

Some vampires smoked—just about the only vice one could employ beyond blood—but Salem didn't, and Kendrick had left that behind a century ago and had no desire to take it up again, especially with the English propensity for smoking harder substances like opium. Opium made the blood taste like sludge, and opium users tended to be wasted and unhealthy. They had designated the billiards room as the location for all vampires who wished to partake, and now the whole rocm smelled like an ashtray.

"I walked her back to our room and ther came down like a good boy," Salem said wryly. "But I didn't care to be ogled anymore, so I stayed in the library. You've gotten some new books. Why behind glass, though? I know you love those historical books, but the children's novels?"

"If you mean the books by a Mr. Anglesy, that is a pseudonym for Genevieve's father, who wrote his adult bocks as E.D. Saxon."

"Did he really?" Salem raised his eyebrows. "And then you marry the daughter. And her father is…"

"Dead, a year ago. But he left her a trunk cf belongings, and I found it when I went back to Oxford. So that's why the books are behind glass. Her father's last gift to her."

"Fascinating." Salem spun the cigar between his fingers. "Well, did the end of the ball survive my absence?"

"It did. I think Genevieve is regarding it as something of a triumph."

"And you're not?"

"Well, I didn't have to draw my sword once, which is both encouraging and also disappointing."

"If you want to trade blows with someone, convince MacPherson to get fitted for a peg leg. You two can go at it with claymores."

"There's a thought," Kendrick mused. "So why are you still up? The last revelers departed twenty minutes ago."

"I wanted to catch you before dawn." Salem pitched the cigar with pinpoint accuracy into the wastebasket. "I felt like I should apologize."

"For what?"

"The state you found the Ossuary in. It feels like it was partially my fault. I killed Theron, after all, and paved the way for Rupert. I know it wasn't in any way good before he took over, and I could not have fixed a broken system when I was broken myself.

But I wanted to apologize and ask what you need." Salem met his eyes squarely.

Kendrick extended his hand, and Salem clasped it. "None of this was your fault, Salem. But thank you, my friend. We can use whatever help you can give. Genevieve has discussed starting a school for any vampires who are illiterate and has an idea for a twenty-four-hour circulation library, catering to humans by day and vampires by night. Either cause could use a book donation."

"I could do that," Salem agreed with a smile. He eyed the clock above the mantle. "I ought to take the dog out. Might as well take your lad's dog as well," Salem said, standing.

Kendrick waited for him while he whistled the dogs from the kitchen, where they were awaiting breakfast, and then followed him out into the garden behind the house. Kendrick yawned as Blaze and Wulfric investigated the garden. The sky was lightening, but true dawn would not be for another few minutes.

❧

Genevieve had finished securing the far curtain and was looking forward to getting out of her gown's trappings. But when she turned around, she was no longer alone in the ballroom.

"You didn't invite me to the ball, Genevieve." Laurent smiled at her, blood streaked across his mouth.

"How did you get in here?" she demanded, going cold at the sight and smell of the blood.

"Why, through the front door."

Oh, no, Robbie—no, Jeremy! Her throat tightened. Her head felt sluggish. She had to stop him.

His face hardened, and he advanced on her. She backed up and circled the room on instinct, trying to get closer to the door. "You ruined everything," he snarled. "You and Elspeth, but *you're* the one who's been whispering into ears and poisoning people against me. I should have taught you your lessons better—should have ripped out every single one of your nails! I should have plucked out both your eyes!"

"*Poisoning?*" Genevieve demanded over the ringing in her ears. "I said nothing that was not true. Your own behavior condemns you!"

"You couldn't be content with your lot in life. You had to go and *change* things!"

"Yes—Yes, I did!" Genevieve stopped and stood her ground. "Being controlled and belittled and abused is not *anyone*'s lot in life, and I will make sure it never is again! You're never going to hurt me or make me feel small again."

"I'm going to kill you!" he growled. "And then I'm going to kill every single human in this house and stain the floor with their blood."

Genevieve saw a flicker of movement behind him. "No," she whispered.

"*Yes*," Laurent said. "That's all they're good for. You can't protect them—and you shouldn't. They're sheep. That's a— *aarghh*!" he yelled as his body jerked.

Behind him, Fletcher, practice foil through the belt at his waist, held grimly to the hilt of the silver knife he had thrust into Laurent's back. He had aimed at the heart—but the angle was wrong. He'd missed.

"Fletcher, *run* and get Kendrick!" Genevieve yelled. Then she smashed her fist into Laurent's face.

She wasn't a helpless human anymore. He could intimidate her all he liked—but she wasn't fettered anymore. He had no power over her.

Laurent growled, trying to both stem the blood oozing from his nose and get a hand on the knife to pull it out. "You little—"

Fletcher pelted away just as Laurent got a hand on the knife and yanked it free. His skin sizzled as he dropped the silver. "Little *brat*—" he wheezed, blood splattering the floor.

"Leave him alone," Genevieve snarled. "Pick on someone your

own size." She hit Laurent across the face again, staining her glove with his blood. Then she dived for the knife and scooped it up. She could feel the silver through her thin gloves, but she held it grimly.

She was free, and she was strong, and there was a house full of people who would come down on his head if she could just keep him distracted and angry enough not to run after Fletcher.

His bloodshot eyes focused on her with a snarl.

She backed up towards the wide ballroom floor, the knife held in front of her. "You think humans are worthless, but look what one boy did! You look down on vampires weaker than you, but Elspeth foiled you! You're delusional, Laurent, if you think this will gain you anything."

He gnashed his fangs, closing in on her. "It will gain me your blood in my teeth!"

"Not if I have anything to say about it," Kendrick growled from the doorway.

❧

"No more hiding in shadows, Laurent," Kendrick declared, stepping into the room and raising his sword. "No more sending others to do your death-deeds. Face me now, according to the traditions you claim to espouse. Face me in trial by combat, though by rights, such an honor should not be given to you."

Kendrick and Genevieve's people crowded in behind him, cutting off Laurent's escape.

"I will not fight a usurper!" Laurent said, his eyes wildly darting for an exit. He reached for Genevieve, as if to snatch her to him like a shield—but she sliced his arm with the silver dagger that had already tasted his blood and ran out of range, traveling along the edge of the room to reach her allies. Laurent howled wordlessly in pain and outrage, and Kendrick felt a rush of pride.

All the blood in him had frozen when he had heard Fletcher's urgent cries. Now he would deal with this tormenter who had hurt Genevieve and so many others—one way or another.

"I gained rulership of the Ossuary fairly. If you had wanted to challenge me, you should have done it in front of witnesses instead of conspiring like a coward. If you will not fight me, then I'll kill you the way you deserve," Kendrick said, advancing on him.

"No!" Laurent shrieked.

"Then will you fight?" Kendrick asked. "Fight or face the dawn. Those are your choices. Choose your end."

Laurent licked his lips. "No weapons in trial by combat! Throw down your sword!"

Kendrick handed it off to Salem, hilt first. "Agreed."

Genevieve reached him and seized his arm, her eyes wide. "Kendrick—"

"All will be well," he said in a low voice.

She took his hand and kissed it.

Then Kendrick stepped forward to meet him.

Laurent would never willingly parley or pay weregild for those he had harmed. He had to be dealt with, here, now. But like all those who traded in fear, this vampire was a coward. Kendrick advanced on him as the household peered in the ballroom doors.

"Get him, guv!" Fletcher's voice called as Laurent backed away.

"Are you going to stand and fight, or run like a dog?" Kendrick asked as Laurent continued to scuttle away from him. "For a man with a lot of big talk, you have no spine when the battle merits it."

"You've turned them all against me," Laurent hissed.

"Have I? Or have you done it yourself, by years of abuse and neglect? Years of oppression? Were they ever *with you* to begin with?"

"It's the right of the strong to dominate those below them!"

"It is the right of every ruler to reach out to those sorely oppressed and save his people. You had twenty years to change your tune. Now we will have a new way." Kendrick feinted for Laurent, who skipped backward.

He could end this here and now, but he wanted to see if Laurent would actually turn and fight.

"The truth is, Laurent," Kendrick said, gesturing to the room, "even if by some chance you managed to strike me down, there are plenty here who would step in to end you. Your vision of darkness and tyranny has no place here. It never will again."

Laurent's face twisted in a mask of rage. "Then if I am to die, I'll take all of you with me!" He lunged for the drapes in front of the windows and ripped them away.

And then, as Genevieve screamed, all Kendrick saw was light.

Chapter Forty-Three

The instant Laurent had reached for the curtains, all the vampires by the door recoiled. When he pulled the fabric down to admit dawn's light to the ballroom, Genevieve screamed, "NO!" She threw herself—threw every bit of her being—forward to try to get to Kendrick, even as hands seized her to pull her back.

Light flashed. She squinted against the brightness. "Kendrick!"

Her voice was lost in Laurent screaming. He flailed in the beam of sunlight. Flames erupted from him in hot, angry tongues of fire. He ran out of the sunbeam, but nothing could stop the blaze. He fell to the ground and twitched, a blackened husk, before finally falling to ashes.

"Let go of me!" Genevieve commanded, fighting the hands holding her. "Kendrick!" Where was he? Where had he gone? He could not have burned before Laurent!

"We can't do anything about the drapes until nightfall," someone warned. "Not unless one of the humans tacks it back up. Genevieve, come away..."

"No! Where is he?" Genevieve demanded, her eyes streaming from the light.

"She's right," Elspeth insisted. "Where did he go?"

"I vow," a wondering voice said from across the room. "I have not stood in the sun in more than a thousand years." Footfalls moved across the floor towards Genevieve. "Don't cry, Genevieve. Not when you're the heroine of the hour." A warm hand encircled hers. "You might drop your veil of protection, though. It is mighty unnerving for a man not to see his own hands."

Genevieve sucked in a hard breath.

Kendrick flickered into view in front of her, holding her hand to his cheek. His face glowed. "You're a marvel, Genevieve."

She threw her arms around his neck. "What happened?!"

"Don't you know?" He laughed. "You saved my life."

⁂

Laurent had forced his way through the front door and badly wounded Jeremy, the footman. But he was alive, and Joseph had been summoned. The ballroom had been closed off until they could deal with Laurent's remains after dark.

As all the vampires still awake filed into the library, demanding to know what had happened, Genevieve threw her arms around Fletcher. "You ran like the wind, Fletcher! But you shouldn't have taken the chance to strike him. It was too risky!"

"I had to! L'go," he wheezed. "Y'r squishin' me."

"How did you come to be there?" Genevieve demanded.

"I was going to practice with my sword before breakfast, but I heard him talking to you and knew that was the bad cove. I couldn't leave him with you, mum!"

Genevieve gazed down into the boy's earnest face. The logical remonstrations that she was a vampire, and an adult, flew through her mind. She dismissed them. "Thank you for being so brave."

He flushed but looked pleased when she kissed his cheek.

"It was a good strike," Kendrick said, setting his hand on Fletcher's head. "I'm proud of you."

Fletcher beamed. "He went off like a ruddy roman candle, didn't he, guv?"

Kendrick laughed. "Yes, very like."

In the library, with everyone yawning and fighting drowsiness but insistent on knowing what had happened, Kendrick said, "When Laurent pulled down the curtains, I looked up and I saw the sun. I thought that was the end, and I lifted my hand to feel the warmth. But I couldn't see my hand. I was invisible."

"I don't know how I did that," Genevieve said wonderingly. "I thought I had lost my talent. I was never able to use it on someone else before. I just...wanted so badly to save you." Her hand tightened around his.

"And it worked," Kendrick said with a smile.

"But you lived! You didn't burst into flame in daylight!" Elspeth gasped.

Kendrick shook his head. "I was standing in the middle of the sunbeam, but I wasn't burning. I can't explain that."

"It's just not possible," Robbie said.

"I can explain," Salem said suddenly from his position by the shelves. "It's because light is a form of electro-magnetic radiation."

"What?" Kendrick said.

"Etienne sent me James Clerk Maxwell's *A Treatise on Electricity and Magnetism* while I was, er, rusticating. Basically, light is a type of wave." Salem moved his hand in the air. "In the eye, you have a lens, which captures the light that reflects into it. In order to see something, a light wave has to—to bounce off an object and hit the lens of your eye."

They all stared at him in varying degrees of understanding.

"Never mind," Salem said, waving that away. "What I mean is —Genevieve's talent must control these light waves. Somehow, she *bent* the light away from you, Kendrick. So we couldn't see you, and you were not burned. Genevieve made you untouchable to daylight."

"As long as someone is invisible," Elspeth said.

Genevieve looked up at Kendrick. "Do you think that's true?"

He grinned. "Do you want to test it?"

"No!" she exclaimed. "I'd rather think it a miracle than chance you catching fire again. It *was* a miracle."

"It was. It was a miracle you were able to react so fast, and a miracle you could use your talent on someone else. Knowing why doesn't make it less wondrous." He wrapped his arms around her.

She buried her face in his evening jacket. "I can barely keep my eyes open."

"Good point. Let's go to bed. Everyone, good morning. We will see you tonight." Kendrick swept Genevieve up into his arms and carried her up the main staircase to their room.

Around them, the city was waking. A new day had broken. A new year lay ahead of them.

Genevieve half-opened her eyes as Kendrick divested her of her evening gown and put her in bed, climbing in after her. She was so tired after a wonderful night and a frightening daybreak, but Kendrick's eyes were still wide open as he lay back against the pillows and stared at the ceiling. No, he wasn't staring at the ceiling—he was staring at the far window, shuttered against the light.

"What did you see?" she whispered.

He turned to her and ran his hand through her hair. "Heaven's candle set in a clear, blue sky." He closed his eyes and admitted, "I thought my doom had come. Judgment, at long last. But there was no judgment. Only light."

"What do you mean?"

"I mean, you are my fate. Had you not left me chiding notes, I would not be here. Perhaps Laurent might have succeeded. Perhaps someone might have achieved his ends earlier with a knife in the dark. But we would not be here."

"Without you, I would not have read my father's last words," Genevieve whispered. "I would never have loved again."

"The path set out by the Giver of Life remains a mystery and is ever passing away, but He saw fit that our paths should intertwine. And that we should relearn hope." He set his forehead against hers.

Genevieve bit her lip against the burn of tears. "What are we going to do now?"

"Do? What we've always planned to. Teach our people to hope. Read good books, love good things. Show the children how to handle a sword."

"Children?" Genevieve murmured.

"You don't think we'll raise just Fletcher, do you? This is a large house. And, if the High King of the World wills it, the years will continue on. And then the end will come."

"Oh, what a lovely way to look at it," she murmured. "But, Kendrick. Will you do me a favor?" she asked, fighting the pull of sleep.

"Anything for you, Jenny."

"The next time someone tries to kill you, will you *get out of the way?*"

Kendrick laughed and kissed her.

Epilogue

❧

DECEMBER 1901, CORNWALL

As the sun set, Genevieve woke with a sense of anticipation. She rolled over and nudged Kendrick awake.

"Hmm?" her husband rumbled, his arms reflexively coming around her.

"Fletcher is coming home this evening. He might already be here!" She beamed. She hadn't seen him and his wife, Liza, and the girls in six months and had been counting down the days.

"August will meet them at the train station," Kendrick murmured.

"But we have to get up!" Genevieve insisted.

"Do we?" Kendrick whispered into her neck.

"Yes." Genevieve laughed. "I'm sure the rest of our guests will be rising as well; it wouldn't do to lie abed with the rest of the house waking."

"I don't know that Salem and Etienne are especially early risers," Kendrick rumbled, but Genevieve was slipping from the covers and donning her dress.

"Come on!" she urged.

"Anyone would think Christmas was today, and not four days hence." Kendrick chuckled, but he got up.

Genevieve, clad in a fashionable gown with a high neckline and a sloped waist, hurried down the hallway. If she went left, she would enter the large system of caves below the cliffs, expanded by enterprising smugglers in days of yore. She would eventually reach the sea far below, smell the salt and hear the low roar of the waves. Some days, she would go and sit and listen and watch the sunlight reflected on the water.

But not this evening. This evening, she hurried up the stairs and into the large Cornish manor that Kendrick had bought two years into their marriage as a retreat from the hustle and bustle and general unhealthiness of London. It was one of her favorite places. The children had loved growing up here.

Kendrick caught up with her in the front hall just as the sound of a conveyance approaching reached their ears. Robbie threw open the door ahead of her, a big grin on his face.

Genevieve stepped out into the evening air as a bright-yellow automobile pulled up in front of the house as neat as one could like. "Oh!" she exclaimed.

But the girls were boiling out of the car as Fletcher and Liza laughed. "Nan! Nan!" the girls exclaimed, their curls bobbing from under their straw hats. "Do you see the car?"

"I do!" Genevieve said, wrapping Samantha and Evelyn in a big hug. They had both grown so much. But then she was abandoned with shouts of "Granda! Did you see the car?"

"Can't hardly miss it, can I?" Kendrick mock-growled, lifting the girls in his arms as they shrieked with laughter.

Liza reached Genevieve and bussed her cheek. "Fletch knew he'd have something to say about the color. It's lovely to see you, Jenny."

Genevieve hugged her and then turned to wrap her arms around Fletcher. "I missed you all," she murmured. The boy—

man now—had grown taller than her a few years after he'd become their son, a mighty feat.

"Missed you too, Mother," Fletcher said, smiling underneath his moustache. "Anyone would think Christmas had come early, the way you ran out of the house."

Kendrick piled the girls into one arm as they giggled and wrapped his free arm around Genevieve. "In her mind, it did."

"When we're all together, it's always Christmas to me," Genevieve said, squeezing Fletcher's hand and leaning against Kendrick. "Come inside, all of you! Everyone is here except Dominic's family; they'll be here tomorrow. I'm sure Addie and Sally have dinner preparations well in hand."

"Nan, will you read us a story?" the girls clamored. "About Wynnflaed? Or Amice, or Hild?"

Genevieve laughed. "I think we can manage a tale or two."

As they stepped into the house, Kendrick pressed a kiss on Genevieve's head. All her people, under one roof, was what she had asked for this Christmas. And he had delivered.

As he always did.

"I love you, you know," she told him, as she often did.

"That I do, Jenny. And I love you too."

Need some more vampires in your life? You can read a FREE short story featuring **Addie and Etienne** if you sign up for my newsletter on my website www.clairetrellahill.com.

And if you enjoyed this story, please consider leaving a review on your preferred book retailer and/or book review site. It really does make a difference. Thank you so much!

Acknowledgments

As iron sharpens iron, so do knowledgeable friends help you polish the areas of your book that you left pretty rough. Thank you to Suzannah Rowntree for her beta reader feedback, in particular for calling me on all my Cockney inaccuracies and the law jargon I got wrong. I love having smart friends. Also thank you for the crusader joke and all the nonfiction recommendations about the time period.

Thank you to Beverly Twomey and Irina, my constant word-getting buddies as we slogged our way to the end of our respective manuscripts. We all need a friend to motivate us. Thank you also to Irina once again for saving my French.

Thank you to whoever wrote the baguette pain-staking joke— I saw it on a Tumblr post, wrote the scene for Addie immediately, and have never been able to find it again. I am not clever enough to come up with puns like that. All credit to the original poster, whoever you are. I hope you don't mind me immortalizing it.

Thank you to Melody, my cover artist, for the best cover I could have asked for. I loved it from the word go and it's sublimely gorgeous. Thank you for waiting for basically a whole year for me to show it off—the book took longer than I thought. But I know the cover is worth the wait.

Thank you to Amy, my copyeditor, for being my comma resource and my word origin fact-checker, and for not being completely exasperated at how much I like to head hop in narration. You caught innumerable little issues in the manuscript, and I am very grateful. Especially for those letters that mysteriously disappeared from words. How did I even manage that? Anyway, you're a lifesaver. Please excuse my hubris for the times I rejected one of your thoughtful corrections based purely on vibes.

Thank you to my parents, who proofread the book and said it was "my best one yet," and also to RJ Anderson, who found all the last minute typos and flubs that inevitably remain until a month before release.

I wrote the big emotional letter in this book on the way home from the funeral of one of my mother's good friends who had known me all my life. She was loving, kind, warm, generous, and loved the Lord so much. Hearing so many people testify to the impact she made in their lives unlocked something that made me able to find the emotional core of this book and really think about what kind of a message one would leave behind if given the chance. So I have to also thank Miss Becky. We love and miss you very much, but we will see you again.

Thank you, as always, to the Lord. You are the resurrection and the life, and no word from you will ever fail.

Semi-Historical Note

Confession: research is usually a draft two problem for me. Other authors may read a lot of books that then informs the plot and structure of their books. I usually hunt for specific details I know I need because I already wrote the first draft and need to back up my ramblings with facts.

However! This time around I read a *lot* of books—some about the Victorian era, but a lot about the Anglo-Saxon era because I was worried about getting Kendrick's characterization right. Those books didn't end up making much of an impact on the general plot, but they did breathe more life into the character and provided extremely helpful details for certain scenes, and I am grateful for them. Thank you to Suzannah Rowntree for pointing me toward several of the Victorian texts. So, in some semblance of order, the books I read, both the nonfiction and the fiction:

The Five by Hallie Rubenhold

How to be a Victorian by Ruth Goodman

Anglo-Saxon Spirituality, trans. Robert Boenig

Jesus through Medieval Eyes by Grace Hammen

The Word Hord by Hana Videen

The Deor Hord by Hana Videen

Mediaeval Feudalism by Carl Stephenson

Sources of English Constitutional History, Vol. 1 by Carl Stephenson and Frederick George Marcham —the source of inspiration for Kendrck's oaths (and some directly lifted)

Britain After Rome by Robin Fleming

Winters in the World by Eleanor Parker, as well as her magnificent blog A Clerk of Oxford

"Beowulf: The Monster and the Critics" by JRR Tolkien

"Widsith," trans. Francis Barton Gummere

Rosemary Sutcliff's body of work, on which I patterned the books by Genevieve's father

I also cobbled together some lines of Beowulf from several sources. I do not claim to be in any way knowledgeable in Old English translation; I merely pulled the phrases and the rhythms of speech together from the versions I read and put them together in a (I hope) pleasing fashion to avoid plagiarizing. Texts I used as a basis:

Beowulf, trans. Seamus Heaney, 2000.

Beowulf, trans. JRR Tolkien, 2014.

Beowulf, trans. J. Lesslie Hall, 1892

Also by Claire Trella Hill

Bonds of Blood

Black and Deep Desires

Parfit Gentil Knyght: an Addie and Etienne Vignette (Newsletter Exclusive)

Every Longing Heart

The Karneesia Chronicles

The Erlking's Daughters

Mistress of Wardwood and Other Stories (Newsletter Exclusive)

The Flight of the Spellbound

The Heartwood's Choice

Tales from Karneesia

When a Dragon Comes Courting

Come by Water

The Shapeshifter Drives a Bargain

The Lost Treasures of Peredur

Aeronwy's Stolen Child (Newsletter Exclusive)

About the Author

Claire Trella Hill will read anything, but fantasy romance and gothic fiction are her favorites. Born and raised in Houston, Texas, she still lives there because she is impervious to 100 degree weather. She also has a bad habit of making her characters in the Sims and continuing their stories. When Claire isn't writing, she can be found with her nose glued to her library app, assisting with the last tricky pieces of a puzzle, swilling Dr. Pepper, collecting vintage romance covers, or cuddling with her cat.

You can connect with her on social media or sign up for her newsletter on her website ClaireTrellaHill.com.